THE
COLOUR
OF
EVIL

The Colour of Evil

A Sebastian Foxley Medieval Mystery
Book 9

Copyright © 2021 Toni Mount
ISBN-13: 978-84-122325-2-3

M
MadeGlobal Publishing

For more information on
MadeGlobal Publishing, visit
our website
www.madeglobal.com

For the fans of Seb Foxley who keep coming back for more.

Toni.

Why not visit
Sebastian Foxley's web page
to discover more about his
life and times?
www.SebastianFoxley.com

Prologue

IF EVER there was a hell-on-earth, this was it, in the city's very heart.

In the rats' nest of alleyways south of Tower Street, Furnace Court was more noisome than most. Sunlight never dared trespass among the soot-encrusted walls, nor tip-toed into the confines where fire burned, smoke choked and the din of metal on metal rang out, assaulting the ears. Yet a man made his livelihood here. Bare-armed and brawny, smut-covered, the smith toiled at his anvil in the near darkness, working by the flickering light of the devil's flames. Sweating, he hammered and quenched, reheated and shaped, forcing his will upon the metals at his mercy. No iron could resist his power.

But such heavy labours were not his sole employment. Elsewhere, in the secret darkness beneath the streets, he had a second, smaller furnace. A more lucrative trade was to be had here, furtive and treasonous, undermining the prosperity of a kingdom. Hamo cared not a jot. In supposed-silver coins, struck with a die stolen from the nearby Tower Mint, there was money to be made – literally.

As the instigator, the greedy genius behind this crime, spread more of the gleaming, underweight groats and pennies throughout the city, strangers began to notice. Such coins undermined their livelihood and must be traced back to the source.

Thus it was that two men, speaking English with a foreign sound, came to a shop, just as the owner was closing the shutters at day's end, demanding to be told the origin of the coins at fault. When no answer was forthcoming, the pair resorted to torture: a thousand small cuts, none fatal, but each draining the victim's strength a little more. Every time they paused, removing the rag from the victim's mouth, they repeated the question:

'Who makes these coins?'

The victim did not know the answer. He had but borrowed them to pay what he owed - exchanging a debt to one for a debt to another.

The cuts continued until the strangers were certain the victim spoke true, by which time only death awaited, but they would not deliver the fatal cut. Time would do that. A clear message needed to be left. And it could not be spoken by the victim. For fear he might name them, they split his tongue in twain – to warn the devious serpent lurking behind the counterfeiting business that they would hunt him down. Then, to show how much they knew of it, they covered the victim's right hand – the guilty hand that passed the fake coins – in shiny pigment, brought for the purpose. And to confirm the warning: that there was no escaping their retribution, they nailed the dying victim's hand to his workbench and left a bag of the false money behind.

The new-minted coins, used to pay debts to the strangers, shone even brighter than silver: the colour of evil.

Chapter 1

Friday, the eleventh day of June in the year of Our Lord 1479 The Foxley House in Paternoster Row in the City of London

I returned home with my purchases of quills and ink, Gawain at my heel. I could have asked Kate or Nessie to buy them, although, in truth, such items were not needed in the workshop. The errand was a means of escape. I entered the kitchen but the sense of something – someone – missing assailed me, like an icy hand clutching my heart, as it always did these days.

Rose sat stitching a pair of gloves of lavender-dyed kid leather, her work so delicate, the stitches were nigh invisible. Little Dickon was at her feet, playing some unknown game with a bunch of straws and a few twigs. Nessie stood at the board, chopping fresh sage from the garden, the kitchen filled with its earthy scent. 'Twas a scene of domestic tranquillity, yet utterly amiss.

My Emily was not there.

I could not get used to the lack – a black hole in my soul that I feared naught would ever fill.

I lifted Dickon from the floor. He laughed, showing off his few perfect white teeth.

'Does my little man fare well?' I asked him. A string of dribble down my jerkin was the answer to my query.

3

'He does very well,' Rose said. 'Dickon, show your Papa how you can play at peep-boo.'

The child put his fists over his eyes then took them away of a sudden, shrieking with delight. I took up a table napkin to assist his game, covering my face with it. He pulled it aside, shouting 'Boo!' It was a merry jest indeed and one he seemed unlikely to tire of in the near future. I had work to do, but what of that? Merriment was hard to come by of late. Thus, I would play with my son a while. He would attain the first commemoration of his birth date in the week to come: the first significant day in his life thus far. I prayed daily that he would see many, many more, as so many infants do not.

'Mercy is coming to dinner,' Rose said, 'That you may see Julia.'

I nodded.

Julia was my daughter, born two months since upon that most sorrowful of days. The widow, Mercy Hutchinson, was the infant's wet nurse but having three sons of her own, including Edmund, who was a little older than Julia, she had taken the new babe to live with her in Distaff Lane until she was weaned. Mercy's other children were Simon, a scholar at St Paul's School, and that scamp Nicholas – a toddling who was trouble upon two legs. I remained uncertain of the wisdom of having Nicholas visit too often, fearing Dickon might copy the elder child's bad habits – biting people being his most recent undesirable trait. But Mercy and my kinsman Adam were betrothed, so I had to make the best of it: Nicholas would one day become a member of the family.

Neither was I able to determine for certain quite how I felt about Julia. Born too soon, she was the cause of my beloved Emily's death. Yet she was an innocent. My father once admitted that he had found it difficult, at first, to forgive me because my mother had died of a fever some days after my birth. I refused to blame my tiny daughter in like manner but realised now how hard it was to form an affection for the cause of so much grief. But Mercy and Rose were determined I should learn to love the child. Hence the nigh-daily visits when they expected me to take the babe in my arms and hold her close, whether I wished it or not.

When Mistress Hutchinson arrived with three children – the two babes being in slings, one upon each hip – with Nicholas held firmly by the hand, I had hardly begun my morning's work. In truth, since the completion of Duke Richard's coat-of-arms, which had engrossed me and filled the bleak days after Em's passing, I found enthusiasm lacking for any new project. This was an experience quite new to me and one I prayed would end swiftly.

A man with a household and children to provide for cannot afford to shirk his duties, idling away the hours, wasting his efforts on inessential tasks. I had tidied the storeroom and checked the inventory so many times. I dusted shelves and swept the shop and workshop – tasks for the lowliest apprentice – rearranged my desk over and over and compiled endless lists. How frequently I sat down to work, all determined, prepared the ink, dipped the pen or brush and then... did naught. I could not settle. Inspiration was there none; my imagination dried up and shrivelled as last autumn's leaf-fall.

I greeted Mistress Hutchinson in the kitchen. As usual, she smiled and handed my tiny daughter into my arms.

'She's grown, has she not, Master Seb? She feeds and sleeps well. You should be pleased with her progress.'

'Aye. You be doing right well in caring for her, mistress. I be grateful indeed.' The mite in my arms looked plump enough but what did I know of babes?

'She'll be waking soon for her feed. Nicholas! Let the kindling wood be, for heaven's sake.'

As usual, Nicholas was up to his tricks. The wood stacked by the kitchen hearth had caught his eye and before anyone could prevent it, he grabbed a piece from the bottom of the pile and brought the heap tumbling down upon himself. There was not so much that he was harmed, merely startled, but began to bawl. The noise roused both babes, Julia and Edmund, as well as upsetting little Dickon, all of them joining in, howling.

How did women ever put up with such din without running mad?

My daughter was wailing now with great enthusiasm, so I handed her back to Mistress Hutchinson right eagerly.

'If you could distract Nicholas, Master Seb, that would help,' she said. 'He likes you.'

I was unconvinced that Nicholas liked anyone and wished Adam would come rescue me from his future stepson but my kinsman was working. It was as well that one of us yet earned his bread and disturbing him would serve no purpose. Thus it was I had two toddlings to keep amused and out of harm's way.

Dickon was ever biddable and easy to distract with clapping games, foolish songs or his favoured rag ball. Nicholas was another case entirely: cast your glance elsewhere for an instant and he would be causing mischief. Only yesterday, he had succeeded in opening the gate into the pigsty. It took Adam, Kate and me – much hampered by Gawain who thought it a right merry game, barking and getting underfoot – to catch the escaped piglet, keep Nicholas from playing with the dung and prevent Dickon from copying the elder child. Nicholas' face and hair were plastered in pig ordure and it seemed all too likely he had eaten some of it. I did not envy his mother having to clean him up after and wondered at the possible consequences of swallowing dung. As it was, he seemed none the worse for it this morn.

During my earlier inventories of the storeroom, I had espied the old sand tray. It had not been used since I first attempted to teach Jack his letters, writing them out in the damp sand with a finger, to learn the shapes and the correct order of strokes in their formation. A waste of effort that had been; Jack was never meant to be a scrivener. But now it might serve to amuse the little ones. Their attempts could hardly be any worse than Jack's, even at their young age.

Having first checked that the pigsty gate was secured, having learned a lesson yesterday, I set the tray down in the yard and tipped the fine sand into it. Nicholas began flinging it around even afore I had moistened it with water from the trough. Dickon received a face-full and some got in his eye, causing him to weep – the best thing since it would wash out the sand but he required consoling. Finally, the sand was evenly spread and dampened and I demonstrated how to draw marks in it with my finger and make imprints with my hand.

Dickon became quite enthralled, poking his finger into the sand, making numerous holes, chuckling all the while. Gawain joined in – whether he intended to or no – making a large pawprint and a noseprint in the midst of the tray. But Nicholas surprised me, drawing circles and swirls and patterns of lines, all most pleasing to the eye. What a revelation that the little scamp could be creative! I regarded him anew.

Had I been unjust in thinking him ungovernable? Mayhap, he misbehaved for why he had naught else to do. His mother was much concerned with his younger brother, Edmund, and now Julia. His elder brother, Simon, had school to think on. Without a father, none had much leisure nor interest in Nicholas. Could that be the cause? I vowed to give the toddling greater consideration. In truth, he looked to be earning it: an hour passed and still he sat content, making marks in the sand, long after Dickon had turned his attention to ants among the cobbles of the yard and Gawain had gone to investigate the denizens of the hedgerow at the nether end of the garden plot.

The difficulties arose in persuading Nicholas to leave the sand when we were summoned to dinner. Then battle ensued over the washing of hands. Oh, well, a man can only achieve so much in a single morn. I thought I had not done too badly, playing my part as a mother hen.

After dinner, as I was ruling margins in readiness for some project, at yet undetermined, Kate came hastening to call me into the shop. Her eyes were wide as Sunday platters, her fingers knotting themselves in her apron.

'Whatever is it, lass?' I asked. 'I heard no commotion.'

'A messenger, master, asking for you in person. An-and he wears the king's livery.'

I was into the shop faster than a cat with its tail afire, then paused. It would not do to appear flustered. I smoothed my hair 'neath my cap and pulled my jerkin straight. My sleeve-ends were ink-stained but 'twas no time to remedy that. I entered the shop at a measured pace, much belied by my racing heart.

'Sir.' I bowed to the messenger, removing my hat.

He greeted me likewise.

'You are Master Sebastian Foxley?'

'I am, sir. How may I serve you?'

'The King's Grace, the Lord Edward, has a commission for you. He has seen your work and approves of it. He would have a book to send as a gift to the Lord of Florence, Lorenzo de' Medici. A trustworthy merchant is to serve as the English ambassador in Florence and he must impress this Medici, who is said to be learned and cultured, as well as much interested in the fine arts of war.

'Therefore, the King's Grace would have a luxurious and elegant Latin copy – and accurate, of course – of Vegetius' *De Re Militari* to be presented upon arrival. The merchant sails at the end of July. The book must be ready well in advance, that the king may inspect and inscribe it. You will oblige His Grace?'

Oblige, I thought? As if I dare refuse the king?

'I shall be honoured, sir, to serve King Edward in any way.'

'That is well. And here are the requirements...' The messenger took a small roll of parchment from his official pouch and passed it to me. It was tied with red ribbon. 'I bid you good day, Master Foxley.' With that, he touched his cap, turned upon his heel and departed the shop.

Supposing the requirements were unclear? What if an unforeseen difficulty arose? Of whom should I enquire? I undid the ribbon and unrolled my set of instructions.

At first glance, they appeared sufficiently comprehensive but one matter remained unmentioned. Neither had the messenger broached the subject: money. How and when would I be reimbursed for my expenses, the cost of materials and the hours of labour needful to complete the commission? The Duke of Gloucester always paid me at least half the agreed sum in advance and the remainder was ever settled swiftly when he received the finished piece. It appeared that his royal brother did not do likewise. In truth, no remuneration whatsoever was referred to in my instructions, no sum agreed beforehand. It gave me pause, considering how best to proceed. I should discuss the matter with Emily...

Oh. I closed my eyes and breathed deeply. I had forgotten for a moment. Mayhap Adam could advise me? Or Rose? Or my old master, Richard Collop?

In the workshop, Adam set down his pen and looked to me, an eager glint in his eye.

'A king's messenger, eh? What did he want, Seb? You're not in any trouble, are you?'

'Nay.' I gave him the instructions. 'We have received a commission from King Edward.'

'Well! What a fine feather in our caps that will be. The name and reputation of Foxley can go no higher. We must celebrate.' He read the parchment. 'Vegetius... in Latin... do we have an exemplar for this?'

'We do not.'

He watched me for a moment.

'Is that the reason for your expression of woe, cousin? Aren't you delighted to be working for the king himself? Or do you not approve of Vegetius? Do you fear the Latin will be difficult?'

'My old master, Richard Collop, has a Latin version of Vegetius and I be certain he will permit us to borrow it since we have so illustrious a customer. And I had copied parts of that same treatise when I was Master Richard's apprentice: the text presented few problems, as I recall.'

'Then why the long face?'

'Payment, Adam: neither the messenger nor those instructions make any mention of how or when or by whom we will be paid for our work.'

'But it's the king... he can afford any and every luxury he has a fancy for. Paying us will be no hardship.'

'Ah, Adam, mayhap you have not lived in London long enough to have heard the merchants, the grocers, the vintners and the fishmongers all griping and moaning about the Exchequer, the Royal Wardrobe and the Privy Purse failing to settle their reckonings. 'Tis well known that the king's coffers are ever bare and he be the worst debtor in the city... in England, for all I know. Many merchants truly fear receiving an order for goods from Westminster, knowing they may wait years for payment, and yet they do not dare refuse. 'Tis as if the king believes the honour of being of service to him be compensation enough to atone for loss of coin.

'Thus, you be correct regarding the gilding of our reputation but what of the cost for so elaborate a volume? We could be the losers in this commission, Adam, and I be uncertain whether the possibility of it inspiring future, lucrative orders from other customers will make good such losses. The bejewelled binding alone, as per the instructions, could cost us a small fortune. That be the reason why my delight stands tempered by caution.'

Adam sighed, his shoulders drooped.

'I hadn't realised getting payment might be a problem. But you'll still accept the commission?'

'Of course. How may I refuse the king? 'Tis a royal command, no less. The matter requiring most thought though is… do we do the work to a reasonably high standard but trim our use of materials to reduce costs? Or do we oblige our sovereign to the utmost of our abilities, stinting naught, and pray that it so impresses him he actually hands over coin for it? I do not know if we even dare send him the reckoning? What be the etiquette for asking money of the king?'

'Who might you ask about such delicate matters, Seb? There must be someone who can advise us afore we begin ordering the finest parchment, gold leaf and lapis lazuli?'

'Aye: Master Collop. I trust his judgement in all things regarding business.'

'But not in his choice of a second wife, eh?' Adam laughed. This had been a source of mystery, aye, and mirth to many of our fellow stationers in recent years. 'She's a dainty piece but not a suitable spouse for the Warden Master of the Stationers' Guild, being barely one-third of his age. She was giving me the come-hither look across the tablecloth at the Whitsun feast, the saucy wench. If I were Warden Collop, I wouldn't trust her an inch or take my eye off her for one moment.'

'Twas but your imagination, cousin, I be certain. Mistress Collop may be young but a good wife for all that. Master Collop would not have wed her elsewise.'

Adam grinned and chuckled.

'You're innocent as a newborn lamb, aren't you, Seb? When it comes to women, at least.'

'That be untrue. I be no fool, cousin.'

He simply laughed all the more, the knave.

TONI MOUNT

Master Richard Collop's Stationer's Shop, Cheapside

Later that afternoon, we made our way to Master Collop's shop along Cheapside, to the north end of Soper Lane, opposite the Hospital of St Thomas Acon. How many times had I made my way here in my youth from my father's house by St Martin-le-Grand, lame and leaning upon my staff, to learn my craft as a scribe, illuminator and book-binder?

Richard Collop had been a good and kindly master to me, realising my talent as an artist early on. Not so my fellow apprentices who made mock of my affliction at every opportunity. Had it not been for Mistress Collop's keen eye – she who had been the master's first wife – my years served there could have been an enduring penance but she succeeded in shielding me from my fellows' worst taunts much of the time. Only occasionally did the eldest of we three apprentices – Guy Linton by name, I recall – manage to hurt me with his words as well as deeds. But that was in the past; matters are quite different now.

'Good day to you, Sebastian, Adam.' Master Collop greeted us as we entered his shop. It was twofold larger than our premises, at least and I noted an impressive array of handsome volumes, set out upon new bookshelves that I had not seen afore. 'Come you through to the parlour and we may share ale and wafers and speak in comfort.'

As we passed the workshop doorway – once so familiar to me – I could not help but glance in. There, at the desk where I used to sit, I glimpsed a dark, tousled head bent low over a ruled page. It might have been me... until the lad glanced up. The snub nose and a thousand freckles scattered like ochre pigment powder across his face were never mine. Then I saw he held the pen cack-handed, as they say, in his left hand.

'That's young Hugh Gardyner, the Lord Mayor's nephew,' Master Collop said, seeing the direction of my gaze. 'God be praised, he's a promising lad and a hard-working apprentice. Unlike so many,' he added, sighing.

Did we not all make that discovery where youngsters were concerned?

'You may recall your fellow: Guy Linton?' my master continued.

Indeed I did: one who would avoid labour whenever he might.

'He was asking after you at the guildhall a few days since.'

'Oh? Did he give a reason?' I asked. 'I cannot imagine why he should. We were never close in age or fellowship except for both being in your service for those times when our terms overlapped – a matter of months only.'

'He never said.'

'I misdoubt he was concerned for my welfare. It must be a matter of business. 'Tis quite an odd happenstance. I pray you, good master, should he ask after me again, if you would kindly enquire of him the reason.'

Master Collop led us to a well-appointed room. A tapestry hung upon the wall. I remembered it: 'Jason and the Argonauts', although lowly apprentices were permitted in the parlour but rarely.

'To what do I owe this pleasure?' our host enquired once we were settled upon a cushioned bench, ale cups in hand. 'You did not come simply to ask after my health and discuss old times, I know.'

I felt a surge of guilt. I ought to visit him more often. His hair remained thick as ever but was now bleach-white at his forehead and around his ears, marking the passing years.

''Tis true, master, for which I apologise sincerely. I have come in need of your sound advice upon a delicate matter.' I sipped my ale, watching my master discreetly over the cup rim.

'Hence why you did not wish to ask me at the guildhall yesterday.'

'The matter did not arise until an hour or two since.'

'Urgent then? Well, tell me of this business that is of such import.'

I delved into my purse and retrieved the little roll of parchment tied with red ribbon. I passed it to my master.

'Tis a commission from King Edward, no less,' I explained. He undid the bow and unrolled my instructions. He read it silently but his lips formed each word. He frowned once or twice and nodded approval at the end. The parchment re-rolled itself as he set it down.

'The instructions appear to be clear enough, but it will be an expensive volume to produce as the king requires. He means it to be an impressive gift indeed. Who is his intended recipient of such an elaborate work?'

'The messenger mentioned the Lord of Florence, or some such.'

'Lorenzo de' Medici,' Adam said, having remembered the name better than I had.

'The expense be my main concern,' I said. 'You will have noted there is no mention of any payments to be made.'

Master Collop read the parchment once more.

'I see your difficulty, young Sebastian.' Almost word for word, as I had explained to Adam earlier, my master reiterated the problem: to make a good copy, well bound, and trust it was found acceptable to the king; or fulfil every last, lavish detail of the commission and pray that we were paid the price eventually.

'Can you advise me, master?' I asked, retying the ribbon and replacing the parchment in my purse. 'For this piece will empty our coffer, if we follow the instructions precisely.'

He rubbed his brow, turning his gaze to the painted roof beams, deep in thought.

We waited, drinking our ale. Adam helped himself to another wafer and a marchpane-stuffed date. I was too concerned for my master's words of wisdom to have any interest in sweetmeats.

'It would be tempting to suggest you complete the work to

a good standard but spend no more than is necessary to make it appear that you have followed the instructions to the letter. No one outside the craft will be able to tell lapis lazuli from the cheaper alternative, azurite. The jewels need not be rubies and amethysts when coloured glass may serve as well. Once the book is in Florence, in some rich man's collection, who will notice if the colours fade forty years hence?

'However, you and I will know. Deceiving the king... it is a serious step to take. You are a man of conscience, Sebastian: could you be easy in your mind, knowing of the deception?'

Master Collop had come upon the heart of the matter. Did I follow the dictates of my conscience or my purse? He knew me well indeed. And there was always the possibility that the king would pay after all.

'I fear I could not, master.'

'Then I believe you have answered your own query. Do you have an exemplar of Vegetius' treatise? You will need an accurate version. It will save you time and trouble, although I know you are more than capable of correcting any errors in the previous scribe's Latin grammar as you copy it: the fewer mistakes, the better, else they may require the layout of the pages to be changed.'

'We have an English version of the most popular Book Three. This we sell as a separate booklet: five copies sold so far this year. Which brings me to the second purpose of our visit...'

'You wish to borrow my complete Latin copy.'

'If 'tis not in use, I shall be most grateful for it.'

'None has worked on it since you left, Sebastian. As you say, the English version sells more readily these days. I will instruct young Hugh to dust it off and bring it along to you at Paternoster Row in the morning. I know he will be glad to have time away from his desk; any errand is welcome.'

I set down my cup and rose to my feet.

Adam did likewise, though he was yet chewing a sweetmeat.

'I thank you, master. You have made my decision for me. I

should ever suffer sleepless nights if I fail to follow the king's instructions as required.'

'Aye. I believed that would be the case.'

'And I shall be pleased to see Hugh Gardyner upon the morrow.'

Master Collop came with us to the parlour door but held my sleeve to detain me. 'If money becomes a problem in this instance,' he whispered so Adam could not hear, 'Officially, the guild has funds to lend out at a most reasonable rate, if required. Unofficially, I also have coin available. And for my best apprentice, this would be loaned at a further reduced rate of interest: that is to say, naught but the capital need be repaid at a time to suit ourselves. Don't let this commission cause you hardship, Sebastian.'

'I be most grateful, Master Collop, both for your advice and your generous offer. Fare you well.' I touched my cap courteously and bowed my head so he might bless me. Kindly, he also bestowed his benediction upon Adam.

'What offer was that?' Adam asked as we returned along Cheapside. I explained about the possibility of borrowing money, though, in truth, such an action would be utterly against my nature.

'I hope and pray that it never comes to such a pass,' I said.

'We're going to make the most extravagant book, then? Cost no object?'

'Aye. Something of the kind. Master Collop was correct: I cannot give less than my very best in working for the king. Mayhap, that be why we were chosen. If our workshop was recommended to His Grace by the Duke of Gloucester, think what he would say, if he e'er discovered I had given his royal brother a shoddy piece and called it craftsmanship. I cannot do that, Adam. I am a better man than that – as are you. We are no charlatans. Together we will do justice to the king's commission and show ourselves worthy of his patronage and our own fair and goodly reputation. I wonder that I had dared consider, however briefly, doing otherwise. Come. Let us tell Rose, Kate and everyone our good tidings.'

Chapter 2

Saturday, the twelfth day of June
The Foxley House

ALIGHT MIST had swathed the city earlier, like a rich lady's gossamer-fine veil, but the sun soon parted the grey drapery to burn bright in a cloudless, azure sky as I opened the shop front, in preparation for Saturday's half-day trading. Of late, I was allowing Kate to deal with customers alone in the shop, she proving so capable, whilst Adam and I had a list to compile of things needful for King Edward's commission.

Parchment – or rather the best quality calf-skin vellum – was specified and headed the list but without the exemplar available to count the folios, it was difficult to judge how many skins we should require. Likewise, the number of illuminated capitals and rubrics for which we would need coloured inks and pigments. Thus, the list was long but much adorned with query marks regarding quantities unknown for numerous items. All we knew for certain were the two oaken boards and their dimensions to form the covers of the book, then to be clad in gilded leather and garnished with gemstones in filigree work. These last would needs be discussed with a goldsmith but were hardly a pressing matter when we had yet to commence writing the book. I was impatient to begin: the end of July was not so far distant – just seven weeks afore the king's ambassador would depart, taking the gift to Florence and the king desired time to approve it afore that. Six weeks at most, I supposed, to create this luxurious volume and time was wasting until I had the exemplar in my hands.

After a good breakfast of bacon collops, oatcakes and honey and a brief exploration of the garden plot with little Dickon and Gawain, I was thinking what might be done to begin the new commission. I fetched our English copy of Vegetius' Book Three and used it to work out likely margin widths and line spacings for the best presentation of the text. Our text was well spread to make it easy on the reader's eye following the lines of words but it might be the case that doing likewise with the whole book would make for an unwieldy volume. Together with the ornate cover, as specified, it could result in a heavy tome, too weighty to hold and read at ease. That was supposing the noble Florentine recipient ever bothered to open the pages over which we would take such care. I made notes and sketched out two possible page designs: one with a well-spaced text, the other more closely set. I wished I had a better remembrance of the book when I worked upon it, copying it out as an apprentice, to improve my Latin and my scribal hand.

At last, Kate called me into the shop. I had described Hugh Gardyner to her beforehand, such that she would recognise him.

'Master Seb! Hugh Gardyner is come,' she cried. 'See what he brings.'

I hastened to greet the lad, Adam following me.

'God give you good day, Hugh,' I said.

The lad removed his cap and bowed to me, then to Adam. He was somewhat taller than I had supposed, seeing him seated at his desk yesterday.

'Good day to you, Master Foxley. Master Collop has sent these for you.' He handed me a well-worn scrip, heavy with the book required – a weighty thing indeed. But 'neath his arm, he carried a linen-wrapped bundle: rolls of calf-skin vellum, smooth and perfect as the Virgin Mary's cheek. Master Collop was generous as ever, knowing our requirements for the king's work.

But I saw then that the lad lacked a thumb upon his right

hand. No wonder he had to use his left, yet that was ever considered to do the Devil's work.

I near made the sign of the Cross at sight of it but refrained. No doubt Hugh saw folk making such a gesture far too often. It must vex and sadden him to be regarded as an instrument of Satan at every turn. I felt an affinity with him straightway forwhy I had suffered likewise as a cripple in the past. How the other apprentices must mock him. Little wonder he was Master Collop's most industrious apprentice. No doubt, he engrossed himself in his work, as I used to do, keeping away from his fellows as far as he might and attempting to avoid their attentions. I also realised why my old master said Hugh would relish this errand, knowing that my own past experiences meant I should offer only kindliness and make naught of the lad's affliction.

'Would you like a cup of ale, Hugh? And some cakes I helped to bake?' Kate offered, overstepping the bounds of propriety. The offer was mine to make but she had forestalled me. Yet, I noted, her smile, lacking for so long, was there, like sunlight shining from her face. 'He is allowed, isn't he, Master Seb?' she said, realising her error.

'For certain. Why do you not fetch it here and Hugh may take his refreshment whilst you await customers. If he so wishes...'

Adam gave me a knowing glance, raising his eyebrows.

'I'd be honoured, master,' Hugh said, his eyes bright with pleasure.

I nodded. It was heartening to see Kate nigh-dancing along the passage to the kitchen.

With Master Collop's copy of Vegetius in my possession, I was eager to begin work. I could now revise the page layout and, with the gift of vellum, Adam could commence ruling up and pricking the folios without further delay.

I returned to the shop but briefly to see that all was well. I found Kate making sketches of Hugh whilst he drank his ale, the pair laughing together. I do believe our Kate has taken a fancy to him and why not? He be the Lord Mayor's nephew after all: a far better prospect for an alderman's daughter than a fatherless joiner like Jack. It was a wondrous thing to have her smiling once more.

'What do you think, Adam?' I showed him a sketch for a large capital letter 'A'. 'The instructions say 'well-decorated' but a surfeit of ornamentation makes the letters difficult to read. I have tried to achieve something betwixt two extremes: sufficient elaboration without rendering the capital illegible. Be this too much or no? I would have your opinion, cousin.'

Adam groaned and muttered under his breath afore setting aside another set of ruled folios.

'I gave you my opinion on the previous five versions of the letter 'A', Seb. The first one was fine – as are they all. Are we to suffer this degree of deliberation over every capital? If so, the book won't be finished before Judgement Day.'

I had closed up the shop at dinnertime, it being Saturday. The afternoon was, of custom, a period of leisure for all but I insisted I would work. Adam had agreed to do likewise but I sensed he was regretting that decision now.

'But 'tis the king's commission. It has to be perfect.'

Adam sighed and leafed through my sketches of ornamented letter forms.

'This one,' he said. 'The first one you did.'

'You be certain? What of this other?' I pulled another sketch to the top of the pile.

'Seb, if you're not going to heed my opinion, why ask for it?'

''Tis rather a debate, I thought…'

'Then you'll have to decide.'

'I shall ask Em what she…'

Adam looked at me, a sorrowful expression moving across his strong features as a cloud passes afore the sun.

I crumpled inwardly. When would I cease torturing myself

in this way?

'I'm going out,' he said, turning aside. 'What say you, we meet at that new tavern by the Bellhouse in an hour? We can try their ale; see if we approve the place.'

'Aye. In an hour, then.' I returned my attention to my little heap of letters, having to dab my eyes with my sleeve. Which of my designs would Em have approved? The choice would have to wait a while.

Saturday afternoon was the time of the week I most dreaded. As well as the commission, the weekly accounts had to be done. However much care I took, no matter how diligent I had been in noting every transaction in the book – whether income or expenditure – the numbers never quite tallied to the last penny. This week – God be praised – the accounts were but a halfpenny in discrepancies and that to our credit, so no harm there. As usual, having put a few pence into my purse and left some in the box for dealings on Monday, I took most of the coin to our secret hidey-hole, Em's and mine, behind the loose brick in the parlour chimney that none else knew of. Surprisingly, the leather bag hidden there was over-full already; no room for more. I wondered how come we were so parsimonious that little, if anything, had been spent of late.

Instead, I went to our bedchamber above stairs where our second and yet more secret place was hidden. Left behind by the miserly Matthew Bowen, one-time master of this house, the heavy image of Our Lady in its leaden frame concealed an aumbry wherein we had discovered Bowen's hoard of gold and silver. Much had been spent since, either by my brother Jude or by me on the fine glazed window there, a newly tiled roof and other repairs to the premises. Whenever there was coin to spare or a gold noble or such from my patron, the Duke of Gloucester, it went into the aumbry behind Our Lady for safe-keeping, against some unforeseen happenstance. I put the extra money away and replaced the heavy picture upon its hook, making certain it hung straight.

The Sun in Splendour Tavern

A new place of refreshment had opened for business, at the northern end of Old Change, beside the Bellhouse. It was likely to compete for custom with the Panyer Inn, across the way, in Paternoster Row, but I was never a great patron of the latter, giving it my custom for no more reason than its proximity to home. Adam and I determined to sample the wares and atmosphere of the new place, acquaint ourselves with the proprietor, whether we liked him sufficiently to become regular customers.

The Sun in Splendour – for so it was called, after King Edward's badge – smelled of fresh paint and new limewash. A piper played beside the door, enticing folk to pause, listen and come along in. Benches stood outside, already crowded upon this sunny Saturday afternoon. And no wonder: the first pot of ale was given free to customers, so we were informed by a comely wench carrying three brimming jugs in either hand to serve the customers.

'Well, I'll certainly come here again,' Adam said, drinking deep of his introductory cup. We had found two stools within, left vacant as a pair of glovers I knew slightly from Ivy Lane departed. Whilst some folk preferred to sit outside, there was yet hardly space left to sharpen a quill indoors.

'The ale will not be free in future,' I said.

'Ale? What of it? That pretty wench yonder is more enticing than free drink.'

I rolled my eyes.

'You will be marrying soon, Adam. Your bride will warm your bed…' The ale was a fair brewing, I discovered, malty and refreshing.

'Aye, but I'm not wed yet. Besides, a man needs a little practice. I wouldn't want to disappoint Mercy on our wedding night for lack of rehearsal, would I now?'

'I know not what Mother Church has to say on the matter of rehearsing for your nuptials.'

'Knowing Mother Church, I doubt they ever thought of the possibility, being no more than a bundle of dry old sticks. They'd be content if we were all monks and lived as hermits; never mind that mankind would die out within a generation. They seem to forget that the Almighty decreed we should 'Go forth and multiply' and I'm more than willing to do my best to obey His command.' He saw my expression and shook his head. 'Come on, Seb: I've not taken any vows of chastity. Have a heart, cousin. Don't think the worse of me. I'll be ever faithful to Mercy afterwards.'

'I suppose, the lass be most fair to look upon… fine eyes, indeed, and a shapely nose…'

'I had not looked so high, as yet,' Adam admitted, grinning.

I feared he was acquiring city ways and prayed he would not become a philanderer, like my brother Jude.

'Beware you do not take more than you bargained for into the marriage bed.'

'She looks clean enough.'

'I do not believe you can tell so easily. Remember those brazen hussies from The Mermaid not so long since. Was it not the case that the most innocent-looking was riddled with sores and had to be barred from plying her trade, so Thaddeus Turner said afterwards.'

'You want I should interrogate her first? Have a surgeon make an inspection?'

'Just be careful, cousin, is all.'

Adam left his stool, moving to cross the wench's winding path among the outstretched legs, booted feet, assorted benches, trestle-boards and sprawled dogs. She was laden with empty jugs and cups but he touched her elbow. She turned to him, smiling, most likely expecting the order for more drink. But Adam was not the only man to want her attention.

As I watched, another fellow's arm snaked about her waist,

drawing her towards him. She turned away from Adam, greeting the other's proprietary gesture with a laugh, bending close to speak in his ear.

I saw the fellow's face: impossibly handsome, fine-featured. He was lithe and tall as he rose to his feet. Adam was good-looking in a rough, countryman's way but could ne'er outshine this Adonis with his elegance of gesture and sweet turn of phrase – not that I could hear his words above the racket of the tavern but they pleased the wench right well, to judge from her expression.

Oddly, I felt I knew his face. Yet that made no sense. I should have recalled such symmetry of feature, the perfect jawline, the faultless brow.

'Damn his eyes!' Adam cursed, coming back to his stool, scowling fit to sour the ale remaining in my cup. He kicked the trestle, rocking the table and toppling someone else's cup – empty, fortunately. Gawain shot to his feet from beneath the board, fearing it would fall upon him.

'Easy, cousin.' I put my hand upon his arm but he shook me off.

'Did you see what that sow's son did? The bastard! I'll have his guts to lace my shoes. He could see I was speaking to her first. How dare he grab her away like that?'

'Mayhap, they be related,' I suggested, soothing Gawain with a pat as I finished my ale.

'Related? Aye, as I'm related to the queen, no doubt.'

'I think we should leave now, afore matters get out of hand.'

'Nothing's going to get out of hand. I'll simply rip out his liver and that'll be the end of it.'

'Nay, Adam. I forbid it. You have more sense than to make trouble over a pair of red lips. Come, Gawain. Home.' I made towards the door, willing Adam to follow me without more ado.

Outside, we passed St Michael's, making for home. My cousin's glaring look betrayed his mood, as did the hefty kick he applied to our back gate.

25

'You break it; you mend it,' I warned him.

'I want to know that bastard's name,' he growled. 'We'll need it for his grave marker when I've done with him.'

'Forget him, Adam. He be unworthy of your ire. Do not let him trouble your thoughts.'

'Easy for you to say. You didn't have a willing wench dragged from your arms by that… that jumped up jackanapes. He needs putting in his place.'

'Well, let some other fellow do it. I do not wish to be bailing you out of the Sheriff's Counter on a charge of breaking the king's peace.'

'The king's peace be damned. 'Tis the devil's neck that requires breaking.'

'The strangest thing is, I know his face, yet I cannot place him.'

'But you never forget a face, Seb. Make yourself remember and tell me his name.'

'Mayhap, I never knew it.'

The Foxley House

The evenings remaining light this close to midsummer, Adam had gone to Distaff Lane to spend time with his intended, Mercy Hutchinson. Jack was also from home, heaven knew where. Kate was in the kitchen with her drawing board, keeping company with Nessie. I could hear them giggling at the other end of the passage, the way young lasses do.

Little Dickon was abed, so Rose and I sat at our ease in the parlour.

'Kate would seem to have regained her merry humour,' I said, as a louder burst of laughter from the kitchen roused me from my study of Vegetius – aye, I was yet at work upon a Saturday eve.

Rose looked up from her neat stitchery, mending a tear in one of Jack's shirts.

'Aye. She is happier, now her flowers have come down at long last.'

'Her flowers?'

'Women's monthly flowers.'

'Oh, aye. What of them?' I did my best to sound worldly-wise but, in truth, all I knew of such matters was that they began when a woman reached marriageable age, ceased when she was with child and betwixt those times the Church forbade husband and wife having bedsport whenever they flowed.

'It could have been shock or grief,' Rose was saying, although she sounded somewhat hesitant and fidgeted with her sewing. 'Such things can cause them to cease a while, you understand?'

'At least we can be certain our innocent maid cannot be with child.'

'Ow! Now look, I have pricked my finger.' Rose set down her mending and sucked her finger, wanting to avoid blood upon the shirt. 'No, of course she can't be. Anyhow, the herbs put her to rights. All is well with Kate now, her humours restored.'

'Meeting Master Collop's apprentice this morn did no harm either: the lass was all smiles for him. Did you see him? Hugh Gardyner, the Lord Mayor's nephew: a good lad, by the look of him. He has my master's approval, leastwise.'

'No, I didn't see him. You think they might be a suitable match?' Rose resumed her sewing.

'What? I had not thought so far, though he be more her equal than Jack, for certain. But Kate be young yet for marriage.'

'But old enough, Seb. You should have a word with her father. We don't want anything untoward to happen, do we?'

'Untoward? But Rose, Kate be a good lass. I know she has – or had – an affection for Jack but naught more than that. Kate knows to keep herself pure for her future husband and if Jack ever attempted… anything inappropriate, she would send him off with a buffet to the ears, or scream. As for Jack, if I suspected aught amiss, he would pay dear for his errors.'

Rose stitched silently and I returned my attentions to reading about Roman military deployment. I know not why but I found it strangely absorbing, though such things held no interest for me otherwise.

'You would make Jack pay? How?' Rose asked after a while.

'What do you mean?' I turned a page.

At my feet, Gawain twitched, dreaming of herding sheep or chasing conies, most like.

'If Jack did something amiss with Kate.'

'I have not considered. Since naught has occurred, there be no reason why I should.'

Rose wore so serious an expression, I closed the book and leaned forward.

'Has some incident come to pass that I know not of?' I enquired, lowering my voice – not that there was anyone to overhear.

She nodded.

'Why did you not inform me of this?'

'Because of Emily. She lay upon her deathbed the day it happened. Your mind had to be upon other matters, Seb. Besides, I said I wouldn't tell, yet the secret gnaws away at me... Now it is over, I feel I must speak of it.'

'Kate and Jack? Together?'

Rose was winding the shirt around her hands in anguish, turning it into a mess of wrinkled cloth.

'I found them in our bedchamber. You may recall that Sunday when the window stuck half-open. We asked Jack to mend it. For whatever reason Kate went to the chamber. I caught them there, upon the bed, their clothing all in disarray.'

'Jack forced himself upon her.'

'She says not. She consented but thought 'twas just a game.'

The book slipped from my grasp to the floor, catching Gawain on the rump and rousing him from slumber with a start. I could barely comprehend what Rose was telling me.

'Do you mean she has lost her maidenhood?'

Rose nodded.

'That cannot e'er be recovered! Dear heaven... what a coil is this? However can I excuse my failure to protect her when her father learns of it? Her future be in ruins; our reputation in ashes when the guild hears what manner of master I be that cannot keep safe a young lass in his care.' I felt I might tear out my hair. Then a worse possibility occurred to me. 'I pray you: tell me she is not with child.'

'No, not any longer... if indeed she ever was. As I explained, her courses have returned, whether by Nature's hand alone or with the aid of the herbs. I feared to tell you, Seb, knowing the trouble this would cause.'

I rubbed my aching temples. Trouble, indeed.

'You should have told me of this afore now.'

'How could I? You were deep in grief. Besides, we knew not whether any harm had been done: a babe, I mean.'

'Harm? She has been deflowered. Is that not harm enough? I shall have to confront the pair.'

'What will you do?'

'I know not.'

How long I sat, I cannot say. My thoughts were in turmoil, my humours seething. I could not find words to speak.

Eventually, I left the parlour and went out through the shop door. I intended to go around to the garden plot, the better to think, but did not dare go by way of the kitchen where I heard Kate laughing yet. If I encountered her at this moment, I could not trust my tongue to avoid uttering words I would regret upon the morrow.

But my respite in the balmy summer's eve was not to be. In the side alley that led to our back gate, Adam caught up with me.

'Well, cousin!' he said, slapping me on the back. 'What a wondrous evening this is. Mercy and me... we...'

I rounded upon him, shoving him away.

'Do not tell me!' I yelled. 'I do not want to know about you

29

and Mercy. 'Tis not my business what you do. I do not care!'

'Easy, Seb. Don't have forty fits on my account. I was going to tell you've we've set the date for our wedding.'

'Well and good. Then you can move out of this house where chaos reigns and the Devil rules. Leave me to sort out this hellish mess.'

'What mess? What's got you all of a lather, Seb?'

'Kate and Jack.' I pushed the gate and went into our yard. Adam followed me.

'Ah, so you've found them out at last. Gone too far, have they? I knew they would.'

'You knew about them?' I propped myself against the apple tree, weary of a sudden.

'Aye. Caught them kissing more than once. It was getting somewhat hot and passionate betwixt them.'

'And you never thought to tell me?'

'Well, I warned them; threatened Jack if he didn't behave. Clearly, that wasn't enough.'

'So, as ever, I be the last to learn of what goes on under my own roof.'

'Sorry, Seb. You had Emily to think of at the time.'

'There was the possibility that Kate had conceived. I suppose you knew that also?'

'No. Christ, Seb. What a bloody fix that would be. She hasn't, has she?'

'Apparently not.'

'God be thanked for that.'

'All the same, I shall have to inform her father. Likely, he will terminate her apprenticeship straightway upon learning I be unfit to stand as her guardian after this. I shall be sad to lose her. She has such talent as would be a pity to waste. And she being a lively lass, brightening the days.'

'Do you have to tell him? Does anyone outside this house need to know?'

'Oh, Adam, do not tempt me to compound my failure with

additional sins. This be hard enough to resolve as it stands.' I picked a sprig of rosemary from the bush Em had nurtured so well. Rosemary for remembrance, as they say. It would ever recall her to mind. I breathed deeply of its cleansing scent. 'Have you ever copied out the Gospel of St Luke, cousin?'

'Aye. Why?'

'And did you ever read the words you wrote?'

'Maybe.'

'Do you recall chapter twelve, verse two?'

'Not especially. What are trying to say, Seb?'

'St Luke tells us: "There be naught concealed that shall not be revealed; neither hidden that shall not be known". You think we could keep Kate's secret indefinitely? That it will not be far worse when the truth is uncovered – as it surely will be – forwhy we attempted to withhold it?'

'Mm, well it'll be your decision, one way or the other.'

I sighed.

'Ever the last to know, yet it falls to me to cleanse the filth from the Augean stables.'

'The what?'

'The fifth labour of Heracles… a monumental task, cleaning up an impossible mess. Read it for yourself. 'Tis in that book of Greek myths upon the shelf.'

'You're too much the scholar for me tonight, cousin. I'm going to bed. Coming?'

'Nay, I shall wait awhile. My mind be in too great a turmoil to be able to rest as yet.

'Don't sit here drowning in melancholy over this, Seb. I know you too well.'

'The blackbird singing his vespers motet in yonder elder tree be company enough and 'tis as fine a lullaby as any. I shall not become mawkish, Adam, but I must think these matters through. Clear my head afore I may seek sleep.'

When he had gone, I sat upon the upturned bucket we use to fill the water trough. The platters of elderflowers, ghostly in the twilight, scented the air. Moths hovered over the lavender and bats flitted through the dusk. As the blackbird sang his orisons, somewhere beyond our garden plot, a babe was crying and the Watch called out the hour of ten of the clock. Night was drawing down.

Eventually, I would find slumber, but requiring peace, instead of climbing to Adam's chamber, I retired to the bed I had shared with my beloved – the first time since I lost her. It seemed a foreign place now.

Chapter 3

Sunday, the thirteenth day of June
The Foxley House

AFTER MASS at St Michael's, I confronted the pair, even afore breakfast, for fear my courage would desert me, if I delayed. Such a situation was so against my nature; Emily would have made a more efficient task of it.

We were in the workshop. Kate sat at her desk whilst Jack leaned against Adam's.

'Sit down, Jack.' I indicated Adam's stool. I could not have the tall youngster looming over me. I stood by the collating table. 'I know what came to pass betwixt the two of you,' I said bluntly, not knowing how else to begin.

'Didn't do nuffink, did we?' Jack said, scowling and folding his arms.

Kate began to sob into her Sunday-best apron.

'It was a mistake... Jack and me... I never thought...'

'Indeed you did not. A moment's consideration aforehand and all this could have been avoided.'

'All wot? Nuffink 'appened; I told you.'

'I needs must inform Alderman Verney of his daughter's fall from grace and you be guilty, likewise, Jack.'

'No, Master Seb! I beg you: don't tell my father. He'll never forgive me. Please, please, I beg you not to.' Kate threw herself at my feet.

It was most disconcerting. I longed to tell her I would not

inform him but how could I? This was so serious a matter: my lapse in the guardianship of the lass and her resultant loss of maidenhood. I felt sure her father would forgive her but never me for my negligence. Kate might fear her parent's wrath but not half so much as I did.

'Do not prostrate yourself, lass. This be my fault as much as yours. The blame lies heavy upon me: I should have observed how you were grown close and instructed you accordingly. I ought to have kept you both from the transgressions and follies of youth but I failed you. 'Tis I should beg your forgiveness for my insufficiency in maintaining the obligations of mastership.'

'Your wot? You mean it's your fault we wos fuckin', cos we didn't know no better?'

'Just so.' I did not reprimand him for his use of common ale-house speech. There seemed little point.

'That's alright then, ain't it?'

'Nay, Jack, 'tis far from being "all right", as you say. The matter be rather "all wrong". The merciful Christ Jesu alone knows how this will end but we have to begin to make amends this day. Thus, after dinner, Kate, you will come with me to your father's house.'

The lass made to object but I stilled her with a gesture to forebear.

'As for you, Jack, you will remain here 'neath Adam's eye, and attend the archery butts with him. There will be no escape to some tavern or other. Upon your return, you will recite the rosary aloud and contemplate your sin all the while we be gone to Walbrook. That be your penance – for the present, until Father Thomas imposes a proper one upon you.'

'You ain't goin' t' tell that mumblin' ol' fart of a priest as well, are you?'

'Enough! Do not compound your misdeeds still further by insulting a man of the cloth. You will keep silent throughout dinner: thus, you can err no more. And, nay, I shall not inform the good Father. Rather, *you* will make your confession to him.'

'I bloody won't.' Jack stood up, overturning the stool with a crash and strode towards the door.

'Indeed, you will. Elsewise, you will be living on bread and water until you do.'

Dinner was a sombre repast. Hardly a word was exchanged betwixt any of us. It was as if a great dark cloud hung over our heads. Little Dickon seemed to sense it too, grizzling fretfully, as was not his custom.

'He has another tooth coming,' Rose explained, then added – and not for the first time –'I shouldn't have told you.'

I nodded, chewing and swallowing my food without any awareness of what I ate. I knew Rose regretted now having informed me, concerning Kate and Jack. But she was right to do so, however unfortunate the consequences.

Alderman Edmund Verney's House, Walbrook

Master Verney greeted us, smiling hugely at the sight of his favoured younger daughter – the elder, like her mother, was never mentioned.

'God's blessings be upon you, Master Foxley, on this fine Lord's Day. Kate, this is an unexpected pleasure. Come in, come in.'

Was the day fine? I had not noticed. Unbeknownst, he was making this harder. It pained me to have to prick his bubble of joy at sight of us.

'God's blessings upon you also, Master Verney,' I said, following him into his parlour.

'Shall you have ale?'

I shook my head.

'I thank you but nay. Yet it may be needful after we have spoken.'

'Well, that sounds serious. Sit down, if you will, Sebastian. Kate, see to the dogs in the yard...'

'This concerns Kate most nearly, Master Verney. I would Kate remained, if you allow.'

The alderman smiled no longer. My formality discomforted him, I saw.

'What has she done amiss? Kate? What have you been doing that your master has so grave a countenance?'

The lass burst into tears.

'I fear the failing be mine as much as anyone's. The lad, Jack, who lodges with us at Paternoster Row – he who was my sometime apprentice – he and Kate...'

Her father leapt from his chair afore I completed the sentence and caught the lass such a blow across her ear, she fell to the floor, sobbing under his wrath.

'You stupid little hussy!' he roared. 'You foolish wench. What are your marriage prospects now, eh? After all I've done to set you up in life... all my efforts... my money wasted on a slut!' Spittle flew from his lips with every word. 'I should throw you out on the street to beg your bread.'

I wondered that he should so readily, upon an instant, accept his daughter's misdeeds e'er they were even named. Why should he think the worst of her without due deliberation? Had she committed errors in the past of which he knew and kept secret?

'The lass should not bear all the blame, Master Verney. I was remiss in my duties as her guardian and Jack, being older, led her astray...'

'She's a slut without prospects and when the bastard is born...'

It took me a moment to realise what he was saying.

'There be no child,' I said hastily. 'Kate and Mistress Glover – Rose – be certain of it.'

'No child? Well, God be praised for that, at least.' He resumed his seat. 'Get up, Kate. Dry your eyes, for pity's sake.

36

Do some useful service: go fetch ale for Master Foxley and me, then leave us. I need to think on this.'

'Yes, Papa.'

For some time, the silence stretched out. I heard sounds from the street beyond the window glass: children laughing at a game; men returning from archery practice at Smithfield, joshing each other over their prowess, or otherwise, with the bow, presumably.

Kate served the ale afore withdrawing. Apart from my thanks for the drink, not a word was spoken.

''Tis not your fault, Sebastian.' Master Verney said at last. 'It seems that Kate is another wayward wench, as bad as her sister. I should have warned you of the likelihood. Maybe I ought to send her to Bedlam also.'

'Oh, no…'

The alderman glared at me for daring to disagree.

'She is a grave disappointment to me,' he continued. 'And what am I to do with the wanton now? You'll be terminating her indenture of apprenticeship forthwith, of course, as is your right, considering her disgraceful behaviour under your roof.'

'Not so, master. I believed you would wish to end the agreement, owing to my negligence, but I be more than willing to allow the indenture to run its course. Kate be a most talented apprentice.'

'It reflects badly upon me and would dash my hopes of being elected Lord Mayor in the near future. All the women of my family have been a sore trial to me over the years on that account. And now, just as I thought to have come through those previous difficulties, this new scandal will ruin my chances yet again. If you could overlook this matter? I'd be content to pay you a goodly sum, Sebastian, if you were willing to keep this quiet, take Kate back into your employ. Will a hundred marks ensure your silence?'

'What?'

'Two hundred, then.'

'Nay, sir. You mistake me...'

'Two hundred and fifty marks.'

'I want no money, Master Verney.'

'You're going to inform Lord Mayor Gardyner, whatever I offer? I can't persuade you otherwise?'

'I swear upon my oath that I shall not inform anyone. My reputation would suffer as much as yours. Kate may return as though none of this ever came to pass. You paid for her apprenticeship when the indenture was drawn up and enrolled at Guildhall. You owe me naught; I require no further monies of you. Never a word of this will pass my lips, for all our sakes. I would ask but one thing.'

'Ask what you wish.'

'Please keep your daughter here for this night. I do not want her under the same roof as Jack. Last eve, I could not rest, thinking how close they lay, even in quite separate chambers. I must make some other arrangements for the lad's lodging. I dare not trust them together again, I fear.'

'It shall be as you say, Sebastian. I'll be forever in your debt, as long as I live.'

'We all of us have been in error, one way or another. I have learned a salutary lesson, Master Verney.'

He nodded and shook my hand right heartily as I took my leave of him. The matter had resolved itself better than I hoped.

But what of Jack?

Upon my way home, I visited Stephen Appleyard – until lately my father-by-marriage and currently Jack's master in the craft of carpentry and joinery – to discuss some change of situation for the lad. Somehow, the matter had to be explained to the worthy carpenter without revealing the true nature of Jack's misdeeds, in accordance with my oath sworn unto the alderman. As ever, I made for my back yet another cross that I must bear in silent suffering. Would I never learn?

As we finished a goodly supper of ham in a spiced broth, I begged attention from all at the board.

'Heed me, if you will.' I tidied my napkin, folding it neatly and cleared my throat.

Adam, Rose, Jack and Nessie sat silent, waiting. Little Dickon gurgled and waved his spoon. Gawain sat up, ears pricked.

'There will be changes made here upon the morrow. They concern you most closely, Jack, but all will be involved.'

'Wot's it to do wiv me?' Jack demanded, snatching another wedge of bread and stuffing it into his mouth, all unmannerly.

'You will improve your behaviour at mealtimes for one thing forwhy, after breaking your fast in the morn, you will be sharing Master Appleyard's board for the foreseeable future.'

'Wot! I'll bloody starve, eating the pig's swill and scrapings the widow serves up.' Jack referred to the kindly neighbour who cooked Stephen Appleyard's meals for him. Never having dined there, I could not say whether he spoke true.

'Then that will be a further cause for you to regret your previous conduct in this house. You will also be lodging with Master Appleyard so, first thing in the morn, you will collect your necessary belongings from your attic and remove them to your new abode.'

'You're chuckin' us out!' Jack screeched. 'You bastard! I wos finking you liked us all this time and you're just as bad as all the bloody rest.'

'It serves you right,' Adam added, unhelpfully. 'You brought this upon yourself.'

'An' wot about Kate?' Jack went on. 'I'll wager a fortune you ain't chuckin' her out on the street.'

'You are not being thrown onto the street, lad. I have arranged a change of bed and board for you is all. 'Tis not the end of our acquaintance,' I assured him. I found it hard to prevent an apology spilling forth from my lips but I must not relent in this matter.

'An' wot of Kate?' he repeated.

'Kate's situation be naught of your concern but she will continue to bide and work here, as afore. That be the reason for your leaving...'

'I bloody knew it! That's not fuckin' fair, that ain't. She did it too. She's to blame an' all.'

'Kate has been punished sufficiently in quite other ways: tormented by fear for weeks that she was with child, then facing her father's wrath and disgust. She too will be making her confession to the priest. She is not being let off lightly; you can be assured of it.'

Rose nodded agreement.

'Kate was beside herself with worry, Jack, as you most certainly were not. Only this last week could we be certain there was no babe to come.'

Jack's eyes flew wide. It was plain that the possibility had ne'er entered his heedless thoughts.

I spoke into the vacant pause as Jack realised how much more grave his predicament might have been.

'This matter will continue to concern us all – and harken well, Nessie – in that I swore an oath to Alderman Verney that this misdeed will ne'er be made known beyond these walls. I informed Master Appleyard that Jack has a serious disagreement, a significant difference of opinion with another of this household. Thus, 'tis better for the sake of peace that both parties have time to cool and settle their humours. I did not name the other party. The truth will remain a secret.

'There will be no boasting of your bedchamber achievements in the tavern, Jack: Kate's name will not be mentioned by you, ever. Do you understand? If I should learn of any rumour besmirching her reputation... well, I be no man of violence but I shall make an exception in that case, Jack.' I turned to Nessie: 'And I be aware of your too-loose tongue, Nessie. You dare to spread one iota of gossip in the market or at the conduit or anywhere else in the city and without and I shall see you regret it lifelong. Now, you will all promise, as I have done, ne'er to speak of this.' I had fetched the Holy Gospel book from its niche in the parlour for this purpose, afore we supped. I set the Word of God upon a clean napkin in the midst of the board. 'Each, in turn, you will place your right hand on the book and swear your oath to keep silent.'

'What? Forever, master?' Nessie asked.

'Aye, forever. Other hand, Nessie.'

Nessie made her oath, then Rose and Adam.

'Now you, Jack, and remember, God be watching you and the life of your soul everlasting depends upon you maintaining your oath for eternity. You will end in the flames of hell, if you break it.'

Jack extended his hand, reluctant as though the book itself would burn him; consume him in a cloud of pungent brimstone smoke. Mayhap Holy Writ could do that to a sinner, if God intended it so but, in this instance, it did not. Jack's flesh remained whole and unsinged.

I exhaled a long sigh. I had not realised how I held my breath.

'That is done,' I said, 'And I pray that Christ Jesu, our most merciful Saviour, may grant us all the grace and strength to keep our oaths. God blessings be upon us all.'

I dismissed everyone from the supper board and took up the Holy Gospel book. I saw that Adam observed me but I could not read his countenance.

'You think I made over much of this matter? That I went too far in having you each swear your oath upon these Gospels? Yet I did not force you against your will, else an oath made under duress would not be binding. You could have refused.'

He shrugged his broad shoulders, so unlike the bowed, narrow form of most scribes. His years as a countryman, labouring in the fields of Foxley village in Norfolk, made him different from the rest of our fellowship members.

'In truth, cousin, I don't know what else you could have

41

done. Come on, 'tis a pleasant evening and a while yet until sunset. Let's take Gawain to Smithfield whilst it's quiet there. I heard tell that tomorrow, they'll start setting up the field for the horse racing and stock sales that precede the Midsummer Revels for St John's Day. You can tell me all about how Londoners celebrate the occasion. I'll be excited to be there and see what befalls. Mercy says the bonfires are so numerous and so large it never gets dark in the city on Midsummer's Night. Is that true?'

Smithfield

Having hailed the gate-keeper, we strolled out of Newgate and turned right, up towards Smithfield. I knew Adam had suggested this walk to raise my spirits and redirect my thoughts. He was a kindly, compassionate fellow, indeed. So I obliged him, telling of past revels but I took in the sights and sounds of a warm, summer eve for the most part.

Upon our right hand, wild roses spangled the hedgerow along the roadside in blushed profusion. The golden crowns at their hearts glowed in the slanting rays of the westering sun, like royal diadems. Bees still buzzed from flower to flower in the fading warmth of day. Meadowsweet spires spilled frothy flowers and honeyed scent upon the air.

It was a glorious evening.

Moths flitted, rousing from their daytime slumbers, but a late-flying butterfly, barred red upon richest brown, crossed our way. Gawain gave chase, snapping and missing. It landed upon a clump of verdant nettles, bold as mercenaries and as well-armed. The butterfly seemed not to notice their stinging weapons, at which I wondered when they afflicted men – and nosy dogs – to our great annoyance.

Gawain retreated from the nettles, abandoning his pursuit of the butterfly. He pawed at his stung snout. Unsympathetic,

Adam and I laughed. For once, it was a relief to find merriment in the misfortunes of another.

The daisies in the grass closed their sleepy eyes. The birds were falling quiet but for the crooning of a lovesome pair of turtle doves in a stand of coppiced hazel and a yellowhammer, chirping out his last short song, until the morrow's dawn-light should summon him to sing anew.

Smithfield lay, a soft emerald meadow, in the gentle light. Coneys cropped the turf and moved away, unhurried, at our trespass. Of course, Gawain thought to play chase with them but they seemed to guess he was of little threat and only in leisurely wise did their white scuts disappear down holes hid 'neath the bramble bushes.

As shadows stretched ever longer, we completed our slow circuit of the Horse Pool where bulrushes stood tall in velvet and yellow water lilies sailed upon still waters. The sky paled overhead to a canopy of crystalline blue, painted towards the west with every hue of amber and copper as the sun sank lower into his feathered cloud-bed. The air felt warm against my cheek: a maiden's caress. We did not speak; words were not needed. My dear cousin knew his sorcery had worked its magic upon me. I was soothed and calm in mind, as I had not been for so long. But as e'er be the way of things, such peace was not to last.

We were back within Newgate, walking along the deserted Shambles. Even upon this, the Lord's Day, the stink of butchery lingered, to be increased tenfold come Monday morn. Gawain went sniffing in corners, disturbed a rat's nest, sending the serpent-tailed creatures fleeing in all directions.

Of a sudden, there came a shout of 'Stop thief!' from farther along Bladder Street. That set off the hubbub of the hue-and-cry. Neighbours hastened onto the street, sounding horns, clattering spoons on pots and pans, adding to the din. It meant Adam and I were obliged to join the chase, pursuing the miscreant, whoever he might be. Adam sprinted ahead, fleet of foot, with

Gawain running at full speed, thinking this a fine game. They turned up Noble Street, betwixt the precinct of St Martin-le-Grand and the Goldsmiths' Hall, disappearing from my sight, along with the crowd of others who ran, hoping to apprehend the villain.

Never much of a runner myself, I soon lagged behind, keeping company with a breathless old man and a woman encumbered with a sleeping infant on her shoulder and armed with a hefty ladle. We would ne'er catch the most sluggardly criminal but the law demanded we make the effort, or be fined for aiding and abetting the same. My hip was hindering my progress, slow as it was, and by the time we reached St Vedast's Church at the lower end of Noble Street, I had to pause to ease my protesting bones. The old man stopped beside me to catch his breath, the woman too.

It was then that I glanced up the alleyway beside the church. A pile of rubbish half-blocked the narrow passage. All was filth and grime and stank of stale piss. Yet there was just light sufficient to see a flash of red: a good shoe, I realised, protruding from behind the unsavoury heap of detritus.

I pointed it out to the old man, then put my finger to my lips.

The old man nodded his understanding. He and I crept forth into the alley. Like so many such passages around the city, this one ended in a blank wall beyond the rubbish. There would be no escape for the vermilion-shod thief – if it were he. I stepped around a broken, handle-less bucket and then a collection of rusted metal odds and ends so as not to alert our quarry. When we drew within a yard or two, we both dashed forward, shouting 'Hold! Hold, villain!'

A middle-aged fellow leaped from his place of concealment and attempted to push us aside. I shoved him in one direction and the old man tripped him. As the culprit staggered back along the alley, into Noble Street, the woman with the infant awaited him. Her skilful use of the ladle without rousing the child was remarkable. She brought it down upon his head, then whacked him across his middle. He went sprawling in the dirt. The clang of metal as he hit the ground revealed his ill-gotten gains, hidden 'neath his jerkin. A gilded candlestick rolled aside, its partner lay sorely dented – mayhap by the ladle blow – beside the fallen fellow. We had caught our thief.

We dragged him to his feet and shook him awake, marching him back to Bladder Street. I had the stolen candlesticks tucked under my arm. The rascal began complaining and attempted to pull free as his senses rallied but the woman threatened him with the ladle and he came quietly, resigned to his fate.

The householder he had robbed greeted us as heroes, the more so when I returned the candlesticks, though he sorrowed at the damage done. We said naught concerning the ladle as the possible cause of the dents.

'Ale! Ale for all!' the householder cried as those who had spent their strength in the hue-and-cry began to trickle back, to report that the thief had got clean away. Most were delighted that we had apprehended the culprit but a few were annoyed to have gone to so much effort for no purpose. Others – including Adam – were disappointed to have missed out on the moment of capture.

'There was naught exciting about it, cousin,' I assured him.

'Did he put up much of a fight?' someone else asked.

I was about to tell him 'nay' but the old man – Todd by name, as I learned – made answer for me.

'I'll say. The devil fought us like... like a devil. Kicking and flailing and yelling filthy words at me, young Seb here, oh, and Alice... her with the babe-in-arms. So we pummelled him and took him by force, didn't we Seb? He was lashing out, all to no avail. We was too much for him, wasn't we?'

The event grew in the telling, Todd elaborating and inventing new details to each new listener who asked. He and I became more heroic in our actions as the evening wore on; the woman, Alice, the true heroine with her ladle, became relegated to the role of a mere on-looker. By the time the city bailiff, my friend

Thaddeus Turner, arrived to take the thief into custody, Todd's tale had become one of knights-errant upon some holy quest. He told Thaddeus how we had wrestled the sword-wielding scoundrel of unsurpassed strength to the ground, despite his casting of evil charms upon us, taking many a cut and buffet in exchange – no matter that we bore not a solitary mark from our encounter.

I shook my head behind Todd's back, such that Thaddeus should see me.

'I shall make a true report on the morrow,' I mouthed to him, not wishing to spoil Todd's hour of glory.

Chapter 4

Monday, the fourteenth day of June
The Foxley House

THAT MORN, I permitted Jack a good breakfast, allowing him second helpings such that he should not think I was sending him away in haste. E'en so, he took his time consuming the meal, far longer than need be. Eventually, concerned that he would arrive tardily at Stephen Appleyard's workshop, I told him to hasten and collect his bundle of belongings.

His face was the very image of one betrayed, disgruntled at the injustice of his predicament.

I had to harden my heart.

'This ain't fair, you knows that,' he grumbled. 'Ain't fair, I tells you.'

'You did wrong; you pay the price,' Adam said as he left the board to go open the shop. 'Now get to work, you idle young toad.'

I touched my cousin's arm, gesturing him to say no more. I did not want Jack's departure to be upon a sour note.

'I shall call by Appleyard's place anon,' I told him. 'To see you settled.'

'Don't bovver yerself on my account,' the lad muttered. He picked up his belongings, which he had left by the back door and slung the bundle over his shoulder. It was but a few items: a clean shirt, braies and hose and a carven creature of a size to sit in a man's hand. I had not seen it afore but it was recognisable as a likeness of his dog, Little Beggar, of late memory. I never knew Jack had made such a thing. It showed a degree of skill with a knife on wood such that was ne'er apparent with charcoal on paper. The lad had a good eye for proportion and representation, after all. He tucked the figure within his bundle, as though none were meant to see it: his privy tribute to a lost friend. It quite put a catch in my voice as I bade him 'God bless'.

Guildhall

Upon her arrival, I set Kate to work with pestle and mortar, doing my utmost to behave towards her as though naught had changed in her circumstances. Why then did I give the lass the most thankless task of grinding a considerable lump of yellow ochre to fine powder? Was it by way of punishment? I could not say. Mayhap, it was.

My next task was to make report of last eve's arrest of the thief to Bailiff Thaddeus Turner at Guildhall though, in truth, I could ill-spare the time with the king's commission requiring my fullest attention. Nevertheless, it was better to get that done than to be interrupted once I had begun my work.

'God give you good day, my friend,' Thaddeus said when I entered his chamber. 'You need not have troubled, Seb. I heard that you have a royal commission to keep you occupied, so I wasn't going to bother you.'

'Why so? Do you not require my report?'

Thaddeus shrugged and held up a cup and jug.

'Ale?'

'Nay, I thank you.'

'I had a most detailed report from that elderly fellow: Todd was his name?'

'Aye, I was there when he regaled us with his extensive piece of embroidery. 'Twas a veritable weaving of myth and imagination. I thought you might want a plain and simple report without extraneous embellishment.'

'In honesty, Seb, I'm not sure what to do about this particular crime. You certain you won't have ale? I would appreciate your opinion on it.'

'Oh, very well but a crime is a crime, is it not? Do you argue otherwise?'

'Sit and hear my arguments, if you will.'

Over ale, Thaddeus told me of the man – the thief we had taken in possession of his ill-gotten gains.

'His name is Philip Hartnell, a most respectable citizen and a cutler by craft. He said he was walking along Bladder Street, passed the house with its window wide to the pleasant evening air when he saw the candlesticks by the open casement. At a glance, he was quite certain they were the same ones he had bought his wife as a wedding gift ten years since. His wife has much fondness for the sticks, so he took them, thinking to please her.'

'Had they been stolen away from him previously, then? Is that the way of it?' I sipped my ale. Thaddeus did likewise afore continuing.

'That was my first thought. I tell you, Seb, it took a deal of cajoling and probing to get the truth out of Philip Hartnell. The candlesticks weren't stolen from him but he apparently gave his goodwife to think they had been taken. The truth is that Hartnell has fallen into debt. He took the candlesticks to a goldsmith and sold them to pay off a sizeable loan. When his wife found them gone, she was much upset – more so than Hartnell ever expected. Thus, he told her they had been stolen, rather than admit his actions and the fact that he was over the ears in debt to a moneylender.'

'An unfortunate situation but how does that excuse his actions of yestereve?'

'It doesn't. Besides, the candlesticks he stole from the house in Bladder Street were never his. Similar in shape but not the same ones.'

'He has no right to them, even had they been the same. He sold them and has had the profit from the sale. Hartnell is a thief and we caught him. He deserves just punishment, does he not? I do not see any reason for your difficulties in this matter, Thaddeus.'

'He has never had any dealings with the law before, Seb. He's a respected member of the Cutlers' Company and a church-warden. He loves his wife and family, works hard and earns a good living.'

'Not good enough, so it would seem, else why would he be in debt?'

'A foolish mistake, he said, though he withheld further details. I had the feeling another woman was involved. In every other respect, Hartnell is a decent citizen. I think he deserves a second chance.'

'What of the house in Bladder Street? The folk he robbed? Not to mention all the neighbourhood having to rally to the hue-and-cry.'

'The candlesticks were returned – dented, it's true but Hartnell says he will pay for their repair. The householder is agreeable. Besides...'

Thaddeus drained his ale.

'Besides?' I prompted.

'Philip Hartnell is not alone, Seb. He is the fourth... no, the fifth respectable citizen that has come to my notice, by one means or another, who has found himself in debt and unable to repay. There's something going on in London, concerning underhanded financial dealings, and I don't like the smell of it.

'Watch your purse, my friend. Every one of them is of middling status like you. Outwardly decent and honest, yet they find themselves in dire need, monetarily. I wouldn't want that to happen to you.'

'Fear not. I owe no man so much as a ha'penny. So you will let Hartnell go?'

'Aye. I think so. Both Newgate and the Counter are overfull of vile inmates. Hartnell is not of their kind. They'd make a hearty supper of him on his first day inside.'

'As you think best, Thaddeus. Forgive me: I must hasten. I have the king's book to begin and another errand to complete aforehand...'

I went to Stephen Appleyard's workshop, not to see how Jack was bearing up – although he did appear to think that to be my reason. He put on a grumpy expression purposefully, as I suspect, when I entered. I had come to collect my gift for little Dickon, the morrow being the first anniversary of his birth. 'Twas a strange thing: the year had passed so swiftly, it was hard to believe and yet it was difficult recall the time afore God had granted us the blessing of this dear child.

I had written out the texts for a special hornbook for his gift, the kind that enables little ones to learn their letters, Paternoster, Ave Maria and Credo. Dickon deserves the best a scribe's son could have. Thus, I had used coloured inks: red for the Paternoster, virgin blue for the Ave and a bright green for the Credo, all on good parchment. Upon a second parchment, to form the reverse, I had written most distinctly each capital letter in the ABC, accompanied by its smaller version, alternating red and blue inks. I filled the remaining space with the image of Noah's Ark, the tiny animals in their pairs, disappearing into the distance, ever smaller around the margins. I hoped it would please him. I had bought a sheet of fine, clear ox horn and had the horner cut it in two, such that the two small pieces of parchment, back to back, fitted betwixt the sheets of horn.

I was well pleased when Stephen showed me the result of his craftsmanship. He had encased and surrounded the sheets of horn in a lime-wood frame – lime being fine-grained and most suitable for detailed carving. He had continued my queue of animals for Noah's Ark around the frame, carving out their likenesses. The pair of horses was exquisitely wrought and the pigs' expressions so comical, I laughed aloud at the sight of them. Upon the frame's handle was carven Noah himself, quite the patriarch with his long beard and stern features, his hand raised in blessing – both of the animals and the young reader of the texts. 'Twas a thing of beauty but also amusing and – as I intended – no common hornbook for a Foxley. My son would learn to read and find the task a pleasurable one, I hoped.

The Foxley House

Back home, a surprise awaited me. Months might pass without my setting eyes upon a piece of correspondence, unless I read it for someone unlettered or of poor sight: most commonly her son's letters for Dame Ellen Langton. Yet this morn three letters had come for me. The first had been brought from the Stationers' Guild, delivered by young Hugh Gardyner - a fact that much delighted Kate. But the others thrilled me more forwhy I knew at once the hand that wrote them: my brother Jude.

I had received but one letter from him since he had departed London at last summer's end, bound for none knew where. That had come with the last merchants' ships of the season, afore the winter storms sent every vessel to seek safe harbour. The letter had been dated to the midst of September, informing me that Jude was in some place called Mechelen in Burgundy. The name meant little to me, my knowledge of the world beyond England – or even London – being sparse, indeed. But he had met the Duchess Margaret – sister to King Edward and Duke Richard of Gloucester – who required me to make a Book of Hours for her, my skills having been recommended unto her by Lord Richard.

That was the last I had heard of my brother, until now.

I had made the tiny book, according to the instructions

enclosed with my brother's letter. I had sent the finished volume – with which I was much pleased – by way of a Dutch merchant risking everything in an attempt to sail home to be with his family for Christmas. I have heard naught of it since. Mayhap I was foolish to send it then and the Dutchman came to grief, lost in the Narrow Seas. I know not of it, whatever the case.

Now I had two further epistles from Jude. Eager as a child, I prised off the waxen seal of one with my knife and read the words, drinking them down as a man denied water for so long. The first was written at Michaelmastide, just a fortnight after the first was sent. I wondered where it had been in the meantime. He had written from a city called Koln, said he was well and travelling with a band of pilgrims, returning home to Florence, having visited the shrine of St Thomas at Canterbury and other holy places. He had become friends with a fellow from Venezia by the name of Alessandro. They intended to cross the Alpines – whatever that may be – afore the snows blocked the passes.

The second letter was bulky indeed. It was, in truth, two letters folded together and, within, a small packet also, wrapped separately. Jude was safe, having crossed the Alps – the same as the alpines mentioned in the previous letter? – that was the main thing and a balm for my heart. In the earlier, written upon St Nicholas' day the sixth of December, he told of Venice. The place sounded such a marvel that I read that part aloud at dinner:

We came by river boat to Venezia… Such a place it is, little brother. Water everywhere. Like Brugge, it has canals but the buildings are so grand indeed. The Doge's Palace is beyond even your imaginings, Seb, like an alchemist's conjuration. I know not how to describe to you such a miracle of intricate carvings and smooth marble and such colours as dazzle the eye. We stay now at the house of Alessandro's parents; I think he calls it the Casa dell'Angelo or some such, where instead of a street below the window, there is a broad canal that

53

*laps against the front door. Imagine if Paternoster Row was
a river! Their house is nigh as grand as the Doge's, if a little
smaller, I believe. In truth, I'm not certain of its extent, but
Alessandro has promised to show me the whole of the Casa
dell'Angelo – it means the House of the Angel – tomorrow.*

The third letter informed me that he was spending the season
of Christ's Mass with the wealthy Baldesi family of merchants
and bankers. They had interests in Florence and Venice but were
at their villa in Ravenna for the celebrations. Part of this letter
was unfit reading for mealtime, so I perused it in silent wise:

*As at Giorgio's house in Vittorio, of which I told you in my
last letter, this place also has a comely daughter and – isn't it
always my misfortune? – she too is betrothed, so I learned last
eve. And who is her future husband? The gouty, one-legged
uncle who's sixty, if he's a day! Can you believe it, Seb? This
beauteous raven-haired creature, Francesca-Antonia, is to wed
that disgusting old man. She confided to me as we escaped the
crowded house to linger under the olive trees in the garden
how much she hates the prospect of being wedded to him. At
least they are awaiting her fifteenth birthday at the end of
January before celebrating these obnoxious nuptials. But I feel
sorry for the lass indeed. To be wedded to Methuselah will be
a torment to her. If his bean-sized prick can ever oblige her,
I'll be surprised. She may be young but seems a lusty wench to
me, if given the chance.*

However, I read aloud the delightful post scriptum:

*You must visit Ravenna, Seb. The gold and colours of the
mosaics in the churches here will have you in an ecstasy. Even
I'm in awe of their splendour. We've never seen the like in
England. My favourite mosaic was in the Basilica – that's
a church – of St Apollinare Nuovo, an image of Christ in
Judgement with St Michael, the good archangel in red, upon
his right hand, and Lucifer in blue, the fallen archangel, upon*

the left. (Lucifer with his straight dark hair had somewhat the look of you, little brother.) Some repairs to a damaged mosaic having been abandoned for the holy days, I picked up a few fallen tesserae. They are my New Year's gift to you, in the little packet, that you might see the colours for yourself.

'You must visit Ravenna…' As if that was ever likely to come to pass. I tipped out the contents of the folded paper packet onto the white linen tablecloth. The tiny squares of glass, smaller than my thumbnail, were coloured with lapis lazuli from Venice, the brightest crimson and gold leaf, imperial purple and silver. We all of us gasped at their shining beauty. Numbered in the thousands upon a wall or ceiling, the effect must be dazzling, wondrous, even magickal to behold.

So engrossed was I with Jude's epistles, I nigh forgot the other letter. Belatedly, I opened it and was much surprised to learn it had come from Guy Linton – he with whom I had been apprenticed to Master Collop – by way of the Stationers' Guild. He had not specified the purpose of his letter except to insist, with much under-scoring, that the matter was 'most urgent'. He wrote that he required me to call upon him this very day. 'Twas hardly a courteous request and one I felt inclined to ignore. Yet he sounded desperate and had once been my fellow. I groaned inwardly, as if I had not enough matters to occupy me already and King Edward's commission not yet begun in earnest. But, out of respect for Master Collop, rather than for Linton's sake, I knew I must go.

Guy Linton's Place, Gracechurch Street

After all these years, I could not understand why the fellow would send such a message, asking me to call. Guy Linton may have been an apprentice with me at Master Collop's workshop, but he was six years or more my elder, completing his term of indenture whilst I had barely begun to learn my craft.

I recall, even when we worked together, he was ne'er especially friendly towards me. Upon occasion, Master Collop would have Guy demonstrate some aspect of our art to me… One time, our master instructed him to show me how to prepare lapis lazuli pigment, if I recall aright. Ever a detailed process, he had no patience and could not trouble himself to demonstrate the secrets to me, watching as I did my best to grind the precious stone to the correct degree – too fine and the pigment would be dull, instead of the heavenly blue desired. Insufficiently fine would have the same result and make the egg tempera gritty. I erred upon the side of caution. Once lapis was ground too much, there was no saving it. Master Collop was unimpressed with my results but relieved that I had not ruined the pigment beyond saving. Had the lapis been wasted, if I had gone too far, it would have cost the business a deal of money. He gave Guy a sound beating for failing to direct me. My fellow ne'er forgave me for that since the thrashing was a thorough one, made the harder by our master's anger.

After that, Guy treated me with contempt, calling me Lame-Duck, and worse, when e'er Master Collop could not hear, for so I was in those days: lame indeed. His sneering disdain and hurtful actions – tripping me, hiding the staff I used to aid my walking and striking me at every opportunity – were the bane of those early days of my apprenticeship. I felt naught but relief when he departed to serve as a journeyman in some other workshop.

In the years since, I had seen him but rarely, passing in the street and at one or two guild meetings, but no words had been exchanged betwixt us, not so much as a greeting.

So why should Guy Linton now be asking me to do him the courtesy of calling at his workshop in Gracechurch Street? It made no sense and I was yet of half a mind to ignore the request. However, curiosity got the better of sound judgement… and we all know what curiosity did to the unfortunate cat.

I made my way across the city. Nigh unto Midsummer so it was, according to the calendar, yet the sky was overcast and a chill breeze blew up river from the east, bearing the scent of the faraway estuary, the stink of the dyers' vats at Whitechapel beyond the city wall and snatches of plainsong chant from Trinity Priory. The wind had twice attempted to rob me of my cap and Gawain's ears were blown aback, his glossy coat rippling.

From the Stocks Market, I went along Lombard Street and found my destination. Guy Linton's establishment appeared prosperous. It stood upon a sizeable corner plot, the house entrance being in Lombard Street, 'neath an elegant tiled porch, shielding from the weather its blue-painted door with the brass lion's-head knocker. A grand place indeed. But I had not been asked to come to the house. This was not to be a social visit and why should it be? We were not friends. I supposed he wished to discuss a business matter. In which case, it would have been more courteous if he did attend upon me, in Paternoster Row. However, I was intrigued to know more.

I found the workshop entrance around the corner, opening off Gracechurch Street, hard by the church of Allhallows. As with the house door, this also had a tiled porch and a striped awning stretched beside to give shelter to the items displayed on the open counter-board. This day, pamphlets were held down with polished brass weights to keep them from blowing away.

Afore I should make myself known, I took the opportunity to assess the standards of workmanship of the pamphlets. I expected them to be of the highest, seeing Guy had been trained by Master Collop, and such grand premises suggested he earned a good living. Thus, I was surprised to see, despite the reasonable penmanship, no decoration but a few plain rubrics. Mayhap, they were done by his apprentices but, if Kate had produced the like, I would not have felt inclined to display them so prominently, as if they were my best wares. Not that Kate's work was ever so dull and mediocre as these.

The few books upon the counter were lavishly bound but,

upon closer inspection, were simply rebindings of old texts and I could find fault with the stitching, blocking and finishing. In one case, the gold leaf was already coming away at the edges from the embossed lettering of the title and the spine was awry, causing the leather to pull unevenly. Such inferior workmanship would ne'er stand the test of time. I admit, I was heartened to learn that Guy Linton's wares were not comparable to mine. Was it just professional vanity on my part that I felt well pleased? Or was it a more personal pleasure because I had no fondness for a fellow who used to bully me in my crippled youth? Yet I wondered how come, with little to recommend his goods for sale, he could afford such a fine house and workshop.

The shop door stood open. Since it faced easterly, bits of leaf, torn blossom and scraps of straw blew in, swirling into corners and ruffling papers. With one last puzzled thought concerning my presence here, I called to Gawain and stepped into the workshop.

A heavy-set man looked up from his ledger. A momentary frown gave way to a smile of recognition.

'Well, Foxley. You decided to come then?' Guy Linton stood up, holding out an ink-stained hand in welcome. It matched my own as I accepted the gesture.

'You requested me to do so, otherwise…'

'You'd never set foot in my workshop from choice, eh? Come along in, have some ale. No doubt you're wondering why I asked you here.'

I followed Guy through a doorway, into a workplace much like that back at Paternoster Row except for its grave air of disorganisation and misuse. A grey-haired fellow was bent over a desk, copying a text at some speed.

'Make yourself scarce, Ralf. Go to the tavern. I have things to discuss – privily – with Foxley here.'

'Aye, Master Linton. How long should I be gone?'

'An hour will do… and no longer, if you want a day's wage.'

Ralf the journeyman departed. An elderly soul, he was just as bowed upon standing as when labouring at his desk. Mayhap, he had some maladjustment of his bones, as I once had, afore the Almighty, in His infinite mercy, granted me a miracle. He touched his cap to me courteously in passing.

Looking around, there was but one other desk. Considerably well crafted and ornate, I surmised that it was Guy's own. There was no sign that anyone else worked here: no indication of an apprentice to learn the trade. Mayhap, that was as well. Unless Guy was much changed by the intervening passage of years, I could not think that he would have patience with an untrained youngster, to instil the rudiments of the craft into a novice's head and guide uncertain hands.

'Sit yourself on Ralf's stool and tell me, Foxley,' Guy said, handing me a chased pewter cup brimming with ale. 'How's business in Paternoster Row these days?'

I moved the stool to avoid a spillage of ink upon the floor and sipped the ale. It was a good brewing.

''Tis passing fair. We have commissions enough to keep us occupied until leaf-fall. And you?'

'No shortage of work for us, either,' he confirmed and yet his eyes slid away and he did not look at me. 'Caxton's bloody contraption should be chopped to kindling, though, denying proper scribes their rightful livelihood. Is the wretch's printing interfering with your profits?'

'It would do so, if we relied on pamphlet sales for our income but we produce other work besides. Illuminated books, coats-of-arms, shop and inn signs and a few portraits, such things becoming the fashion of late.'

'Aye, I saw the portrait you did of Ol' Collop last year to hang in the Stationers' Hall. It looked very like the miserable bugger, I'll give you that.'

I disapproved of his speaking so disrespectfully of our one-time master but held my peace, drinking the ale to cool the beginnings of anger's heat. I had painted a likeness of Master Richard Collop last autumn, when he was elected to replace the

felonious Clifford as Warden Master of the Stationers' Guild.
It was the least I could do after his intervention had restored
my reputation and returned my name to the guild roll. I had
asked no payment since it was a gift, yet I had been repaid right
well because the portrait brought in a number of commissions,
serving to advertise my skills.

'Have you ventured into other fields?' I asked.

'Indeed I have and most successfully too. A month since, a
wealthy vintner commissioned me to paint his portrait.'

'Ah.' I finished my ale, still no wiser concerning my visit here.
Was idle chit-chat Guy's only purpose? I doubted it. 'I thank
you for the ale, Master Linton, but I too have work demanding
my attention.'

'Don't go, Foxley. Have more ale. I need your advice.'

'My advice? Concerning what?'

He made to refill my cup but I covered it with my hand,
shaking my head. It was a strong brew and I would not spend
the rest of the day half befuddled.

'The portrait. Don't get me wrong: 'tis well-executed, finely
painted but... well... it just doesn't look like the bastard that
sits for it. I can't get a decent likeness, however much I repaint
the damned thing. I thought you might...'

'Might make suggestions? But how can I when I have ne'er
seen the subject? I may advise upon methods of applying paint
but not upon improving the likeness.'

'Well, that's why I asked you to come this morn. I have to
go to the vintner's house after dinner for his next sitting but
he's getting impatient, wanting to see what he's, er, paying for.
I daren't show him. He's not much to look at anyway but the
portrait makes him look like a bloody gargoyle with a toothache.
I just can't get it right but I can't see where it's wrong, either.
I need your help, Seb. That's the truth. I can't afford to fail in
this commission.'

So, it was 'Seb' now, was it, in friendly wise? Not 'Foxley',
nor 'Lame-Duck'. At least I understood his purpose.

'Will you help me, for the sake of our shared apprenticeship? So Ol' Collop may keep his good name as a master and teacher of fine craftsmen? Please?'

'Oh, very well, but only for Master Collop's sake. Show me the work afore your appointment with the sitter.'

Guy took a stout board, draped with a linen covering, that leaned against the wall beside his desk. He hesitated, reluctant to reveal his unsatisfactory handiwork.

'There!' he said, shoving it at me and turning away. 'Don't tell me how inept it is. I know it's a poor effort but this is my first portrait. I can improve, if you tell me what I've done wrong.'

I removed the cover and took the painting to the window, the better to view it in the light of day. Guy was correct: it was a poor effort. There was no need for me to belabour the fact. Whether it looked like the vintner or not, the arrangement of the sitter, full face, was ill-chosen. The velvet hangings of a golden hue were expensive, no doubt, but only served to reflect upon the sitter's complexion and turn his skin to the unhealthy jaundiced colour I observed. The hands were as shapeless as uncooked sausages, the face quite out of proportion, the ears far too large – unless the sitter was a very strange-looking fellow, indeed. There were so many things amiss with the portrait, I hardly knew what to say of it. In truth, to begin anew was likely my best advice but if this was Guy's first attempt at portraiture, that was not helpful and unlikely to assist his improvement for the future.

'In the main,' I said, ''Tis the proportions of the face. Unless your sitter has no forehead to speak of, and exceptionally prominent cheekbones... Look at my face: 'tis of reasonable shape. See how my eyes be roughly halfway betwixt the crown of my head and my chin. And the tops of my ears be level with the bridge of my nose. Do you see that?'

Guy frowned at me, squinting, then nodded.

'Now look at your painting. Can you see that the eyes be too high, making the nose and cheeks over long and no room for the forehead? Remember what Master Collop used to tell us whenever we attempted to draw anything living, whether a flower, a butterfly or a horse: "Draw what you truly observe with your eyes; not what you think you see in your head". I fear you have failed to observe your sitter truly. Therein lies your problem.'

Guy looked about to object to my lecture but then shrugged and sighed.

'I ne'er paid much heed to Ol' Collop when he prattled on about how to draw. I'm not much of a one for sketching; curlicues and vine leaves are decoration enough to my mind. I don't hold with filling the margins with a host of worms and weeds and such like.'

'But you sketched out your sitter's pose and a rough likeness before you began the painting proper...'

'Why would I waste my time? He wants a portrait, not a pile of loose papers.'

'The preliminary drawings be for your benefit; not his. They enable you to recall the pose for subsequent sittings, to ensure the image of the figure will fit the board, else you may find you cannot include the top of the head...' I looked once more at Guy's work. 'That is what happened, is it not? That is why the sitter has no forehead: when you did his hat and his hair, there was insufficient room for it. This will not do; you cannot expect anyone to pay good coin for it. I fear 'tis fit for kindling wood and little else. I suggest you return the fellow's down payment and apologise; admit to him that you cannot do it.'

'I can't. That's why you have to help me, Seb.'

'Return the money...'

'Oh, for Christ's sweet sake!' Guy closed his eyes as a man in pain. 'There is no bloody money. I owe him a-a huge favour... he said he will consider it repaid, if I paint his portrait for him. He's seen the likeness you did of the previous mayor before the new fellow was elected.'

'Humphrey Hayford.'

'That's him. The vintner admires it, apparently, and… well… I told him… I painted it.'

'You told him that? How dare you claim my work for your own? The guild will hear of this.' I slammed my cup down upon the board, unmannerly, and made to leave.

Guy rushed to block the door, barring my way. His face was pitiful. He was wringing his hands.

'I'm so sorry. I swear I'll make amends to you, Seb. I know I was wrong but matters are desperate. If I don't do this portrait, all sorts of horrible consequences will follow. I have no choice. Now do you understand? Please. You must help me. I'm begging you…'

I must be a lackwit to have embroiled myself in Guy Linton's mess, he being no friend to me. Mayhap, I considered what Master Collop would wish of me. Or the reputation of the Stationers' Guild. Or could it be my own vanity that urged me on, convinced I could surpass my fellow's feeble attempts and put him to shame? Whatever my reasoning, I did not do it that Guy could save face. But, fool that I be, I agreed to abet him in his subterfuge. Naught else in my profession thus far has caused me greater trouble.

Chapter 5

Monday afternoon
Mallard Court in Gracechurch Street

THE VINTNER, Clement Mallard, lived in a grand place
further up Gracechurch Street, opposite the Leadenhall.
Guy Linton's premises had impressed me but this establishment
was close kin to Crosby Place, where the Duke of Gloucester
resided when in London. I recalled that it had also been built for
a wealthy merchant, the grocer John Crosby. Clement Mallard
could likewise afford a similar fine house, with its grand gated
entrance into a paved courtyard and marble steps leading up
to the great hall beyond. It was as well that I be familiar with
Crosby Place, else I may have felt intimidated by Mallard Court.

I followed Guy – apparently, we were upon such terms
now that the use of first-names was permitted – up the steps,
into the hall. I remained somewhat behind him, posing as his
humble assistant. Thus was I laden like a pack-horse, carrying
the offending portrait and a good deal of artist's paraphernalia
besides my own scrip. I disliked this subterfuge more with each
passing minute.

'You're late, Linton,' Mallard growled by way of greeting.
'And who's this?' The vintner waved his hand vaguely in my
direction, frowning. 'I don't want anybody coming here,
uninvited. You know that.'

'Ignore him, Master Mallard. He's only my assistant. I needed
help, carrying my stuff, is all.' Thus, Linton introduced me. 'Set

up the easel, brushes and pigments there, by the fireplace,' he instructed me, 'And then sit out of the way, behind my line of sight, and keep silent. Don't disturb me at my work.'

I made no answer. The reply that sprang to mind was not of a suitably servile nature but I did as bidden. I sat just behind and to the left of Guy, such that I might view the sitter from the same angle, taking out my charcoal and cheap papers ready pinned to my drawing board in such wise as not to attract the vintner's eye. I had commenced my first sketch afore Guy had even settled the half-painted portrait upon the easel and dipped his brush.

The subject had little to recommend it. A true likeness would not be one that any but the blind could possibly take pleasure in gazing at. I should not want it hung upon my wall. The expression would turn ale sour and set children wailing. In truth, the physical features were of common proportions – not as Guy had painted them – and naught out of the ordinary, topped by thinning grey hair. But the eyes held such malevolence as I had ne'er espied in any other. If the eyes be the windows of the soul, as we be told, then this one must surely be beyond saving, belonging to Satan already. I was hard-pressed not to cross myself. Suspicious brows were drawn low over these twin pools of darkness, as though to keep their secrets hidden. Even as I drew them, I shivered. Creating their likeness chilled me.

The skin had an unhealthy, jaundiced hue – Guy had painted it aright; it was not wholly caused by light reflecting from the golden curtains – and lay upon the bones beneath like a creased bed sheet. Every line bore the mark of ill-humour. These were not the characterful wrinkles of old age but the deep-scoured imprints of malice and spite. It was hard to gauge this sitter's age at all but the gnarled fingers, contorted by swollen joints, suggested three score years, or thereabouts, at least.

But, as Master Collop used to instruct: I drew what I saw; five minutes of worthwhile observation giving birth to a few lines of exactitude. In a short space, I had the sketches required of the sitter and tucked my board away in my scrip, out of sight, glad to turn my eyes to more pleasing views.

The parlour at Mallard Court was well appointed. A gilded ceiling looked to be well constructed and I noted the carving on the beams of what I first thought to be a skein of geese in flight. But no. Of course, they were ducks: mallards, a play upon the vintner's name. A carven mantle surrounded the fireplace, and here, too, images of ducks outnumbered all else. I had ne'er considered these birds to be evil creatures. My son loved to watch them swimming on the water of the Horse Pool and they gave me pleasure also, admiring the iridescent plumage of the drakes, their determined waddling gait upon land. Yet these ducks looked to thirst for blood. I turned away to gaze out the window. I was becoming over-fanciful, imagining such foolish things as ill-intentioned ducks.

When Guy breathed a heavy sigh and turned to me, holding out his brushes, indicating that I – being but his lowly assistant – should clean them, the vintner pushed out of his cushioned chair.

'Show me the portrait,' he demanded. 'I have waited long enough to see your handiwork, Linton. I will see it – now!'

'No, no, Master Mallard.' Guy threw a cloth over the portrait, despite the likelihood that the last strokes of egg tempera were yet wet. ''Tis ill-luck to see it in its unfinished state.'

'Who says so?'

''Tis a well-known fact, I assure you. Isn't that right?' Guy looked at me, his desperation clear.

'I have heard it said,' was all I would offer in support.

'Next time, it will be finished, master, then you can view it as you wish. I promise you.'

Master Mallard muttered to himself, glaring at Guy.

'Next time, then, and woebetide you, Linton, if it's not finished. I've wasted enough time on this damned porterate business. I have more important matters to attend to.' With that, he stomped out of the parlour, leaving us to clear and tidy away the materials and equipment. We had not been offered so much as a cup of water and the chamber had grown stuffy and over-warm as the afternoon sun poured through the glazed windows. In truth, with the need for subterfuge ended, I stood back and watched Guy pack up his things. Every craftsman has his own way of it, I told my conscience; better if he does it himself. Indeed, he 'tidied' his things much in the manner of his workshop – that is to say, in careless wise, with no thought to ensuring his brush-ends would dry in goodly shape nor securing his pigment pots to preserve the precious powders. E'en so, I helped him carry his stuff back down Gracechurch Street to his house where he had manners enough to offer me ale.

'How do you wish me to portray the man?' I asked as we sipped our cups. 'If I paint a true likeness, I doubt it will please him but aught else will be an untruth.'

'That was part of my difficulty, Seb, having to invent a new face for the old bugger. A proper likeness will never do: he'll murder me if he doesn't have a far more pleasant appearance in the portrait. You understand my dilemma?'

'I do but I mislike the thought of producing a counterfeit. Wilfully creating a fake image is not my way.'

'But all images are fakes, are they not? You create a likeness of a man, yet it isn't the living, breathing person, is it?'

'Nay, I suppose that be the case.' I yet felt discomfited at the thought of purposefully changing the appearance of Our Lord God's handiwork. The Almighty had created Clement Mallard as suited His divine purpose. Who was I to say it should be otherwise?

'Surely, 'tis no worse than a woman lightening her hair with camomile water, or an old man hiding the grey of his beard with walnut juice? I don't see your difficulty, Seb.'

I was unsurprised that he could not. Guy Linton and I had so few matters in common. Finer feelings were not among them.

'How will you proceed?' he asked. 'When can I have the portrait finished? You saw how impatient he is become.'

I heaved a sigh. I should have to confess my error at the first opportunity and beg Our Lord's forgiveness for tampering with His creation.

'I shall do it this eve. The figure must be re-done entirely but I may leave the setting for the most part as you have painted it. That much, at least, will be your own work. There be naught amiss with your methods. But hear me, Guy, this will be the only occasion upon which I rescue you from the hole you have dug for yourself. Do not claim my work as your own e'er again. I do this for Master Collop alone, not for you. Do we have a firm agreement on this?'

'We do, Seb. And I'll not forget the favour I owe you for saving my reputation – and my neck.'

'I have not done so, as yet. It will depend on whether Master Mallard approves the work once 'tis completed.'

'And he's hard to please; that's for certain. But I'm grateful all the same.'

I left Gracechurch Street to walk home, encumbered by the portrait – well wrapped in cloth for I would not want anyone to see it and think it my handiwork – and a box of Guy's pigments for he had made use of some I did not have in my workshop. Our deception required that the materials remained consistent.

The Foxley House

Gawain greeted me at the kitchen door like a long-lost lover. It was rare that I should leave him at home but Guy had warned me that the vintner had even less liking for dogs than he did for his fellow men. Besides, Gawain would have attracted more attention to me – he being of a size and enthusiasm for life that was impossible to overlook.

Rose, Nessie and Kate were in the kitchen and such laughter filled the place as I had not heard for so long. Rose was mixing a batter, Nessie was stirring the pottage pot and Kate was arranging the tablecloth upon the board but such outbursts of merriment hampered their tasks. Kate dabbed tears from her eyes and Nessie clutched her ribs with one hand whilst stirring the pot with the other.

'Clearly, I have missed some fine jest,' I said, setting down my burden to pat the dog and take little Dickon upon my knee.

'You've not heard such stories in your life, master,' Kate said. 'Rose met someone at the market in Cheapside who told the most wondrous tales. Tell Master Seb, Rose.'

'Come, Rose, I should appreciate a cheering story, after the dire company I have endured this afternoon.'

'Which shall you hear? The one about the pot-herbs is most amusing.'

'Whichever pleases you, Rose.'

'Well, this tale was told to me at a market stall selling the new season's radishes and beetroots. A fine-looking woman spoke to me, saying she was but lately come into the city from Oxenford. She was enquiring as to my opinion of the produce for sale and went on to tell me of the doings of some rascal scholars at the university in Oxenford.' Rose laid aside her whisk of rushes and left the batter to stand.

'It seems that a townsman was boastful of the pot-herbs he grew in his garden, claiming his radishes were the size of a man's fist, the beetroot the size of his head – which must have been enormous, what with so much boasting – and the parsnips as long as his arm. Now the townsmen and the scholars never see eye-to-eye on anything – so Eleanor said (that being the woman's name) – and the scholars determined to teach the man a lesson.

'Upon the next moonlit night, so they could see what they were about, armed with digging tools, the scholars crept into the man's garden and dug up his choicest roots. Then, they sliced off the leafy tops and planted them back in the earth. They stole back to Merton Hall, where they lodged, and gave their

TONI MOUNT

ill-gotten pot-herbs to the cook. Next day's dinner was a feast
compared to the poor stuff that was usually served up, such that
the Master himself commented upon the improvement and said
how much he enjoyed the meal.

'It was a week later that the townsman noticed that some
of his crops were wilting somewhat and wondered at it. Upon
looking more closely, he discovered the theft and was sure he
knew the culprits. So he went straight to the Master of Merton
Hall, demanding recompense for his losses. The Master realised
what had happened, that the good dinner he had enjoyed came
from the man's garden so he dared not admit it and, of course,
the evidence was long gone, eaten by them all. In a quandary,
the Master spent his own money, buying the best pot-herbs he
could find in the market and, on the next moonlit night, went
along to the townsman's garden, intending to replant the roots.
But the man was watching, fearful lest the scholars came to steal
more of his crop, and he caught the Master in the act of digging
the earth with a heap of fine pot-herbs lying by his feet.

'Oxenford was up in arms next morning, demanding the
Master – ever considered the most honest of fellows – be
dismissed as a thieving rogue. Only his scholars owning up to
their crime got the Master out of trouble and they were let off
with no more than a reprimand because they had saved him.
The man got his pot-herbs, the stall-holder made a good sale,
Merton Hall's cook was given money enough to improve the
poor food and the Master maintained his good reputation.

'Is that not a fine tale, Seb? Though Eleanor told it better,
doing all the actions, voices and expressions. Quite the
mountebank is she. Such a crowd gathered in the market to
hear and see her performance.'

'My sympathies be for the Master,' I said. 'He alone appears
to have been the loser in this, purchasing all those pot-herbs to
no avail on his own behalf.'

'It's only a tale. Who's to say it ever happened?' Rose said,
returning to her batter.

70

'Then what be its purpose? An imagined tale must have a moral, else why tell it?'

'Oh, Seb, you take everything so seriously. Mayhap, 'tis simply meant to amuse, naught more. Now let me get on, else there'll be no supper.'

True to my word, afore supper, I set out all in readiness in the workshop to repaint Guy's portrait as soon as the meal was done. How fortunate that at this time of year the light lingered beyond nine of the clock. The guild had regulations forbidding work by candlelight, knowing poor standards would likely result. Not that it mattered so much to me in this case. What cared I for Guy's reputation? Not a jot. But I did care for Master Collop's as the man who once trained us both, so I would do the best I might to improve Guy's poor efforts. I should do the face and hands first, whilst the light was at its brightest. Less vital matters, such as draperies, could be done in the more uncertain light later, if it took me so long.

My first task was to paint out the entire seated figure with a yellow ochre under-layer in order to begin anew. Guy's figure was too cramped at the top of the board such that the head had been depicted overly small in proportion to fit it in. This could not be remedied without repainting the sitter as a whole and the elaborate chair on which he was seated. Mayhap, this was likely to take longer than I expected at first glance. Oh well, I had committed myself, so it must be done.

Out of kindliness, not duty, Kate mixed the egg tempera and pigments for me, as required, and washed brushes. Rose kept me supplied with cool ale as the evening wore on. I worked without any respite more than to step back to observe the progress of the whole. And if paint had to dry afore adding further layers and details in one part, I worked elsewhere upon the image for a while. In truth, on a warm midsummer eve, the egg tempera dried swiftly, which was helpful. With constant reference to my sketches, I recreated the portrait.

It ought not to be termed 'a likeness' for it was not. Rather, it was a more acceptable semblance of a man whose true likeness none would desire to look upon, even the sitter himself. I did, however, repaint the hands – Guy's sausage-shaped fingers – as they truly were: gnarled and bent. They were naught to need disguising but a worthy badge of age, in my opinion. That much at least of the sitter's image would be the truth, not counterfeit.

My greatest change was made to the eyes, giving them a mild expression. I could not produce the malevolence of that gaze that made me shudder to think on it. No man's soul could be so black as I had seen through the window of his eye. It must have been a trick of the light, I convinced myself. That was it: the fault of a sunbeam, trapped for an instant at the exact moment when I drew his features.

I went to the trouble of painting a small but perfect image of a mallard drake in the bottom left-hand corner. I thought it appropriate and would appeal to the vintner's vanity, being the sitter's name and cognisance. I know not why I made the effort on behalf of Guy Linton, a fellow for whom I have ever had little liking and now, after this, even less respect.

The portrait proved to be a deal of work and dusk had fallen by the time it was done. I kept my fingers crossed that it would look as well in daylight as it appeared to do in twilight. I would rise right early upon the morrow to make certain it would pass a sharper-eyed gaze than could be given now.

'Seb? Are you done?' Rose asked.

'Aye, just these brushes to rinse and stand.'

'I'm not sure I like the look of this man,' she said, viewing my handiwork with her head upon first one side, then the other.

'In which case, 'tis probably not so wide of the mark and should be recognisable, forwhy he be no lovable fellow. I did not take to him in the least.'

'Where's Kate?' Rose asked.

'Abed. She was yawning and the hour grown late. Has Adam returned from Distaff Lane as yet?'

'Aye. He's in the kitchen, talking with Thaddeus.'

'Thaddeus? At this time of night?'

'That's what I came to tell you, Seb. Thaddeus came to say that a man's been murdered.'

'Oh, Christ have mercy.' I crossed myself. 'But what does Thaddeus want of me now? Note-taking, I suppose. Well, he must wait upon the morrow. In any case, he will have to find some other scribe. I have the king's commission to fill my time.'

Having covered the portrait and put my brushes to dry, I went to the kitchen. Adam and our visitor were drinking ale, seated at the board. I refused the offered cup, having had my fill.

'What brings you here, Thaddeus, my friend? Rose mentioned a murdered man. No one we know, I pray?'

'You know him after a fashion, Seb. 'Tis the fellow you apprehended during the hue-and-cry yestereve. Philip Hartnell, if you recall?'

I nodded, remembering the name.

'What came to pass? Did a fellow prisoner slay him?'

'No. I released him, allowed him to return home. He is – was – required to pay a fine and recompense the owner of the damaged candlesticks but how can that be done unless he be at large to earn money? He was killed in his workshop around suppertime. His goodwife was visiting her sister in child-bed but had prepared his supper for him beforehand. When she returned, she found him dead. I fear it was a terrible sight that greeted her, Seb, and most strange.'

'How so?' I enquired, finding my interest roused despite my better judgement. I pulled out a stool and joined them at the board. 'Strange in what manner?'

Adam poured more ale and for me also, though I drank quite unaware.

'Thaddeus says the fellow was tortured first,' Adam said.

'Aye, that's so. A multitude of knife cuts all over him – and done with one of his own blades, by the look of it – he being a cutler, as I told you this morn. No single injury was sufficient to kill him but with so many, he bled to death. It would've been a slow and painful death, I fear, poor fellow.'

'And that's not the strangest thing, is it, Thaddeus?' Adam went on. 'Tell Seb what you told me.'

'His right hand…' The bailiff paused, staring into the contents of his cup. 'His hand was pierced and nailed to his workbench. Then…'

I winced at the thought of the agony that must have entailed.

'Then his hand was painted silver. That's the oddest part of it. What could that mean, Seb? Does silver paint have some significance? You're the only man I could think to ask. Do you know of any special meaning for such a colour? Why would a killer waste such a precious pigment? I'm supposing silver paint is costly stuff: am I right?'

'You be correct, Thaddeus, although silver be less expensive than gold or lapis lazuli or even saffron. Was it applied as silver leaf or shell-silver?'

'I've no idea,' Thaddeus said with a shrug. 'What's the difference? See? I knew you were the right man to ask.'

'Silver leaf, like gold leaf, comes in thin sheets, finer than a hair's breadth and is applied as a layer. Shell-silver is the powdered metal mixed with egg white – we call it glair – and painted on with a brush, much like other pigments. The same can be done with gold or even tin.'

'Which is cheaper? Leaf? Or this shell stuff?'

'The shell-silver but not by so much. Its advantage be that it goes further, being painted on, it can be spread across the surface, unlike leaf which simply sits where 'tis applied. Does that aid you at all?' I yawned behind my hand, unable to stifle the urge any longer. 'I could show you both leaf and shell forms in my workshop, if you wish? I have gold leaf but not silver, at present. But there be some powdered silver which I may mix for you to see how 'tis done.'

'It would be of greater assistance if you came to view the body and told me what was used and whether it might have any bearing upon the case.'

'But not now.' My voice held a pleading note. I felt weary indeed.

'In the morn, afore Prime, if you will. A corpse does not keep well at this time of year. It will stink all too soon, I know.'

'Aye. I shall be there. I leave you in Adam's company to finish your ale.' I made for the stairs but paused. 'Where does the body lie?'

'In St Mildred's, in Poultry.'

I knew of the church. It stood beside that grim edifice of the Sheriffs' Counter prison.

'May Christ in His mercy keep you safe this night,' I said in blessing and made to seek my solitary bed in the chamber overlooking the street. Exhausted as I was, I knew restful slumber was not assured me. As so often, my body desired rest but my mind busied itself with all manner of matters, anxieties and concerns and, unlike my bedside candle-flame, could not be stopped with a puff of breath.

I lay in the darkness, fretting. The chamber was over-warm, so I felt my way to the window – its glazed panes Em's pride and joy – and opened the casement. The air without was no cooler than that within and came with a stink wafted from some nearby latrine pit, accompanied by the sound of a wailing babe and a dog yapping somewhere, streets away. London was ne'er silent. The night airs lay too heavy to refresh. Mayhap, a summer storm was brewing upriver: the direction from which rain and thunder came most usually. As I listened, a distant rumble confirmed the likelihood. I brought the stool and set it by the open window, off to one side, such that I might view a thin sliver of the western sky, beyond the turret and gables of the Bishop's Palace.

Sure enough, the waning moon already edged towards a cloud bank, seeking to hide her face from the approaching storm. Lightning flashed, far brighter than moonlight, casting momentary sharp shadows which then dissolved back into the night's gloom, as though they had ne'er been. Thunder rolled across the skies.

Gawain whined and hid 'neath the bed. He was much afeared of storms, the foolish creature.

The moon was gone. Raindrops the size of groats pattered down. The air cooled and an errant wind blew the rain in through the casement. I should have watched the storm but, having to close the window, I retreated to my tangle of sheets in search of elusive sleep. Since Morpheus failed to oblige me, I lay, listening to the warring of the elements above the rooftops.

Gawain joined me, lying close at my side. It felt comforting to have someone living and breathing and sharing my bed. Em would have disapproved right heartily. I must have found solace too in running my fingers through the dog's fur, as I used to with Em's hair, forwhy black and white strands were woven around my hand next morn.

I wakened afore cockcrow, surprised to realise that I had slept better than I ever had since my grievous loss.

Chapter 6

Tuesday, the fifteenth day of June
St Mildred's Church in Poultry

THE RAINSTORM had refreshed the city as Adam and I made our way to St Mildred's Church, Gawain trotting by my side. It was early as yet, a little after four of the clock in the morn. Few Londoners were about so early but the sun was up and ready to illumine the day, casting bronze and copper shafts along the length of Cheapside and Poultry. A few stallholders were setting up their trestle boards and arranging goods for sale an hour hence, when the market bell rang, signifying the opening of business. Of course, a few shifty-eyed forestallers hung around, hoping to beat the bell, if the beadles were insufficiently alert so early as this.

Steam rose from wet cobbles and cracked crusts formed on patches of mud by the conduit. The overnight rain had dampened down the dust of the streets and a band of argumentative sparrows bathed in haste in a puddle afore it should disappear. The air smelled more wholesome also.

The bailiff awaited us at the church door in company with a scowling priest. St Mildred's was cool within the grey stone walls. Not so the humours of the priest Thaddeus had roused from his bed to fetch the key. He was much put out by our arrival at that untimely hour, well afore the office of Prime.

'This needs to be done early, Father,' Thaddeus was explaining. 'The dead can't wait upon your convenience in this warm weather.'

In the porch, I set my burden to lean against the wall. I had brought the wretched portrait with me, concealed 'neath its cloth. St Mildred's was more than halfway upon my path to Grace Church Street, and I would not trouble myself to make the journey twice to oblige Guy Linton. I had far better things to do this day than waste more time than was needful upon him.

However, Philip Hartnell was another matter – a Christian soul requiring justice be done. If I might aid Bailiff Turner in his search for the man who denied the cutler his rightful term of days in this world, I would do so. The cutler had been a misguided thief himself – as I knew full well – but that did not give another the right to rob him of his life and send his soul, all unshriven, to Purgatory.

'Will Coroner Fyssher be joining us?' I asked as we went through to a small chapel dedicated to St Mildred. 'I suppose you have informed him, Thaddeus?'

'I told him in person last eve, before I came to you, Seb. No doubt but he's still abed. You know the coroner as well as I do. His work is a duty he would rather shirk and put upon others' shoulders whenever he may. Yours and mine, like as not.'

I had little liking and less respect for London's deputy coroner, William Fyssher. An idle and inefficient fellow, he was ever more concerned for giving as little time and effort to the pursuit of justice for the dead as he could manage. That was never my way, nor the bailiff's, although, upon occasion, Thaddeus had so much work required of him by the city authorities, he could not be as thorough as he wished. Thus, I felt more inclined to assist my friend, rather than the coroner.

The remains of Philip Hartnell lay upon a trestle board, serving as a catafalque, set by the Rood Screen. As yet, the parish's common coffin had not been brought, for St Mildred's must surely have one; most churches in London did so. A cleric was upon his knees at its head, having kept a vigil through the night. The body was decently covered in a white sheet but staining had occurred upon the pristine linen.

'The deceased has not yet been washed and shrouded, as per your instructions, Master Bailiff,' the cleric said as we approached. 'But it should be right soon. 'Tis an abomination to leave it so in God's house.'

'I know, I know, Father Simon, and it will be done,' Thaddeus said, his hands extended in a deprecating gesture. 'But first, my colleague here must examine the remains. He has skills in observation that most of us lack. If we are to solve this murder, Master Foxley must see and learn all he may from the victim before any clues are hidden away within a shroud. Now, please to step aside, Father, and let Master Foxley do what he does best.'

'He won't defile this holy place, will he, spilling blood?'

'Rest assured, he will not.'

I had already folded back the sheet as Thaddeus joined me.

'Father Simon fears you may be about to intrude upon the body, inwardly. I said you would not.'

I nodded.

'This was an outward assault. All the injuries be external. In any case, I be neither surgeon nor butcher to go cutting into a body. I ne'er have done so and have no intention to the contrary.' I examined a myriad of small incisions down Philip Hartnell's pallid cheeks, the blood now dark and dried. None was sufficient to have killed him but each was precise and done with a small, keen blade.

Thaddeus took a cloth-wrapped item from his scrip.

'This is the knife used. See the dried gore? Hartnell's stepson has identified it as one of the cutler's own making, taken from the display in the shop.'

'I shall examine it after, if I may. Let us finish here first, such that Hartnell's family can prepare him for his obsequies and burial. I would not delay them any longer than necessary.'

The body yet wore its blood-soaked shirt but the garment was cut to shreds. The injuries had been inflicted through his clothes, for his hose were likewise in tatters. I waved away the gathering flies that would hamper my work, drawn in by the odours of blood and death. I examined the right hand: a shocking sight with the piercing nail yet in place, hammered through into his palm from the back. It had not been done easily. The bones in the back of his hand had been crushed. Had he survived, likely it must be amputated and his days as a cutler ended.

'They nailed his hand to his workbench,' Thaddeus reminded me.

'Why would they do that?' Adam was acting the scribe this day, making notes at my dictation.

'To keep him still whilst they painted his hand, maybe. Or as a message... or a warning? No need to write that down, Adam, 'tis no more than supposition.'

I examined the painted hand closely, using the scrying glass to observe how the pigment had been applied. It had been daubed on, probably with a piece of cloth. I returned to his shirt sleeve. A part had been torn – not cut – away and might have been used to smear on the pigment. Intriguingly, I realised it was not shell-silver that covered the hand like a glove but shell-tin, a more unusual but cheaper substitute. The perpetrator had come prepared with that paint and, mayhap, also bringing the long iron nail, yet had brought neither blade to cut nor rag to apply the colour. Had he brought the hammer required, I wondered?

'The hand was not nailed to secure it whilst it was painted but afterward,' I said. 'See here? The nail has passed through the wet pigment, taking it into the wound. Will you both aid me in turning the body, please?'

The cutler's back was more deeply scored. The loss of blood must have been considerable, each cut weakening the victim a little more. The unfortunate man had had no swift and painless death.

'In short,' I said aloud as realisation dawned upon me, 'I believe the victim was subjected to torture. Someone was desperate to gain information from him.'

'Do you suppose he told them what they wanted to know?' Adam asked but then answered his own query: 'I suppose that's unlikely, else why would they kill him after he had told them?'

'To silence him, either so he could not inform others or so he would be unable to reveal his murderer's name. Might you aid me to turn him one last time, please? Then we may leave him in peace.'

My last task was one I had delayed, being reluctant to perform this undignified intrusion. It was not easy to prise open the mouth, the rigours of death having clamped the jaw but the stiffness was passing off. I had already noted the caked blood about his lips and thought the poor fellow, in agonies, might have bitten his tongue. I was mistaken.

His tongue had been slit in twain, in the manner of a serpent's. The gory mess quite turned my stomach. I saw Father Simon scuttle away in haste and heard the sound of retching through the open vestry door. Adam looked somewhat green also.

'The brutes,' Thaddeus muttered behind his hand. 'I've seen enough of this. Are you finished here, Seb? I pray God you are, before we all empty our bellies on holy ground.'

In answer, I did my best to conceal the worst by forcing the jaw closed once more and covering Philip Hartnell's ravaged face with the sheet.

'I shall need to see the victim's workshop, Thaddeus, as the scene of the crime afore the place be cleaned up and put to rights. There may be more to learn from it.'

The bailiff agreed.

'I left instruction it was not to be disturbed until you'd seen it. There is more grim and gruesome horror for us to bear, I fear.'

Adam was shaking his head, an expression of dismay upon his face.

'If you prefer, cousin, you need not accompany us,' I said, taking pity on him. 'Instead, you might do me another service.'

'Anything in preference...'

'Call at Edmund Shaa's goldsmith's shop upon your way home and place an order for more gold leaf, if you will. We shall be much in need of it for the king's commission, once we make a proper start upon that work.' I turned to the young cleric – the one who had kept the night vigil. He appeared tired, knuckling his eyes like an infant, yet seemed to have borne the examination of the body better than the rest of us. 'May you provide me with water to wash my hands?' I had no intention of getting gore upon my attire and scrip. Nor would I wish to attract the wrong sort of attention from Gawain, awaiting us out in the porch, unless he had wandered off, in search of some more interesting diversion, such as a butcher's stall or a cookshop.

The cleric gave me such a look, as though I had asked him for the moon but went into the vestry to fetch what was needed – with utmost tardiness. If he had all day to waste, I did not. I called out to him and bade him hasten which earned me another glowering look upon his return. I was supplied with a dented basin, a scant cupful of cold water and a threadbare towel.

"'Tis holy water. All we have. 'Tis not meant for the likes of you to rid your hands of filth. Treat it with reverence, as you should.'

Now I understood his reluctance and made my ablutions accordingly, much chastened by his rebuke. I did wonder why he could not have walked the few paces along to the conduit in Cheapside to fetch some water of humbler kind.

With my hands not only cleansed but sanctified, I thanked the cleric and returned the basin, ready to commence the next unpleasant step in the investigation: the examination of the scene of the murder.

Philip Hartnell's Cutler's Workshop, where Bucklersbury joins Poultry

Not far from St Mildred's, Thaddeus took me to a small but well-maintained shop. It seemed that Hartnell purchased his blades ready-made from a blade smith forwhy there was no forge for working metal. Rather, it seemed his trade involved much leatherwork, bone-working or carpentry in making the handles into which the blades were set afore being polished, honed and finished for sale to customers. The place looked to have been well-ordered afore the killers came to do their worst. Stuff upon the higher shelves stood neatly arranged, tools hung each from its rightful peg.

But now dried blood splattered the walls and had congealed in pools upon the workbench and the floor beneath. A stool lay broken and a hammer and a collection of sundry items were strewn across the earthen floor, mayhap swept aside from the workbench. The victim had put up quite a fight, which furthered my surmise that there was likely more than one perpetrator – an idea supported when I identified at least three different sets of footprints having trodden the blood across the floor. I sketched their forms in case they should prove useful in some way in the future.

'Er, Seb,' Thaddeus said, hesitant as he watched me drawing, 'I fear those footprints maybe mine and the constables'. And those smaller ones maybe Mistress Hartnell's, since she discovered her goodman's body. The son and stepson also came in here to aid Mistress Hartnell in her shock and grief.'

'Oh. So not a useful clue, then. 'Tis a pity, Thaddeus, that you could not keep this place free of other folks' boots. Can you recall if there were any marks, other than those made by the family, afore you all traipsed through the blood?'

'Nay. I truly can't remember whether there were or not. I

suppose we could make comparisons with your sketches, see whose footwear fits and if there be any belonging to strangers.'

'Aye, we could. Or rather you can, my friend. I shall give you my drawings when I be done, let your constables do the work.'

I took time also to examine the hammer. Like the nail which had pierced Hartnell's hand, the hammer also showed smears of shell-tin upon its face, mixed now with dried blood. The victim must surely have cried out as he was tortured. Why had none of his neighbours come to his aid? I must enquire of them, when time allowed – or, more rightly, Thaddeus should.

I searched in the most obvious places first and quickly retrieved the piece of cloth, torn from Hartnell's shirt sleeve and employed to daub the shell-tin all over his hand. As to the meaning of that, I yet remained mystified. But seek as I might into every corner of the workshop, there was one item I failed to discover.

'They took the pot of pigment away with them after their gruesome business was done,' I said to Thaddeus as I recorded the fact in my notes. 'What is more, I believe they brought it with them for the specific purpose since I can find no trace of such a pigment – or anything similar – having been used by the victim in his work.'

'Is that important?' the bailiff asked.

'It proves that the painting of the hand was planned afore they came.'

'But why? What does it mean?'

'I know not. See here though, Thaddeus, a set of five knives lying upon the counter-board, ready for sale.' I picked up a finely worked eating knife, set in a bone handle carven with a vine-leaf design. 'Five being an odd number for a set, do they, by chance, match the murder weapon you have?'

Thaddeus showed me the linen-wrapped knife he had in his scrip. Removing the cloth revealed an identical handle. It did indeed match the remainder of the set.

'Where was it found?' I asked.

'In the midst of the floor, just flung aside after, by the look of it.'

'Which sets us another conundrum: was it the case that they arrived here unarmed and grabbed whatever instrument came to hand when the situation became heated and violence ensued? That seems unlikely.' I answered my own question. 'Rather, the use of his own creation against him must be part of the message.'

'What message?'

'I have not the least idea, Thaddeus, but it may be of greater import to ask for whom the message was intended? His family? His fellow cutlers? Other thieves, mayhap? We must not forget that the victim attempted to steal those candlesticks from Bladder Street upon Sunday eve. If I were you, my friend, I believe it might be worthwhile to make enquiries of the fellow who raised the hue-and-cry. He had a motive of sorts to take against Hartnell, although this crime appears to far exceed any petty act of revenge.

'For certain, this was not an act of hedge-breaking gone awry,' I continued. 'In plain sight upon the counter there be a bag of coin.' I fetched it but frowned, feeling the weight of it. So many pennies should weigh heavier, I thought. I tipped a few coins into my hand. They shone brightly and must be new-minted. By chance, I dropped one upon the countertop. My frown deepened.

'What's amiss, Seb? You look perplexed.'

'So I am, Thaddeus.' I unfastened my purse and took out a penny, much used and rubbed. I dropped it on the counter. It tinkled like a tiny bell. Once more, I did likewise with the bright new coin. It did not ring with the same note. I dropped the other coins from the bag, one after another. All made the same dull, lower note as they struck the hard wooden surface. Being a sometime chorister, I could discern the different tones, as others might not. 'Another task for you, my friend,' I said. 'I suggest you take these to the Goldsmiths' Hall and have them assayed.'

'Are they underweight?' the bailiff asked as he watched me

replace the pennies in the bag. 'I believe that to be the case but, worse yet, I do not think they be of silver. These be counterfeit coins; they do not ring true. Try the test for yourself, if you will. It may be that Philip Hartnell's murder had naught to do with a pair of dented candlesticks; that he was in far deeper trouble.'

Having left my sketches of the footprints for Thaddeus and his constables to make use of as best they might, Gawain and I had continued on to Gracechurch Street, taking the completed portrait to Guy Linton. I received scant thanks indeed for my hours of toil last eve, not so much as an offer of cooling ale or water for my companion. I made a mental note not to spend time and effort obliging the ungrateful wretch in the future. In truth, I regretted having made a decent piece of work of it, knowing Guy would be given credit. If it was not for the respect I bore Master Collop, I might have chopped the portrait to kindling with an axe and burned it in my hearth.

The morn was well advanced now, the streets bustling and the day becoming increasingly warm. Gawain's tongue lolled and dribbled. No doubt, if he could, he would have shed his thick coat of fur. I sweated 'neath my jerkin but only a common labourer would be seen in his shirt upon the city streets. Like Gawain, I would have to bear the heat clad as I was, for the sake of propriety.

The Foxley House

It seemed no work had been done 'neath our shop sign of the Fox's Head during my absence forwhy, as I turned into Paternoster Row, I espied Adam leaving the Sun in Splendour Tavern. I heard him call out to someone as he departed, waving his hand. To judge by his broad grin, he had spent a right pleasant hour or two, supping ale and joshing with friends and now it was drawing nigh unto the hour for dinner, I doubted a pen-stroke of work would be achieved until after the meal.

Adam must have read my displeasure writ plain upon my face as he made excuses afore I said a word.

'I was much in need of a cup of strong ale, Seb, after what we saw in the church. I couldn't stomach it; had to settle my humours, else I was in no fit state to work. I'm not so used to such sights as you are.'

'Did you visit the goldsmith, as I asked?'

'Of course. I'm not shirking my work, if that's what you're thinking,' he said hastily, having read my thoughts. 'Master Shaa said he's short of gold leaf at present. He needs to acquire some Venetian ducats from the Italian Baldesi bankers in Lombard Street and hammer the coins down. He'll send word to us when the leaf is ready. I asked him to set some aside.'

''Tis as well then that we have sufficient to make a start upon the royal commission.' I almost enquired whether the business of asking for gold leaf had taken all morn but held my peace. Adam was an industrious fellow – for the most part.

'Oh, and that rascally fellow was in the Sun again.'

'Who?'

'You recall him, the good-looking devil who robbed me of my sojourn with the tavern wench.'

'You were not tempted to commence to brawl with him again, I trust?'

'Nay. We fell to talking, John and me. That's his name: John. I told him what we'd been about this morn, why I was so in need of a good pot of ale. And upon hearing that the dead man was Philip Hartnell, John said he knew of him and wasn't surprised... that Hartnell was not so respectable nor blameless as folks believe.'

'He may well be correct at that,' I said as we entered the house through the side gate. Adam had had his reviving ale but I had not and I intended to remedy that afore I set to work –

both matters being too long delayed.

'Did Guy Linton approve the portrait?' Adam asked as I helped myself to ale from the jug in the kitchen.

'After a fashion. He said it would "serve". Offered me no thanks whatever for my time and labours. Remind me ne'er to oblige the wretch again in future. I know he believed it my duty to aid him for the sake of Master Collop's reputation but his discourtesy concerning it was insupportable, as though I be a slave with no choice in the matter.'

'Perhaps you should charge him a fee anyway? It will dissuade him from asking ever again.'

'Aye, mayhap I should.'

At that moment, Rose returned, her basket filled with market fare on one arm and my son in the other. I hastened to assist, taking little Dickon from her and setting him upon his feet – an action for which he showed his great disapproval by commencing to wail.

'The poor lambkin dislikes this hot weather,' Rose explained, 'What with those new teeth to trouble him too. I'll give him a soothing drink and put him down for a nap. I want him to be in a merry humour for his special dinner.'

I poured ale for Rose – she looked in need. A strand of fair hair had escaped her cap and clung damply to her flushed cheek.

'Special dinner?' I queried.

'Oh, Seb, you can't have forgotten. We discussed it last eve at some length over supper: Dickon's birthday dinner. Mercy is bringing Nicholas and Edmund and little Julia, of course. Dame Ellen and Grandfather Appleyard are coming too. And Jack, no doubt. None of us could be there, in Norfolk a year since, to celebrate his birth, so I thought – and you agreed – we should have an anniversary feast instead.'

'I agreed?'

Rose, Adam and Nessie all nodded.

'I had not forgotten the date but I do not recall any such discussion.'

'No doubt, your mind was set upon that damned portrait,' Adam said. 'But you certainly said "Aye" when Rose suggested it.'

So it was that we celebrated my son Dickon's first birthday with a fine dinner. We had aloes of beef sprinkled with vinegar, ginger, cinnamon, and pepper with crumbled egg yolks. Rose had made a colourful salat of tiny onions, parsley, chives, sage, borage, mint, fennel, rosemary, garlic, watercress and purslane. The platter was decorated with flowers: blue borage, purple chive-heads and rosemary and wild rose petals. Although it was not a fast day, battered whitebait was served – they being Dickon's favourite. The second remove – no expense spared – was a cream tart flavoured with sweet cicely and an apple curd, marchpane sweetmeats and best white wheaten bread in honour of the day, dressed with parsley butter. Rose had done us proud. I doubt King Edward at Westminster had a dinner any better than ours and, if he did, I wager he did not enjoy it half so much.

Fortunately, Julia and Edmund, the babes, slept throughout and Dickon and even Nicholas, mercifully, were in good humour and well behaved. When the platters were cleared, we retired to the parlour. Jack, Kate and Nessie had to be content to sit upon the floor with too few stools and insufficient room for the kitchen benches with us all there together but 'twas a right merry company. Stephen Appleyard had brought his flute, Adam had his gittern and I sang whilst others joined in, clapping hands. Rose and Kate found space enough to dance in the passageway, through the shop and out into Paternoster Row.

There, Mercy Hutchinson took up the dance with Jonathan Caldicott, our near neighbour, much to Mistress Caldicott's disgust. Jack clod-hopped with Nessie, treading on her toes more often than not. For a one-time would-be acrobat, he could be right clumsy in the dance. Folk spilled out of the Sun in Splendour Tavern across the way to join in the merriment. That ribald fellow with the handsome face was among them – John. He linked hands with Rose and Kate and others joined them in a circle dance, which soon filled the street. I kept a close watch upon him with pretty Kate. I would not trust him one inch.

Ale jugs and cups appeared as if by magick to be shared by all. I know not who paid for it. Mayhap, I did.

As I began to sing 'Summer is a-coming in', young Nicholas Hutchinson instigated a game of chase with Dickon and some other toddlings, racing or lurching precariously, depending how steady they were upon their feet, weaving around the adults' legs. When Gawain added his great furry self to the game, tripping up the dancers, good-natured chaos ensued.

'What are we celebrating?' Jonathan asked as I paused in my singing to take a sip of ale and assuage my thirst. Rousing ballads of 'Robin Hood and the Tanner' and 'The Outlandish Knight' had quite parched my throat.

''Tis the first anniversary of my son's birth.'

'What! One year old already?' his wife exclaimed. 'Why, it seems but yesterday that I first saw him when your Emily – God rest her soul – showed me a bundle of swaddling no longer than my forearm. How time has flown.'

Both Jonathan and I made the sign of the Cross and whispered 'Amen'.

Aye. Emily should be here, sharing in her son's day of celebration. Of a sudden, I had no more voice for singing. I crept within and hid in the workshop, shedding my tears, privily. I would not cast a sorrowful shadow upon such a joyous day.

Chapter 7

Wednesday, the sixteenth day of June
The Foxley House

NO MATTER what befell, this day, I would make a proper start upon King Edward's copy of Vegetius' *De Re Militari*. It could be delayed not a moment longer, else the book would ne'er be completed in time, afore the twenty-fourth day of July. Five weeks be hardly time enough for so splendid a work as this royal commission. Every day, every hour, must be expended upon it without my attention being diverted elsewhere.

I set to work that Wednesday morn an hour afore Prime, determined to have the first part of the book well in hand ere I broke my fast. Adam and Kate joined me later, at the time appointed to commence the day's work. Adam set a platter of honeyed oatcakes beside me and a cup of ale.

'You missed breakfast,' he said.

'Aye. I needs must get on with this. I have copied out the first gathering and begun the second. My thanks for the cakes.' I took a bite, elbowing Gawain's nose aside when he thought to share it. 'Kate, if you would please to prepare some shell-gold, enough for the eight-line opening vignette and the five initials following, in the way I showed you last week.'

'Aye, Master Seb. And what other pigments will you be needing?'

'Lapis lazuli and vermilion. Together with the gold, that will be the three colours of the Royal Arms. I shall keep the initials simple but bright – and luxurious. Elaboration will take time we do not have. Oh, and I shall need, er, malachite also, if you would, Kate.

'Adam, if you could begin the third gathering, I shall sketch out the under-drawing for the first of the full-page miniatures. 'Tis those that will take most time.'

With Adam requiring the exemplar copy to be open at the third gathering and myself requiring the fourth folio of the second, we could not work together without turning from one page to another and back again, in danger of losing our place and making mistakes. So, since Adam be a fine copyist, I left him to work unhindered whilst I began to paint the first of a dozen full-page miniatures. A score of half-page miniatures was also required. I had a deal of work to do. To produce a detailed full-page image could take me a day. It was as well that the hours of daylight were at their greatest length but I dare not produce anything less than my best. The trouble be that a man's hand, eyes and mind can only labour for so long afore his standard of craftsmanship deteriorates through weariness.

Thus, with the under-drawing for the miniature sketched out and ready for the application of gesso, I marked each area with the letter indicating the colour I intended to use – L for lapis lazuli, M for malachite, etc. as is the artists' tradition – I went out into the garden plot to stretch my legs, straighten my back and rest my fingers.

It was a fine June day with a cooling breeze chasing lambs-wool clouds across an azure sky. Rose was hoeing weeds from among the pot-herbs, her skirts kilted up, out of the way. Little Dickon, sitting in the dirt at her feet, was examining a snail as if it were a precious emerald. Such be a child's fascination with the world.

I crouched down beside him.

'See here, little one. You recall your sore finger of yesterday?' I took his hand and found the tiny mark upon his thumb where he had caught a splinter. 'If you take the snail, thus, and wipe his slime upon your hurt, it will heal right readily. Do you see?'

Dickon gazed up at me, large-eyed, as if inwardly wondering whether Papa was the fount of all knowledge or simply somewhat insane. Whatever his final decision, he returned to the serious study of the snail, poking a finger into the shell, trying to pull the creature from its sanctuary.

'He tried to eat it earlier,' Rose said, watching him, smiling the while. 'I told him only French peasants eat snails, or so I've heard tell. True Englishmen eat roasted beef and, in special cases, battered whitebait, of course.' She moved along the row of red caboches and stooped to pick off a caterpillar. 'Here, Dickon. Here is a new beast for you.' She held out her hand so Dickon could watch the creature's odd, looping gait. 'Nay. Don't put him in your mouth. See how he walks.'

I stepped back, observing them: Rose and little Dickon. How like a mother and her child they seemed. In truth, she was a mother to him. They laughed together and she smoothed my son's dark hair from his brow with a gentle hand.

'After we have dined,' Rose said, pushing tendrils of her fair hair back into her cap, 'I shall take Dickon up the lane beyond Newgate, if you agree, Seb? I want to gather meadowsweet from the hedgerow there before everyone else takes it all. It's in full bloom now and will scent the parlour floor when I strew it there. Some I will use to make the headache remedy, as Em showed me how to do.'

'Take him by all means but have a care, Rose. 'Tis not the safest part of the city and there be much activity up by Smithfield as incomers have begun arriving for the Midsummer Horse Sales. Thaddeus' constables have had to break up a few brawls there already, so he said.'

'Fear not, Seb. We'll be safe enough.'

Refreshed but thoughtful, I returned to my desk. Seeing it anew, I added a few lines to the image of soldiers readying for battle. It was a sight I had not seen, except in other images, but I could picture it in my mind's eye, hear the rasping of sand on steel as the esquires polished their lords' armour, the hammering as new arrowheads were forged, the screech of blades being sharpened on whetstones. The hurrying and scurrying as preparations were made for war. I tried to depict these things as well as what the eye would see, trying to bring a flat image to life.

'Shall I sketch in the foliage in the margins as I go for you to paint after?' Adam asked, shaping a new quill to his liking.

'No need. I was thinking of interspersing English oak leaves with swords, arrows and the like. It will be something different and suitable for a warrior's instruction book.'

'You think English oak is a good idea? The book is going to Florence remember.'

I shrugged.

''Tis a gift from the King of England. The recipient should be reminded of that whenever he turns the page. Besides, for all I know, oak trees may grow in Italy too. I shall ask Jude when I write to him... whenever I next have time to spare. And whilst we be thinking upon English images, I intend to have St George arrayed for war on the frontispiece. Or be George too much our own English saint? What be your opinion, Adam?'

'They worship the same God in Italy; praise the same Christian saints as we do, isn't that so? In which case, I'm sure George will be acceptable, especially if you give him a marvellous and ferocious dragon to slay. Everyone enjoys a colourful dragon, the more formidable, the better. You're brilliant at creating such beasts. Do you remember the sign you painted before Christmas last for the Green Dragon tavern? That was as magnificent a beast as I've ever seen. Such a one must surely meet with approval. Aye, Seb, St George will make a most excellent frontispiece.'

And so we laboured diligently until Rose called us to the kitchen for dinner. I was glad of the respite. Having determined to keep fine detail to the least that would suffice, my cramped fingers and sore eyes brought realisation: I had been painting every rivet in the armour, each filament in the fletching feathers and all the hairs in a horse's mane. I could not prevent myself from doing the best of which I was capable. At such a rate, it would take until the long day's end to complete the miniature – too long.

Twelve full miniatures taking a day each; twenty half miniatures at half a day... that meant twenty-two days' work. Add in the marginal decoration and the initials... another five days at least. Without labouring upon the Lord's Day... I tallied upon my fingers... that meant I had thirty-three working days until the book must be presented at Westminster and twenty-seven days' worth of illumination work to do. That would leave but five days for collating, stitching, trimming and the elaborate binding of gilded leatherwork, tooling and embossing to be done, not to mention the gold filigree and gemstones for which the book would have to be left with Edmund Shaa. 'Twas not enough time. I must find ways to speed my progress. What a task I had! The very prospect was sufficient to give me nightmares. No wonder my head ached at the thought of it.

I cannot say what we dined upon. My mind consumed by the puzzle of fitting a quart into a pint pot, as they say, or rather two months' worth of work into one, I did not hear the rapping on the shop counter-board.

'Shall I see who that is?' Kate asked. 'Rose has gone up Smithfield way, to gather herbs and blossoms.'

'What be amiss?' I queried.

'A customer in the shop.'

What manner of artisan was I, leaving the shop unattended? 'Aye. Well done, lass. I did not hear a sound. Did you, Adam?'

My cousin mumbled a reply, being fully engrossed in his penmanship. Glancing over, I could see page after page of faultless script appearing under his hand. Adam was a fine scribe, indeed, heaven be thanked. Mayhap, he could do some of the marginalia when he was done writing, as he had suggested. If the marginal decoration had to be simplified, then so be it.

'It's an urchin with a letter, Master Seb,' Kate said, bouncing back into the workshop. 'Says he won't hand it over 'til he gets the farthing he was promised.'

'Well, I promised naught. Here...' I fished out a coin from my purse. 'Give that to the young rascal.'

''Tis a whole penny, master.'

'No matter. Tell him to be gone, then you may serve in the shop a while; best not leave it unattended: any rogue might help himself to our wares.'

The letter, when Kate brought it, proved to be from Guy Linton. Ah, a word of thanks, at last, I thought, breaking the wax seal. But it was not. Instead, it was another plea that I attend him at once, this very afternoon. Some new dire situation must have befallen. He did not say what it was, and I felt not the least inclined to learn of it. If he must see me, he would have to come to Paternoster Row. I had not time to spare to trail across the city on his behalf, yet again.

I threw the letter aside and returned to painting a bowyer, bundling bow-staves into a barrel for safe-keeping. I delineated the figure's jerkin in malachite green, as marked earlier with an M, though he sported the Duke of Gloucester's white boar badge plainly upon his sleeve. That was my decision: to include a reference to the king's brother in the book. It contented me.

With but a horse and groom to paint, I took another walk out to the garden plot, to rest watery eyes and flex cramped fingers. Nessie was gathering lavender flowers to dry and strew among our winter woollen garments to keep the moths at bay. Clearly, it was the season for such activity.

Gawain joined me. He attempted to herd the hens into a corner but they were having none of it. Feathers flew as birds fluttered up to the pigsty roof or took to the apple tree where he could not harass them.

'Save your strength, lad,' I told him, laughing. ''Tis too hot for such antics.'

He came to me, tail wagging, expecting praise for his efforts.

I patted him and he rolled on his back in hope of a belly-scratch. I obliged him.

'I see you have time at hand, enough to frolic with your bloody dog. Why did you not come as I asked?'

Guy Linton stood in my garden, uninvited, and giving not so much as a greeting. I wished to send him off with a few choice words but, as ever be my way, courtesy prevailed.

'Good day to you, Master Linton. I have much work to do, so I pray you, state your business directly if you will.' I did not go so far as to offer him ale, though that would have been proper for a visitor. His manner did not sit well with me.

'It's the portrait...'

'If aught was amiss with it...'

'No. Ol' Mallard approved it right heartily. Much favoured the duck you added.'

'Then all be well. Now, you must pardon me. I have a royal commission in need of my attention.'

'But, Seb.' Guy caught at my sleeve to delay my return to the workshop. 'That's the problem. He thought it so fine a likeness, he's commissioned me to paint his son, the son's wife and their children. And this time he will pay me for it. I need the money, Seb. You have to help me. I'll give you a share, say, one-tenth. I'm not an unreasonable man. We can discuss terms, if you wish?'

'Nay. Not again. There be naught to discuss, Guy. I shall not paint another portrait for you to claim as your own work. I made it clear to you: I would save your reputation but once. I even showed you how to improve your art. If you cannot do the likeness yourself, then you must admit your failing. Or find some other foolish artist to abet you in your subterfuge.'

'How can I do that? You're London's only portraitist, Seb. There's no one else can help me. Please... I beg you, my dear friend... for Master Collop's sake.'

'Do not bring his good name into this as you did the last time. I told you "nay" and that stands as my answer. Go home,

Guy, practise with chalk and charcoal. You know the rudiments of drawing as Master Collop taught us. I cannot and will not do your work for you. I bid you good day.'

Gawain growled, showing his displeasure also.

With that, I brushed past Guy, leaving him in the garden to return to my work, collecting some ale from the kitchen as I went by. I noticed my hands shook somewhat. Sharp words were never my way but I had no choice. Even if I wanted to aid him, I had not the time to do so. Guy had created his own mess and would have to deal with it.

'You told 'im well, master,' Nessie congratulated me with her gap-toothed grin. The lass had witnessed all. She was tying the lavender into bundles to be hung from the rafters to dry. It scented the air pleasantly – a perfume that was supposed to soothe.

'Aye, but I wish he had not asked.'

Unbelievably, I found my thoughts turning to what I might say in a letter of instruction that I should send to Guy, guidance as to the better drawing of a likeness. But there was little point in that. What would I write but "Observe, observe and observe again"? There was naught else to say and he knew that much as well as I. I would not trouble myself to write to him but put all such concerns aside.

Seated at my desk, I took up my finest brush and dipped it into the white lead pigment to add the glint of sunlight on a polished armour breastplate. And yet Guy Linton's face, his desperate expression as I abandoned him, kept leaping into my mind, unbidden.

I laboured on, steadfast, until Rose called us to supper.

Over mussels in a green sauce, the talk was all of what was afoot at Smithfield. Rose had seen tents pitched, striped in gay colours, and swarthy traders from foreign lands exercising their beasts upon the field.

'You must go look at them, Seb,' Rose said. 'They're not like the heavy dray-horses or the coursers or palfreys we usually see. I asked about them and the fellow said they were from Araby: fleet of foot but lightly built. They had such pretty faces. Dickon quite took to them.'

'Rose! You did not take my son so close to these strange beasts? And you spoke to some incomer concerning them? I warned you to have a care. Whatever were you about?'

'Oh, Seb, we did but watch from afar and I spoke to no incomer but a London ostler who knew of these beautiful horses. He is Mistress Fletcher's ostler at the Hart's Horn. I know him vaguely.'

'Ah. Forgive me, Rose. I misunderstood. I did not mean...' I stabbed a juicy mussel with my knife somewhat more forcefully than intended, splashing sauce upon the board. I chewed the delicate morsel. 'Did you find the herbs you went searching for?' I asked quietly, hoping to make amends.

'Aye. Armfuls. Did we not, Dickon?' My son waved his spoon in agreement. 'He helped pick some and I think we were the first to gather the meadowsweet, for we had the choicest of blossoms. I've already strewn the parlour floor, as you'll appreciate after supper. It smells so fresh. The rest I have put to steep overnight, ready to boil up tomorrow to make the remedies. Which reminds me, I must buy honey at market to sweeten it. Meadowsweet smells delicious but tastes bitter otherwise. Oh, and Dickon found a mouse's nest attached to the tall grasses, all neatly woven as any basket. You should be proud of him, Seb, he was so gentle with the tiny creatures, watching but not disturbing them.'

'I be proud of him, whatever the case.' I wiped my mouth upon my napkin and leaned across to kiss his soft, dark hair where it stuck up in unruly tufts since his nap. He had had a long walk for a toddling and quite an adventure, by the sound of it.

'Master Seb,' Kate began in that tone I knew so well. 'Master... how would it be if you allowed me to paint something in the margin of the king's book? Naught too large. I thought

99

I could do King Edward's sun in splendour badge, just once… just so I can say I worked on a royal commission.'

'You have ruled a goodly number of pages for it, lass. That be a most valid contribution. The work would not look so neat and regularly set without your fine lines and measured margins to guide our hands.'

'But nobody notices the lines once the text is written and the miniatures done. Please, master… I did some sketches whilst I was in the shop – but only when there were no customers. Oh, please let me show you. I'm sure you'll like them.' Liquid brown eyes beseeched me.

I must have looked doubtful indeed.

'At least take a look at the lass's sketches, cousin,' Adam said, elbowing me in the ribs. 'Can't hurt, can it?'

'Nay. I-I shall look at them, most certainly, but cannot make you any promises, Kate. You do understand that?'

'Of course, master, but I know you'll like them right well.'

When supper was done and, by custom, the day's work ended, I permitted myself a half-hour in the parlour afore returning to my desk. The freshly-strewn herbs were fragrant indeed and to be enjoyed. However, there were yet three or four hours of good light that I could ill-afford to waste but a short respite, sitting with Dickon afore he should be abed, was time well spent.

He sat upon my knee as I showed him the beasts of Noah's Ark on his new hornbook. What with the celebrations of yesterday, we had not the leisure to study it 'til now. My son appeared much taken with the serpent that wound down one margin and the lion snarling below the coloured letters of the alphabet, running his finger over the shapes whilst I retold the story of Noah, not forgetting the rainbow at the last, arcing over the Paternoster Prayer on the other side. But all too swiftly, Dickon's head drooped and his eyes closed. Rose took him away to his cradle.

Afore I could wet my lips after story-telling, Kate hastened to thrust a paper into my hands. Her eagerness overflowed like

THE COLOUR OF EVIL

a stream in flood. I set the little hornbook upon the shelf, out of harm's way.

'What do you think, Master Seb? Are my suns in splendour good enough? Look at this one: 'tis not a sun at all but the white rose of York surrounded by the flaming rays of the sun. I saw it on his tabard when the king's messenger first brought the letter about the commission. Is it fine enough to be used? I pray you, master: say that it is. Or this one: a proper sun with pointed rays like a star and a crown...'

As bidden, I examined her drawings. In my mind, I had already planned out the decoration for every page but, since only one gathering had the under-drawings completed, there was yet scope for change within other gatherings not so far delineated. In truth, Kate's work was of the highest standard: designs of which no artist could be ashamed but justly proud. But pride be not a vice to cultivate in any young apprentice, therefore fulsome praise must be restrained.

'You have done well, lass. I approve the rose en soleil – for so the device be termed. You say you copied it from the messenger's badge?'

'Upon his tabard, aye. I'm so pleased you like it. Will you let me draw it in a margin somewhere – small and in a corner. Please say you will, Master Seb.'

'I shall think deeply upon the matter. I promise no more than that for the present, Kate.'

'Oh, but, master...'

'Do not vex me. There be much to consider afore I decide. Now. I have a miniature to finish whilst the light lasts. I bid you all good night and may Our Lord Christ keep you in His care.'

At last, the first miniature was completed. I had laboured long. Adam assisted in tidying away my pigments and put them safely in the box. The parchment folios were pressed flat on the collating table 'neath brass weights. Now my cousin and

I sat over our last few sips of ale in the kitchen by the light of a solitary candle. Rose and Kate were long since gone to their beds in the chamber above, where little Dickon also slept these days. Nessie had withdrawn to her curtained alcove beside the chimney, taking Grayling the cat with her for company. We could hear her snoring gently and kept our voices low so as not to disturb her.

Gawain was the first to respond to an unaccustomed sound: a scratching noise coming from along the passage to the shop. The dog came alert from his slumbers 'neath the board. He stood facing the passageway, his hackles rising upon his neck and a threatening growl rumbling deep in his chest.

'You hear that?' Adam whispered.

I nodded, reaching for a hefty fire-iron on the hearth.

'Did you bar the door and shutters when we closed up?'

I nodded again.

'Give me a moment.' Adam slipped out of the kitchen to the yard, returning with the axe we used to chop kindling for the fire.

Thus armed, we went silently along the passage. I held the candle high in one hand, the iron in the other. Gawain came stealthily, growling, but keeping behind me. The parlour door stood closed on the right but I lifted the latch and looked in, thankful for well-greased hinges. There was naught amiss.

The next door to the right led into the shop. Nothing untoward was apparent there. I checked the bar on the door to the street. It was firm in its hasps. The shutters were likewise in their proper place.

There came a sudden clatter and a smashing of pottery vessels. The intruder was in our workshop to the left of the passage. I reached for the latch, lifted it and pushed the door wide, the fire-iron raised high.

'Show yourself!' I cried. 'No, no!'

Something burst forth, straight into my face. I swung the iron in defence and felt it hit a target but I dropped the candle, plunging us into darkness. I stumbled back from my unseen assailant and fell on my backside. My heart was pounding fit to break my ribs and something tickled my face, causing me to sneeze.

Gawain tore into the room, courageous of a sudden, barking madly.

Adam was striking tinder and groping on the floor for the candle. When he relit the flame and it steadied, he began to laugh.

'By the saints! All that for a bloody chicken. You did for it, Seb: broke its neck by the look of it.' He picked up a sorry bundle of feathers from the floor, pushing Gawain aside when he would have it. More feathers floated around. 'A chicken dinner for us tomorrow.'

I clambered to my feet, wiping feathers from my mouth and nose, sneezing again.

'Must be Caldicott's birds have escaped again.' I spat out more filaments of feathers. 'It must have come in afore I closed up and wandered into the workshop... then was unable to get out.'

'His loss is our gain. Seems only right, Seb, after the consternation and trouble it's caused us. Look at the smashed pots! 'Tis fortunate it didn't break any precious pigments but the pounce and sand have made a mess indeed.'

'We can clean it up in the morn,' I said, turning as Rose and Kate appeared in the doorway, clad in their night robes.

'We'll all help,' Rose said. 'But you're bleeding, Seb.' She wiped my forehead with soft fingers.

'Am I? The bird came at me, aiming its beak straight at mine eyes. Mayhap, I be fortunate it pierced my forehead and did not blind me.' I felt chilled and shaken of a sudden and slumped upon the nearest stool.

'We heard Gawain making such a din; thought we were to be attacked in our beds.'

'Aye, our great protector...' I fondled Gawain's soft ears. 'Our brave knight be naught but a silly coward. Be that not so,

Gawain, you foolish creature?'

'Come back to the kitchen,' Rose said, taking charge of the situation. 'I'll make mulled ale for us all and for you a posset as a restorative. I'll put some salve on that cut, it looks sore.'

In truth, I hardly felt the hurt, for the present, leastwise, but I was most certainly shaken. Though I dared not admit to it, knowing Adam would laugh right heartily at me, if I did, I had been much affrighted by that wretched bird and was all unsteady.

A posset cup of hot milk, honey, cinnamon and nutmeg, whipped together to a froth, settled me well enough.

Chapter 8

Thursday, the seventeenth day of June
The Foxley House

RIGHT EARLY, afore Prime, Rose aided me in cleaning
up the mess in the workshop, sweeping the spilt fine sand
and ground chalk into separate heaps, in the hope that some of
each might be saved for use. We hoped in vain. I needs must
purchase supplies of both anew. I was much displeased at the
unexpected expense, and yet more so when I discovered chicken
droppings splattered upon my desk, stool and our precious
collating table. This last, I ever kept pristine and its present
condition was demoralising indeed. I knew chicken dung clung
like glue and would take a deal of effort to scrub off.

'I'll do it after we have broken our fast,' Rose said. 'Hot water,
lye and sand should get it off. I've cleaned stickier things from
the kitchen board before now – usually little Dickon's honeyed
pottage or egg yolks. As for your stool, why not use one from
the kitchen until this one is scrubbed and dried.'

I nodded.

'And I shall make use of Kate's desk,' I said. 'I cannot
work upon damp wood. The lass can serve in the shop in the
meantime. Oh, no. Look at that, Rose. The wretched bird
must have roosted upon that shelf there.' I pointed to where I
kept my brushes and quills upright in pots. ''Tis all soiled with
dung and feathers. And my best squirrel-hair brush... ruined.' I
sighed and rubbed my brow only to recall, belatedly, the injury

there: another score I would have to settle with my neighbour concerning his accursed bird. 'I shall have this matter out with Jonathan straightway.'

'Why not wait until after we've had our bread, bacon and ale?' Rose said, resting her hand upon my arm.

'You think to distract me?'

'Nay, but your humours are hot, that gash on your forehead looks red and angry and... Besides, Seb, you know full well Jonathan is never the first man from his bed. Likely, he's yet sleeping.'

'Well, his unholy cockerel gets us up and to our work right early. Why not our neighbour also? I should drag the rascal from his pillowed rest. I know not why I put up with him and his chickens. Why can he not keep them safely housed, as we do ours? And the damage done will neither be cheap to repair nor swiftly put to rights. My most favoured brush... I doubt Giles Honeywell will have another just so and I was using it to paint the miniature yesterday. 'Twill not be easy to replace it.'

As Rose suggested, I held my peace until after we had eaten. She soothed my forehead with a cooling salve and advised – should Jonathan vex me further – I breathe deep and count to five afore giving him answer. That such sage advice was needed demonstrated how I was becoming a fellow quick to anger these days, since Em's passing. God rest her dear soul. I know not why it should be. 'Tis a trait I must endeavour to curb.

I rapped upon my neighbour's door, somewhat hopeful that he might be still abed and my racket rouse him untimely.

'Jonathan Caldicott!' I cried, hammering on his door once more so hard that I hurt my knuckles. 'Get your idle carcass from betwixt the sheets. I have matters to raise with you.' I sucked at my scraped skin. 'Come. I do not have the day to waste upon you.'

The window above the street was flung open.

'Then come back tomorrow.' Caldicott's shout was followed by the flood of night soil emptied from a chamber-pot.

THE COLOUR OF EVIL

I hopped back in haste as the unsavoury deluge nigh doused me. My shoes were splashed and some misbegotten passerby laughed aloud.

Adam came out to join me.

'Leave it, Seb,' he said loudly, speaking so our neighbour must hear. 'We'll take the bastard to law instead. See how he likes the fat fines he'll have to pay.' His ruse proved successful.

Jonathan stuck his sleep-dishevelled head out of the window. 'I don't owe you devils a penny. What's this about fines, eh?'

'Compensation!' Adam yelled back. 'Your bloody hen wrecked our workshop last eve. You owe us for the damages done and the things that must be replaced. I've written a list here.' He unrolled a lengthy strip of paper and read aloud: 'Twelve sheets of finest calf vellum, a new collating table, two ounces of gold leaf, lapis lazuli, vermilion, dragon's blood, saffron, rose ochre, gum-tragacanth, four sable-hair brushes, a half dozen of squirrel, two of badger...' He named the most expensive items any stationer might have. Being a stationer himself – if not one of note – Jonathan knew the value of such things.

'We do not possess dragon's blood, saffron, rose ochre nor sable-hair brushes,' I said to Adam.

'Shhh, cousin. He doesn't know that. He deserves to have to pay.'

I saw then that Adam's paper was blank.

'I don't believe you. You're a lying scoundrel, Armitage.' Jonathan shook his fist at us, leaning precariously from the window above.

'You should keep your hens safe. One of your chickens attacked me. See here.' I pointed to the gash on my forehead. 'I should also be compensated for the mess and breakages it caused.'

To my dismay, Jonathan began to chuckle.

'Poor ol' Seb: hen-pecked as ever. No doubt, it was defending itself, knowing you for a fox. Ha, ha.'

''Tis no laughing matter, Jonathan.' I regretted mentioning

the injury and it now throbbed the more.

'So where is my hen you say did so much damage?'

'In the cook-pot, where it belongs,' Adam told him, grinning in anticipation of a tasty dinner.

'You have no right. That's my wife's bird. If you killed it, you should give it back to us.'

'It was self-defence... a lawful slaying,' I said, sounding lame. Self-defence against a scrawny bird? It was humiliating.

'I'll take you to the law over it. You owe me for the hen: a fine layer, that one.'

'You dolt! You don't even know which one is missing,' Adam said, clenching his fists.

'No. Well, I'll take you pair of thieves to the law over it, all the same.'

Heaven be thanked; at that moment, afore we found ourselves become the miscreants in the matter, Bailiff Thaddeus Turner arrived.

'The law is here,' he announced. 'What's amiss, masters? 'Tis early in the day for fiery tempers, unless last night's over-indulgence of ale is still to blame.'

'Foxley killed our chicken.' Jonathan determined to speak first.

'I knew not what it was in the dark. And such chaos it has caused in my workshop.'

'No doubt there are arguments on both sides,' the bailiff said, 'But I have more heinous crimes to investigate than your dead bird, Master Caldicott. If it was in someone else's workshop, 'tis a case of trespass. One of my constables will deal with that later. For the present, I need to speak with Master Foxley.'

'Oh, aye, and take his part... harken to his tale but not to mine,' Jonathan shrieked. 'I know you, Turner: always ill-favouring me because we're not friends, like you and Foxley. I'll complain to Lord Mayor Gardyner about you, failing in your civic duties, so I will.'

The bailiff shook his head. His usual upright stance

was slumped.

'You be weary, Thaddeus, at so early an hour? Come, take ale with us.'

He nodded and came with Adam and me into our shop.

'That's the way of it, is it?' Jonathan went on. 'Currying favour as ever, Foxley, you filthy arse-licker.'

I turned my back upon my neighbour with his foul words. Thaddeus must surely have come with some purpose other than peace-making in Paternoster Row.

'You have something to say, Thaddeus?' I prompted as we shared ale but the bailiff remained silent. 'You have uncovered some clue concerning Philip Hartnell's murder, mayhap?'

'Mayhap. Aye. But 'tis ill-tidings, Seb.' He drank long and sighed, easing his shoulders as though they ached and troubled him. Bearing over-much responsibility upon them? 'There's been another man slain in much the same way. I was called to his workshop soon after first light. His journeyman found him when he arrived to begin work.' He paused, staring down at his well-worn boots. 'You know him, Seb, so his journeyman informed me. He visited you here just yesterday. The journeyman said he returned in sorrowful wise, distraught, so he said.'

'Guy Linton? Do you speak of him?' My first thought – one that I would have to confess and do penance for – was of such relief it came close to being pleasurable: that the portrait of the vintner's family was no longer a cloud upon my horizon. It could be forgotten as though Guy had ne'er asked me concerning it. But then alarm flooded through my veins, my heart's pulse hastening. Did Thaddeus think I had to do with his murder?

'I'm sorry to tell you so plainly of your friend's death.'

'Friend? Nay, Thaddeus, I hardly knew the fellow. We were apprentices together for somewhat less than a twelve-month serving with Master Richard Collop. Guy Linton was my elder by a number of years. Master Collop alone made the link betwixt us. Otherwise, we had naught in common and I had not spoken with Guy until this week past.'

'Why did you meet up again of a sudden?'

''Twas not my choice,' I said. The conversation was proceeding upon a path I did not want to tread: the act of subterfuge with the original portrait was best kept hidden. 'Guy was in need of assistance with a particular commission. He believed I might render him aid in the completion of it.'

'And did you?'

'I offered advice.' Which was true enough but certainly not the whole truth. I hated deceiving Thaddeus.

'That was yesterday?'

'Nay; a few days since. Yesterday, he came to request that I do more than give advice. I told him I had not the time. That be all. We have a commission of our own to complete for King Edward that must take precedence above all else. I could not assist Guy, even had I wished to.'

'Did you realise how greatly your refusal upset him, as his journeyman reports?'

'He seemed dismayed. I would not think he was so much distressed. Mayhap, some other greater problem had arisen?'

The bailiff looked downcast.

'May I have more ale?'

'Tell me in all honesty,' I said, refilling his cup. 'Do you suspect my involvement in Guy's death? I would rather know how the matter stands.'

'What! Of course you're not a suspect, Seb.'

'That be good to hear, indeed.' I felt the tautness in my body melt away like snow in sunlight.

'Since I already know of your royal book – of which we spoke in full already –'

'Oh, forgive me. It does fill my every thought of late.'

'– and having learned that you were acquainted with Guy Linton, I am reluctant to ask... but would you be able to spare an hour, cast your knowledgeable eye over the scene of the crime? 'Tis a great imposition, I know, but you're the best man in London for the task, elsewise I wouldn't make so onerous a

110

request of you...'

Guy Linton was not my friend. I could hardly care any less about him in other circumstances, but every man was entitled to live his span of years, as allotted by the Almighty, and not have it curtailed by some felonious act. Guy deserved justice like any victim and since Thaddeus had need of me to help bring that about, my conscience would give me no rest, if I refused.

'Aye, I shall come,' I said, fetching my cap down from its peg. 'Permit me to fetch my scrip. Adam, if you will continue with the Vegetius text...'

'You don't want me to come with you and take notes?'

'The book cannot be abandoned. And have Kate go to Giles Honeywell's stall in St Paul's to purchase what we need to replace: pounce, sand and whatever else was spoilt last eve. Rose promised to scrub my desk and the collating table, so they will be unusable for a while. They will dry whilst I be gone.'

'You want the lass to buy you some new brushes as well, since they were ruined?'

'Nay. Those I must select for myself, to suit the way I work and make use of them.'

'Is all this down to your neighbour's chicken invading your workshop?' Thaddeus asked.

'Aye, it caused a deal of trouble and affrighted us.'

'Not to mention the damned expense,' Adam added, 'And we're far behind as it is. Don't keep Seb away too long, Thaddeus, else you'll have the king himself to answer to, if his book isn't finished in time.'

Guy Linton's Workshop in Gracechurch Street

We entered Guy's workshop 'neath its tiled porch. This day, there was no striped awning erected to shield the counter-board, which had not been lowered. Thaddeus went through into the workshop. If, upon my previous visits, it had been a place much disorganised, now it was a scene of chaos. One of the constables guarded the mess. The air was befouled with the metallic tang of blood and something else besides.

The grey-haired journeyman – Ralf, I recalled – sat upon his stool as afore but was not working. Why would he when there was no longer a master to pay his wages? I knew naught of the relationship betwixt them but Ralf looked to have shed tears, dabbing his eyes upon his sleeve.

'You'll want to question him. Ralf Reepham,' the bailiff said, nodding towards the aged fellow. 'He found the body. Gave him a nasty shock.'

'Reepham? Once a Norfolk man, mayhap? I shall speak with him directly, then he may leave; go home or to the tavern. It seems a cruelty to have him stay.'

I went to him. Since his bent back made looking up at me an impossibility and there being no other vacant stool, I had to crouch. This questioning then must be brief, else my hip would complain.

'Ralf. Your loss must grieve you and I apologise for having to question you at this time.'

'If you think I weep for him, it's not so, Master Foxley. He was mean spirited, worked me hard but paid me little. He only kept me on because I came cheap. Yet it was the means of earning my bread. Since my back went awry, nobody else wants a twisted up journeyman, though my fingers work as well as ever. How will I earn a livelihood now? That's what worries me.'

Now that I knew his name, I could hear a faint echo of Norfolk lingered in his voice.

'For the present, Ralf, I would have you turn your mind to the matter of Master Linton's death. How were things arranged here when you first arrived this morn?'

'As now. I haven't touched anything. Didn't want to, what with all that blood. Then I sent an urchin to fetch Bailiff Turner and when he came, he told me not to move anything or try to clear up. As if I would. Why should I care about this shambles?'

'Why, indeed. I thank you for your time, Ralf. Unless Bailiff Turner has questions, you may go home. Where be your house, if we should need to speak with you again?'

'House? Tush! I lodge in a poky room – a storeroom – at the back o' the Boar's Head in East Cheap. Leastwise, I do for now, 'til I can't pay the rent come Saturday. Then, who knows where I'll lay my head?'

The journeyman shuffled off and I eased myself up from my crouched position. My hip creaked in protest, causing me to wince. Discomfort aside, I could delay no longer the purpose for which Thaddeus had brought me here. Guy Linton's ornately carved desk was a sight of horror. Like Philip Hartnell, Guy had been tortured with a myriad of small cuts. His penknife lay bloodied beside him so, as afore, the felons had made use of the man's own tools. Yet a stationer has little use for a hammer so, mayhap, they had to supply that upon this occasion. I could not see one lying about and there was no escaping the fact that one had been employed: Guy's right hand was nailed to his desk in like manner as with Hartnell's. It too had been daubed with a silvery pigment. I also saw a bag of coins, which I pointed out to Thaddeus.

'Far too light,' he said, weighing the bag in his hand. 'Just like last time. Constable!'

'Aye, sir?'

'Take these to the Goldsmiths' Hall for assay, Angus, and don't think to spend them on a cup of ale along the way. They're counterfeit coins, if I'm any judge.'

'What did the goldsmiths have to say concerning the previous bag we found at Hartnell's workshop?'

'Almost all of tin, mayhap with a dash of copper, they think. And worse yet, they say similar forgeries are being found, here and there, about the city in increasing numbers. The lord mayor and the council are very worried. And, no doubt, you can guess who is supposed to track down the devilish coiners and bring them to justice?'

'You?'

'Aye. As if I have time when I'm not trying to discover murderers. I tell you, Seb, my job needs an army. One man alone can't do it all.'

And there was I begrudging him my aid. What a selfish dolt was I? Thaddeus laboured far harder and longer than an illuminator ever did.

'See, here,' I said, returning my attention to the clutter on Guy's desk. 'This be of considerable interest.'

'The pigments? What of them, Seb? They're the tools of his trade. I see naught unusual in that.'

'But look more closely at these oyster shells.' Like us, Guy mixed his dry pigment powders with beaten egg yolks in shells. At present, only the powder had been put into the shells, of which a box of unused ones sat on his desk. 'Can you see that some shells have bloodied finger marks upon them... and this spillage of azurite powder?'

'What of it?'

'I think he was tipping the powders into the shells even as he was dying, his hand already nailed down, having to do it in unaccustomed wise with his left hand.'

'Why would he do that? He was never going to use them, was he?'

'I know not but there be another odd circumstance. He has set out four shells containing blue. Why so many? And then he has lined up the shells in a straight line across his desk.

Guy was not a man of tidy habits, as you can observe from the workshop otherwise. Why would he make such a neat and ordered line even as he breaths his last? These pigments were of great significance to him, Thaddeus. I feel it in my bones.'

I took out my pen, inkpot and paper and sat at Ralf's abandoned desk to make a note of the pigments the dead man had arrayed before him. Right to left, they be named dragon's blood, realgar, azurite, lapis lazuli and another lapis, a second shell of azurite (somewhat spilt), malachite and crimson lake. Why so much blue? Was there a pattern, I wondered? If there was, I did not have wit enough to discover it.

My final and most gruesome task had yet to be accomplished. I performed the office right swiftly: it took a few moments to prise apart the stiffened jaws. As expected, yet to my great horror even so, Guy's tongue had been slit in twain. The purpose of so vile an injury was as mysterious as the line of pigment pots.

'We must endeavour to find some common thread betwixt the two victims, Thaddeus. These were no random murders.'

'What could it be? Both are – were – respectable artisans, owning their own shop.'

'Aye, and the shops be not so far distant, one from the other. However, Philip Hartnell had a family; Guy Linton does not.' I chewed my pen. 'The one had recently been engaged in an act of thievery,' I said, recalling the hue-and-cry in which I had played a part. 'Had Guy Linton e'er been involved in some crime of which you know, Thaddeus?' I nigh bit my tongue off, realising what I asked. Guy had recently committed an act of subterfuge and I had abetted him in counterfeiting his work. I would do better to keep silent.

'Not that I know. His name rang no warning bells. If he was up to no good, I have yet to hear of it. Can you think of anything else that might connect them, Seb? Or shall we consider the matter over a jug of ale, if you have finished here?'

'Aye. I can think of naught else I need to see. There are no footprints in the blood as there were at the cutler's place. Did your constables determine to whom the marks belonged?'

'All fitted the family's shoes, so unless his wife or sons killed him...'

'They provided no useful clue, then. You do not believe his family to be guilty, do you?'

'No, Seb. All have alibis and, besides, they don't seem the sort to commit such a ghastly crime. Could a wife do that to her husband? She wouldn't be strong enough, in this case. As for the sons... could any man hate his father so much?'

'I solved a case a while back, afore you were the bailiff, in which a son slew his father. He did hate him but – as you say – even so, he killed him with a blow. Naught so grisly as these two deaths.'

'Shall we take that ale now?'

'Nay, my friend. I have much to do but if you give me leave, I offer to go tell Master Richard Collop about Guy.'

'Are they relatives, then?'

'I do not believe Guy has any family – if he does, Master Collop will know. Guy was once his apprentice and, thus, his one-time master be the closest thing to family. Shall I inform Master Collop?'

'Aye, it'll spare me an irksome task. I hate telling folk of a horrible death when they know the victim. I'll be pleased if you would; if 'tis no trouble?'

'I have business with Master Collop in any case. I shall make a fair copy of my notes for you when I may. It might not be possible this day, but as soon as maybe. God be with you, Thaddeus.'

The Stationers' Hall, Amen Lane

It happened that Master Collop was not at his shop in Cheapside. Neither was Hugh Gardyner, though that be by the by. A less courteous apprentice informed me, rudely, that if I wanted to speak with his master – and I relate his words exactly – 'The ol' goat was at the hall in Amen Lane'. Such insolence! I would report the rascal directly.

Arriving at the Stationers' Hall, I had to curb my impatience yet further forwhy Warden Master Collop was dealing with another matter, talking with some considerable degree of animation to a man wearing his official alderman's robes. Since such attire was not for everyday wear, I supposed his visit must be of importance. At length, I succeeded in catching my old master's eye and could see he would much appreciate any excuse to be done with the alderman.

I moved forward, removing my cap and bowed.

'Ah! Master Foxley,' the warden spoke as if he had not noticed me afore. 'You bring me news of that urgent matter we spoke of earlier?'

'Indeed I do, Master Collop,' I replied, realising his subterfuge.

'My thanks, Alderman Faring, for bringing these facts to my attention. Now, if you will excuse me, I bid you good day, sir.' With that, the robed official was dismissed. I wondered at my master's daring as he turned to me, smiling. 'Sebastian. Good day to you and I'm grateful for your timely arrival. 'Tis the third time in a week that the wretched fellow has accosted me and thinking this time to impress me by wearing his regalia – in which case he was much mistaken. So, you wish to speak with me, Sebastian?'

''Tis sorrowful tidings I bear, unfortunately, Master Collop, concerning Guy Linton,' I said, in truth, being curious, wanting to know about the alderman's complaint.

'Oh, no. Got himself into yet another tight corner, has he?'

'I fear 'tis worse than that. His journeyman found him dead in his workshop this morn.'

'An accident?'

I shook my head.

'Murdered.'

'Poor fellow. May God receive his soul.' Master Collop crossed himself, as did I. 'I suppose Bailiff Turner has called upon you to determine what came to pass?'

'He has. But I came to enquire of you, master, whether Guy has any family to inform, or to take charge of the funeral arrangements?'

'I don't believe so; not any longer. His father yet lived when Guy was serving his apprenticeship but that was all he had by way of relatives. He ne'er spoke of there being anyone else, and I know his father died, leaving him the shop in Gracechurch Street a few years ago. Guy inherited the business, along with his father's ageing journeyman, Ralf. Is he the one who found the body?'

'Aye, Ralf Reepham. It was a great shock to him but – so it seemed to me – there was little affection betwixt him and his master.'

'Are you suggesting Ralf may have killed him?' Master Collop stepped back in surprise.

'Nay, you mistake me. Bailiff Turner and I suspect naught of the kind. Ralf would not have sufficient strength to... do what they did.'

'They?'

'Two men at least; mayhap even three. They held Guy down.'

'And you have an idea who they are, these devil's spawn?'

'Not as yet but we are doing our best. 'Tis early days, although Guy be not the first to suffer at their hands.'

'There are others? By God's sweet mercy, Sebastian, what is our city coming to, eh?'

'One other, a cutler by trade, Philip Hartnell. He lived not

THE COLOUR OF EVIL

far from you, master.'

'Hartnell! Aye, I know him – knew him – well. A respectable neighbour. His poor wife... I must pay her a visit, offer my condolences and any assistance she may require. 'Tis a wonder I had not heard of his passing.'

'I believe Bailiff Turner requested the family not to cause alarm by telling the neighbours too much. But I would ask you, master, concerning Ralf Reepham. Might he be considered a worthy scrivener, reliable and skilled?'

'Why? Not thinking of employing him, are you?'

'Aye. He was so forlorn, saying he had a roof over his head but only so far as the end of this week and bewailing the unlikelihood of earning a wage anywhere else. And I be falling behind hourly with the king's commission. If Ralf be dependable, I have need of an extra journeyman. What do you think, Master Collop? Will I regret the day if I offer him employment?'

Chapter 9

Friday the eighteenth day of June

I HAD SPENT the previous afternoon and this morn working on the miniatures for Vegetius' book for the king but it was painstaking work.

I had discussed the matter thoroughly with Adam as we dined yesterday and he agreed with me that it was worth taking on Ralf Reepham to help us with the commission, if the fellow was willing. Thus, last eve, we sought out the journeyman, finding him at The Boar's Head Tavern where he lodged.

Much as I expected, the man was overjoyed at my proposal that he should work for us at Paternoster Row, the more so when he learned Adam was not only of Norfolk but one of the Foxley Armitages. Though he did not know Adam personally, his family in nearby Reepham – the Meadows – had been acquainted with the Armitages in the past in friendly wise. Once such knowledge was exchanged, I discovered my presence at the board in the rundown tavern to be superfluous. These Norfolk men surely know how to chew the cud together, chattering on and on, singing the praises of their beloved shire, relating tales of the places and people they knew in common.

In the end, I left them to their jaw-wagging and strolled back home, taking Gawain along Cheapside. Although it was past eight of the clock – as told by St Martin's bell – it would remain light for another hour and I had no need of a torch to light my way. As I walked, I envisaged Guy's line of shells, pigment-filled, attempting to unravel the mystery. Why two shells each of azurite and lapis lazuli? Why was the colour blue of such importance? Was it to do with St Mary, Ever Virgin, traditionally depicted gowned in blue? Had Guy been attempting, at the last, to pray to Her, beseeching Her aid at the end? Mayhap, it was, in some way, an artist's prayer. Cudgel my wits as I might, I remained as baffled as afore.

The Foxley House

I set to right early this morn to begin the miniature of St George as the frontispiece for the Vegetius. In the meantime, Adam had returned to The Boar's Head to fetch Ralf and aid him in bringing his few belongings to our house. Aye, matters had progressed during my absence last eve – Ralf was now to bide with us, sharing Adam's chamber. I never thought the matter through so far, seeing our paying of the journeyman's wages as enabling him to continue lodging at the tavern, as afore. But, as Adam argued, 'twas a lengthy walk for the elderly man with his bent back and, since we had room enough to spare, would it not save a deal of time if Ralf slept 'neath our roof? The logic was impeccable but I felt wary of the addition of a man we hardly knew to our household. However, my cousin being adamant, that was to be the way of it.

I forewarned Rose, Kate and Nessie concerning an extra place to be set at the board for breakfast. I hoped that sharing food with Ralf would be the best means of introduction, that he might meet us all and we begin to know each other's ways. He seemed personable enough last eve at the tavern and I prayed none would find any reason to object to him. After all, if Jack was acceptable to the womenfolk, then Ralf should be also, for I had heard no foul language from him. He neither spat nor belched over his ale as some do and his habits appeared reasonable, on brief acquaintance, leastwise.

Ralf joined us, removing his cap and bowing to Rose and Kate. Even Nessie received a mannerly greeting which pleased her much. Little Dickon was patted upon the head, as was Gawain. We took our places at the board, Ralf seated beside Adam. I said a grace and we tucked into roll-mop herrings and new bread.

''Tis a fine meal, Mistress Glover,' Ralf said, wiping his platter clean with the last morsel of his bread and sucking on his few remaining teeth.

'Have some more fish, if you will?' Rose offered. 'And please call me Rose, Master Reepham.'

'Aye, then "Rose" it shall be, so long as you call me "Ralf", and I will have another roll-mop, if I may.'

Thus, Ralf's coming to us appeared painless. Not so, his climb to Adam's chamber to stow his belongings. He had a deal of difficulty upon the outside stairs, puffing and wheezing and having to pause to catch his wind. And 'twas not so many steps – only a dozen. This was a problem neither my kinsman nor I had foreseen.

'This damnable bent back...' he explained once he had caught his breath, '... leaves no room to breathe deep. But fear not, it bothers me little otherwise. You'll see... I go back down steps as easy as you do.'

I nodded, hoping he spoke true.

'I could get some timbers from Stephen Appleyard,' Adam said, 'Build a second handrail on the left hand, so you can pull yourself up using both hands.'

'No, Adam, that's not my difficulty... just getting my breath is all. I manage well enough.'

However, matters resolved themselves in more advantageous wise in the workshop. Ralf was to work at the desk used previously by Tom Bowen, my one-time apprentice and late journeyman. Once seated there, he looked quite at home, sharpening quills to suit his way of working and pinning out parchment ready for ruling.

I returned to my St George frontispiece, designing how the coiled dragon should lie, entwining the hooves of the knight's steed in the foreground as the evil beast thrashed in its death throes at the bottom of the image. Having had it brought to mind of late as the colour of evil, I marked the dragon's scales with the letters 'S-G' to remind me to paint them later with shell-gold. But first, I had to mix and apply the gesso to those parts that were to be covered in gold leaf: George's halo and the quarterings of his shield. These last I would then paint over, opposing quarterings in azure and vermilion and, when dried, I must remove the pigment with delicate touch to reveal golden fleurs de lis upon the azure ground – these for the arms of France – and the three lions upon the red ground for the arms of England. Only then could I paint the rest of the image. With so much involved and no time to be wasted, nevertheless, I would do as a good master should and have Kate assist me, such that she might learn the craft secrets of making gesso and applying it.

'Take the powdered chalk and tip a few spoonfuls worth into the mortar,' I instructed. 'Now add a little white lead and a dash of the reddish-brown ochre – not too much. Aye, that be about the correct amount. Now mix the powders thoroughly, Kate.'

'Why do we add ochre, master?'

'A little colouring aids us once we put the gesso on the white parchment to see where we have placed it, to make certain we do not leave gaps where there should be none.'

'Won't the red colour show through the gold and spoil the look of it?'

'Nay, lass. In truth, it does show through somewhat but gives the gold a warm glow, improving its appearance most agreeably. Keep mixing, Kate… until 'tis all of the same palest rosy hue… aye. Now put it upon the marble slab. Add a drop of honey. This begins to bind the paste and, later, aids the gold leaf to adhere to our little gesso cushions. Good, that be coming along well but now we must thin it, to make it useable. Egg glair goes in next.

You recall that I showed you how to beat the eggs last week?'

'Aye, master.'

'I asked Rose to whip some egg whites for us after we broke our fast. Fetch them from the kitchen, if you will, lass?'

'You take a deal of time with your 'prentice, Master Seb,' Ralf said as Kate scuttled off to the kitchen.

'How else will she learn our craft?'

'Master Linton never had the patience for it. He had a few 'prentices over the years but they never stayed long. None did their full term and learned little from him. What they did learn was mostly what I showed them how to do. Mind you, Master Linton might have given the youngsters little instruction but he was free enough with the rod. Many a beating did he give out.'

'And what did you teach them, Ralf?' I asked.

'Well, though I says it myself, I know all about mixing the stuff you call gesso – I just call it a plaster because it needs to be as smooth but runny as a medicinal plaster. And gold leaf – I've always been good with that fine, tricky leaf.'

''Tis as well to know. If I fall any further behind with this commission, I may have to call upon your skills. Ah, Kate, you have the eggs. Now see this watery portion at the bottom of the bowl?'

'Shall I throw that away?'

'Indeed not! That be the part we require. Pour it on the mixture... carefully now. Keep it to the midst of the marble slab. Now mix it with the palette knife. Try to avoid spilling it over the edges... aye... well done.'

'It's very lumpy.'

'Aye. 'Tis too dry. We need a little rainwater.'

'There's scented water in the bucket for hand-washing...'

'Rainwater be preferable, Kate.'

'Why?'

'In truth, lass, I know not but 'tis the way I was taught and, since the method has not failed me yet, I will hold to it.'

'I'll fetch some from the butt, then. It's a good thing we've had so much rain of late.'

'And you're honest too,' Ralf said, continuing our conversation in Kate's absence. 'Master Linton would never admit he didn't know something. His answer to young Kate's question "Why?" would've been "Because I tell you so!" No patience had he.'

I thought upon Ralf's comments as I awaited the lass's return. If Guy Linton was such an impatient, surly fellow, who could say how many enemies he had made down the years? Apprentices denied their full term of indenture. Disgruntled fathers who had paid him to train their sons only to have them learn little and suffer too many beatings. If the man had many enemies, Bailiff Turner's task would be the harder.

'How much water shall I use, master?'

'Add a few drops at a time. It will not do to make it too thin. It would run all over the underdrawing.'

'What if I add too much?'

'That would be a sorry thing. We would have to add more of each of the dry ingredients to achieve the correct consistency.'

'Like making bread dough.'

'Aye. Not unlike that. But then there would be more gesso than I can use afore it sets hard'

'Couldn't we save some for the morrow?'

'Nay. Once the glair and water be added, it must be swiftly used. You have the mixture correct, I think, but keep turning it with the palette knife until it be silken-smooth and without any bubbles. If you leave bubbles, they will burst as the gesso sets and leave little pits. The surface must be as perfect as we can make it.'

I watched as Kate worked the paste, blending and smoothing.

'Will that do, master? My arm's aching.'

'Aye. That be sufficient, lass. Bring the clean bowl and scrape it in. Do not waste any, leaving it upon the marble. Now I may do my part whilst you rest your arm. Come watch me; see how to apply the gesso to the vellum. I use a quill pen. Not a brush. I pour a drop or two only... just a little in the centre of the shape to be filled, then use the pen to guide it into every corner. I must act in haste, else it will begin to set. There! I have done St George's halo. Next, the shield. This being a larger ground, I need more gesso and it will take longer to set. But, e'en so, I waste no time. Just push the paste to the point of the shield… thus… and 'tis done.'

'Why don't you use a brush, master?'

'However thoroughly I might wash the brush after use, the least trace of gesso remaining would set hard and ruin the brush. Quills come more cheaply and be easier to clean.'

'What do we do now?'

'We set the page aside to allow the gesso to dry and harden overnight. No more may be done to it until the morrow, when I shall show you how to smooth and level the surface and apply the leaf, trim and burnish it. In the meanwhile, I have other miniatures to do, laying out the underdrawings and denoting the pigments to be used. Why do you not go fetch ale for us all, lass? The chalk dust in the air makes my throat dry indeed and everyone else's also, no doubt. Then you may aid Rose in the shop. I be certain she will be grateful for that, having much to do elsewhere.'

I settled at my desk, pen in hand, ink pot opened, ready to begin a drawing of men training their destriers for battle. This was but an excuse to draw horses – a subject much to my liking – but was an aspect of war dealt with in the book. As Vegetius wrote: *busy occupations in deeds of arms profits more to keeping knights in good health than physicians or medicines.* That must likely apply to their horses also and why should I not indulge my fancies once in a while? The full-page miniature allowed for five horses, each in a quite different pose: one being saddled, another at the trot on a long rein; a third with its rider charging at the quintain; the fourth being shod by a farrier and the fifth rearing up, tumbling its rider from its back. For this last, I composed a story in my head as I outlined it, as to why its rider deserved to be unhorsed and humiliated. It made me smile to think upon the beast taking its revenge for some act of mistreatment.

Afore I knew, Rose called us to dinner. I must cease allowing my imagination to conjure such foolish tales. They achieved naught but wasted time. I should work more swiftly if I kept my thoughts upon the task in hand. However, during the meal, I found myself wondering again if Guy had been murdered as an act of revenge? If so, then the same perpetrator likely also had a grudge against Philip Hartnell. I must enquire of Thaddeus, how his investigation was progressing – if it was.

'Seb!'

'Aye?'

'I pray you, pass the salt,' Adam said in a tone suggesting he had asked more than once.

'Forgive me. My thoughts were elsewhere.'

'And where was that? The pages of Vegetius?' Adam suggested.

'Drawing horses,' Kate offered.

'Thinking of a pretty wench, maybe?' Ralf asked, knowing me not.

I shook my head.

'None of those. I be considering these two murders of late, wondering what the victims had in common. There be something we have overlooked but I know not what.'

'I wouldn't worry your head about it, Master Seb,' Ralf said. 'Guy Linton's not worth the headache it'll cause. Besides, 'tis the bailiff's work, not yours.'

'My cousin oftentimes helps the bailiff solve crimes,' Adam told him, then went on to tell Ralf all about our search for a missing child, not so long since, and our misadventures across the river. There was a deal of embellishment, embroidery and exaggeration, all of which had the old man wide-eyed with wonder.

'Don't believe everything Adam relates,' I warned him. ''Twas more about mud and lost boots than deeds of valour.' I passed Rose my empty bowl for washing, realising as I did so that I could not recall having eaten the contents nor what they were. 'Come, we must return to our work, although I should visit Giles Honeywell to purchase the brushes I need to replace those that were ruined. I shall require them in the morn.'

As we went to the workshop, my ears were yet sharp enough to hear what Ralf whispered to Adam behind his hand: 'Your kinsman's a hard taskmaster but at least he drives none harder than he drives himself.' At which Adam chuckled and answered: ''Tis but for your sake, to make a good show. Mostly, he's as idle as the next fellow.'

I did not much like my cousin's disparaging remark and hoped it was made in jest. I ne'er considered myself a lazy man but might I seem that way to others? I opened my purse to make certain I had sufficient coin to buy the items I required. There was sufficient.

'I be going to Paul's, to Giles Honeywell for new brushes,' I said.

'Pity you can't have the ones from Linton's workshop,' Ralf said. 'He always bought naught but the best of everything, yet I never saw him use them. Don't know how he could afford such expense; we didn't make much profit. In truth, I reckon he ran up debts everywhere. I know he hadn't paid the apothecary for inks for months because the fellow came in person to demand payment only a few days before Linton was... aye, well... And I know he owed money to that miserable vintner he was painting the portrait for and seeing he didn't much like wine, it can't have been that he was paying for. If you ask me, there was more going on betwixt them two... I never took to that man.'

'Indeed. No matter. I shall return in haste.'

St Paul's Cathedral

I strode directly to Honeywell's stall in the cathedral nave, intending to waste not a moment in idle talk, certain Giles would serve my needs.

'Good day, Master Honeywell.'

'And good day to you, Master Foxley. How's business? Are you well? And that little lad of yours...' Giles was ever a one for gossiping.

'All as it should be, I thank you. But I be falling behind with my work and I require three squirrel-hair brushes of differing sizes, if you please?'

'But you bought all my best ones not so long since. What do you do with them? Eat them?' He laughed.

'They were all ruined by a, er, stray chicken.'

Giles laughed louder.

'You hear that, Hal?' he said to the fellow on the neighbouring stall – likewise a stationer though he dealt more with the necessaries of book-binding than illumination. 'Brushes got eaten by a chicken. How did that happen, then?'

'Please. Just show me your selection of brushes.'

'I've only got badger or horse-hair. I haven't had time to re-stock the squirrel since you bought the last lot. I could get some in a week or so.'

'Nay. I have need of them directly.'

'Sorry, Master Foxley. Hal! Do you have any squirrel brushes to sell?'

'Nope,' said his neighbour. 'Try Joanna Crabtree, down by the font. She sometimes has squirrel. If not, her goodman makes brushes. You could order some special.'

'My thanks. I shall enquire of her.'

It took an hour of vexation afore I managed to purchase what I needed.

Joanna Crabtree had plenty of brushes but none suited my

exact requirements. The shafts felt heavy in my hand and would make the fine details of painting difficult to achieve. Of course, I might trim the brush-heads to shape and shorten the shafts to reduce their weight but they would yet be unwieldy tools. I did not want to make do but would have the best for the king's commission.

Eventually, I found a weasel-faced little fellow in the south transept, a pedlar with but two brushes for sale from his pack. Had I not been desperate, I should not have asked to look closer at his wares. Yet, as happenstance would have it, the brushes were beautifully made and perfectly balanced for me. Brought from and made for the illuminators at Lincoln Cathedral, he told me, and the price he asked was far cheaper than at any stationers' stalls. A bargain, indeed. So much so, I told the fellow to keep the ha'penny change he offered.

'Next time you visit Lincoln,' I said, 'Any good brushes you can buy, fetch them back for me and I shall pay you well. You can find me at the sign of the Fox's Head in Paternoster Row.'

Content with my new brushes, I hastened home, knowing much precious time had been lost.

The Sun in Splendour Tavern

Having paid Ralf his first day's wages, he insisted that Adam and I join him at the tavern, to share a jug at his expense, to celebrate his change in fortune, working with us and biding 'neath our roof.

I was not much of a mind to do so, certain the Norfolk men would have a good deal to say to each other and few words for me, as at the Boar's Head yestereve. But Ralf insisted and it seemed churlish to refuse. Yet I proved correct. The pair was soon bent over their cups, heads together, chuckling over jests peculiar to their home shire – merry jests beyond a Londoner's comprehension. Thus it was that I fell into conversation with – of all people – John, our very own Adonis of Farringdon Ward, he with whom Adam had nigh come to blows, recently.

The handsome fellow approached me as I sat back, leaning against the wall, sipping my ale and, quite plainly, uninvolved in the conversation at the other end of the board.

'Good even to you, Master Foxley. I see this stool is vacant. May I sit?' At least he had manners enough to ask and, since the tavern was somewhat crowded, I could hardly deny him the empty seat.

'As you will.'

'I'm glad of the chance to speak with you, Master Foxley.'

I did not much approve his free usage of my name when I did but know him as John. Neither could I imagine what matter he might possibly wish to discuss with me. Fortunately, he had a full cup of ale in his hand, so I did not feel obliged to share our jug with him. As it was, Adam and Ralf had nigh drained it to the dregs in any case.

'Concerning what? Your name be John. I know naught else of you.'

'Ah, how discourteous of me. John Rykener, at your service, good master.'

The name chimed with some distant memory but I could not own it for the present.

'You know my name, Master Rykener. How come?'

'I am no man's master. All call me John… when the occasion suits.' He smiled, showing even white teeth. 'I know of you from your kinsman, Adam, and other sources. Adam told me you were aiding Bailiff Turner in investigating the death of the cutler, Philip Hartnell. I have information that may be of value to you.'

'Of value? Do you mean to say that you require payment for it? In which case, I recommend you take this valuable information to Bailiff Turner at Guildhall. I have little to do with such matters and less interest. Tell the Bailiff…' I rose to leave but John held my arm in a graceful but firm grip.

'The bailiff and I are acquainted but not in any amicable wise – if you take my meaning.'

'You have fallen foul of the law at some time, then.'

He shrugged.

'In a way. 'Tis enough to say I do not want to take my knowledge of Philip Hartnell's affairs to him but I would tell you, if you will listen. And I didn't mean to suggest that my information came at a price but rather that it could be of value in bringing Philip's killers to justice.'

I sipped my ale, thinking the while.

'Very well. Tell me what you know and I will inform Bailiff Turner of it, if I see it as relevant. Master Hartnell was a friend of yours?'

'More a good customer than a friend. But he told me much of his affairs.'

'And what manner of craft or service do you provide that a customer should reveal his business to you?'

'A very personal service. Intimate, in fact. You'd be surprised at the things folk tell you as you lie together, sweaty and satisfied, afterwards.'

'What!' I almost toppled off my stool, aghast at this revelation. 'B-but you… you be a man! How could you and Hartnell…'

John laughed so loudly heads turned.

'Keep your voice down, Master Foxley.'

''Tis you that laughed aloud.'

'Aye. The look upon your face… how could I not laugh? This is London. Everything on earth goes on in this city… every vice, every crime man can invent. Besides, I never said I lay with Philip as a man. He preferred me as a lady, Eleanor.'

'Eleanor! I remember now. You accosted me in Southwark at Eastertide, you disreputable… rascal.' I had difficulty finding a word to describe this creature that could be man or woman upon a whim. I brought to mind the lovely-seeming creature in

Bankside. Aye, with gorgeous hair and faultless complexion…
'Twas the same who sat here now.

'You recall me, at last. It took you a deal of time and there
was I thinking I was a memorable sort.' He drained his cup and
beckoned the tapster to refill it. 'But forget that now. Do you
wish to learn of Philip's affairs or not?'

'Not if they involve such… such goings-on.'

'I swear I'll not mention that side of our business but he was
deeply indebted. Did you know that?'

'I know he pawned his silver candlesticks.'

'Tush. Trading pennies. No. Philip owed hundreds of marks
to the Italian bankers in Lombard Street. They were demanding
payment and he feared them so. And how did he pay them? He
borrowed more money elsewhere from folk even more dubious
than the Italians. All he did was spread his debts yet wider across
the city, owing larger amounts to more people. It didn't surprise
me, Master Foxley, to hear one of his creditors grew tired of
waiting for repayment.'

I sat silent, thinking a while. It seemed to make sense in some
ways and yet…

'Why would a creditor kill him? If the man had no money
to pay, pawned what he owned of any value, how was a creditor
hoping to collect his due, if the debtor could no longer earn
any coin? His estate could pay off some after his death but, if
what you say be true, there be little possibility of it covering all
his debts.' I was about to tell him how the victim was tortured
but did not do so. That was not yet common knowledge and I
kept my tongue in check. 'Do you know the names of those he
borrowed from, perchance?'

'I've told you enough. I'm not doing the bailiff's job for him.'

'But you do know who?'

'Maybe. Maybe not.' The rascal rose, drank his ale and
banged the cup down upon the board, causing Adam and
Ralf to start from their conversation. 'I'll leave you to pay my
reckoning,' he said, 'Seeing you owe me.'

'What was that about? What did John want with you, Seb?' Adam asked, seeming surprised that I was yet there in the tavern with them.

'Naught. Naught at all. I want no dealings with his kind. Be you coming? I shall want to bar the doors at home.'

'No. We'll stay awhile,' Adam said. 'We can go up to our chamber through the yard. We'll not disturb the house and I'll fasten the side gate after.'

'Then I shall bid you good night, cousin. Ralf.' I nodded my farewell and left them to their ale. My thoughts, I confess, were not of the most charitable towards the denizens of the Sun in Splendour Tavern – any of them. Hopefully, a fair night's sleep would improve my mood.

Chapter 10

Saturday, the nineteenth day of June
The Foxley House

THE DAY was young. When there was yet a little moisture in the air, the early morn was a perfect time to apply gold leaf. I showed Kate how to smooth the gesso with a penknife, gently paring away any high points which inevitably appear as the centre tends to sink a little as it dries. Once the surface was even, I explained how to use the flat, brush-like gilder's tip to pick up the thin gold leaf then, having breathed a damp breath upon the gesso, how to lay the leaf thereon.

'It sticks as if by magick, master,' Kate said, delighted.

'It does indeed. Now cover the leaf with the square of silk and press it into place all over the gesso.'

'Why do we use silk?'

'Forwhy we do not want to mar the gold with the sweat from our fingers. That would spoil the gleam of it. If you would please to pass me the burnishing tool...'

'It looks like a fang with a handle.'

'And so it is, lass: a dog's tooth, although Master Honeywell insisted it was a wolf's tooth when I purchased it, I suspect otherwise. See how the excess leaf comes away at the edges, wherever there be no gesso beneath? You must have a care not to push into the vellum around it, else as the pigments be applied after, there will be a danger of too much gathering in the grooves or dents you have made by accident. There. See how the gold shines bright as the sun in the heavens? And it will ne'er tarnish but look the same a hundred years hence.'

'Truly, master? What a wonder. Is it finished now? Must we leave it to dry?'

'Nay, 'tis ready for painting but first, fetch a clean pigment brush and that small pot on the shelf there... the one with the stopper. Aye, that one. Now see here, Kate, upon the desk, the tiny crumbs and flakes of gold. Brush them all into the pot. Do not lose them to the floor.'

'But they're too small to use.'

'Gold be too valuable to waste. When we have collected more, we may sell them back to the goldsmith to be re-hammered into leaves again, or use them ourselves, pound them into powder, add egg glair and make shell-gold. It is then used just like any other pigment for the details of illuminated initials and the like.

'I think you have learned much this morn, Kate. Why not take some respite from work? Gawain would appreciate some exercise, if you would oblige him? But keep away from Smithfield. There be many strangers there for the horse sales next week. You may visit Dame Ellen or Mistress Hutchinson, if you wish, but do not make a nuisance of yourself. I do not want Dame Ellen complaining to me that you ate all her almond wafers, as last time. Return within the hour.'

Kate laughed at my litany of instructions and danced out of the workshop, calling to Gawain. How the lass did cheer me.

I settled once more at my desk, uncovered a shell of vermilion pigment and dipped my brush.

I was deeply engrossed in my work until someone rapped upon the door jamb loudly enough to attract my attention. I glanced up and was so shocked to see the figure standing in the workshop doorway that I could not find words at first.

'Jude!' I managed to say at last, rising from my stool.

'Well met, little brother!' He held his arms wide, grinning.

'Well, don't just stand there, gaping like a stranded salmon; come greet me as you should. Your prodigal brother has returned!'

I dropped my brush and flew to him. He clasped me to his breast, tighter than any lover.

'Have you missed me, Seb?' He pushed me back but gripped my shoulders, looking me over.

'Missed you? You nigh ripped my heart in twain when you left that day, of a sudden.' I choked back tears. 'Of course I have missed you, you errant knave.'

'I see you're skinny as ever. The Moody Mare refusing to feed you, eh? And where is she? Spending all your hard-won coin at market, no doubt.'

I knew he spoke in jest, but...

'I suppose my letter ne'er caught up with you. I wrote, telling you: my beloved Em has lain in St Michael's churchyard since Eastertide.'

'Oh.' He released his hold upon my shoulders and stepped away, taking time to look about the workshop where all attempts at worthwhile labour had ceased. 'And everyone else? They're all well?'

'You will recall our kinsman Adam, though your acquaintance was but brief.'

The men exchanged greetings, but there was a coolness betwixt them. Jude had taken no liking to Adam upon their meeting in August last. I believed then that Adam's coming to dwell with us was one cause of Jude's departure, among others.

'And Kate Verney...'

'How could I ever forget our merry lass? How d'you fare, Kate?'

She left her stool to make her courtesy.

'Very well, Master Jude, thanking you.'

'And this be our new journeyman, Ralf Reepham.'

'My replacement?' Jude quirked an eyebrow.

'Nay. Tom Bowen's more like and a worthy one.'

'You kicked Tom's arse finally. Well done, little brother.

We're well rid of one idle jackanapes. What of the other?'

'Jack be learning joinery and turning with Stephen Appleyard and showing more skill there than he did here. He bides at Stephen's place also.'

'I suppose that foolish wench, Nessie, is still here?'

'Aye.'

At that moment, Rose came in, carrying a dish of strawberries in one hand and holding little Dickon by the other.

'We were in the garden, picking strawberries. We heard voices. Did we not, Dickon? Thought your guests might enjoy…' Her eyes fell upon Jude and all colour fled her cheeks. They regarded one another in awkward silence for an uncomfortably long moment, then she said: 'I'll leave the strawberries and have Nessie serve you ale. I have dinner to prepare.' With that, Rose returned to the kitchen, taking my son with her.

'Whoo!' Jude blew out a breath. 'I never thought she'd still be here after…'

'After you abandoned her on your bridal day? Where else would she go? Dear Rose has been a Godsend to us, keeping this household from falling into chaos and ruin since… since Em's passing. I know not how we might manage without her hard work and gentle care. She loves little Dickon as if he were her own child, organises meals and laundry, the garden plot, the larder and all manner else of womanly chores.'

'And warms your bed?'

'How could you dare say that, Jude? I be widowed but two months since and would ne'er treat Rose so, e'en had Emily been gone a twelvemonth and more.'

'Still of a monkish disposition then, Seb. It's a wonder you managed to beget a son at all.'

'I have a daughter also.'

Jude laughed heartily.

'Well, that's a surprise, indeed. When did you fit that in? Two babes within less than a year. Remarkable. My congratulations, little brother. You must have some fire in your blood after all.'

I was about to give answer but another shock occurred. A raven-haired lass walked into the workshop without a by-your-leave and grabbed my brother's arm.

'Jood. Will you leave me all day waiting? I tire of a parlour. I have admired the hangings too well.'

'Oh, aye.' For once in his life, it seemed Jude was at somewhat of a loss. 'Seb, this is Francesca-Antonia. Chesca, this is my little brother, Sebastian.'

'I be honoured…' I hesitated, not knowing how to address her but I made my bow anyway. 'Welcome to Paternoster Row.'

She made her courtesy to me then caught me all unguarded, embracing me and kissing both my cheeks.

'Brother Sebastian,' she said. 'I have hearing of you greatly.'

'You have?' Did she think I was a monk or friar?

'Jood told me all of you. I am much in happiness now and properly Mistress Jood Fossley. Did I say that right, Jood?'

'Leave off, Chesca. Adam, for Christ's sake, take her… show her Paul's spire or some such.' Jude shoved the lass at Adam, who had good grace and manners to do as he was bidden, however discourteously. 'A word, Seb, in the yard.' Jude took me by the sleeve and dragged me along the passage, nigh knocking Nessie aside with her tray of ale cups.

'I fear a word will not suffice,' I said as we hastened through the kitchen, where Rose stood intent upon the sage she was chopping, and went out to the yard. 'Who is that lass, Jude? You best explain.'

'Aye. It's a long and complicated story…'

''Tis rarely otherwise with you.' I braced myself against the trunk of the apple tree, prepared to listen to his tale. Whether I would believe it or no, was another matter.

'Did you not get the letter I sent you from Venezia at Christmastide last? I'm sure I mentioned Chesca in it, about how she was destined to wed some ancient step-uncle or other. It was horrible to watch, Seb, all during the festivities, the old lecher was pawing at her; couldn't keep his hands off her even as we ate at the board. I could see how Chesca did all she could to avoid him, pleading a headache every eve, so she could escape to her chamber.

'Of course, they couldn't wed without a dispensation from the pope, being related. And before the documents arrived, it was Lent, so the marriage was put off until Easter. Then the dispensation came, and Chesca was in tears, knowing there was no way to avoid it, dreading the end of Lent.

'Well, by that time, I'd had my fill of Venezia…'

'Had your fill? Or wore out your welcome?'

'You know how it is, Seb. I tire of the same sights, the same bed.'

'And your hosts tired of you?'

He shrugged.

'Maybe I had over-stepped the mark once or twice.'

'With the daughter of the house? Oh, Jude, do you not know better than that? She cannot be any older than Kate.'

'You make it sound… sordid. It wasn't like that. And she'll be sixteen years come next spring. Old enough. Anyhow, to return to my story… I'd already booked passage on the first ship of the season, sailing from Venezia, bound for the Isle of Cyprus. I told Chesca she could come with me, avoid this hateful marriage. She was that eager, it was all I could do to make her keep our leaving a secret. We escaped the house at dead of night, upon a Sunday, as it became Monday, the day the ship sailed. Thanks to my skills at subterfuge, we made our escape without any trouble.'

'Oh, what have you done, my foolish brother?' I sighed and shifted my position against the tree. This was taking longer than I feared.

'I paid for our passage but then I realised a difficulty. There were other travellers bound for the Holy Land, calling themselves pilgrims. Huh. The way they ogled Chesca, there was nothing holy about their thoughts or intentions, so… What else could I do to protect her? I let it be understood that we were man and wife. There. I've told you now.'

'But you are not truly wed.'

'That's not the worst of it. Our ship was damaged in a storm and the winds blew us off course. We landed in a place called Cecily, I think it was. Something like that. From there – I'd had enough of stormy seas – we took a shorter passage to Marsay. We still had to sail because Cecily is an island, I discovered. Marsay is in France, if you don't know. I was determined to travel the rest of the way on dry land as far as possible. Chesca kept pestering me, saying we must marry but I could put her off until the end of Lent.

'Now, I must admit, Seb, the little French I know served me ill. The accursed Frogs don't even speak their own tongue decently, such that an educated Englishman can understand it. But Chesca managed to make them understand most of the time and she wanted us to celebrate Easter in proper fashion with a feast. As the end of Lent was fast approaching, she made all the arrangements with the oaf who ran the inn where we were staying – a flea-pit of a place not far inland from Marsay. Those wretched Frogs know how to overcharge, I can tell you. Never go to bloody France, Seb, the place is full of thieves, vagabonds and rogues and the stink! Makes a London privy smell like a rose garden. Now where was I?'

'Not far from Marsay with Chesca arranging the Easter celebrations…'

'Oh, aye. So Chesca invited the whole damned village, so it seemed. Everyone from the baker to the bee-keeper, the miller to the blacksmith. And, of course, the bloody priest. I swear it wasn't my fault, Seb. I couldn't make out what they were jibber-jabbering about. Their Latin was as bad as my French. Wine flowed freely… I had no idea what was going on. The first I knew, they were hustling Chesca and me up to our chamber in the inn and there it was, all decked out and garlanded with flowers: the bloody marriage bed and the damned priest dousing it with holy water. I don't know how it happened.'

'You must have given your word of consent, else it would

not be a valid union. Did you do that? Did you give consent?'

'I suppose so. The priest asked me a question or two that I couldn't understand. I just answered "aye" or "nay"; "si" or "oui" or "non" to help the conversation along. It was all a terrible mistake, Seb, and you've got to help me undo this bloody marriage.'

'But why? Chesca is a beautiful lass and if you love her…'

'Of course I don't bloody love her. And her family will give me such grief when they learn of it. They'll hang me by the balls and shred me, bit by bit. The Italians have a terrible way of avenging any dishonour done to their family. They have a special word for it: vendetta. Makes me go cold just thinking of it.'

'Do not concern yourself, Jude. Her family is far away.'

'No, they're not. They're right here in the city. They're the Baldesis – the fucking bankers in Lombard Street. I should never have come home. You've got to help me.'

'I do not see any way.'

'You've got to persuade Rose to help. If she stands with me before the Church Court of Arches and we swear we were wed before I left England – as we intended if things hadn't gone awry for me – then my marriage to Chesca will be annulled, won't it? It'll be as if it never happened. Talk to Rose for me.'

'Nay. You distressed her so; abandoned her once, leaving her humiliated. Why should she want to be your wife now? And what if the Court of Arches did find in your favour? You would then be regarded as wed to Rose – a married man in either case. Besides, what then of Chesca? Will you abandon her in a strange land? Having taken her maidenhead, do you cast her away like a broken pot?'

'Taken her maidenhead! You jest. Alessandro – did I tell you of him? – a couple of lusty lads and a servant or two had all been there before me. Chesca was no virgin bride, I can tell you.' Jude shuffled his feet, frowning at his dusty boots. It was as if I could see his mind working behind his frowning brow, thinking upon some new strategy. Then he said, 'Think how badly you'll feel,

Seb, when they find me dead, cut to ribbons in a dark alley. And they surely will, if you don't help me.'

'Do not try to wring my conscience as you have wrung my heart. You dug this deep pit for yourself; 'tis up to you to climb out of it, Jude. Do not involve Rose nor me, entangling us in your coils of deceit and untruths. I know not whether to believe half of what you tell me.'

'Then hide me, at least. I'm your brother, for Christ's sake. You owe me that.'

'I owe you naught, Jude. I cannot help you. I have but lately saved this workshop – my workshop – from ruin, restoring the reputation you destroyed.' Even so, I felt such unease at his words, I began to wrestle my thoughts – aye, and my conscience, just as he had foreseen – as to ways that I might aid him.

Rose had prepared a good dinner but the air was fraught with tension. Few words were exchanged among our company at the board, bar a request for bread or to pass the ale jug. Jude poured ale for Chesca. She sipped it and pulled such a face.

'This dog's dung – I will not drink any more. You!' She pointed at Rose. 'Go fetch wine. Never serve this at me again. And you English: why you have servants eat with you? This not happen in Italy. Servants eat with their kind.'

I was upon my feet in an instant as Rose made to leave her stool.

'Rose! Pay no heed to her.' I turned to my brother's wife. 'Speak not to Rose in such wise. You may be a guest, but do not think to order Rose as you would one of your servants at home. Jude. You best instruct your goodwife as to the ways of conduct in this house.'

I sat down, shocked by my own words and lack of courtesy. All the same, I meant what I said.

'Jood. I will stay here not two instants more. Take me from these bad people. I not like your family. They pigs, barbarians.' Chesca flounced out of the kitchen and along the passageway. 'Jood!!'

'Now see what you've done,' Jude roared, taking up his platter and throwing it across the board, food and sauce and all. He stormed off and I could hear him repeating his wife's name in a quite different tone, pleading almost, as he followed her out, slamming the street door behind them.

I told myself that I did not care.

Little Dickon was howling. He hated disharmony as much as I and I lifted him from his chair, hushing and rocking him, comforting him, comforting myself, mayhap?

Having said Rose was no servant, I felt obliged to assist her and Nessie in clearing up the mess Jude had caused in his anger. However, as I encouraged Gawain to devour the edible scraps, the situation gave me pause. I wondered how Rose's place in our household should be described; how outsiders regarded her: not quite sister nor mother nor wife nor mistress of the house, yet somewhat of all those things. How did Rose see herself?

It being Saturday and a half-day of labour, the shop was closed for the afternoon and the others were at leisure, to do as they pleased. But my labours could not end so readily. Disconsolate and out of humour, I determined to engross myself in my work, applying gesso to another miniature. But matters did not proceed so well.

The afternoon was hot and the gesso began to set in the bowl afore I had finished. Once hard, it was of no use, yet such a small area remained to be covered, it was not worth mixing a new batch. Another nine miniatures remained to be done but were, as yet, undrawn. I would have to leave making more gesso until I had sketched out further images. But that meant the miniature in hand would not be ready for painting upon the morrow – or rather, on Monday, if I dared to rest upon the Lord's Day as I ought. Gesso must be left to dry overnight afore laying on the gold leaf. That could not be done once painting began, for fear of spoiling the colours whilst burnishing the metal to a high shine. All this was further delaying the king's commission.

Then, as I sorted through my scrip, in search of a sketch done a few days earlier, when I had espied a man in the street with a face well suited, as I thought, to be that of Julius Caesar, I found my notes made at Gracechurch Street. I had promised a fair copy of them to Thaddeus as soon as I might. And I recalled the information gleaned from that strange creature, John Rykener, at the Sun in Splendour tavern last eve. I had quite forgotten all that concerned the murders.

Could this day be any worse? Could anything else be required of me? Might one more straw be added to my burden of responsibility without breaking me? It seemed the Devil himself determined to find out.

As I put aside my half-painted miniature and covered the pigments with a damp cloth against drying out, I heard a knocking at the street door. Whoever it was, I had not the time to spare and ignored the summons. Let Adam or Rose deal with it. Yet, though I took up my pen to copy out the notes made in haste previously for Thaddeus, the hairs upon my neck prickled.I headed the page *Notes made at Guy Linton's Place in Gracechurch Street* and began to write.

'Seb, I apologise for interrupting your work but a clerical gentleman awaits in the parlour,' Rose said.

'Can Adam not deal with him, lass? I have that much here to do.'

'Adam has gone to visit Mercy Hutchinson in Distaff Lane; said not to expect him back for supper.'

I sighed and laid down my pen, having written but a sentence or two. It seemed events conspired against me at every turn. Afore any task was completed, Fate added two more to my ever-lengthening list. I began to wonder what would happen if the king's commission was not finished in time: the possibility grew hourly.

'Oh. I see I have no choice in the matter, then. I trust the cleric's business will not take long, else my mixed pigments will spoil. Did he say what he wanted?'

'No, Seb, but he asked for you by name and said he comes on Bishop Kempe's behalf. Shall I serve ale?'

'It would be a courtesy, but I fear to encourage him to linger. What can the bishop want of me? If he wishes me to sing for some visiting dignitary, he must find another chorister. I have had no time e'en to practise the new anthem of the precentor's devising, in readiness for the Feast of St Paul, which comes hard upon us.'

'I'll wait a while then.'

'Aye. I thank you, Rose.'

I went into the parlour in trepidation, I know not why. I could recall having committed no offence against Holy Church of late. I did not recognise the visitor. A tall man of erect bearing, he wore the scholar's plain garb, rather than clerical vestments. His grey hair suggested middle age but his eyes were keen as he looked me up and down, as a horse-trader might assess a palfrey for sale.

'Sebastian Foxley,' I said, making my bow. 'You would speak with me, sir?'

'Permit me to introduce myself, Master Foxley. I am Geoffrey Wanstead, currently in the service of His Grace, the Bishop of London.' He returned my bow in courteous wise. 'There is a matter that the bishop would have me explain to you and ask your advice upon.'

I realised then that I had little choice but to gesture him towards the cushioned settle, sensing this matter was going to consume a deal of precious time.

'How may I be of service to Bishop Kempe?'

'It has been brought to the bishop's notice, Master Foxley – and to mine – that you have considerable experience in certain aspects of scribal hands, parchment, inks and such like. In short:

the historical uses of these things.'

'I do?'

'I heard tell that you were able to distinguish betwixt certain documents for the lord mayor's office, to determine which were legal and which were counterfeited.'

'Oh, aye. That was a few years since, during Robert Bassett's term. I had forgotten.'

'Well, others have not. Your skills are remembered by both the Stationers' Guild and the City Council. Your knowledge saved the latter a deal of money, avoiding the excessive expense of lawyers, as well as a loss of income, had you not been able to show certain documents to be false. You are a man of considerable abilities, Master Foxley.'

'I was content to be of service, sir.' My face flushed hot at his words of praise and I wished I had not asked Rose to delay serving the cooling ale. I was much in need of a sudden.

'And now Bishop Kempe would likewise make use of those same talents. The matter is become of such urgency that, if you be at liberty now, I have permission to explain the situation to you directly, although the documents in question are in the keeping of the bishop's librarian. You will have to come to the bishop's palace to view them, when convenient. Do you have the time, at present, to hear of these troubling concerns the bishop would have you look into?'

What could I say? Honest man that I be, I yet had not the courage to speak the truth. How could I tell the bishop's man that I had work enough and to spare upon the king's behalf? The king must surely take precedence above a bishop but the king's man was not seated on the settle in my parlour, pinning me with a sharp eye.

'Aye, sir. Please explain the problem. I shall listen well. But first, let me ask for ale. Explanations be ever thirsty work.'

Geoffrey Wanstead remained for an hour. We drank a jug of ale. A second hour passed and still he talked. I asked Rose to bring another jug. With every word spoken, my spirit sank lower.

The bishop's man departed at last. I bade him farewell at the street door.

'No! No! No!' I cried as I shut it behind him. 'I can do no more! Jesu take pity upon me. Ask not more of me.' My clenched fists came away from my head with handfuls of hair entangled. My heart pounded as though rabid wolves pursued me. I knew not what I was about.

'Hush. Hush, dear one. Calm yourself.' Rose murmured soft words as she held me close.

There in the passageway, I unburdened the weight of tears and distress upon her sturdy shoulder.

Rose understood. She ever did.

Chapter 11

Saturday eve
The Foxley House

I FORCED MYSELF to finish copying out the notes for
Thaddeus and added a few lines concerning what John
Rykener revealed to me the day before. It was not the neatest
piece of writing but it must serve as it was. Only Rose's sage
advice to me: 'You can but do one thing at a time, Seb', enabled
me to get it done at all. 'One thing at a time' would be my
watch-word from now on, else I should drown 'neath the
weight of work.

I knew Thaddeus was not one to work upon a Saturday
afternoon – much like everyone else – but Saturday eve was oft
a busy time for the City Bailiff, what with too much ale flowing
after the week's wages being paid. Therefore, I half expected
my friend might be at his post at Guildhall, in case of trouble
arising. I was glad to leave the house for a while, taking Gawain
along for company.

The air felt heavy, storm-laden, and thunder rumbled around
the skies. As yet, I saw no lightning and the rain held off. I took
my cloak, though I hoped not to have to wear it – the heat of
the day lingered still.

Guildhall

At Guildhall, I proved correct in my assumption. Thaddeus was there, organising the evening's duties with the Sergeant of the Watch and the constables.

'Greetings, Master Foxley,' he called to me. 'I'll be with you shortly, Seb. Did you bring the notes?'

'I did, Bailiff Turner,' I replied formally, seeing he was in company with those under his charge. But what you will make of them, I know not, I thought.

'What's this?' he said when, at length, I gave the papers into his hand. 'Crossings-out? This isn't like you, Seb. Not your usual immaculate work.'

'Forgive me. I hope they be legible enough.'

'What's amiss, eh? You want to tell me over a cup of ale?'

''Tis so plain as that, then? I did not mean to make it obvious. This day has been fraught, indeed.'

Over the ale jug in his chamber, I told my friend of Jude's return. Thaddeus knew Jude of old and sufficiently to realise that turmoil was like to follow wherever my brother came. This could well mean additional work for the bailiff. I did not tell him the details of the ill-conceived elopement of the foolish couple but I mentioned that in the near future – if it had not come to pass already – the Baldesi family in Lombard Street would likely hear of it and find some way to make their grave disapproval known. To my brother's cost, no doubt. It could mean trouble and it seemed wise to forewarn Thaddeus of the likelihood.

'I'm grateful for the timely information, Seb. I'll have my constables keep a subtle watch upon Lombard Street and suggest you tell your brother to behave unobtrusively and keep away from that part of the city.'

'You think Jude will take the least notice of my advice? I may as well advise the sun to stand still in the heavens or the tides to cease flowing in the Thames.'

'Aye. I know you'll have a hard task there but tell him, all the same. More ale?'

'A little, if it please you. I shall do what I may concerning Jude.' I took a sip. 'But of other matters... last eve I had speech with that strange one: John Rykener. You recall him? Calls himself – herself – Eleanor upon occasion.'

'I remember. He would seem odd company for you to keep, Seb.'

''Twas not my choice, I assure you. He approached me, having learned that I be involved in the attempt to unravel the mysteries of two murders. It seems John knew Philip Hartnell well. I did not enquire too closely regarding the nature of their companionship but I have included what John revealed to me at the end of the notes I gave you. 'Tis not much but it seems Hartnell was greatly indebted to the very family I mentioned afore: the Baldesis.'

'A coincidence, you think?'

'I know not.' I stood, pushing my stool 'neath the board. 'I must go home, Thaddeus, and thank you for your time and ale; your listening-ear. I needs must work upon the King's book afore dark, although it seems the sun has departed afore its time.'

'Aye. I suspect you're going to get wet, my friend. May God keep you and yours this night.'

'And you, Thaddeus. Come, Gawain. Make haste, lad, else we shall be drenched.'

Beyond the door, in Guildhall courtyard, the rain began tumbling from clouds as black as the Devil's soul. Lightning split the heavens and thunder crashed, sending Gawain cowering into a corner of the building, his tail betwixt his legs, whimpering.

'Come, you great coward.' I had to shout above the noise of lashing rain and the next deafening drum-roll of thunder. But my dog refused to obey. I could not leave him there nor could I carry the great foolish creature. Angered at the thought of being compelled to waste precious time, I dragged him from his corner and pulled him back within the building to shelter and wait out the storm. There, he huddled so closely upon my feet, he nigh toppled me.

'Still here?' Thaddeus said, seeing us – a most bedraggled sight we must have been.

'Aye. Gawain will not brave the storm. He fears thunder so.'

'Well, I doubt there'll be light enough for you to work until the clouds clear, anyway.'

'Mm. You be correct.'

'More ale?'

'Why not.'

'We shan't be disturbed, I'm sure. Malefactors, felons and mischief-makers tend to stay home in such weather. Come, I'll find you a towel to dry off.'

The Foxley House

Upon our belated return home, Rose – bless her – had delayed supper until our coming. However, my brother was there afore me, as was his wife, ready seated at the board.

'We'll be staying here, of course,' Jude was telling Rose as I entered the kitchen from the yard, trailing water across the flagstones, for it was yet raining, though the thunder had passed. Emily would have scolded me; Rose said naught of it. Neither did she comment upon my brother's assertion. 'We'll sleep in the master bedchamber at the front. Seeing you're a bachelor once more, Seb, you can share my old chamber with Adam.'

I did not trouble to point out that Ralf now slept there also. It would be somewhat crowded with three of us in that chamber. Jude would not be bothered by the inconvenience caused to others.

'So be it,' I said, with a shrug. I fetched a towel to dry my dripping hair afore doing my best with Gawain's sodden fur. He rewarded my efforts by giving a thorough shake and spraying us all with water drops. Most laughed but Chesca began to berate me, the dog and the company for wetting her gown. Being of silk, it showed the damp splashes.

'Stop that, you stupid wench!' Jude shouted. 'I told you to watch your bloody manners. You want I take my hand to you?'

Chesca shook her head and began to weep. Of a sudden, she was but a child, not a woman grown.

I felt sympathy for her, aye, and discomfort at my brother threatening a lass. 'Tis the law that a man may chastise his wife, by deed as well as word, but I loathed such actions. I had ne'er laid a hand upon Em, unwilling to countenance any such cruelty. I could not harm her, whatever her shortcomings, and never had. Now Jude threatened violence 'neath my roof.

'Not in this house, brother,' I said. 'No one suffers beatings here and that stands for visitors also.'

'Visitors? We're not bloody visitors; we're family. And if my wife deserves punishment, I'll do as I think fit and it's none of your business.'

'Not under my roof.'

'Your roof? I own half this bloody place.'

'You did once but not any longer. You took your share in coin when you left to go upon your travels, remember?'

'I never did.'

'You signed the document to prove it. It had to be thus, else the guild would not let me resume business here. You were forbidden; your name struck from the guild roll, if you recall? 'Twas your one gesture of recompense afore you departed. I have the deed safe, if you would see it?'

'I don't care.' He thumped the board with his fists, causing the cups to jump, the full ones to spill ale upon the white cloth. 'I won't have you telling me how to treat my damned wife, here or anywhere else. If she needs a beating, she'll bloody get it.'

'And your welcome here will end upon the instant. I mean it, Jude.' I noticed then that Chesca's cup had spilt red wine. Rose must have troubled to purchase some to please her, following the tantrum at dinner.

My eyes met my brother's across the board; grey and azure. He looked away first.

'Did I tell you of the carnival in Venezia on Shrove Tuesday?' he said, diverting everyone's attentions from his moment of defeat. 'No? Well, there were water pageants and everyone wore masks, so you can guess there was a lot of things going on, all bloody secretive... cut-purses were the least of it. Alessandro – I spoke of him, didn't I? He lost his purse. Two local families involved in a feud for years seized the chance of attacking each other under cover of the mask-wearing and milling crowds. Knives flashed and then came some tremendous blast and a gout of flame and two of their number fell. One died in a blood-splattered heap. I thought it must have been a cannon shot but Alessandro said no, it was some new devilish contraption: a gunne so small two men could carry it, set it up and fire it. On the street! Not a siege engine nor defender of the town walls. It killed folk enjoying the day without warning. With such a thing secreted under their cloaks, felons might waylay any fellow just going about his business and blow him to pieces. No need to accost him; simply blast him as he passes by. Is that not Satan's very own accursed invention?'

'Wouldn't be very secret, though, if it made such a noise,' Adam observed. 'A bow and arrow could do as much and silently. I can't see a weapon of that kind being used in London... or Norwich come to that. Every true Englishman would choose the bow, if he had to.'

'Maybe so, but there are Frenchmen, Italians, Flemings and Bohemians here too. Those buggers might well take to hand-gunnes, content that the racket would put the fear of God into every innocent. It scared you half to death, didn't it, Chesca?'

'No. It never did so, Jood. I hear gunnes before. It only fright thin-blood English like you.' She laughed and I saw my brother's brows draw down but he had the good grace to say naught, not with me present, leastwise. What he might say later, privily, was not my concern, though if Chesca appeared in the morn with bruises to show, Jude would hear my opinion, whether he wished to or no.

After supper, the others retired to the parlour. No doubt, they would be regaled with more of Jude's adventures and enjoy the tales he told. Indeed, I heard much laughter and jocundity wafting across the passageway, into the workshop, where I made use of the remainder of the daylight to complete the underdrawing for another full-page miniature. This showed men working a great siege-engine known as a trebuchet. I had ne'er seen such a thing but both Master Collop's Latin Vegetius and our little English version of the third part of *De Re Militari* had diagrams of the contraptions. I believe them little used these days, cannon being more efficient at demolishing stone walls and the like, but the trebuchet made for a more interesting subject to depict.

Having completed the drawing, there was yet time afore dark to consider the pigments to be used in painting it. The great beast of a thing lobbed a stone heavenward and I thought to do the missile in gold leaf, as if catching the sun as it flew to smite down the enemies of God. The instructions for the king's book demanded much use of gold and, there being neither saints nor angels nor kings in this miniature, I could not think what else be deserving of gold colouring. However, a lion rampant in the bottom margin could receive like treatment, so I marked it with a letter 'g'.

Crimson lake would be the soldiers' caps, those who did not wear armoured head-coverings, thus I wrote 'c-l' in those parts. The armour could be of shell-tin – of discomforting memory – but as I wished to employ vermilion close by for their hose, shell-tin would not blacken as shell-silver might in the vicinity of this vivid but troublesome red pigment. I labelled the areas accordingly: 's-t' and 'v'. The trebuchet would be in shades of brown and yellow ochres to appear of wood. Still, the ropes could be of azurite to enliven the look of it and its wheels of bright tawny realgar – I must remember to warn Kate ever to have a care in the use of this last, it being a foul poison, if a fine pigment. I marked these parts 'b-oc', 'y-oc', 'a' and 'r', as appropriate. The pigments for the horses and dogs which populated the miniature I should decide upon later. For the greens of grass and bushes, weld, verdigris and malachite in varying tints might suffice. For the present, I had achieved a fair evening's work.

'You coming to bed or not, cousin?' Adam put his head in the doorway as I closed the inkpot and set the drawing aside, covering it with a cloth. I did not want any uninvited fowls spoiling the fruits of my labours again.

'Aye, shortly. Have the others retired as yet?'

'Everyone but us two. 'Tis late and Ralf will be snoring already. In which case, you may be in need of this.' He held out his hand.

'Sheep's fleece?'

'I borrowed it from Mercy this day. She works as a spinster, you may know, whenever Nicholas and the babes allow. I asked her for the fleece to stuff my ears. As you'll learn within the hour, Ralf snores worse than a sow in a thunderstorm. You'll be needing it, if you hope to get any sleep at all.'

Adam proved correct. Although my cousin and I shared the comfortable bed, whilst Ralf used the pallet with a featherbed atop, sleep eluded me. Even with my ears stuffed, Ralf's hearty rumblings reverberated around the chamber, keeping me awake despite my weariness. How I begrudged Jude the use of my solitary chamber as I lay counting the journeyman's in-drawn breaths and exhaled snorts. The night was too hot to bury my head 'neath the pillows, so I abandoned the bed and crept out, down the outside stairs, to the yard.

The garden plot was cool, the air refreshed with the night scents of woodbine and lavender. Moths flew, pale in the starlight, and bats flittered, black against the velvet sky. An owl screeched and, somewhere close by, cats yowled.

I set the old bucket under the apple boughs in such wise that I might lean against the trunk of the tree. Upended, I heaped some sacking upon it for a softer seat and, resting my head on my folded arms, I slept at last.

Sunday, the twentieth day of June

It being nigh unto midsummer, the sun rose early indeed. How long I had slept, I know not, but time enough in that bent position that my spine and neck were stiff and aching and my backside quite numb. A bucket with a sacking cushion does not make for an easeful bed, as I discovered. I rinsed my hands, face and neck at the water trough in the yard, rousing myself to wakefulness. Whatever the hour, it seemed a sin to waste this God-given daylight. Thus, I might go to the workshop to begin anew. The cool of morning would make the gesso less likely to set hard afore I finished applying it.

However, clad in naught but shirt and drawers and not wishing to disturb my bedmate in order to dress, I hoped none would see me so. It seemed an unlikelihood. Who would come to the workshop at such an hour? St Martin's bell had chimed four as I washed. Quietly, I poured a cup of ale in the kitchen and took an egg from the earthen bowl upon the shelf. Nessie did not stir in her alcove beside the chimney but Gawain awoke. Poor creature, of late, he was become used to keeping me company abed but last eve, there had not been room enough in Adam's chamber for a great hound, breathing hot vapours, as well as three men. I be sure Gawain believed he was in disgrace for some misdeed when I had told him to remain in the kitchen. But how to explain to a dog? Now I made much of him, praising him, fondling his soft ears and stroking his fur. How else might he know I was not displeased with him? When I split the egg,

157

lifting out the yolk and straining the white through my fingers into a bowl, needing the white part alone for the mixing of gesso, I rewarded Gawain with the yolk. He licked my fingers clean of every speck of yellow.

Having made the egg glair, I mixed it with the powdered chalk and other ingredients upon the marble slab until the gesso was perfectly smooth and of the correct consistency. I then began to apply it to the underdrawings, just as I had shown Kate. So content was I in my work, I began to sing a joyous *Jubilate*, quite forgetful of the need for quiet, so as not to disturb the rest of the household.

So enrapt was I, it came as a surprise when Rose entered the workshop with Dickon in her arms.

'Working, Seb? Upon the Lord's Day? Whatever are you about?'

'It seemed a sin to waste the God-given light when I might use it in service to the king. I shall make my due penance.' I stood, easing my back, yet inclined to stiffness after a night of discomfort.

'Seb!' Rose averted her eyes and turned away. 'You're quite undressed.'

'What? Oh, aye, I had forgot.' I resumed my stool such that the desk hid the worst of my embarrassment. 'Forgive me, lass. I must go to my chamber for my Sunday attire.'

'You cannot. Chesca is yet abed, claiming an indisposition.'

'Then I must wear yesterday's hose and jerkin to church.'

'Where are they?'

'In Adam's chamber.'

'You cannot come through the kitchen. Kate and Nessie are there, preparing for our breakfast upon our return from St Michael's.'

'Then what am I to do? Would you have me use the street door to go around the side of the house to get to Adam's room?' I saw then that she was smiling behind her hand, mayhap upon the brink of laughter. I found naught amusing about my predicament.

'Fear not. Amuse little Dickon and I'll take Chesca some wine. Whilst in the chamber, I may fetch your Sunday best.' She set my son in the midst of the workshop floor. 'Don't go anywhere,' she said as she left, closing the door after.

I wondered if she meant the child or me. As if I dared venture from behind my desk in my nether-clouts.

'Come, little man, let us amuse ourselves. Shall we play at 'peep-boo'? Papa will hide his face behind this cloth and…'

'So this is where you hid yourself.' Adam burst in. 'Christ on horseback, Seb! What game are you at? We're ready for church and you're still half-naked.'

'You think I be ignorant of it? 'Twas ne'er my intention. Now, have pity and close the door.'

'You think to spend all day in here, skulking?'

'Skulking? Rose has gone to my chamber to fetch my garments…'

'What a relief. Can't have you frightening the goodwives, scaring the ladies and giving children nightmares, showing off those terrible skinny, hairy legs of yours and all else, can we now?'

''Tis no jest.'

'No? Wait until I tell the congregation why you're late for mass.'

'You would not be so cruel.'

'If I don't tell, your brother surely will.' Adam went off, chuckling, not even troubling to shut the workshop door. Why did they delight so in mocking me?

St Michael le Querne's Church

I arrived at St Michael's just in time for Low Mass and suitably attired in my Sunday blue doublet and a decent pair of hose. But Adam and the others – except Chesca – were there afore me and, to judge from the amused smirks and giggling from my fellow parishioners, he and Jude had likely done their worst to discomfit me utterly. Even Dame Ellen wore an unbecoming grin at sight of me and turned to her fellow gossips who made but a token gesture to conceal their mirth behind their aprons. I was a laughing stock.

'Smile, Seb,' Rose whispered. ''Tis not ill-meant. Folk want something to cheer them at this time. Dame Ellen said there are a few cases of plague down by the Steelyard. Such solemn tidings put us all in need of laughter.'

'But why at my expense? Why not some other's? No one be mocking Jonathan Caldicott for his hair standing on end and his shirt hanging. Or Ralf with his shoes unfastened. I come in good order and respectable, yet folk cannot hide their amusement.'

'Don't take it so to heart, Seb. We all hold you in deepest affection.'

'Truly? Sometimes, it seems otherwise, Rose.'

'Oh.' In answer, she kissed my cheek, her lips cool upon my flushed skin. At which point, the Eucharist bell rang and our attention demanded by sacred matters.

The office was done and we received Father Thomas's departing benediction.

'When you fetched my clothes, Rose, how do you think Chesca was faring?' I enquired as we waited in the churchyard for Ralf to catch up. 'I pray she be not sickening, not with the pestilence returning.'

'Chesca isn't sick.'

'Then why does she claim to be indisposed and not attend church?'

'Jude told her to.'

'He fears the Baldesis will recognise her? Why would they? The Italians do not attend here.'

'It has naught to do with them, Seb. It's you he would hide her from.'

'Me? Why?'

'Because of what you said last eve.'

I went then to Em's grave with its wooden marker upon which I had scored her name. I bent the knee and laid the posy of rosemary – for remembrance – saying a prayer for her dear soul and making the sign of the Cross.

When I had paid my respects, it took me some moments, firstly, to recall what I had said yesterday and then, secondly, to determine Jude's reason for concealing Chesca in the bedchamber.

We returned along Paternoster Row, Rose beside me, leading my little son by the hand.

'The wretch has beaten the lass, has he not? After my explicit warning, he has left her bruised and battered. 'Tis intolerable. He must go. I care not where.'

'But where will they stay?' Rose asked. 'Last eve in the parlour, Jude admitted he had no money left.'

'That explains much. Little wonder then that he returned, no doubt hoping I may aid his purse; supply his lack. But upon this occasion, he will meet with disappointment. I refuse to give alms to this undeserving beggar.'

'You can't throw them out, onto the street, Seb.'

'I have said naught concerning Chesca. The lass may stay. My brother cannot.'

'But they're wed. You can't come betwixt a man and his wife.'

'Then Jude will have to decide what be more important to him: to abide by the rules of my house and have bed and board or to ignore them and make the best of it in some bug-ridden inn, if that be all he may afford.'

'So you'll give him a second chance, Seb? He said you would.'

'He said! You mean to say he would have you plead with me on his behalf? The Devil take him!'

'Please, Seb, let them stay...'

'You would beg on behalf of the rogue who abandoned you at the church door?'

'For Chesca's sake… What if she's with child, Seb?'

'With child! Oh, most merciful Lord Jesu, let it not be so. Another of Jude's kind? Is there not trouble enough in the world as it is? I could not bear it.'

We turned down the alleyway and entered the yard by means of the side gate.

'I hear you taking my name in vain, little brother?' Jude threw his arm across my shoulders with such force I staggered somewhat. I shrugged him off.

'You take advantage of me at every turn. Jude. You go too far, harming Chesca after I forewarned you of the consequences, if you did so.'

'The little cow deserved it. Besides, I only tapped her. She bruises too easily.'

'All the more reason why you should not lay a hand upon her. You can be a brute at times, as I have come to realise.'

'Me? Who cared for you all those years you were a cripple, sneered at and mocked? Who saved you every time you stumbled? Who wiped the shit from your face when urchins threw it at you? You're an ungrateful toad; I thought you were a better man than that. For once I ask something in return and this is how you repay me? You would cast me aside, throw me out on the street… yet call me "brother"? You're a heartless bastard, Seb. I'm ashamed to say we share blood.'

I knew he spoke truly, some of what he said, leastwise. He did care for me in my youth, when I had been bent-backed and lame. But he had profited much from my labours even then. Yet my gratitude for his past fraternal benevolence could not out-weigh what he had done since: the nigh-ruination of all we had worked for. Neither did it absolve him of his guilt in humiliating dear Rose a twelvemonth since, nor now in striking a young lass. Whether she be his wife or no, I could not condone cruelty of any kind.

Chapter 12

Monday, the twenty-first day of June
The Foxley House

L AST EVE, I chose to sleep in the workshop upon a straw-stuffed palliasse on the floor. It was more comfortable than the upturned bucket in the garden and quieter by far than sharing Adam's chamber, attempting to sleep to the accompaniment of Ralf's trumpeting snores. With a good pillow for my head, I passed the night well and woke refreshed this morn.

Being a Monday, there was no need to feel the least guilt in commencing work right early, though I had yet to make amends with a penance for my labours of the Lord's Day, previously. The gesso applied yesterday had dried upon the miniatures, so I set to smoothing the surfaces. There was yet a trace of dampness in the air afore the sun's heat increased over much. Thus, it was the perfect time to lay on the gold leaf. If matters proceeded without upset, I should have the gold parts finished and burnished afore breakfast.

At least this day I was suitably attired when Rose and little Dickon came to bid me 'Good morn' and inform me that the mess of eggs with herbs and honey cakes were ready at the kitchen board. I left the gleaming gold and went to break my fast.

And there was Jude seated in my place at the head of the board, spooning egg into his mouth.

'Could you not wait? I have yet to say grace.'

163

'I said it on your behalf, little brother. The eggs were going cold.'

'God give you all good day,' I said, remembering my manners, belatedly, and greeting the company. I noted one missing person. 'Will Chesca be joining us? I have not seen the lass since Saturday.' I sat on a bench, squashed betwixt Ralf and Nessie, the latter seeming to wax broader by the week and taking up more than her allotted space upon the seat. Mayhap, we fed our serving wench too well. 'Jude, I would not have you usurp my place as master of this house. It undermines my authority.'

My brother laughed out loud, choking on his honey cake.

'Authority! You? Seb, you know full well you have all the authority of... of a new-hatched chick. I usurp naught. Now cease your prattle and eat your bloody food. Stop making so much fuss about who says grace. I doubt God bothers to listen to you anyway. The prayers of a mouse, not a man...'

'I shall not bide here and suffer your insults!' I clambered from my tight perch, all undignified. 'If required by any respected person, they may find me fully employed at my desk, earning my bread.' It was a feeble repost. Jude likely would not realise my barb was aimed at him – one who assiduously avoided earning his keep. His laughter followed me back to the workshop: the one place he was not allowed, by ruling of the guild, and would have no desire to enter, in any case.

I returned to my pigments, selecting those required to complete the frontispiece: the full-page miniature of St George. The vibrant malachite ground colour of the dragon was fully dry now and ready for the details of the scales and claws to be painted on in shell-gold, so they should shimmer in the light and bring the beast to life. I also required the brighter red of kermes grain to highlight the folds of the saint's cloak from the darker red shadowed areas of crimson lake already done. I would then paint the shell-gold spear, overlying the cloak, piercing the beast's side and the gore spilling forth from the mortal wound.

What more suitable pigment for that than dragon's blood itself? And for the small area of sky, I had marked with 'l' for lapis lazuli… But, mayhap, having second thoughts, why use the most expensive of pigments upon it? Azurite would serve well enough and save a few coins, seeing I was unlikely ever to be recompensed in full for this book.

'Kate, lass, I pray you, fetch some azure pigment for me, if you will? I have changed my mind about using lapis.'

'Aye, master. Did you finish the drawing of the, er, treber-thing? You said you would show it to me and explain what it does. And you promised to show me how to paint the look of wood.' She set the required pot of blue before me.

'You mean the trebuchet? Aye. I finished it yesterday. 'Tis covered by that cloth over there. Look at it by all means but I be uncertain I can explain its workings to you. As for painting a wood effect, I shall show you later, when I be done with St George here.'

She lifted the cloth from the other miniature, now with its gilding done and ready to paint, studying it with care, her tongue poked at the corner of her mouth – her sure sign of concentration.

'Master?'

'Mm?' I loaded my brush to apply the kermes grain and worked it to a fine point afore applying a line of highlight, so the folds of the saint's cloak no longer seemed flat upon the page. Master Collop had taught me this trick to deceive the eye.

'Master, why have you written 'dog' on the drawing?'

'Nay, lass. I have drawn a dog into the scene, but I did not write it.'

'But you did. You have written it on the treber-thing.'

I frowned. I could not recall doing such a thing. Then I realised.

'You mistake me, lass,' I laughed. 'You read the letters on the hurled rock: 'd-o' and 'g'. They indicate gold to be used with dark ochre over to give it shape and shadow.'

'Ah! That makes sense then. Shall I fetch us all some ale, master?'

'That would be welcome,' Adam said afore I could reply and without glancing up from his neat lettering.

'And then you may serve in the shop awhile,' I said. 'Let Rose be about other matters. I be sure she and Nessie yet have the wet linen to see to, upon a Monday. D-o-g,' I muttered to myself and chuckled anew afore returning to my miniature.

My good humour was of short duration, I fear, forwhy my neighbour, Jonathan Caldicott, called out my name from the shop. We had ne'er been close friends but after his behaviour last Eastertide, I had lost all respect for that gutter-snipe and trusted him not. Besides, his arrival always seemed but the precursor of trouble and the business of the wretched chicken was yet fresh in my mind. What did the wretch want of me now? I sighed, cursed silently and washed out my brush with due care – the fellow could wait.

'Seb! I would speak with you,' he shouted.

Since I would not invite him into the workshop for all he was, supposedly, a fellow guildsman, I must go to him.

'Good day, neighbour.' I remembered my manners if he did not. 'What is it you require that you would raise the hue-and-cry, bellowing like a crazed ox?' I turned to the counter-board to tidy the pamphlets displayed, though they lay straighter than a draper's yardstick.

'L-listen, Seb...' Jonathan was twisting his cap in his hands, making a dishrag of it. 'Now I know you d-don't owe me any favours much – except for the chicken, of course. You owe me for that, most certainly...'

'I do not. As Bailiff Turner told you: if you believe you have a case, then take it to the law. Be off with you. I have no intention of discussing it any further. I bid you farewell.'

'No, no, Seb... have a heart, can't you? You know I can't

afford to pay lawyers' fees and the rest. And 'tis St John's Day, come Thursday...'

'Then enjoy the bonfires and celebrations.' I made to return to my work but he blocked my way.

'I will, if I'm not in gaol by then.'

'Why? What mischief have you caused now?'

'None. But you know what happens on the twenty-fourth day of June.'

I looked at him but remained silent. His eyes glanced hither and yon, unable to settle.

'All the city rents fall due on the quarter day. You know that.' He picked up a pamphlet of William Langland's *Piers Plowman* and fanned the pages.

I took it from him and replaced it with its fellows, smoothing it flat.

'I do not pay rent,' I said. 'I bought this house and shop outright. I owe no man and that includes you, Jonathan, so get you gone from my premises.'

'But, Seb... I'm only a few shillings short. Please... I beg you...'

'You be asking me to lend you money? I cannot believe such temerity. After the trouble you caused me, you expect me to make a loan unto you? I be no money-lender, no unChristian usurer. You mistake me, if you think...'

'Just a few pence, then, betwixt friends. I'll pay you back, I swear to Christ.'

'You will not, forwhy I shall not lend you a farthing.'

'Think of it as alms for the needy of the parish, Seb.' He held my sleeve. 'Would you see my Mary homeless, wandering the streets, begging her bread?' he wheedled. 'And who knows what sort of disreputable, drunken, foul-mouthed neighbours you might get in our place. Think of the bad language, the unruly behaviour your little son might see and learn from them. Think how their kind might leer at your Rose... torment young Kate and thieve the stuff from your garden plot...'

By the time the wretch had turned our neighbourhood into a midden of crime, I was reaching for my purse, fool that I be.

'Take it.' I put a handful of coins, uncounted, into his outstretched, greedy hand. 'And do not ask me ever again. Now go. Get out of my shop.'

Incredulous, I watched as the knave remained, counting out the money I had given him.

'Five-and-twenty pence and three farthings... Could you not...'

'Out! And show not your face again. If I see it, I shall not be the master of reason but strike it full square.'

Jonathan gave me such a look – of disbelief at the threat, no doubt – but slunk off, his fist tight around the money.

I was unsure whether I meant what I said but, watching him depart, how sorely was I tempted to hasten him on his way with the toe of my boot. I realised I had been holding my breath and blew it out. Feeling the first stirrings of a headache behind mine eyes, I put my hand to my brow.

'Are you alright, master?' Kate asked.

'That man would try the patience of Job.'

'Will he pay you back, do you think?'

'In kind? Nay. In the like degree of trouble: most probably.' I looked to my depleted purse. A few coins yet remained. 'Here, Kate, take these to Master Lewis and purchase more dragon's blood pigment, if you please. I have used more than I reckoned and will be in need by afternoon.'

'How much shall I get?'

'Whatever amount three pence ha'penny will buy. 'Tis all the coin I have to hand, at present.'

'Who will watch the shop, master? Shall I fetch Rose?'

'I shall serve in your absence, lass.' In truth, I was yet unfit for the delicate application of colours. My nerves, strung taut as bow-strings, would not make for a steady hand, nor my aching head for a keen eye. Sitting in the shop would provide respite, so long as no other customer of Jonathan's kind came to annoy me further. The wretch had put me quite out of sorts.

A plump merchant required a Latin primer for his son who was now of age to have a tutor. Anyone who could afford to hire a tutor for tuition at home must have wealth enough that I showed him a Latin primer of good quality, bound in blue leather. I had penned it myself, so knew it to be accurate in grammar and finely set out in excellently clear lettering. I asked a most reasonable price of fifteen pence but it seemed he was inclined to quibble until a handsome young woman entered the shop and, of a sudden, the fellow paid quite readily, his gaze turned upon the newcomer.

As I wrapped the book in a linen square to keep it clean, the merchant paid his respects to the lady, bowing low and sweeping off his hat in a lordly gesture. He announced his name and smiled at her, creasing his fat cheeks.

The fine woman turned from admiring a pretty little volume of poetry and I experienced difficulty in keeping a bland expression upon my face. It was no woman but that strange one: John Rykener, in his guise as 'Eleanor'. She – or he – (I never knew which) gave the merchant her fullest attention, a beguiling smile, as though he was some godlike creature she had awaited all her life. Dark eyelashes fluttered. Laughter tinkled like a Moorish-dancer's bells. I recalled that sound all too well.

It was clear to me that she had followed the merchant into my shop with every intention of capturing her prey, as a cat waylays a mouse. And now, cat-like, she would play with him a while afore revealing her claws to the unsuspecting victim. The pair left the shop, arm-in-arm, but 'Eleanor' glanced back at me, over her velvet-clad shoulder, winked and mouthed 'See you in the tavern, later, Seb'. As if we were firm friends! And using my premises as a place to ply her counterfeit trade… Far from improving, my headache grew worse and little wonder that it did so.

'Master Foxley.' The next person through the door was not a customer. It was Geoffrey Wanstead, Bishop Kempe's man of letters. I felt as though I had been felled by a blow to my breast. 'My lord bishop's librarian and I have been waiting for you, Master Foxley. You did not come as arranged.'

'Sir, I, er... Did I not say I would come this afternoon?' In truth, I could not recall what I had said. 'Forgive me if...'

'We agreed upon the forenoon. The bishop is in haste to have this matter dealt with.' Master Wanstead fixed me with his eye. Dagger-sharp, his glance would pin me down.

'*Mea culpa.* I forgot what was decided. The fault be mine entirely. I shall come now, if 'tis convenient?'

Wanstead nodded.

I hastened to the workshop to fetch my scrip.

'Adam? Could you mind the shop awhile, if you will?'

'Where's Kate? I'm in the midst of this.' He waved his pen at me.

'The lass be upon an errand. The bishop's man has come for me. I was supposed to go to the library at the palace this morn to examine some documents suspected to be false. I forgot all about it and must make amends immediately. I apologise for disrupting your work but 'tis urgent.'

'Aye. I suppose part two of Vegetius can wait a while.' Adam left his desk. 'I wish you good fortune in appeasing the bishop's wrath, Seb.'

''Tis Master Wanstead's displeasure I fear the more. Ask Rose to set dinner aside for me, if she may. Do not wait upon my return. I know not how long this will take.'

The Library at the Bishop of London's Palace in St Paul's Precinct

Master Wanstead referred to the attic chamber at the head of the stair as 'the library' and introduced me to Brother Henry, the librarian. Yet no books were in evidence. Instead, there were great oaken chests, locked, stacked around the walls. Chests full of precious books, I supposed. And the librarian had a mighty ring of keys dragging at his girdle, such that he clanked like a Newgate gaoler when he walked. A dusty little man with a protuberant wart upon his forehead seeming to support his tonsure, he looked too frail to bear the weight. A curt nod and a sniff were his greeting to me when I removed my cap and bowed. I dare say I deserved no better, having kept him waiting all morn.

A board of considerable age, much wood-wormed, stood in the midst of the chamber with a stool. Two cheap tallow candles were ready for lighting, an uncovered inkwell and pens provided, together with a palimpsest of parchment, scraped clean of its old writings for reuse. At least I was not expected to provide my own necessities. Upon the board was a wooden box, lying on its side with the lid opened back. Within, were parchment rolls, ribbon-tied, two dozen or more. Was I supposed to examine them all?

Brother Henry brought a taper and lit both candles.

'You'll have a care with the flames. These documents must not come to harm. At least, not until we know which ones are faked.' The brother scowled at me, pulling the wart down betwixt his brows. It was hard to keep from staring at it, the eye drawn to it, unerringly, as iron to a lodestone.

'I shall take care,' I assured him, purposefully looking away. Yet I wondered why this windowless chamber served as a library. Reading required light but candles were e'er a danger close to old parchments. Why did they not use a well-lit chamber? No doubt but a building the size of the Bishop's Palace must have rooms to spare, better suited for the purpose.

Brother Henry sniffed significantly, extinguished the taper and departed, his monkish sandals slapping on floorboards that creaked alarmingly 'neath even his slight weight. It was miraculous, indeed, that the floor supported the great book-chests at all. How long afore it would surely collapse? I could but hope – seeing how Dame Fortune had turned against me of late – that this day would not be the day it succumbed to the burden of books.

I had hardly seated myself upon the stool provided – it wobbled, I discovered – when Master Wanstead took a parchment from the box, undid the ribbon, unrolled the document and thrust it 'neath my nose. Of course, it promptly re-rolled itself. None had thought to provide weights to prevent this. Wanstead huffed and tutted and went off to remedy the lack by which time I had supplied my own river-pebbles from my scrip. He huffed again at having troubled to fetch a couple of brass weights in the shape of a matching pair of sleeping hounds.

'You could have let sleeping dogs lie,' I said. It was a feeble attempt to lighten the situation and I should have spared my breath.

Wanstead looked at me, frowning. I suppose levity was beyond him. He bent low at my elbow, leaning forward over my shoulder.

'Now this is the document of which I… er, his grace, the bishop has most doubt.' He tapped at the parchment with an ink-stained finger. ''Tis a dubious piece of script. And what of this date, eh? See how it is written? A half-decent scribe would never write it thus and this here… Look at it!'

'I will indeed look at it, sir, given leave… and room enough to do so.'

He moved back a little.

'You asked me here to examine documents concerning which you seem to have made up your mind beforehand. Why do you require my services, if you know already which be false or otherwise?'

'Well... Bishop Kempe requires certainty in the matter before we take it through the Court of Chancery.'

'Aye.' I smiled up at him, all the while knowing how churchmen guard their cash more surely than their holy relics. 'You would not want to waste coin, paying lawyers' fees and then discover your opponents' documents be true and your own of doubtful provenance.'

'Exactly so.'

'The humiliation would be beyond bearing... for you.'

'Aye, so just see that you find the faults in this charter and this with the green ribbon. I marked it so you'd know.'

'Sir. I will examine these in my own way. Do not tell me which you believe or desire to be found counterfeit. My mind must be unbiased, if you want a true account of them. Now, I pray you, step away and allow me to begin my work – unhindered, if you please.'

Wanstead did as I asked but I felt he hovered, watching over me, as a kestrel with a vole in its sight. How did he expect me to work, thus observed?

Nonetheless, I began examining the parchments. Master Collop had instructed me in the study of old documents, oftentimes of a Saturday afternoon, when my fellow apprentices were at leisure, enjoying themselves. Since they ne'er wanted the company of a lame duck, dragging along, slowing them down, I was content to learn other skills at my master's behest. How to discover the true origins of a warrant, charter or deed was among the knowledge I thus acquired.

The first three parchments passed any test I could apply – whether that would please the bishop or not. But the fourth was another matter. Supposedly a charter dated to the long-ago time of the first King Edward and the twenty-first year of his reign, the parchment and the seal appended were in agreement with such an age. However, other details were not. Being a church document, the year 1293 was also designated as to the year of the reign of the Holy Father in Rome. I recalled that year as being extraordinary in that there had been no pope – my reason for remembering it. Yet the date was noted as the fifth year of Pope Nicholas IV. But Nicholas had died after just four years as the incumbent of the Holy See in 1292 and his successor, Celestine V, had not been elected until the summer of 1294. Had the charter been written at the time, the scribe and those concerned in the matter would have known that. It was a basic error. And the scribal hand was of a later style, likely of an early date in our own century. The charter involved a property in the county of Essex, given to St John's Abbey in Colchester by the owner, Walter Marley, in exchange for prayers to be made in perpetuity for him and his heirs for the good of their souls. Quite how that concerned the Bishop of London was not my business. I set the document aside and made my notes upon my observations.

By the end of the afternoon, I had perused every document and set seven of them to one side as being suspect. My reasons for selecting them were varied. Though dated to the late thirteenth and early fourteenth century, two of them were quite plainly written on new parchment, the waxen seals still bright red with no sign of ageing, the ink sharply black and the hand of the modern style. They were amateurish efforts at counterfeiting that anyone with eyes to see could have recognised as faked. Three were copies made of St John's Abbey's account books made at various dates betwixt the reign of the second King Richard and the fifth King Harry of Agincourt fame. They were of interest because in each case, the income from the property in question in the first charter had been inserted into the accounts afterwards, evidenced from the fact that despite the records being in different hands, the first and the last more than forty years apart, the insertions were all in the same hand and with the same misspelling of the word 'sterling' as 'sterrling'.

The final document was a later deed, transferring ownership

by the heirs of the aforementioned Walter Marley of a plot of land adjacent to the first property. This was a recent document – no subterfuge required to make it appear ancient, dated to the eighth year of our present King Edward's reign: 1468. It purported to be witnessed by the lord mayor, Ralph Verney, who signed himself as holder of that office, and both his sheriffs: William Constantine and Henry Waver. But I knew Ralph Verney, he being Kate's uncle. He and the named sheriffs had indeed held office in the same year but in 1465, if my memory served me correctly.

My work completed, I realised I had not been offered so much as a cup of water throughout my hours of toil. I was thirsty, indeed. I left my uncomfortable seat to stretch the knots from my spine. Turning, I saw Geoffrey Wanstead had not departed but was slouched upon a book chest in the corner, sound asleep. On the floor by his feet was a jug of wine and an empty cup. What a selfish oaf! I crept close and helped myself to the wine.

'To whom should I apply for the reckoning for my services?' I asked loudly, rattling the pewter jug and cup together.

He awoke suddenly, looked about, wide-eyed and blinking like a startled owl.

'What? You haven't finished yet.'

'I most certainly have. I made detailed notes for you on every document I found to be untrue. Seven of them all together. I have set them aside for you. Upon Saturday, we agreed a halfpenny per document...'

'Oh, you remembered that well enough, though you forgot to come this morn, as arranged.' He snatched the wine cup from me and drank what drink remained.

'I had much upon my mind, made my apologies and completed the task in one day, as demanded of me – all nine-and-twenty documents. Now I be weary and would have the monies owed: fourteen pence and one halfpenny, by my reckoning,' I said, emboldened by the parlous condition of my purse.

'I will deduct a ha'penny since you helped yourself to wine without permission.'

'I have laboured eight hours without refreshment. What do you expect of me? I would have asked, had you not been sleeping.'

'Wait here. Don't touch anything – especially not my wine. I'll fetch your payment and be done with you.'

Wanstead left. I resumed the wobbling stool and waited. And waited. The ill-mannered wretch was taking his own good time. My belly rumbled and my mouth felt parched.

Eventually, he returned, a small money bag in one hand and a paper in the other.

'Sign this receipt,' he ordered.

'I shall see the coin afore I do, sir.' I liked this fellow less with every minute that passed.

He muttered something about 'accursed scriveners' but emptied the money onto the board.

'Count it, if you must, but hasten. I am taking supper with the bishop, shortly.'

I counted the coins. They were correct in number: fourteen pence, less a halfpenny for my solitary mouthful of wine.

'These are not acceptable.' I slid three coins towards him. 'They be counterfeit. I have seen their like of late. They be of tin mostly, not silver as the sterling coins of the realm must be.'

'Don't be absurd. They come from Bishop Kempe's coffers. How dare you insinuate…'

'I insinuate naught but state the true fact, sir: these coins be faked. I refuse to accept them as payment.'

'Take them or be damned.'

'Nay. If I take them, they shall be presented to the city bailiff first thing in the morn, and he shall be told how I came by them. By midday, the lord mayor will know of the bishop's – or your – involvement in spreading counterfeit coins about the city. 'Tis a treasonous act, as you be aware, no doubt. Now pay me with true coins or matters could become embarrassing…'

Wanstead went to his own purse and took out a few pennies to sort through.

'By the Rood! I've got two of those shiny things here also. What do I do about that? I've been cheated by some tradesman or other.'

'I suggest you check the bishop's coffers and your own and take any dubious coins directly to Guildhall. Only in that way can you avoid any accusation of spreading false monies.'

'But where are they coming from? Who is putting them about?'

'I know not. Now... the three pence you owe me? I would have them afore I leave.'

Wanstead sighed, added three good coins of his own and replaced the total of fourteen pence back in the bag.

'Take it. Sign the receipt and go! Be gone, you caitiff.'

Caitiff? I could have him for a slanderer, calling me a base and despicable fellow. But I was beyond caring, wrote S.F. upon the paper and departed, glad to breathe the cool air outside. My headache was now of such proportions, my head felt to be the size of one the boulders I had drawn, about to be slung by the trebuchet.

Chapter 13

Monday eve
The Foxley House

AT HOME, not only was my dinner waiting, long gone cold upon the hearthstone but, had I returned any more tardily, my supper would have been sitting beside it.

'Oh, Seb, I was becoming so worried,' Rose greeted me, concern writ clear in her eyes. 'You must be so hungry. What shall I serve you? Shall I warm your dinner over a pan? Or shall you have supper whilst it's yet hot? Everyone else has eaten.'

'Just supper and little of it, Rose. My head be thumping and plaguing me so. If you have a remedy to hand, I should be grateful.'

'My poor Seb. You look that worn. I'll prepare some meadowsweet for you.'

I admit I did no justice to the bacon and pease pottage the dear lass set afore me. But the ale and the remedy both I drank down swiftly. The noise that Kate and Nessie were making, clattering pots as they washed them, proved beyond bearing.

'I shall seek my bed, Rose, rest whilst the remedy goes to work. I fear I be fit for naught else.' I went to the foot of the stair.

'Don't go to your bedchamber, Seb.'

'Oh? Why ever not, pray?'

'Your brother and Chesca are there, making full use of your bed, by the sound of it.'

I had heard no such sounds but neither was I paying attention to much besides my indisposition. I sighed.

'What of Adam's chamber? Do not tell me Ralf has retired and be snoring already.'

'Nay, not retired but he and Jonathan Caldicott are playing Nine-Men's-Morris there. They seem to have formed a friendship.'

'They had better not be gambling under my roof, not after Jonathan borrowed the money from me to pay his rent.'

'You lent that man money? Whatever were you thinking? You know silver runs through our neighbour's fingers like water through a sieve.'

For a moment, it was as if Em had returned to scold me. The hairs prickled upon my neck and I shuddered. Her voice was so like...

I shook myself free of the memory.

'I know... but I was perplexed... unable to see any other means of persuading him to leave the shop. It was a mistake. I suppose I must content myself now with my palliasse on the workshop floor.'

'Adam's working there, making rapid progress on the Vegetius.'

'The settle in the parlour then, too short though it be...'

'Or you could use the bed Kate and I sleep on. We'll not be using it for an hour or two.'

'My thanks. A few hours should see my head restored.' I did as Rose suggested. Little Dickon was slumbering like an angel in his cradle at the foot of the bed, thumb in mouth. I removed my boots then lay, yet dressed, upon the coverlet, grateful for the soft pillows. I was somewhat aware that Gawain came to lie at my side but sleep claimed me after that.

Some while later, Rose awakened me with a gentle touch upon my arm.

'Seb? It's nigh time for Kate and me to come to bed.'

'Eh?' I rubbed sleep away with my knuckles.

'You're in our chamber...'

179

'Oh, aye. I recall now.'

'Are you feeling any better?'

I sat up, thought upon the matter, collecting my wits. The headache was no more.

'Much improved. I thank you. Come, Gawain, off the bed, you idle beast.' I pulled on the boots I had discarded anyhow a while since. 'What hour is it, Rose?'

'Ten of the clock just gone. St Martin's bell chimed before I woke you.'

'How rude of me to keep you from your rest. Forgive me. I knew not how long I slept.'

'You were in need. I could see that. Was your work for the bishop so taxing?'

'Nay, but hard upon the sight. And naught to drink all the while did not help. Then that fellow Wanstead attempted to pay me with some forged coin. I was having none of that and told him so right plainly but it all took time.'

'Did he give you proper coin after?'

'Eventually.'

'Seb, we need to speak of money, you and me. Not now. The morn will be soon enough. But we must discuss the matter, privily.'

'Be there a problem, lass? Is the glover not paying you fairly for your beautiful work? I shall have words with him, if 'tis the case.'

'It has naught to do with him. But the morrow will suffice to speak of it. God keep you this night, Seb.'

'And you, dearest lass.' I kissed her forehead and departed, finding Kate upon the stair. 'God bless you, Kate. Sleep sound.'

'You too, master.' She was giggling as I went down to the kitchen, hungry, despite the lateness of the hour.

I lit a taper from the banked embers of the fire that I might see what I was about. The house was quiet. Grayling, our mouser, stretched before the hearth, yawning hugely, the way cats do. I found my dinner platter upon a shelf, covered with a cloth. My appetite was such that I could not be bothered to stoke the fire to life, heat water and warm the food, so I ate it cold, sharing the cheese dumplings with Gawain. The cat regarded me with hopeful eyes but if she was hungry, there was a mouse behind the wainscoting in the parlour I had heard of late, scrabbling around.

Having eaten, I felt alert, too much awake to sleep again, as yet. Since I was once more destined to lie upon the palliasse in the workshop to pass the night, I would go there now, to avoid disturbing Nessie in her chimney-corner bed, taking the candle.

The guild forbade working by candlelight and rightly so as no man could do full justice to his craft by an uncertain, flickering flame. Thus, I dared not work upon the king's commission but I could find other matters to occupy a mind not yet inclined to rest. I took out the notes I had made at Guy Linton's place, remembering there to be a puzzle I thought to unravel. Was it truly only upon Thursday last? It seemed so long ago that I made these scribblings, recording the oyster shells, lined up by a dying man's left hand, each containing a pigment, ready for a painting he would ne'er execute. I was certain they held some hidden meaning, a message I should comprehend yet had failed to do so, thus far, at least. I had written:

Right to left, dragon's blood, realgar, azurite, lapis lazuli and another lapis, a second shell of azurite (somewhat spilt), malachite and crimson lake.

'Why so much blue?' I had made a note to myself. 'Red, tawny, blue x 4, green and red.'

Guy Linton was right-handed, I knew that, but must have arranged the shells left-handedly. I thought about it, wondering how I might manage if forced to do likewise. I picked up a piece of charcoal and attempted to write my name. I discovered it was easier, if I made the letters backwards. It was also better to make the marks from right to left, to avoid smudging what was already written. Somehow, it felt more natural. Could Guy have left his message in backwardwise? I rewrote the list in reverse order. It made no more sense than afore. Then it occurred to me of a sudden: d-o-g. Kate had laughed, seeing I had spelt a word upon the miniature of the trebuchet, whereas I was indicating the pigments to be used in the customary manner. What pigments had Guy lined up? Crimson lake, malachite, azurite, lapis lazuli (twice), azurite, realgar, dragon's blood. Then I wrote them as I would have done to indicate pigments to be used: C-L, M, A, L, L, A, R, D-B. Ignoring the final letter B, Guy had spelt out a name: C Mallard. It could not be a coincidence and it explained the use of the blue pigments more than once each.

I had solved the puzzle. But what did it mean? Was Clement Mallard, the vintner, Guy's killer? Or had he paid others to do the deed? Or was he the reason or cause behind Guy's death? If so, did the like apply to Philip Hartnell's murder also? Did the cutler have any connection to Clement Mallard? For all that I seemed to have unravelled one mystery, its solution but served to raise a number of new queries in its place. Upon the morrow, I needs must inform Thaddeus of my discovery, that he and his constables could question Mallard. I would be interested to hear his answers.

Tuesday, the twenty-second day of June
The Foxley House

We had broken our fast and I was preparing to go to Guildhall, to tell Bailiff Turner of my deductions, when Rose caught at my sleeve.

'Seb, when I collected the eggs this morn, I saw something amiss with the henhouse. Before you leave, I think you should take a look. Come, I will show you.' She led me out of the kitchen, across the yard, beyond the pigsty to the garden plot. There she stopped, beside the lavender bushes.

I walked on, towards the henhouse and the ivy-draped privy at the farthest end of the plot.

'You said aught was amiss with the henhouse,' I queried.

Rose shook her head.

'The henhouse is as it should be. But I would speak with you, Seb, where none else can hear.'

'Oh? There be some matter causing you concern, lass? Tell me.'

'Firstly, I would apologise for yesterday. I had not the right to speak to you as I did.'

I frowned and shook my head, recalling no offence.

'I scolded you for lending money to Jonathan Caldicott. 'Tis not my place to speak to you in that manner. A wife may have the right but I do not. Please forgive me. I will guard my tongue in future.'

'Ah, Rose. Think naught of it. You were correct in all you said. I was foolish to give him so much as a farthing. I shall ne'er see it returned. Forget it.' I made to go back towards the house.

'Seb, you are kind to forgive me but there is another matter, concerning money. I don't want to speak of it but can see no other way. I apologise for it before I ask…'

'Ask for what, Rose? Do not fear.'

'Since Emily passed to God – may her soul rest in peace…' Rose made the sign of the Cross, as did I. '…I have been using the money she'd earned and put by in the cracked jug upon the larder shelf to feed us. I have also spent the few pence I've earned from the glover. But since your brother and Chesca came and I bought wine for her… the jug is empty. I need to ask you, Seb, for money to go marketing. The larder is quite empty.'

I laughed, embarrassed at my own thoughtlessness.

'Oh my sweet Rose. What an inconsiderate churl I be not to have thought to give you money.' I embraced her. 'You should not be reluctant to ask, neither spend your own coin upon the household. In truth, the other Saturday, when I did the accounting, I wondered why our coin purse was over-filled, that we had spent so frugally, yet our board was generous as ever. I ne'er realised Em hid her own monies separately.'

'Aye, that's what has kept us fed since Eastertide. I knew of the jug in the larder. She told me of it, saying you knew not that it existed.'

'I did not. But I will share the secret of our household finances with you, Rose. 'Tis only right since you perform the office of Mistress of the House. There be a loose brick to the right-hand side of the parlour chimney, halfway up. Lift it out and a leather bag lies hid behind it. Do not go there now. Wait until the house be quiet. I would not have them all learn of it. But here, you require coin now for marketing...' I took from my purse most of the money Geoffrey Wanstead had paid me yestereve. 'Take this but look closely upon any change given you by the traders. There be counterfeit coins about in the city.'

'How shall I know them?' Rose took the pennies I offered.

'They be... well... more silvery than true silver, shinier. And weigh lighter. If you drop a true coin, it rings, bell-like, but the fake coins sound dull. They be harder to dent with your teeth than proper sterling silver forwhy, so I was told, according to the goldsmiths, they have a little copper added. You must refuse to accept them or, if the trader denies you, take them straight to Guildhall. Otherwise, 'tis a crime to pass them on, knowingly.'

'I'll be careful, Seb, and thank you for being so understanding.'

''Tis I should be grateful to you, Rose, managing to keep us all fed for so long on so little coin without complaint. I ne'er realised.'

'In truth, Seb, there was quite a lot of money in Em's jug and I'm not sure she didn't have more hidden elsewhere. Her business was proving most prosperous. More than she told you, I suspect. She called it her 'ransom'. I don't know what she meant by that. But, anyhow, purchasing wine for your brother's wife took the last of it. 'Tis gone now.'

'Her ransom? How strange.' I turned aside. 'I must be away

to Guildhall myself, now, Rose. Last night, I solved part of the puzzle concerning Guy Linton and needs must inform Bailiff Turner of my deductions. I intend to be back afore dinner.'

As I walked along Paternoster Row and into Cheapside, I thought deeply upon Rose's words. Ransoms were for the purchasing of freedom, were they not? Had Em been intending to escape our marriage, somehow? It was a dreadful thought that oppressed my heart with sorrow. Had my wife, whom I adored, loathed me so very much? I could not help that my eyes pricked with salt tears.

Guildhall

Thaddeus Turner greeted me with a smile, though a weary one. At least he appeared in reasonable spirits as we met in the doorway of his chamber.

'God give you good day, Bailiff Turner.'

'And you, Master Foxley. I've run out of ale, else I'd offer you a cup. It was a long night last night and a lack of good drink not the least of my problems. I'm bound for the tavern to buy more. Come with me to The Cat's Whiskers over the way. I'll tell you of all that went on last eve and you may tell me your news – I can see by your face you have something on your mind. Not ill-tidings, I trust?'

The Cat's Whiskers in Catte Street was an old building that might well have fallen down had it not been propped up by its neighbours on either side, like a drunkard on a Saturday eve. Its roof of thatch drew low, frowning over the entrance as though scrutinising any would-be customers but I knew the ale must be good forwhy the place supplied the lord mayor at Guildhall. The smell of malt hung in the air, evidence of a fresh brewing.

There were few drinkers so early but the tapster brought a jug and two cups straight to us as we took the stools by the window.

Having set them down on the board, he tugged his forelock to Thaddeus and then to me.

'Thank you, Peter,' my friend acknowledged as the fellow poured the frothing, golden liquid.

'Can I get yer aught else, Master Bailiff? Joan's made cheese an' onion bread and a coney stew, if'n you're wanting to break yer fast, sir?'

'Aye, both would be welcome. Same for you, Seb?'

'Nay. I be obliged for the offer but I ate my fill at home.'

Gawain gave a whimper of disapproval from 'neath the board. Sometimes, I be certain he understands words such as 'cheese' and 'coney' – two of his favourite foodstuffs – and I was denying him. Mind, he had already devoured a bacon collop, a square of cheese and little Dickon's dropped oatcake, so the creature was by no means starving, as he would make out. I have to admit, though, when my friend's meal was served, the delicious savoury aromas of fresh bread and stew caused my mouth to water. But greed be a sin and I would not be tempted. I sipped my ale instead.

'Last night, Seb,' Thaddeus said betwixt spoonfuls, 'There was such a to-do at Smithfield. A fight amongst the horse-dealers encamped there. So many bloody noses and broken heads, you would scarce believe.'

'I pray there were no mortal wounds.'

'One for certain: an Irishman stabbed through the neck. A mishap, so his friends claim. Another two or three have injuries that might go either way. There's no telling as yet, Surgeon Dagvyle declared. Blackened eyes, split lips, a Fleming with a broken arm... the place looked a veritable battlefield.' He wagged his spoon in emphasis. 'Me and my constables arrested eighteen miscreants, apart from the injured. Angus the Scot – one of my men – took a knock that made him see stars and young Thomas Hardacre has a black eye to show for our efforts. We hardly had space to lock up so many and the magistrates will be busy 'til week's end, dealing with the offenders.' Thaddeus took a bite of bread and chewed, looking thoughtful. 'In truth, dozens more of the rascals should have been taken and charged but we'd need an army of constables to do it and a place the size of Newgate to keep them in. I'll be glad when this damned horse fair ends on Friday. It's been naught but trouble this year.'

I nodded.

'As shall I. The Horse Pool at Smithfield be my customary place of quietude but there be no peace to be had there at present. The incomers be raucous as magpies.' I drew my finger through the wet ring upon the board, left by my cup. 'Do you know the cause of the brawl last night?'

'Too much drink, women and money, no doubt. One or the other, if not all. 'Tis usually the way of it. But money may be the important reason in this case. Faked coins were certainly mentioned by more than one of those arrested. Complaints were made that horses had been bought and paid for with coin that wasn't true silver. Like those you brought to me. I have to look into the matter; try to find out the source of this counterfeit money.' Thaddeus wiped his platter clean with the last morsel of bread. 'I don't suppose you have any idea as to where I should begin my quest, have you, Seb?' He popped the bread in his mouth and turned his attention to the ale.

'I may have a name for you in that connection.'

'Heaven be thanked, if you have.'

'Clement Mallard, a vintner in Lombard Street. I know not the connection but Guy Linton left us a puzzle, if you recall? The line of shells full of pigments?'

The bailiff nodded.

'I unravelled the mystery last night. Guy had spelt out the name, C. Mallard.' I went on to explain how illuminators indicated pigments as an aid to memory though I realised, as Thaddeus began to bear a weary expression, that he had no need of such details. The fact of the name was sufficient.

'Shall we go speak with this Mallard fellow?' my friend said when I ceased my monologue abruptly. 'Are you acquainted with him?'

'We met but once. I went to his house, accompanying Guy
Linton. Guy was painting Mallard's portrait and was needful
of my advice concerning it but the vintner barely acknowledged
my presence. I doubt he would remember me.'

'Do you want to come along with me anyway?'

I thought upon the matter. Of course I wanted to unravel the
mysteries of the two murders and the counterfeit coins – if the
two were even connected – but my conscience cried louder each
hour that I did not give my attentions to the king's commission.

'Two minds and two pairs of eyes are better than one,'
Thaddeus continued. 'And I may well need a taker of notes...
What do you say?'

Clearly, he wished me to go with him to Lombard Street and
would find a reason for it. I had not refused Guy Linton, who
was ne'er much of a friend to me. Why would I not oblige my
true friend in like manner?

'I shall come but I gave my word that I should be home afore
the dinner hour.'

'Then we must make haste. I wouldn't have you break
a promise.'

Mallard Court in Gracechurch Street

I led Thaddeus to Clement Mallard's place in Gracechurch
Street, opposite the Leadenhall. As we went through the gated
entrance and crossed the courtyard to the marble steps, my
friend whistled, gazing around, impressed by the grandeur of
the vintner's house.

An elderly woman crossed the courtyard to a side entrance.
She was struggling with a basket laden with linen, clean and
neatly folded.

'Good dame, let me aid you,' I said smiling and hastening to her. I lifted her load from her arms.

'Thank you, young master.' She pushed open the side door and held it that I might enter. 'Just set it down there, if you will. There's not many youngsters these days as will help the likes of me. Scared of my warts, so they are.'

It was true. Her face was betokened with an alarming array of large warts.

'Do I know you, lad?' She looked at me, her head cocked like a blackbird's, listening.

I was amused to be reckoned "a youngster" and "a lad" at my age but perhaps I seemed so to one of such a weight of years.

'Sebastian Foxley, at your service, good dame.' I bowed.

'I've heard that name of late...'

'Forgive me. My friend and I have business with Master Mallard.'

'Well, I wish you good fortune with him, the old warlock.'

I bowed again and returned to my friend who yet stood upon the steps, gawping at the hall's fine facade.

'I knew there was money to be made in the wine trade,' he said. 'But this place is fit for a prince. I'm in the wrong business, Seb, if I ever hope to make my fortune. Look at those windows! So much glass! How can anyone afford all this?'

'You are not likely to be half so impressed by the owner. Oh, and to forewarn you: he dislikes uninvited visitors.'

'That's too bad. He can't refuse the city bailiff.'

We mounted the steps to the impressive portal of Mallard Court. Thaddeus knocked loudly upon the oak with his bailiff's staff of office with its gilded finial and the city's coat-of-arms. He was not in the habit of carrying it with him but I had advised him that it might be as well to bring it, to make an impression of authority. He straightened his shoulders, the better to display his city livery with its badge emblazoned upon his chest.

A servant opened the door to us. The fellow's haughty expression may have looked well upon an emperor but appeared quite absurd on a menial, even though he was better clad than

Thaddeus or me. I remembered him from afore, upon my previous visit with Guy, though I doubt he recognised me. My visits here seemed to require I play the part of Everyman's lackey. Why would anyone recall my presence?

'City Bailiff Turner to see Clement Mallard.' My friend could put a most authoritative ring in his voice when he chose.

'Is my master expecting you? If not, then casual callers are not permitted.'

'I am not a casual caller,' Thaddeus growled. 'Now step aside and go announce us to your master.'

The servant did not move from barring our entrance into the great hall.

'My master is not available at present.'

'Then he'd better make himself available... Now!'

'I shall enquire.' Seeming unruffled, the servant stepped back and made to close the door in our faces but the bailiff's staff prevented it.

Uninvited, we crossed the threshold into the hall.

'Tell Mallard I have questions to ask and be quick about it. And give me no nonsense about his being unavailable, or I'll have you arrested for obstructing a city official in pursuance of his duty.'

The servant stalked off, head held high, like an offended lordling.

I had rarely seen this side of my friend afore. He could be quite impressive as an officer of the law but, left alone for the moment, he looked around the sumptuous hall in wonder.

'Watch out for the malevolent ducks,' I whispered, nudging him with my elbow to gain his attention. It would not do for the servant to see him awestruck. I pointed at the evil-featured birds carven into the lintels above the doorways and windows and on the beams above us.

'They look blood-thirsty indeed.' Thaddeus grinned.

I was unsure whether, in this instance, a merry countenance was any more appropriate than one of wonderment but, as soon as the servant returned, the bailiff resumed his stern expression.

'Wait here. My master will summon you anon.'

'Indeed he will not. Where is he? I will speak with him now.'

The servant did not answer but his eyes flickered towards a particular doorway.

'I believe we shall find him in the parlour yonder, Master Bailiff,' I said, remembering the whereabouts of that chamber from my previous visit.

The servant scowled and attempted to deny us entry but Thaddeus shoved him aside with his staff and strode through the doorway. I followed after, attempting to emulate the bailiff's impressive length of stride. I could not but refused to be cowed by the least degree. I gave the servant what I trusted to be a withering look. It had no effect. Mayhap, it was a skill requiring of practice.

The man whom we sought half-rose from his chair, his lined face contorted into a wrathful scowl. If looks could kill – as the saying goes – Thaddeus and I would be dead as Mallard's hearthstone in that instant. He raised his stick against us as though to fend us off.

'What is the meaning of this intrusion? Phelps! Phelps!' he shrieked. 'Who are these blackguards you've allowed in? Get them removed at once. At once, I say.'

That devilish face… I recalled how last time I had felt the urge to cross myself at sight of it. I had the like desire no less upon seeing it again and I sensed the bailiff, likewise, was somewhat taken aback by the visage in that he hesitated to speak.

'Clement Mallard,' Thaddeus said after a pause during which I saw him visibly brace himself. 'I am City Bailiff Turner. I have questions to ask of you and it would be as well for you, if you answered them truly and honestly to the best of your knowl…'

Mallard stepped forward and struck the bailiff with his stick across the upper arm.

'Out! Out of my house. You have no right to trespass here. Go now before I beat the pair of you. Out, I say. I won't warn you again. Phelps! Show them the door. I dare say they're too stupid to find it for themselves.' The old man resumed his seat, still waving and threatening us with his stick.

'I shall return with my constables to arrest you.' Thaddeus said with every ounce of authority, although I saw him rub at his arm.

'On what grounds? You have no cause, you fool. I'm a respected citizen. You can't arrest me for refusing to listen to your pointless questions. As for answering them... I have no reason to assist you – or that lack-wit mayor that you work for – and I will not be commanded by any gutter-scum in his employ.'

'A murdered man's last message consisted of your name.' Thaddeus was certainly persistent. 'Guy Linton's dying words were "Clement Mallard". Why would that be? In what connection did he know you?'

In childish wise, the vintner gazed around, refusing to look at us. He began to hum, loudly but tunelessly, to demonstrate that he neither saw nor heard the bailiff. He was giving insult to the office of city bailiff and to the lord mayor whom Thaddeus represented. But what could be done? He was correct: for the present, at least, there was no cause to arrest him.

At length, the bailiff turned and strode out of the parlour, head high but eyes afire with anger. I followed him.

Thaddeus did not stop but made straight for the gate across the courtyard. His fists were clenched. Now was not the time for soft speech, not when his humours were boiling over like an unwatched pot on the flames.

'Hsst! Master Foxley.' The old dame came hobbling over to me, her basket now empty of clean laundry.

'How may I aid you now?' I touched my cap respectfully. I reined in my own ill-temper. It was not the washerwoman who was at fault. 'Shall I take your basket for you?'

'No. I need no aid. Never did, even when it was full, but it seemed unmannerly to refuse a courteous offer from a handsome young man.'

'Oh.'

'But I recall your name now... where I heard it. Ralf told me... said you'd offered him work as a journeyman. That was a kindly act.'

'You know Ralf Reepham?'

'Aye, we're old friends. Met in our youth when Ralf first came to London. I've always been the washerwoman for the unmarried men of Gracechurch Street – them with no wife to do their linen. I washed for Master Linton as well as sly-faced Mallard, the miserable old curmudgeon. And something was going on betwixt them two, I know.'

'Guy Linton was painting the vintner's portrait.'

'More than that. Things I've seen; things I've heard, Master Foxley. I'm not just a fine looking woman...' She laughed at her own jest. 'I've still got my wits and my hearing's sharp as it ever was. Money. That was at the root of it. Money. And a great deal of it. Take my advice, young master, and stay away from Mallard. He's an evil piece of Satan's own connivance. And more dangerous than he looks.'

'I shall heed your warning, good dame. I can well believe what you say be true.'

'Remember me to Ralf. I doubt I'll be seeing much of him now he lives with you, over Paul's way. Tell him, Joan Alder sends her regards and hasn't forgotten he owes her a pot of ale.'

Chapter 14

Tuesday
The Foxley House

JUDE AND Chesca appeared at the board in good time
for dinner. I had ceased enquiring their whereabouts or
intentions. My brother seemed a stranger to me since his return
and as the answer to any of my well-meant queries concerning
their activities for the day was usually a shrug or a "what has
it to do with you?" kind of expression, I no longer troubled to
ask. I could but hope he was conducting himself in a manner
unlikely to bring the name of Foxley into disrepute once again.

'Ah, Ralf,' I said, pulling a heel of bread to mop up the spicy
sauce Rose had made to go with our beef pie, 'Joan Alder sends
you her regards and reminds you that you owe her a pot of ale.'

'You saw Joanie? Didn't know you knew her, master.'

'I did not until an hour since. We met at Clement Mallard's
house. She brought his clean linen as Bailiff Turner and I arrived
and she spoke with me again after.'

'How is she? Still over the ears in other folks' dirty
washing, plainly.'

'Aye, but lively enough for all her years.'

'All her years, you say? We be of an age, master, me and
Joanie. Were right close, once upon a time, 'til she wed a fellow
with better prospects than me, though nothin' much came of
it. Reckon she knows she made a mistake there.' He chuckled
at the memory. 'She was a fine-looking lass in them days.' He

sucked on a mouthful of succulent beef. 'She wed this fellow, Hamo by name. He were a blacksmith by trade – and skilled, I'll give him his due. But he was a rotten apple, that one. Joanie walked out on him after a year or so. He beat her bad and was into all sorts of – what's the word? – nefinous business.'

'Nefarious?' I suggested.

'Aye, that's it. I b'lieve he's still around, unlucky for Joanie, 'cos otherwise she could've found a new husband. A decent one… like me. But there it is: the way o' the world.' He chewed thoughtfully with his few remaining teeth.

'Why she not poison him?' Chesca suggested. 'A Venetian woman get rid of unwanted husband. Phtt! And he gone. Then she marry better for love. Jood will tell.'

'Be quiet, you stupid wench,' Jude scolded. 'And don't get any ideas on that score, either. Drink your wine and then I'll take you to the horse fair. If you don't behave, I can bloody sell you, you silly mare. There's cockfighting there this afternoon and I might wager a penny or two.'

'Do not waste your coin, Jude,' I said. 'A few bedraggled feathers are not worth the risk.'

'Did I ask your opinion, *little* brother? And keep your bloody long nose out of my business, if you know what's good for you.'

Thus was I reprimanded, even in my own house.

'How goes the Vegetius text, Adam?' I asked, turning to my cousin, changing the subject.

'Better than you might suppose. I can but hope you approve.' Since he wore a doubtful expression, my heart leapt, fearful of what had been done during my absence that morn.

'Why? What has occurred?'

'Naught untoward, I swear. But we have done much to advance the work.'

'How so? Tell me, Adam. Keep me not upon tenterhooks like a worn tapestry.'

'Well, now, it seems Ralf here…' he patted his fellow journeyman on the back, grinning the while. 'He has unused talents, especially in the application of gesso and gold leaf – skills Guy Linton had no use for – but he hasn't forgotten how, have you, Ralf?'

Ralf blushed and fidgeted upon the bench.

'Indeed he hasn't,' Adam went on. 'So betwixt us three, for Kate assisted the burnishing, we've done the gilding. Fear not! We did exactly as you marked it to be done.'

'How much did you do?' I chewed my thumbnail.

'All the gesso that was dried since yesterday, Ralf has gilded. All the parts on the miniatures you had already drawn, Kate mixed the gesso and Ralf laid it in place. 'Tis now left to dry.'

'In a single morn you have done all that? There were three pages ready for gilding and two requiring gesso...'

'Well, we just set to and got it done, the three of us together. No distractions. Rose served in the shop and we laboured without pause, did we not?'

Kate and Ralf nodded agreement and all were well pleased with themselves. 'Tis hard to describe my trepidation, my anxiety that the work had been done in too great haste and would prove to be of a poor standard. For the king, it had to be perfect and what should I do or say if I found it shoddy? If it had to be done over again, there was no saving my underdrawings nor the gold leaf. It would be a great deal of work and materials all gone to waste.

I said naught more upon the matter but the wild strawberry mess with almond wafers took all my attention, seemingly. I was but delaying the moment when I must see their work, praying it was not beyond redemption.

'Come then,' I said at last. 'Show me.' I pushed back my stool and herded my journeymen and apprentice towards the workshop. My stomach churned - too many strawberries, most like.

Adam and Ralf lay the newly-gilded miniatures upon my desk, that I might examine them. I held each one to the light in turn. I did not speak. Next, I was shown the work with gesso.

My stomach settled and I felt the tension dissolve from my limbs. I could breathe easy.

'Your work be of the finest. I be more grateful than I can express. My thanks for all you have accomplished this morn – all three of you are to be commended.'

Adam gave a whoop of delight. Kate danced around the workshop and Ralf nodded, knowing he had done well indeed.

I had ne'er felt such a great wave of relief, a burden lifted. The reputation of the Foxley workshop was safe and in good hands. And who could have thought my approval would mean so much to them? Were my words of praise so rare a thing?

'We was right worried what you'd think and say, Master Seb,' Ralf admitted. 'Didn't know if we'd done the right thing.'

I smiled.

'You have. And taken a weight off my mind forwhy there be no reason now that the king's commission cannot be completed in time. I was wrong to assume I must do so much myself. I should have realised you all have talents sufficient to the task and put my trust in you. I apologise for doubting you. You in particular, Ralf. If I had known…'

'Aye. Well, we'd best get on with it, then,' Adam said, looking somewhat discomfited by unexpected words of praise. All the same, he was grinning widely as he poured fresh ink into his well and sat at his writing slope.

I went to my own desk, ready to put the coloured pigments in place on the ready-gilded underdrawing but then a thought came to me. The areas of colour were marked out as to which pigment was to be used. If I was found to have lacked trust in my fellows, I should remedy that now.

'Kate, lass, how would it be if you painted the ground colours on this miniature for me? After all, you have prepared all the pigments in readiness for tempering. Leave the faces and hands of the figures for the present. I will show you how to do those upon some other day but lay on the colours as indicated – not too thickly but as I have taught you.'

'Oh, master. I've wanted so much to do some part of the king's book. I'll not spoil it, I promise you. My father will be so proud when I tell him.'

That afternoon, the workshop was as industrious as any beehive ever was. Everyone went about their allotted tasks with such goodwill and eagerness. I should have changed the way of it afore now, putting more faith in their abilities. I knew now they would not disappoint me but continue to earn the good reputation of the Foxley workshop. I was content to do the underdrawings for the two remaining full-page miniatures.

Wednesday, the twenty-third day of June
The Foxley House

The morn had witnessed further, excellent progress upon the Vegetius and I felt well pleased and reassured. I had now commenced the cartoons for the half-page miniatures – a score of them required in all.

The one small cloud in our privy azure sky occurred when Jude came to see what we were about. My brother stood, hands on hips, like a monarch surveying his lands. He approached each desk in turn, peering at us, inspecting our progress and put me quite upon edge, wondering what disparaging comments he would make.

'Do they always work like this, little brother?' He spoke as though Adam, Kate and Ralf had not ears to hear. 'Or are you just trying to impress me with your skills at keeping an orderly workshop?'

'We were not to know that you would come, see what we do. Why would I have put on a show for you? I can tell you in any case, they work as well without me looking over their shoulders every minute. Ask them.'

Jude simply pulled a face and left us. I was pleased, knowing he was vexed to have seen naught of which he could make complaint. If he had e'er believed the business would founder without him, he now saw his error, for rather it thrived in his absence. Was he envious, I wondered? Could he be jealous of my success, mayhap?

I hoped not for, in the early days, I could not have survived without him. We were equal in partnership then and it was a sorrow to me in its ending. It was a dreadful admission to make – and silently – but, although I should love my brother until time's end, I no longer felt the same affection for him as I once had done. He was much changed since our days of closeness and, in all likelihood, so was I. I wished he would go from my house – an unChristian desire indeed. He caused naught but disruption and extra work and expense. Quite how he yet had money to spend, I could not hazard a guess and did not want to enquire. I prayed it was come by honest means.

Nonetheless, I was in good humour. When Mercy Hutchinson came with the little ones, as was her custom most days, I took my tiny daughter from her more readily than usual. Ever wary of holding so young an infant, I was becoming used to her. For once, Julia was neither sleeping nor wailing but looked at me with great guileless eyes. Such innocence... how could I not love this motherless mite? I knew both Rose and Mercy feared I might not for reason of the grief her birth caused but they should not concern themselves. Julia was already a beloved child though I was uncertain how to demonstrate it to one so small and without comprehension. I could but think loving thoughts as I held her and hope she felt the tenderness, somehow.

Thus, when Thaddeus, his timing faultless as ever, came to have speech with me just as dinner was about to be set upon the board, I was of a humour to greet him right heartily. Since Jude and Chesca did not appear to be joining us, there was food aplenty for my friend to share our meal forwhy Rose had troubled to prepare meats enough for my brother and his goodwife also. Jude was an unmannerly scapegrace not to have spared her the effort and cost by informing her they would be eating elsewhere. No matter, with the bailiff, Mercy and little Nicholas dining with us, naught would be wasted. Mussels and crabmeat in a chive and mustard sauce, topped with crisp breadcrumbs and served with fresh green peas and mint from the garden plot, the first of the year: Thaddeus had chosen well his hour to call by. The peppered and sugared strawberries, decorated with blue borage flowers and the frilled leaves of Our Lady's mantle, did not sit long upon the dish either. Was the expense of powdered sugar meant to sweeten my brother, or to impress Chesca? Rose did not say, but we all enjoyed them in their brief season.

'I'm returning to Gracechurch Street this afternoon, Seb.' Thaddeus said having sucked the last of the strawberry juice from his fingers and wiped them on his napkin. 'Will you join me?'

'Is there any chance that Clement Mallard will do other than send us off with ill-words sounding in our ears this time? Do you have a warrant to question him or just cause to search his place?'

'Oh, just cause, indeed, you'll be pleased to hear. Not against the old man in person but against that high-and-mighty servant of his: that insolent wretch Phelps. Come, I will explain all to you as we walk. And bring your writing stuff, if you will?'

'I knew you must have some other purpose in inviting me, Thaddeus, apart from the gratifying prospect of bearing witness to you scoring a mark off one so deserving. I am to play your humble clerk yet again, I suppose?'

Mallard Court in Gracechurch Street

We came to Mallard Court once more but its fine facade no longer enthralled Thaddeus.

'Shall you knock, as last time? Or shall we find the servants' entrance?' I asked.

'Why trouble ourselves when, like as not, the fellow we seek will open the door himself?'

Thaddeus proved correct. Phelps did indeed open at our knocking, imperious as afore.

'You.' Somehow he contrived to make so small a word sound a great insult. 'Again.'

'Aye. Us again,' Thaddeus said, grinning in triumph. 'And with a warrant this time, signed and sealed by Lord Mayor Gardyner as chief magistrate of the City of London, so stand aside.' The bailiff shook the parchment 'neath the fellow's elevated nose then entered the hall without breaking step.

'I'll inform the master.'

'Don't bother. Just show us to your quarters. 'Tis you upon whom this warrant is served.'

'Me?'

'Indeed. You.' Thaddeus had his petty revenge, employing the exact same tone as had been used upon us and smiled. 'Edward Phelps. That is your name, is it not?'

'W-well, yes. But I've done naught amiss to bring you here.' Of a sudden, his demeanour was not so haughty and a definite pallor made known his fear.

'Edward Phelps, you stand accused of feloniously and maliciously passing counterfeit coins other than the sterling coinage proper to this realm with treasonous intent to undermine the aforesaid sterling coinage proper to this realm, to the great inconvenience of our sovereign lord, King Edward, and all the peoples of this Kingdom of England.' Thaddeus had not unrolled the parchment to read it out. Nay. He knew every word of it by rote and relished each one, the taste of it upon his tongue, the sound of it in his ear.

I had ne'er seen my friend take so much pleasure in exercising his authority.

'What! But I never did any such thing.' Phelps's hands went

to his breast as if to steady a racing heart. He took an uncertain step back. 'Who dares accuse me so? I am innocent of the charge, I swear before God and all the saints in heaven.'

'Then you can have no fear of showing us your quarters; that we may make diligent search of the same.'

'I don't understand,' Phelps wailed, his voice aquiver.

'You paid a quarterly reckoning of £2 13s and 4d to a tailor in Threadneedle Street and another quarterly settlement of £5 18s and 11¼d to a grocer in Leadenhall. Both reported receiving counterfeit coins among those in your payments.'

'T-that wasn't my money.'

'You're a thief also, then?' Thaddeus looked upon the verge of laughter, eyes merry, the corners of his mouth twitching.

'No! I was settling Master Mallard's accounts. It was his money. I was but the m-m-messenger. You cannot accuse me. The coins were in small pouches, ready counted. I never so much as set eyes on them. How was I to know they weren't proper sterling? I just paid them over, I swear to you.'

Nevertheless, Thaddeus went through the motions of making a cursory search of the fellow's bed and coffer in a space so small that outstretched arms could touch either wall. Phelps might be grandly attired at his master's expense to make a fine show but the remainder of his possessions were few and mean.

All the while, I stood by and watched. The space was such that I could not assist the search and, besides, it took the bailiff less than the time to say a Paternoster and an Ave to rummage through the coffer and unmake the bed. Thaddeus found naught of interest yet, to judge from his expression, he was not disappointed but took delight in the tangle of linens he left.

I began to feel some element – small but real enough – of sympathy for Phelps, the hapless servant, guilty of no more than running his master's errands.

'You enjoyed that, you rogue,' I chided my friend as we departed the premises.

'Aye. As did you, no doubt.'

'Not so. Phelps be of little account, yet you made him feel even less worthy. I do not wonder so much at his assumed airs and graces now, seeing he has naught else to his name. Besides, it was a pointless exercise. You did not find anything and yet I think you ne'er expected to, did you?'

'I got what I wanted.'

'Exacting your revenge?'

'Not at all, Seb. You don't think I'm so petty-minded as that, surely?'

'In truth, I wondered...'

'Phelps told us it was his master's money, already counted out to pay the tradesmen. That's what I wanted: someone to connect Mallard to the false coins. Now I can apply for the warrant I need to search all over this house and Mallard's warehouses and any place else that he owns.'

'Forgive me, Thaddeus. I underestimated you, aye, and discredited you with possessing a meanness of spirit, undeservedly. I beg pardon for that.'

'Don't. I admit, I most thoroughly delighted in seeing that odious lackey writhe like a worm under my boot. You owe me no apology. This was a fine afternoon's work. On the morrow, I'll serve the second warrant with constables at my back to enforce it since, no doubt, Phelps will have forewarned his master. Shall you want to be part of that, Seb?'

'Why would you have need of me, Thaddeus, when you have burly constables to assist?'

'Aye, they're brawny fellows, Seb, but they lack your sharp wits and keen eye. You may recognise false coins better than they... or me.'

'For knowing counterfeit monies, a goldsmith will be of better use to you.'

'But I know of no goldsmith I can trust as well as you. You unravelled the mystery of the pigment shells. None else could have done that. You set us on the path to Mallard's door in the first instance.'

I sighed. My friend was appealing to my vanity. Flattery was e'er a persuasive weapon with me. *Mea culpa.* Thaddeus understood my weakness too well.

'Then, I suppose if you truly require my talents… but if there be any who make their objections known, concerning your searches, by physical means, I be no man for violence, you realise. A broken hand be more than I dare risk with the king's commission yet unfulfilled.'

'That is the work of my constables. Fear not, Seb, I won't expect you to be a party to any brawl that might result. Just keep your eyes open for anything – I know not what – out of place. That's all I ask of you.'

'Then I shall come. At what hour will you want me?'

We parted company by Old Jewry, where Thaddeus turned off Poultry towards Guildhall. I continued along Cheapside, construing arguments in my head as to why I required to be absent from the workshop, yet again, upon the morrow. I realised with a jolt that I had no reason to contrive my lawyer's suit. I had to excuse my actions to none but myself. Emily was no longer my keeper nor captain of my affairs. Then a wave of remorse washed over me forwhy I had felt such relief.

The Foxley House

I arrived home in good time, afore supper was to be served. Rose and Nessie were preparing the meal at the kitchen hearth. Little Dickon played 'neath the table board but he crawled out from amongst the trestles upon sight of me, pulled himself upright and tottered towards me, grabbing my hose to maintain balance.

'Well done, little man,' I commended him, swept him up and kissed him heartily. When I set him down, he grabbed at Gawain's fur instead, chuckling merrily. The dog's forbearance was exemplary, as always, never minding the tail-pulls or ears poked or paws trodden upon. I noted then that one in the kitchen wore a frown of discontent. Most unusually, it was Rose.

'Be aught amiss, lass?' I asked. 'You appear vexed.'

'They're back.' She cocked her head towards the passage that led to the workshop and parlour. 'I fear, I haven't enough supper for all. I wasn't expecting them.'

I could hear Jude's voice issuing forth from the parlour, Chesca laughing.

'Mayhap, Mistress Routledge's cookshop can supply the lack. Nessie, here, take this and go see what be available.' I sorted through my purse and found a half groat – definitely of silver.

With Nessie scuttling off, Rose turned to me.

''Tis as well you came, Seb. I have not coin enough.'

'Did you not look where I told you, in the parlour chimney? I said to take what you required.'

'I did so before your brother returned. Seb... the bag was empty. There were no coins.'

I stared at her, shaking my head.

'But that cannot be. 'Twas overfilled upon Saturday last. I could fit no more in the bag. I have not taken so much as a penny from it since. How can it be empty? There has been no sign of any thievery, has there? Besides, 'tis well hidden, as you must have discovered.'

'I fear you must have misremembered. Could you have put it elsewhere?'

'There be naught amiss with my memory. I did put money elsewhere as it could not all go in the bag but it was full, as I told you. You say the bag remains hid there but empty?'

'Aye. What do you make of it?'

'So much loose coin would be troublesome to carry for a thief in haste. Why would he not simply take the bag to keep it in? Unless he took a handful at a time, at leisure, to refill his own purse.'

'You know who took it, Seb?'

'Apart from Emily and me… and now you, Rose, but one other person knows of that hiding place behind the brick. Jude.'

'But surely he would ask you and not just help himself. He would say something…'

'Would he? Perhaps not. My brother thinks I owe him. He believes he yet has the rights to half this house; this business.'

'But you said he signed it away. That the guild forced him to.'

'They did upon the business side but, at the time – you may recall – Jude had run the workshop into such a mire of debt and difficulty, it was nigh worthless. Wanting money enough for his travels, he also made the house over to me, such that I gave him every penny I could raise to buy his half share of it. In truth, the amount I could come by in so short a time afore he departed, it may be that I paid somewhat less than the full value. Not by much – a few marks or so – but enough that he feels I owe him more.'

'Even so, if that's the case, why would he not ask you for it?'

'Forwhy I gave him short answer when he did so a few days since.'

'So he has helped himself without a by-your-leave.'

'It would seem so, Rose.'

'Leaving us no money to fund your work nor put food upon the board. What does he think? That money sprouts like weeds amongst the worts or rains down from heaven?'

'Knowing Jude, I doubt he thought at all. Just took what he wanted.'

'But all of it! Every penny! How could he do such a foolish, discourteous thing?'

'Sweet Rose, you of all people must know what my brother be capable of. Not marrying you was the most foolish and discourteous action of all. Wedding that silly foreign child was nigh as bad. He will come to regret both, if he does not do so already.'

'But what shall we do about the money? Will you demand he returns it?'

'He will deny he took it and I have not the evidence to prove his guilt.'

'Then how can I feed us?'

'The brick in the parlour was not the sole place of secret keeping. Fear not, lass, we shall not starve but neither shall my brother remain here, since I cannot trust him.'

Later that eve, I had words with Jude in the garden plot. In the soft moth-light, with swallows wheeling and piping in the dusk, I was forced to make the most difficult decision.

'Jude, you must leave this house. You be no longer welcome 'neath my roof nor at my hearth. I be right sorry for it but it cannot be otherwise.'

'What! How can you say that? I'm your brother; your flesh and blood. This is my home as much as yours. Call yourself "Christian", you bloody hypocrite? Will you throw Chesca on the street? She's a child in a strange land. You can't expect...'

'You married her, Jude. Chesca be your responsibility, not mine. As to what I can and cannot expect... I expected more courtesy from you than we receive. I did not expect you to rob this household of every penny we had put by.'

'I never did such a thing. How dare you accuse me?'

'I accuse you forwhy, other than Emily – God rest her soul – only you and I know of the loose brick in the parlour chimney. Upon Saturday last, the coin bag was full. Now 'tis empty. How else can you explain that unless you have been helping yourself?'

'Why blame me? Perhaps your precious bloody Adam took it. Or Nessie. How do I know you haven't told half the street about where you hide your damned money?'

'Then, if all know of it, why did naught go missing afore you came?'

'It must be Adam's doing. He doesn't like me. He's bloody jealous of me, the snivelling bastard. He'd do it in the hope you'd blame me. I know it.'

'If you knew our kinsman better, you would realise that be not his way at all. He might tell you to your face, if he disliked you, but ne'er would he do anything so underhanded as you suggest. Adam be an honest man, which, I be sorrowful to admit, you are not.'

'Honest! You call the man who displaced me here honest?'

'You displaced yourself. You left of your own free will. Now you return and think you can take what be no longer yours.'

'Are you calling me a thief? A bloody hedge-breaker? Yet Adam is treated as your brother and I'm not. You're a false-hearted, *sanguinosso, maledetto traditore*.'

'I refuse to argue the case with you, Jude,' I said, having no idea what he had called me but it sounded bad enough. 'Mayhap, a court of law would call you "innocent" for lack of proof but you know you stole the coin, as do I. We both know the truth of it. Thus, since my trust in you lies forever broken, you and Chesca will leave upon the morrow. I be sorry for it but can see no other way.'

'If we were in Venezia or Firenze and you betrayed me like this, I'd bloody nail you. That's what Italians do to the likes of a fucking Judas.' With that, he turned away and stormed back inside the house.

Even from the garden, I could hear his feet thundering up the stair and the chamber door – *my* chamber door – slamming at the farthest end of the house, rattling the shutters and likely raining dust from the roof-beams. His furious temper had not mellowed one whit during his time in strange lands.

Chapter 15

**Thursday, the twenty-fourth day of June.
The Feast of St John the Baptist.
The Foxley House**

I HAD SLEPT on the straw-stuffed palliasse upon the workshop floor last night – in hope of it being for the final time. I passed the dark hours better than I expected, considering my conscience might well have driven away slumber. But it did not. Should I feel guilt at having told my brother to go? Mayhap, but I was relieved rather than discomfited by what I had done. If that was wrong and against the love a true Christian should bear his brother, it could not be helped. Later, I would confess my sinful lack of fraternal feeling and do due penance but not this day. The Feast of the Baptist was a holy day of celebration, albeit, Bailiff Turner would not suffer every Londoner to enjoy it as he pleased. If Thaddeus had his way, some would end the day behind prison bars.

It was a fine morn. The sky was painted the hue of the Virgin's robe and veiled with a gossamer-fine mist overlaying the halo of the sun's golden light. Already, upon street corners and in marketplaces, folk were piling up kindling in readiness for the St John's Night bonfires. Along Cheapside, groups of apprentices huddled, plotting their mischiefs for later. It was to be hoped naught too rowdy or violent was being planned but these things could get out of hand with little encouragement. A few pots of ale too many and a good-natured game of football could turn riotous so easily.

I had been in Norfolk this time last twelvemonth. In Foxley village, the celebrations had been in a similar vein but smaller. Just two bonfires: one for the upper end of the village and one for us at the nether end of The Street. Good humour had prevailed throughout, although the wrestling matches were keenly contested with mighty Cousin Luke – he of blessed memory – proving the victor over all, to no one's great surprise. Adam had won the yard of ale prize as best archer of the day, I recalled, and shared it with me forwhy, so he said, I had shouted by far the loudest in urging him on at the butts. That had been a merry interlude and I smiled at the thought of it.

This St John's Day seemed like to be somewhat different, beginning with the serving of the city bailiff's warrant. But later, both Adam and Jack were hoping to outmatch each other at the archery over by Smithfield. And Kate wanted to watch the horse racing there on this last day of the horse fair, when the finest of the beasts would be put through their paces, shown at their best to fetch the highest price. Noblemen and wealthy merchants would rub shoulders with humble tradesmen and apprentices, all sizing up the horseflesh afore placing their wagers.

Thaddeus had said, in passing, that he intended to be there also – in part, out of duty to ensure fair dealing and in part to enjoy the spectacle – so I doubted the execution of this warrant would take too long. I suppose it depended upon how many premises Clement Mallard owned and to what degree his warehouses were full of stuff to require searching through. But the day promised to be a hot one and how much time would the constables want to spend in a dry and dusty warehouse, sweating their way amongst barrels of wine with not one cup of it to drink when idle pleasures were to be had elsewhere in the city?

I awaited the bailiff outside Leadenhall, as arranged. Most of the traders had closed up their shops for the holy day but, as I stood upon the corner, I was approached by a woman vending hot peas-cods from her tray. A lean fellow with a donkey – both man and beast wearing woven hats to shield against the sun, the latter with holes cut out for its ears – had fresh-gathered strawberries from Kent, still with the morning dew upon them. They were as rubies in his baskets but I had eaten too many of late from our own plot.

Another huckster tried to sell me a cup of clover-mead by which I was tempted. But mead be strong stuff and the hour too early, a little after Prime, and I had to keep a clear head. Thaddeus wanted the use of my sharp wits and keen eye: befuddled with mead, I would be of little worth to him.

A pedlar would have me purchase a tin trinket or a ribbon for my sweetheart, encouraging me with a knowing wink. A pie-man cried his wares of mutton in gravy or beef with mustard and the scents wafting from his tray were enticing. I was offered fresh nutmegs or cloves from the Indies; flavoured sugars, apricocks or stuffed dates from the Levant. It seemed I might buy anything in the world, if I waited there much longer.

Thaddeus arrived tardily but soon enough to spare my nigh-empty purse greater temptation. He was in company with two constables. I had expected more for the searches to be made.

'The others are keeping watch for trouble,' he explained when I asked. 'So many apprentices idle, so much strong drink on sale...'

'Indeed. I have already been offered mead at this hour. By midday, half the city could be staggering drunk and looking for a fight. So how thoroughly do you intend to search?'

The bailiff shrugged.

'We'll see. The warrant is valid for a sennight, so if we don't have time this day, we can continue tomorrow. By the by, this is Thomas Hardacre.' He nodded to a young fellow the size of a barn door who grinned beneath a tangled thatch of fair hair. 'This is Master Foxley. He's assisting us this morn.'

'I know you,' Thomas said, his grin widening. 'I arrested you at Eastertide last.'

'Aye, well, that's in the past,' Thaddeus reproved him. 'Master Foxley's on the side of the angels now. Our side. So mark him well. And this is Angus.' He indicated the second man. 'A Scotchman, poor devil, but he knows his business as constable, so we overlook his grave fault,' he said, laughing.

'Pleased to meet ye, laddie.' The Scot was grey-haired, wiry, his complexion that of man who was out in all weathers – a one-time mariner, or the like.

'God give you both good day,' I said. 'I hope I may be of use to you in this search but any arrests, assaults or confrontations, I leave to you entirely. I would have you understand that.'

The constables eyed me, up and down.

'Lamb to the slaughter, elsewise, a skinny mouse like you,' Thomas commented. Angus, the Scot, just nodded.

'Right. First, you'd best put this on, Seb. You're officially my assistant for the day.'

Thaddeus gave me a tabard to pull over my head and fasten with ties at each hip. I think the ties were intended to be at the waist but most constables were far larger men than me. Little wonder then that it was too wide also. I straightened the garment to ensure the city's coat-of-arms on the front was prominently displayed but, straightway, it was obvious that it would keep slipping off one shoulder or the other.

'Now to Mallard Court to serve our warrant,' the bailiff continued. 'I can't wait to see the vintner's face.' With that, he crossed the way into Gracechurch Street, leading us through the gates of the grand house.

Mallard Court and other Mallard Premises

'The old bugger must be rich,' Thomas muttered as we stood at the great door. 'I'm going to enjoy turning this place inside out, rummaging through his damned finery.'

'No. You will have a care, young Tom,' the bailiff said. 'Master Foxley needs to see things as they stand or lie, not overturned and strewn all about. This will be a diligent search, not a destructive one. Leastwise, not until after Master Foxley has done his observing,' he added with a gleam in his eye that boded ill for the vintner's luxurious possessions. My friend had not forgiven the insults suffered at Mallard's hands previously.

As it came to pass, at first, it seemed we could as well have spent the morn quaffing ale in the tavern. We found naught of interest though we searched the great hall and parlour, the kitchen, all three bedchambers, the buttery and pantry and various storerooms. Coffers and chests had been emptied and beds dismantled. All the while, Mallard stood at each door in turn, waving his stick, cursing us, until in one of the storerooms, the bailiff told him to be silent afore barring him within. We could hear him hammering at the door and yelling as the constables poked through a barrel of salt fish and sloshed wine casks about – aye, and sampled the contents – to be certain that was all they contained. But we found no counterfeit coins nor smithy equipment for making them. I do swear that Thaddeus and his constables enjoyed themselves. I felt naught but frustration at the waste of time and effort.

'Mallard be a man of business, Thaddeus,' I said, watching as he savoured a cup of filched wine and the others raked through piles of neatly folded linen, tossing clean sheets upon the floor. 'Yet we have failed to find any coin whatsoever. No doubt his servant forewarned him to remove his monies. He must have an accounting house elsewhere, somewhere to keep his books, ledgers and tallies and cash at hand.'

'Where do you keep your accounts, Seb?'

'The accounts ledger and order books are kept in the storeroom in the workshop. The money I keep… Wait. Thomas, Angus… leave the linen. Return to the bedchamber and the parlour. Look behind the hangings there.'

'We did that already,' Thomas said.

'So you did but tap the panelling all along. If it rings hollow at any point… And then we must lift down the new portrait of Mallard in the parlour. I recall that it replaced a small tapestry there. Look out for misaligned stones in the chimneypiece. And whilst you be about it, notice any loose flagstones underfoot or creaking boards upon the floor.'

'Floors always creak, laddie,' Angus said, admiring a silver ale cup he had found in the buttery, polishing it on his sleeve.

'But this house be newly built. Creaking boards may be worth a second look.'

'Put the cup back, Scotchman,' Thaddeus warned mildly. 'We're here to investigate, not help ourselves. You've had your free wine, now do as Master Foxley says. 'Tis a fair possibility the old devil hides his money somewhere conveniently close at hand.'

For some reason I could not explain – a pricking of thumbs but no more than that – I felt drawn to the portrait in the parlour. It was odd to look upon my work, knowing it was credited to another. Adjusting my borrowed tabard so it did not hinder me, I lifted the portrait down from its peg on the wall and set it on the floor to lean without damage. The peg was of brass, not wood, and shaped, most fittingly, as a duck's head. Mallard must be proud of his likeness, mostly counterfeit though it was. Perhaps it was the true image he imagined of himself.

The oak panelling was of the highest quality timber and craftsmanship, as I had noted upon my first visit with Guy Linton. I ran my fingertips over the smoothness of the surface and particularly along the nigh-invisible joints betwixt the panels, alternately painted in golden yellow – a beautiful ochre, I thought, to match the hangings – and malachite green. I fancied I found a groove where the yellow met the green but it could have been the panels' natural joint. My fingernail definitely fitted in the gap. I tapped at the wood, here and there, but could detect no change in the sound. Each piece was as solid, or as hollow, as the next.

I stood back to observe the panelling as a whole. I could

just make out, as the light caught it, the rectangle of brighter paint where, until recently, the tapestry had hung, protecting the pigments. It was obvious that the new portrait was differently shaped, taller and narrower. In truth, it was poorly placed. The ceiling was high and the image could have been viewed to better advantage if it was hung higher. In which case, I should have required a stool to climb upon to lift it down. I was glad not to have been forced to do so: I was ne'er one for climbing and disobliging my hip.

Then the truth occurred to me, like a candle kindled inside my head. Of course, it was low down that the old man might reach it. No clambering on stools for one of his age and uncertain balance, walking with a stick as he did.

I traced the groove all around with my fingernail until it caught upon something just below the duck's-head peg. I pulled at the brass peg, wiggled it, but to no avail. Then I tried twisting it. It turned with a most definite "click" and whatever mechanism had impeded my nail was withdrawn.

'Bailiff Turner!' I called out. 'Thaddeus! See here. Bear witness, if you will.'

Not only Thaddeus and the constables hastened to my summons but Phelps and other servants came running to see what was amiss. I opened back a square section of the panelling to reveal a sizable aumbry within the thickness of the wall. Then I lifted down small coin bags by the dozen, handing them to the bailiff.

To judge by their expressions, the servants, including Phelps, had no knowledge of this hoard until now. Thomas's jaw dropped lower with every bag removed and Angus's eyes shone brighter. Then we examined the contents of each bag. The faces of the onlookers changed as we revealed that the miser's treasure was not entirely of silver. For every bag of true sterling silver coins, there were at least three of counterfeit tin discs. Despite the warning of our coming, Mallard believed his secret to be so well hidden, there was no danger of us finding it – so he thought. By the time I had emptied the space, we had eleven bagfuls of silver and forty-one of tin-and-copper fakes in two separate heaps upon the floor.

Weary but elated, I hitched my tabard into place again and grinned at Thaddeus.

'I hope you be satisfied with our morning's labours, Master Bailiff?'

He returned my expression of triumph.

'Aye. Not so bad on your part... for a lowly assistant.' He clapped me upon the back hard enough that I had to steady myself against the panelling. I grabbed at the open door, catching something with the open armhole of my overlarge tabard. The door promptly folded back further, spilling me on the floor. I heard a collective gasp but I was not the cause of the assembly's surprise. I was deluged with small stones pouring down upon me, or so I felt. No, not common pebbles. A small coffer had overturned, its contents falling out like spilt water. Gemstones, pearls, amber and jet rained down, followed by the box itself, which clouted my ear.

'So we'll get all this back to Guildhall and put in safe-keeping for the morrow,' Thaddeus said, making no comment concerning my predicament but struggling not to laugh out loud as he hauled me to my feet. 'Tom, Angus, go fetch the old devil from the storeroom. Let's hear what he has to say about his secret cache of treasure.'

As I stood and pulled my jerkin and tabard into place, more gemstones tinkled to the floor: a huge pearl, virgin-pale and larger than my thumbnail, bounced upon the tiles. A piece of polished sunset amber fell and a small, dark cabochon, likely a sapphire or emerald but I could not tell which without holding it to the light. I picked them up and put them with their fellows as Thaddeus collected the jewels back into the box.

'Do you suppose he forges the coins himself?' Thaddeus asked as I returned the tabard to him. 'We found no smithy equipment there, did we? Oh, keep the tabard for the present.

You may need it when we search Mallard's warehouse down by Galley Quay.'

'Smithy work takes a deal of strength. Mallard looks too fragile. Besides, I would not reckon him a man inclined to soil his hands, if he may avoid it.'

'Do you know of anyone who might suit the part?'

'Nay. Do I look the sort to have dealings with smiths?'

'I was thinking that Philip Hartnell, our dead cutler, might have had to do with blade smiths and the like. And even you might know of goldsmiths, having need of metallic leaf for your illumination work. You mentioned leaf of tin one time, did you not? Mayhap the coins are the work of a tinsmith. There can't be so many of those about. What say you, Seb?'

We were walking where Gracechurch Street becomes Fish Street, closer to London Bridge, afore turning left along Thames Street. At the farther end of Thames Street, close by the Tower of London, we came to Mallard's wine warehouse opposite Galley Quay. The Custom House on the riverside was busy indeed, whether it was a holy day or not, with much coming and going as assessments were made, fees negotiated and paid. Whether upon incoming or outgoing goods, King Edward would have his due. The tide was, likewise, ignorant of feast days and brought trading ships upriver to London, whatever the calendar declared.

A broad-beamed merchantman was being off-loaded of its cargo of Baltic timber with much sweating and cursing by all concerned. Mind, the scent of resinous wood made a pleasant change from the river's usual odours of rotting fish, seaweed and foul mud.

Soon, we were sweating also, if not cursing like the stevedores, though I suspected Angus's Scottish mutterings were blasphemies in his own tongue. The warehouse was vast, the stale air so heavy with the fumes of wine and vinegar, it seemed we might become drunk upon it. Squeezing betwixt lines of barrels – my thin frame and narrow hips meant I was put to that task particularly – poking into cobwebbed corners and searching high and low produced naught but dusty tabards, grubby breeches and a deal of sneezing. In short, despite our efforts, we found naught here to implicate Clement Mallard in any crime greater than poor housekeeping. But the counterfeit coins had to be made somewhere and the vintner had possessed far too many to have come by them accidentally in doing everyday business.

Needless to say, our triumphant humour of earlier was fled by the time we four sat in the Star Inn in Bridge Street, washing the dust from our throats with jugs of ale. Thomas took his first draught, rinsed it around his mouth and spat into the floor rushes.

'A mouth full of bloody grit was all we got out of that,' he complained. 'And Meg'll be berating me when she sees my breeches. I put on my best pair, seeing 'tis a holy day and now look at 'em – filthy. You want any other places searched, you can call someone else, Bailiff. I'm done with it.'

'You'll do as you're told, Thomas Hardacre. That's what you're paid for,' Thaddeus told him.

'But 'tis a bloody holy day, after all.'

'Cease your whining and drink up. We have a counting-house to deal with next.'

'I'd rather quell a riot, any day.'

'You may get your wish, later, when the apprentices' unaccustomed bellies get a skin-full of strong drink. Come on.' Thaddeus paid our reckoning and led us out of the inn. The sun was high, a disc of burning brass, scorching our faces.

I said naught but felt as Thomas did: that I had done enough rummaging and sorting through other folks' properties, to no avail. If he was being paid for his trouble, I was not.

Mallard's counting-house was a few doors away from the Star Inn. It was a small, two-roomed place betwixt St Magnus Church and Bennett Hepton's fishmonger's house and shop – he who had lately wed Emily's friend and fellow silkwoman, Peronelle Wenham. The counting-house had a secure lock and a stout door but Thaddeus' warrant had required the vintner to give him the keys. And much foul language and protest had ensued afore the bailiff wrested the keys from the old man's belt.

The rooms here were cleaner than the warehouse had been, mayhap, forwhy Mallard himself worked here, leaving those in his employ to do the heavy labour down by Galley Quay. The first room was furnished with a heavy desk with a writing slope, two carven chairs and a coffer that put St Michael's parish chest to shame. The chest bore no fewer than three weighty iron locks and was bound to the floor with chains that appeared hardy enough to raise the Tower of London's drawbridge. No man was going to run off with Clement Mallard's strong-box, that was certain.

After a deal of fiddling with keys to find which one fitted which lock, Thaddeus lifted back the lid and we all leant in to observe the contents. If we had hoped to see heaps of gold and assorted valuables, we were sorely disappointed. The coffer held five huge ledgers and a very small bag of perfectly genuine coins.

'What a bloody waste of time,' Thomas yelled, kicking the desk hard, then wincing. It was a stout piece of furniture indeed. 'That's it, Master Turner, I'm ending my work here, whether you agree or not.'

This time, Thaddeus merely nodded. He, too, was disappointed by our findings. But Angus went through to the back room, yet hoping to discover some incriminating evidence. He returned, laden with a second chest, a far smaller casket, and put it on the desk.

'You got a key for this, Bailiff?' he asked.

'No. I have but four: one for the door lock, three for the coffer. All too large to fit this.'

'I could break it open,' Thomas offered. No doubt he could but Thaddeus shook his head.

'I told you we would make diligent search, not destructive. Leave it there. We'll take it with us; open it later.'

Meanwhile, I was looking through Mallard's hefty ledgers.

The accounts in the earliest book went back nigh unto four decades. I be no expert in such matters but they appeared much like my own accounts, except that the amounts recorded were, for the most part, significantly larger. Nevertheless, they seemed innocent enough for one involved in the lucrative wine trade. The two consecutive ledgers were much the same and dated up until Lady Day of 1471. The next, a thinner volume tied closed with laces, began at Lady Day 1478 – last year. Clearly, I had them wrongly ordered and was about to look at the only remaining ledger when something caught my eye, a name: Philip Hartnell. So I read the entry more closely. No mention was made of barrels or pipes of wine. This was a monetary transaction only.

Being unfamiliar with the unChristian practice of usury, I was unsure how such illicit acts might be recorded but it appeared to me that I had found a connection betwixt the murdered cutler and Clement Mallard. I turned the page, running my finger down the columns, and there was Hartnell's name, again and again, each time with an amount of a few marks noted beside. And then I found another: Guy Linton and the borrowed amount recorded would make a wealthy duke blanch.

'Look here, Thaddeus,' I said, forgetting to address him formally. 'I believe I may have found what we require. 'Tis something most incriminating, unless I be greatly mistaken.' As we looked through this particular book, we realised it had naught to do with wine trading and all to do with money lending. 'Clement Mallard be a usurer, by the look of this.' I tapped the entry with my finger. 'What think you of the possibility that the coin he lends be not all of them of honest sterling? In that way, he will only be giving out a portion of the amount he claims and when the debtors repay the sum, no doubt he will make certain all the coin be genuine. Thus, he makes considerable profit, exchanging counterfeit for genuine.'

'It makes a reasonable explanation,' Thaddeus said, staring

down at the numbers, pulling at his earlobe as he considered. 'But why then would Mallard murder those who owe him? A dead man can only repay so much from his estate and, since both Hartnell and Linton needed money, likely their businesses were not overly prosperous. Why kill them when, if they were yet working, more of their debts could be repaid?'

'I cannot hazard a guess at that… not without a deal more thought upon the matter, at least. You be correct: slaying your debtors makes little sense. Moreover, I cannot imagine the old man could kill two fit and able younger men. We know at least a pair of felons were involved, one to hold the victim still as he was tortured by the other. If Mallard hired men to do his dirty work, that would cost him. Such as they be unlikely to do the deed without payment. Mallard would lose rather than make money. I remain unconvinced that he be involved in the murders. Besides, he had just commissioned Guy Linton to paint another portrait of his son's family. Why would he do that, if he planned to have him killed?'

'To allay suspicion, mayhap?' Thaddeus' earlobe was turning crimson betwixt his fingertips – so much thought was doing the appendage no good at all. 'You're the clever one here, Seb. You'll have to solve this puzzle also, as you did the mystery of the pigments. I'm relying on you.'

'You put much upon me, then. I can make no promise not to disappoint you. I have not the knack of knowing other men's minds. However, I believe there be another path yet to be explored.'

'Oh. And what is that?'

'Rest assured, my friend, I shall inform you as soon as I know myself.'

In truth, I did have the seed of an idea but it was by no means ready to be shared and, unfortunately, its further growth might require that I spoke with my brother, Jude, if I could determine his whereabouts.

The Foxley House

Back at Paternoster Row, the dinner hour was long gone but dearest Rose had kept a platter aside for me upon a shelf in the larder, where the dog and cat could not help themselves. Afore I should eat, being so hot and dusty, I unlaced my jerkin to give it a good shaking, out in the yard. As I shook it, something flew out, catching the light, then pattered on the cobbles. I searched and found it, washing it in the water trough. Of all things, it was a fine, polished emerald stone, much the size of my smallest fingernail. It must have lodged in my clothing when Mallard's treasure chest fell upon my head. Such a thing of exquisite beauty, I would show it to the others afore I returned it to Thaddeus.

Whilst I ate, the workshop being closed for the holy day and kitchen labours abandoned for now, Rose, Adam, Kate, Ralf and Nessie sat at the board with me, to harken to my tale of that morn's affairs. Much laughter ensued when I told of the little box of jewels falling on me but all fell silent, gazing upon the emerald. It winked, green as a cat's eye, in the palm of my hand.

'Are you going to keep it?' Adam asked, turning it in his fingers so the light shone through it. 'Is this payment for your time and trouble, assisting Thaddeus? I reckon you deserve it.'

'Deserve? Mayhap, I have earned some recompense but hardly this. It must be worth... I know not how much but a thousand times more than the few groats I have earned this day. Besides, it belongs, by rights, to Clement Mallard.'

'And did he ever come by it rightly? I doubt the devil did. Why should he have it and not you? And you say there were plenty more in the box. He won't miss just one. Anyhow, when he's hanged as a usurer, he isn't going to know nor have any use for it, is he?'

'Adam, do not tempt me. Such beauty of colour does hold much appeal for me, I admit, but what would I do with it? I should likely donate it to a godly cause, but it be not mine to give. I shall return it to Thaddeus in all honesty, as I said.' I folded the stone within a clean napkin and put it in the midst of the board whilst I finished my platter of bacon dumplings and green peas, fresh from the pod.

The others departed to their chosen pursuits for the afternoon. Adam set off for Smithfield, to the archery contest, taking Kate along to watch the horse racing. I noted that she took her drawing stuff too – a conscientious lass, indeed. Ralf said he would likely join them later, in company with Joanie Alder. Rose and Nessie left with Dickon, intent upon joining Mercy Hutchinson and taking all the children to the horse fair.

I sat, finishing my ale, enjoying the quietude of an empty house, yet my hand kept straying to the napkin, opening it to reveal the gem, then coving it again. It was, indeed, a fascinating colour that called to my artist's nature. I determined I must put it out of sight – aye, and temptation's way – within the aumbry in my bedchamber, to keep it safely until it could be returned to the bailiff.

In the chamber I used to share with my beloved, I opened back the heavy-framed image of the Virgin that served to conceal our secret place, intending to add the emerald to the valuables within. I would not carry it about my person, fearing to lose it. Here I kept Em's sapphire wedding ring, the pearl brooch I had purchased, intending to give it to her in celebration of the birth of our second child. Of course, she had ne'er received it. Our supply of gold and silver leaf, as well as monies saved from my commissions and the surplus coin which, last week, could not fit into the bag in the parlour chimney – all were stored here.

Except that they were not. The aumbry was empty but for a single scrap of silver leaf which floated out upon a draught as I opened the little door.

What a fool was I to expect otherwise!

Years since, Jude had been the one who discovered our miserly old master's hiding place. As my brother knew the secret and had slept in my bed these nights past, why would he not take all it contained when I told him to go? He had already taken every penny from the parlour chimney. Why did I dare hope he might refrain from taking all the rest? Did he realise his thievery left us penniless? Could he be so heartless as that?

I sat upon my neatly-made bed, yet clutching the emerald in the napkin. What was I to do? I confess I did no better than succumb to despair, weeping bitter, angry tears.

Chapter 16

Thursday afternoon
Around the City

THAT AFTERNOON, with Gawain by my side, I visited
all my brother's favoured haunts of old, in search of him
or tidings of some kind as to where he and Chesca might have
found lodgings. At first, I was so angered, I could hardly think
what I would do, if I discovered him, other than have it out
with him, fists and cudgels, or whatever came to hand in that
moment. Such a foolish notion. As my anger began to cool
and ebb away, I realised how absurd that would be. Jude would
have me at his mercy afore I could recite a single Ave Maria and
I should have naught but bruises to show for my misguided
challenge. I might have more success, if I went to him, holding
out my begging bowl, in hope of some morsel of charity. Not
that that was likely to prove worthwhile either. Jude was ne'er
the giving kind, not of his coin, leastwise.

My temper was not all that seethed. The afternoon
shimmered in a heat haze. The hot cobbles could be felt
underfoot, e'en through my leather boots and my hair clung
wetly to my brow and neck. Gawain's tongue lolled and dripped
but he found a horse trough to quench his thirst outside The
Barge. This inn in Bucklersbury had rooms at reasonable prices
where Jude used to go with his cronies upon occasion. It was
worth enquiring within. Besides, walking the city streets was a
dry occupation.

A cooling cup of ale would be welcome indeed but I had counted the coins in my purse – a third accounting increasing them by not so much as a farthing. I possessed a half groat, two pennies and five halfpennies. A grand tally of sixpence ha'penny to keep the household and pay my journeymen's wages on Saturday! And I had thought to give them a little extra in token of their fine work upon the king's commission. More like, I would now have to ask them to buy tomorrow's bread for the board. Rose might have a few pence remaining of those I had given her from my payment for the examination of the bishop's suspect documents. There were takings from this week's book sales in the box – if Jude had not filched them also.

Of my brother, there was no sign and, when I made enquiry of the innkeeper, he declined to answer unless I bought a drink at least. Thus, I was about to leave The Barge, without information and parched as ever, when someone called my name. It was a woman's voice.

'Master Foxley? Is that you, young man?'

I looked about me. Being a building of great age, the inn was a gloomy place, having old-fashioned, narrow windows. A pale hand waved above the heads of other customers, beckoning.

'Come join us, Master Seb.' This voice I recognised. I pressed through the crowd towards the board in the far corner.

'Mistress Alder. Ralf,' I greeted them, touching my cap to the washerwoman.

'Since you gave us the half-day off, I reckoned I'd make good my debt to Joanie, like you said she reminded me. So here we are, supping ale. Will you take a cup with us, master? Looks like you're in need.'

Ralf's offer could not have been a more welcome one, so I smiled and squeezed upon the bench beside the journeyman. Gawain went under the board, out of the way of so many feet.

'Ralf was telling me how you approved his just-so and gold-leafing, Master Foxley,' Joan Alder said, finding someone's abandoned ale cup, wiping it out upon her apron and filling it from the jug.

'I told you, Joanie: it's gesso, not just-so.'

'Aye, well, whatever it is, sounds as though you've made yourself right at home in Master Foxley's workshop.' She passed me the ale. 'Better than that tight-fisted Master Linton you used to work for. You know he still owes me tuppence for his last four lots of laundry. What am I? A saint to toil for naught? It's not fair, the way some folks treat others, is it now?'

'Don't speak ill o' the dead, lass,' Ralf said, patting her hand, reddened from years of soaping and boiling linens.

'Well, I for one bless you, good mistress, for this ale.' I drank deep of it but then thought to make the remainder last a little longer.

'You're welcome to – ' Mistress Alder gaped for an instant then disappeared 'neath the trestles with the speed of an apprentice evading his master's birch. 'Don't let that pig see me, Ralf,' she said in a muffled voice. 'Keep him away, for the love of St Mary.'

Ralf turned, glancing towards the entrance, then turned back swiftly, pulling his cap low.

'Master, take Joanie's seat, if you will. Spread yourself.' Ralf eased along our bench to take up more room as I moved to sit upon the stool opposite, attempting to arrange my feet around Gawain's great furry heap under the board without kicking the washerwoman. Quite how there was room enough for them both in so cramped a space, I was unsure.

'From whom does she hide?' I whispered, leaning across, close to Ralf. I noted then her cup, yet full: clear testament to an absent third member of our party. I passed it down to her without looking and felt a hand take it from me 'neath the board.

'See the fellow just come in the door? Good thing he must be nigh blind in here after the bright sun outside. I'll keep my head down. He knows me, knows I get on well with Joanie.'

A wide-shouldered fellow, built like the barbican of the Tower of London, surveyed the crowded inn, squinting in the gloom. His was an intimidating presence; his beard, a thick black tangle of brambles, hid half his face. He held his arms, the size of a bull's haunches, away from his sides, his chest so massive, his limbs could not hang straight as those of normal men.

'Who is he?'

'That's Hamo, Joanie's one-time husband. A blacksmith by trade, I swear he used to use poor Joanie like his anvil, the swine. Him and me have had words in the past. It never ended well for me or Joanie.'

'He has a look about him,' I said in a hushed voice. 'Bent upon trouble, that one. See how the other customers stand aside for him. Oh, Ralf... I fear he comes this way. Put your head down as if sleeping off your drink.'

Ralf did so and I swiftly pulled his cap lower yet, such that only his sparse grey hair was visible around it. He could have been anyone but I had forgotten his bent back.

Too late. Hamo had already seen my journeyman's misshapen form and the blacksmith made straightway towards our board.

'Ralf Reepham,' he growled, grabbing the older man's hair and pulling his head up. 'I told ye t' stay away from me drinkin' places, didn't I?'

'Hey! Hold off!' I told him. I was ignored.

'If ye're seeing that bitch o' mine agen, ye knows what t' expect.' Hamo dragged Ralf's head further back – a position his spine could hardly achieve. Poor Ralf's face showed his agony; he tried to push Hamo off but he might as well have tried to fend off a falling boulder.

'Leave him be, you wretch,' I cried. 'You be causing him much hurt.'

Hamo turned his eyes upon me.

'Whoever y' are, shut yer mouth, 'less ye want t' eat yer own teeth.' He returned his attention to Ralf. 'Where's the bitch? Haven't seen her earnin's fer months.'

'She owes you nothing,' Ralf managed to say. 'Let go,

228

I beg you.'

And that was the moment I made a terrible error. I threw the contents of the ale jug in Hamo's face. I could have done no worse if I had poked a baited bear in the eye.

Hamo roared and flung Ralf aside like a rag.

Customers fled to the farthest corners, though few left the place. Nobody wanted to miss this entertainment.

Still dripping ale, the blacksmith grabbed the front of my jerkin in one massive hand and hoisted me aloft.

'Ye skinny yard o' piss!'

I kicked out and flailed at him but if he felt my blows at all, he did not mark them. He hefted me outside to the horse trough as though I were but a penny-weight burden, dropped me in the water and pushed my face under.

When he let go, I surfaced, gasping and spluttering, only for him to submerge me a second time. When next he left hold, mercifully, he walked away, shaking water off his hands.

Folk were applauding his performance, cheering. No doubt, they thought it a right merry holy day jape. But a couple of fellows had courtesy enough to haul me out of the trough. I might have thanked them heartily had they not been laughing so hard at my humiliation. I coughed, spat, wrung out my cap and perched on the edge of the trough to remove my boots and tip the water from them.

By the time Ralf, the washerwoman and that useless dog of mine – who had not so much as barked a protest at his master's mistreatment – came out to see how I faired, at least I was upright. Water pooled around my feet as I dribbled and dripped like a leaking conduit. Earlier, I had desired cooling. This was not the means I then had in mind but cool I was, if ungrateful for it.

At least, on such a day, my attire would dry swiftly but with squelching footwear, I no longer wanted to go searching for my brother. He would enjoy overmuch the state of me, after my involuntary bathing. And what would Chesca think? A half-drowned rat was not an exemplary impression to make upon one with such airs. I needs must return home, mission unaccomplished, to change my clothes.

I was surprised when, halfway along Cheapside, Ralf managed to catch up and walked back with me. Was Mistress Alder not better company than a wet, disgruntled master? Mayhap, he thought I required safe-conduct, if I was not to suffer further humiliation. Not that any man could have protected me from that monstrous Hamo.

'I wanted to thank you, Master Seb, for speaking up on my behalf. I should have warned you not to. I'm right sorry your courage led to a dowsing but it could've been worse. Hamo's a bully. His dealing is usually more violent than that. He must be in an agreeable humour this holy day, or too hot to make a proper brawl of it.'

'Are you telling me I was fortunate? Fortunate to be publicly humiliated? I could as well have spent the day in the stocks, pelted with dung and rotten cabbages.'

'Aye, but this way you don't stink so bad.' Even Ralf found this amusing. I could detect a hint of laughter in his words. Such knavery from one of my own household was hardly to be borne.

It was as well that Adam would be from home, elsewise, my cousin's mirth at sight of me might know no bounds.

The Cardinal's Hat Inn, Cheapside

Dried off and wearing my Sunday best shoes in preference to oozing boots, we all of us – the entire household along with Mercy Hutchinson and all the children – went to the Cardinal's Hat in Cheapside where was promised an evening of fine music. Minstrels with shawms, flutes, sackbuts and tabors tuned up for an hour or two of dance and song. I determined to enjoy myself, setting aside the memory of my earlier soaking. However, paying for our ale could prove a problem. I had no choice but to tell Adam and Rose of our parlous situation and, upon counting our coin, we none of us had above a few pence in our purses. It might have to be a dry evening, or else we must make do with ladles of water at the conduit.

Ne'er a dancer – one episode of high spirited cavorting upon the birth of my son in Foxley village a twelvemonth since not withstanding – I watched, wistfully, as Adam danced every jig and reel with our womenfolk. Rose, Mercy, Kate and even Nessie, who ambled like a carthorse, were led around the floor in turn, spilling out into Cheapside to whirl around the Cross.

Our own Jack and Stephen Appleyard were there and both found willing partners. Jack made up in enthusiasm what he lacked in finesse whilst Stephen demonstrated surprising grace and sureness of step. Kate sought out Master Collop's apprentice, Hugh Gardyner. He might have difficulty doing strip-the-willow, what with his hand without a thumb, but naught was amiss with his elegant footwork. They made a handsome young couple – aye, and suitable. I should mention it to her father sometime soon.

The long, hot twilight of midsummer witnessed much pleasure, laughter and merriment. The little ones, curled together on a heap of blankets like a litter of pups, slept through the noise, somehow, and Gawain and I kept a watch upon them. Dickon sucked his thumb and hugged his rag ball. The troublesome Nicholas slumbered like an angel and the babes, my Julia and her nursing sibling, Mundy, likewise looked innocent as saints. Mercy's other son, Simon, was chasing around with his schoolmate, Will Thatcher.

How startled was I when Will's mother, Beatrice, came over and seized my hand.

'Come, Master Seb. My Harry's knee's plaguing him. You will partner me in the dance, won't you? Can't bear t' see you missing the fun, nor me. Come on.'

I tried to object but she was deaf to my pleas and dragged me forth to join in a circle dance. It was not that I was ignorant of the steps required. I had watched this dance many times. But I had suffered public embarrassment once already this day and to repeat it by tripping over my feet and sprawling upon the floor would be unbearable. Yet Beatrice insisted.

So I danced. A circle dance and a reel with Beatrice, another circle dance with Rose, during which, whilst stripping-the-willow, I found myself holding John Rykener's hand. He wore velvet skirts in his role as Eleanor, graceful and light of step as any maid. Only his saucy wink as we parted company again was less than demure. I then partook of a jig, partnering Peronelle Hepton – Wenham, as was – with her new husband's permission. This last being the final act for my reluctant hip. I subsided onto the steps of the Cross, there being no benches or stools unoccupied in the inn, sweating and panting but laughing all the same.

'Such unaccustomed exercise; you'll be needing this.' Adam grinned and handed me a brimming ale cup. Thought you said you couldn't dance.'

'I cannot. Not one step more, cousin. I be blown.' I sipped my drink, not chancing to enquire who paid for it.

It was then that I espied my brother. He and Chesca stood beyond the ever-growing pile of kindling that would shortly become the largest of the city's celebratory bonfires. Those with an eye to caution were filling buckets at the conduit for fear stray sparks might alight upon roofs or bushes and set up a blaze. Fortunately, there was little wind to make it too much of a likelihood.

Ale cup in hand, I made my way around to Jude on the far side, discovering I was limping a little from my aching joint. Quite what I should say to him, concerning the money, I knew not. It seemed unmannerly to spoil a joyous evening with harsh words and anger. In the event, it was my brother who did the talking.

'Ah, well met, little brother,' he greeted me. 'And you read

THE COLOUR OF EVIL

my thoughts: ale!' He took my cup and drained it in a single draught, smacking his lips when he was done. He gave me the empty cup and wiped his mouth on his sleeve. 'You should have come with us to the horse racing earlier. We had a bloody fine afternoon's sport, did we not, wife?' He pulled Chesca to him in a tight embrace and gave her a resounding kiss. I saw that he was somewhat glassy-eyed. My ale was by no means his first drink of the night.

'Chesca's my good luck charm... aren't you, dear heart? We won! For once, we bloody won. She insisted I put a big fat wager on the sorriest bloody nag outside a knacker's yard, 'cos she felt heartsick for it and it bloody won, didn't it? Talk of fucking miracles. So I reckon I owe you a portion of my winnings, seeing you lent me...'

'Lent you! I ne'er...'

'Here.' Jude unfastened his purse.

I had not noticed the weight of it, bulging and dragging at his belt. He was fortunate no cutpurse had thought to relieve him of it.

'Go. Have a good time at my expense.' Laughing, he gave me a fistful of coins. 'Show me your purse,' he said, peering into its bare interior as I was about to put the coins in it. 'Whoa. You're poorer than a bloody church mouse, Seb. Have some more.' He took another handful and tipped them in. I dare say, upon the morrow, he would regret it but he was generous in his drunken state, I admit.

'My thanks, Jude. Have a care this eve; keep that purse out of sight.'

He waved aside my warning and went off along Cheapside, his arm tight around Chesca's waist. I was unsure quite who was supporting whom as they wove their way through the crowds of merry-makers. I wondered if he would have any coin remaining by morn, whether gambled, drunk or stolen away.

I returned to the steps of the Cross where Adam sat, staring into his empty cup.

'Where be Mercy?'

'Feeding her Mundy within.' He nodded towards the inn door. 'Woke up, howling, so she's soothing him.'

'You want that cup refilled?' I asked.

'We can't afford it.'

'We can now. My brother just repaid his debt – somewhat of it, at least.' I gave him my cup also and coin enough for us all to enjoy refreshment.

He grinned and went to shoulder his path betwixt numerous, jostling folk, in search of a potboy. Until his return, I observed the dancers, lacing patterns, skipping and spinning. I waved at Master Collop who watched his young wife measuring steps with an alderman whose name escaped me. Jonathan and Mary Caldicott galloped by, hands clasped, up one column of dancers and down the next. Then I saw our Kate, dragging a clod-footed watchman along, his cudgel banging at his thigh. Half London was here, enjoying the celebrations.

'Did Rose find you?' Adam said, returning with our ale.

'Nay. Why?'

'She's looking for you to lead her in the last square dance. Here she comes. You best brace yourself, else she'll be gravely disappointed.'

Kate joined us also, having despaired of the watchman for a partner.

'You lead her then, cousin. My hip be untrustworthy now.'

'I'm spoken for. I'm dancing with Mercy. Pen and Bennett Hepton, Beattie and Stephen – would you believe – but we need you and Rose to make the square. Come. Stir your idle backside, can't you? One last time, eh? For Rose?'

'Go on, master. You make a fine couple.' Kate added her voice to the argument.

Oh well: for Rose. Much against my better judgement, I left the step, handing my cup to Kate for safe-keeping as Rose came over.

'My lady Rose,' I said formally, bowing low. 'I would be truly honoured and take the greatest pleasure if you would permit me to escort you in this last dance.' I kissed her hand, playing the court gallant.

'Well, sir knight,' she said, eyes sparkling as she gazed at me. 'Since I see no line of other suitors vying for my hand...'

'Then more fool they for being blind to the most perfect, the sweetest flower in all England.' I led her out to form the square with the others. I hoped she could not see how I gritted my teeth for the pain and prayed silently that I should survive the dance without mishap. Once worn, my hip could be a chancy thing.

The music began. We were the fourth couple and thus the last to make our stately measure, up and down, her hand resting upon mine, stepping with pointed toe and making our courtesies as we turned. I achieved that much well enough. But then we eight joined hands and circled round. I nigh stumbled but Rose and Peronelle on either hand kept me from falling. Then we had to repeat it all again. The measured steps I could manage but the final circling was likely to be fast as a last flourish to end upon. And so it was. Adam and Bennett Hepton pulled us round at a furious pace. My left hip gave out, as I feared it might. I tumbled and, though I released her hand, Rose fell atop me, followed by Adam, Mercy, then everyone else. I felt mortified at the bottom of a heap of arms, legs and writhing bodies.

In the event, seven dancers untangled themselves, giggling and laughing, brushing down skirts and retrieving caps. No one called me a fool, nor pointed me out as the cause of it all. Adam and Rose assisted me to my feet and Kate hastened over with my ale. I was spared humiliation, Jesu be thanked.

The others went off to light the first of the St John's bonfires but Rose and I returned to the Cardinal's Hat, where Nessie, with Gawain's aid, had been keeping watch over the babes. The inn was emptying now and stools stood vacant. I grabbed one and eased down awkwardly upon it.

'Nessie,' I said. 'You may go join the others at the bonfires. I will look to the children.'

She was gone afore I completed the sentence. Who knew she could move with such alacrity?

'And what of you, Rose? Do you not wish to share in the lighting?'

She shook her head. Much of her hair had cascaded from her cap when we fell and, though she attempted to tidy it, long tresses lay in disarray over her shoulders. The hue of ripened wheat but shimmering like starlight on water, I longed to stroke her hair.

'I'm sorry about the dance, Seb. I should have realised your hip...'

''Twas I asked you, if you recall.'

'Aye, but you only did it to please me, you great chivalrous knight.' She smiled. 'I liked being called a lady, even in jest. But it was one dance too many for you. I'm sorry for that.'

'Rose. If not for my leg, I should dance every dance with you through all eternity.'

'There you are: playing the court gallant again with your foolish, pretty poetry.'

And yet, in that moment, I felt that I truly did mean those words. Mayhap, I had consumed more ale than I thought.

The fire was lit. All cheered and drank to midsummer and a good harvest coming, if the Lord God and the weather continued to oblige. Flame gathered strength and leapt higher into the star-speckled night. Young fools dared each other to dash as close as they might without singeing. One caught his trailing sleeve afire and was doused by his fellows. A dancing circle formed around the blaze, singing the traditional song, accompanied by beating tabors to keep the rhythm.

I did not join the dance this time, which proved fortunate. A stray spark caught the dry grasses by the entrance to the alleyway, where I leaned, watching. The grasses flared up, threatening the low corner of a thatched byre. I found a water bucket close at hand, intended for the purpose, and extinguished the greedy flames ere damage was done. It would not be the last unintended fire of the night – it never was. St John's Night in the close-packed city was not without hazard.

The flames were yet leaping but most folk were too weary as we all escorted Mercy Hutchinson home to Distaff Lane, the sleeping children being more than one woman could carry alone. I bore Dickon in my arms as I made my way, trying my utmost to refrain from limping but my gait was uneven, all the same. Adam carried his soon-to-be stepson, Nicholas – a heavy load in more ways than one. Mercy had her own infant, Mundy, and Rose cradled my tiny daughter, Julia.

We left Adam saying a fond farewell to his beloved and assisting her in settling the babes abed. Only Dickon was coming home with Rose, Kate, Nessie and me. Stephen Appleyard went to his house alone, Jack having disappeared with some fellow apprentices hours ago. I prayed the lad might not get into mischief nor trouble the Watch.

Weary though we were, Rose and Kate yet had life enough that they danced along, hand in hand, singing as we turned into Paternoster Row. I watched Rose with new eyes now. Why had I not realised what beauty dwelt 'neath my own roof? I suppose I had seen naught but my Emily until now and Rose had been my brother's intended. I would ne'er trespass on another man's claim. But Emily – may God assoil her – was no more and foolish Jude had wed elsewhere. Adam had found Mercy, their nuptials planned for September, after harvest. But I had no one and neither did Rose. Was this meant to be?

At least I had my own bed in my own chamber this night but, though weary of body, my mind was yet wakeful. Sleep eluded me.

Belatedly, I recalled that money was not all I had meant to speak of with Jude. I also wanted to enquire of my brother what he had meant when he spoke of the Italians 'nailing'. After all, that was what had been done to both the murder victims, their right hands literally nailed down. I was beginning to wonder – what with money being so involved in all this matter – if the Italian bankers might have some connection to these vile crimes.

But that was for the morrow. As Dame Fortune would have it, our most recent parting had been in friendly wise and not as previously. Who could say what my brother's temperament might be in the morn, what with an ale-heavy head and, mayhap, an empty purse. I would take the risk – except that I knew no more where he might be then than when I had searched this day. No matter. I would not think upon that now.

I composed myself, lying back upon the pillows and closed my eyes. Far beyond the open window casement, the distant sounds of folk yet merry-making drifted in, along with the scent of wood smoke. I turned my thoughts to wheaten hair and sparkling eyes, smiling and at peace with myself.

Chapter 17

Friday, the twenty-fifth day of June
The Foxley House

FALSE COINS were becoming a plague in the city. This morn, when I took time to look more closely at the coin Jude had given me last eve, quite a number of them proved counterfeit. What had seemed to be a generous repayment of fifteen shillings and ninepence of the £5 and more that he owed me – not to mention the jewellery – was not. The true value of the money, after purchasing a jug of ale at the Cardinal's Hat, was less than a mark. Twelve shillings and seven pence, to be exact. I should have to go to Guildhall and hand over the false coin, along with Mallard's emerald, to Thaddeus. But every time I did so, I lost out, as did every honest citizen who did right by the law. It was a grave situation – one I could ill afford, at present.

Ale-heavy heads were no excuse: work upon the Vegetius for the king's commission had to resume in earnest come Friday morn. I believe I was least afflicted; Ralf the worst, mayhap forwhy he had commenced drinking at The Barge after dinner the afternoon previously. I had drunk but little then, afore the beast Hamo had disturbed us all and Joan Alder took to hiding 'neath the board. Later, until I acquired coin from my brother, Adam and I had been all but dry.

It was as well that my cousin and I were sufficiently alert, for I had the last few half-page miniatures to draw and Adam was to embark on scribing the most important Part Three of the book, filling in the text around the pictures already gilded and painted. Any errors he made now would cost us dear in materials and the labour that had gone before.

Kate had all the ingredients prepared to make the gesso when required. Ralf would then use it on the sections of the miniatures I had marked for gilding. In the meantime, the old journeyman nursed a sore head, perched upon his stool with naught else to do.

'Master, me and Joanie were right sorry for what happened at The Barge, yesterday.' Ralf was clearly thinking on a matter I preferred to forget. 'That Hamo's a real piece o' work; no doubt about that.'

'So what happened?' Adam asked. 'Do tell us, Ralf.' My cousin was all ears. I had told him naught of my previous humiliation and had no intention that he should hear of it now. He would likely laugh so hard, his penmanship would suffer.

''Tis of no consequence,' I said, eager to change the subject. 'Rather, I would know more of this Hamo. Who is he, Ralf?'

'Well, Hamo was – is yet – Joanie's husband, as I b'lieve I told you already. But he treated her so badly, the Church Court agreed she could leave his house; no longer owed him marital rights, nor anything else a wife should. Though Hamo doesn't see it that way, the Devil take him. He still reckons he can use Joanie whenever he fancies a bit o' bedsport... saving your innocent ears, Mistress Kate. But things got worse back in the springtime. You see, Hamo, for all his hateful ways, did have a decent job, working as a smith at the Royal Mint at the Tower of London.

'I've no idea what came to pass – not sure Joanie does either, though she may know more than I do – but, any road, Hamo was dismissed, of a sudden, from the workings there. Don't surprise me. 'Twas a wonder they kept him so long, what with his temper and rudeness and idle ways, not to mention the drinking. I s'pose he's short of coin now. That was likely why he came after poor Joanie yesterday, insisting she owed him her earnings from the laundering, which she don't. The court made that plain enough: that her earnings were her sole means of livelihood and naught to do with him any longer.'

My mind leapt far beyond the underdrawing of the great bombard I was designing, taking its likeness from our English exemplar of Vegetius. In truth, I knew no more of cannon than I did of the far off Land of Prester John but I could make a good copy.

'He was employed as a smith at the Royal Mint, you say?' I dipped my pen, casually, and drew the wheels upon the cannon carriage – each with a single curving stroke. 'Thus, he would know well the making of coins.' I did not add 'whether false ones or true' but that was my thought.

'I dare say he would, master. Joanie may know more of it. Why?'

'Do you know where Mistress Alder can be found, Ralf? I think I may visit her after dinner.'

'She'll most likely be in Crooked Lane, off Fish Street, but her laundry deliveries take her all along Gracechurch, Candlewick and East Cheap. She bides halfway along Crooked Lane, beyond St Michael's, coming from this direction, opposite the well where she gets her washing water. You want me to show you, master?'

'Nay. I thank you for your kindly offer, Ralf, but 'tis a lengthy walk. I shall find it.'

'Not so far, master, that I haven't been to see Joanie since I came here.'

'Oh. Very well, then, if we can get the gesso applied and to set...'

Work proceeded at a reasonable pace in the workshop. Our one problem was storm flies sticking in the gesso afore it dried. Mayhap, they were the harbinger of bad weather to come later in the day. Even so, the last few underdrawings were completed and marked out for the application of gesso or pigments, as

I deemed appropriate. It was a relief to have achieved these – the only part of the commission I did not yet feel happy about permitting others to do. With a little time yet to spare ere dinner, I gave thought to the cover of the book. The king's commission required it gilded and bejewelled but now I could not afford to pay a goldsmith. It could not be that I would fail in this requirement. To have exquisite pages bound in a plain cover would not do. Then I recalled Jude's gift to me. Might I use the mosaic pieces from the walls of a church in Ravenna to decorate the king's book? This would not only save time in taking it to a goldsmith for bejewelling but spare me the cost.

I fetched the tiny glass jewels and tipped them out upon a sheet of clean paper where they winked and sparkled in the light. I arranged them, here and there, moving them about with a damp brush. I could produce any number of pleasing designs and there were sufficient pieces to adorn both front and back covers. But the front cover required something even more special at the centre to build the pattern around.

I wondered if I dare... Mayhap, I would. Had the Almighty not seen fit to put it in my hands? Was it for this very purpose? From my purse – where I had put it with the intention of taking it to Thaddeus – I took out the napkin-enwrapped emerald and set it in the midst of the mosaic. I moved a few glass pieces to accommodate the gemstone. Not only did it look well, in truth, it was perfect.

'What do you think?' I asked Adam.

He came to see my handiwork.

'For the book's covers?'

'Aye. Do you think I dare make use of Mallard's stone?'

'Most certainly. Ralf, Kate, what say you to this? We can use rabbit glue to fix the mosaic squares. How best to fix the emerald, do you think, Seb? It wouldn't do to have it fall off and be lost.'

All agreed the use of the gem was a righteous act and that it was ever meant to adorn this commission. It was more

242

befitting a king's or nobleman's possession than a vintner's. In the meantime, I must give thought to the method of its fixing. Adam was correct: it would be piteous to lose it during its journeying to Italy.

Joan Alder's House in Crooked Lane

After a dinner of oysters in a green sauce, Ralf and I, with Gawain at heel, walked slowly to Crooked Lane, pausing now and then to allow the old man to catch his wind. There was no cause for haste, although behind us, upriver to the west, clouds were mounting higher. The storm flies told true, so it seemed, but overhead, the skies were yet a spread coverlet of blue. We likely had time enough.

The scawagers had cleared away the ash of last eve's bonfires but the taint of wood smoke lingered, hanging in the heavy air. Blackened circles on street corners showed where the fires were lit and one or two roofs of thatch bore testament to strayed sparks with wet patches encompassing spots of charred straws. But it seemed the city had done well this year, avoiding blazes beyond control.

Ralf knocked upon the door in Crooked Lane and called out.

I noted the well-swept step and fresh limewashed plastered walls. This was a house of goodly keeping.

No one answered Ralf but, as we turned away, he deliberating upon where next to try, Mistress Alder appeared around the corner, carrying a large basket of someone else's soiled linen.

I went to aid her but she shook her head.

'I'll lose my strength, if you aid me too often, young master. Let me fend for myself but I thank you for the thought. Did you want me?'

'Indeed, good mistress. I have questions to ask of you, though I doubt you will approve the subject.'

'Questions, eh? Well then, you'd best come indoors. You, too, Ralf. I dare say you came for the mead and naught else.'

'I, well... since you're offering, Joanie, I may as well partake...' My journeyman looked a little sheepish, caught out in his wily intent.

Mistress Alder's house was well-ordered and spotless, much as I expected from its outward appearance. Two small rooms looked out upon a yard where tubs of linen in soak stood on low trestles. One room was full of linen, hung over cords strung from wall to wall, some of it yet dripping. The laundress took us into the second room. Here she lived among further evidence of her toil and trade: baskets of neatly folded, snowy linen, awaiting return to her customers.

'How do you know which linen belongs to which household?' I asked mystified.

She laughed.

'Is that what you came to ask me? Bless you, master: each line of washing, every basket has a coloured ribbon tied. You see? That blue ribbon there marks Mistress Tuffnell's washing – all them babe's tail-clouts and swaddling bands. The plaited ribbon is Master Carfax's shirts and drawers. And Master Mallard's stuff is in the basket with the dark green ribbon – as always. Mind, I'm not sure what's to be done with it now. What with him in prison... who'll pay for its lavering?'

Mistress Alder shrugged at her own query and bustled about, fetching clean cups and a flagon. She poured generous measures of liquid gold for each of us.

'You could go to Mallard Court with it, as you normally do,' I suggested. 'The servants there will be in need of their clean clouts, whether the master be at home or no. Mayhap, Phelps will pay you your fee.' I tasted the mead. It was cool and strong. I must sip in moderation.

'Him? His purse-strings are knotted as tight as his master's. But no matter. What did you come to ask me? It weren't about washing, I know.' She drank her cup down as if it were water and replenished it; Ralf's also. Mine remained nigh full but she topped it up anyway.

'Nay, indeed. I wished to learn more of Hamo.'

'Because the fat rascal dunked you? I warn you, good master, go after him and he'll likely do the same again, if not worse. Stay away, I should.'

'I have no intention of seeking him out, good mistress, not without assistance, leastwise. I wish to learn more of his past employment at the Royal Mint within the Tower. What do you know of that?'

'Not so much.' She chewed at her nether lip, thinking. 'They dismissed him in April last. Eastertide it was. There was rumours of things going astray from the mint; dies, I believe it was. But whatever went on, they couldn't prove it was Hamo's doing, else they'd have arrested the ol' wallidrag for thievery and they didn't. Reckon they thought it was him though, else why would they tell him to go and never come back?'

'Do you know about the work he did there? As a smith, was it not?'

'Aye. He smelted the silver and made the blank coins, ready for the dies to put the king's head on them. Why do you want to know?'

'You may have found fake coins crossing your palm of late, mistress. Someone is forging them and...'

'And you think it could be Hamo.' It was a statement, not a question. 'I can well see that skabbit skarth up to no good, doing just that, though... well, he's not so sharp-witted. I can't think he'd be devious enough to plan something like that. But if you're going to accuse him, take an army with you, young master. You know what he's like.'

I most certainly did.

'To your knowledge, mistress, has Hamo ever had any dealings with Clement Mallard?'

'How did you know of it? Aye, afore he lost his place at the Tower, he did some repairs to them fancy gates at Mallard

Court.' She pulled at her lip again with her forward teeth. 'You know, I thought at the time that miserly old curmudgeon seemed to have paid him over well. He was so loaded with coin for two days' work, he didn't pester me for my laundry earnings for weeks.'

'And where might I find Hamo's workshop now, good mistress?'

'Well, he has a place – a hovel at best – down by Galley Quay. You know it?'

'Aye, and 'tis close at hand to the vintner's warehouse. I doubt 'tis naught but a coincidence. Does he have his furnace there, also?'

'Nay. The hovel is too small. He used to have his furnace at the farthest end of Tower Street and may have yet. There's an entrance to some old tunnels there that run under the Tower. The entrance was blocked up years since but Hamo found they were a quick way into the fortress. Aye, and a quick way out without being inspected for filched silver from the mint. I think he set up a little forge there, within the entrance, but I've never been inside. I'm not one for tunnels, you see.'

'Neither am I,' I admitted. 'I experienced those tunnels myself once and would not repeat it for a king's ransom. But where might I – we, Bailiff Turner and I – find this entrance, should the need arise?'

''Tis off a yard – Cutpurse Yard, I think it's known as – in a narrow passage called Furnace Alley. In truth, that may not be its name but Hamo calls it so. There's a sort of hovel built there to hide the way into the tunnel. But don't go there, young master, without armed men, if you value your life. The bailiff is not enough. You know Hamo's strength of arm as well as I do.'

'I shall have a care for that, fear not.' I stood and touched my cap to her. 'I thank you, mistress, for both the mead and the information. I must go tell Bailiff Turner what you have told me. Fare you well, good mistress. Ralf? Will you come or stay?'

'I'll finish my drink then make my way back to Paternoster

Row, master, at my own pace. Unless you need me at Guildhall to speak with the bailiff?'

Guildhall

It was decided. Thaddeus said that we should seek out the forge this very afternoon: 'Strike whilst the iron's hot', as he put it so appropriately. However, despite Mistress Alder's insistence that we should take an army along with us, the bailiff thought otherwise.

'I'd prefer to use a little subterfuge... investigate the situation quietly,' he said. 'As yet, we have no cause to arrest or even suspect this fellow Hamo. If we find evidence of crime, then I'll fetch the constables with me to take him in charge. But if I do that in the first instance and find naught, I'll look a fool and he'll be forewarned to dispose of anything incriminating in his possession elsewhere. By the by, that casket we found at Mallard's counting-house contained two coin dies, both genuine, stolen from the Royal Mint. I know not how he came by them but they put the vintner at the heart of this counterfeiting business.'

'Hamo was thought to have filched them,' I said. 'That be the reason he was dismissed, though it could not be proven.'

'Not if the stolen items were in Mallard's possession. That would explain why they weren't to be found with Hamo but I suspect he has use of them – or did 'til now. What say you, Seb? Do you think you and me and your dog can manage a little espying? Do you want to join me?'

'I suppose so.' My doubt sat plain in my voice. 'But, if you allow, I would have my cousin come also. Adam be right handy in, er, physical situations.'

'Aye, if the presence of a third party will ease your mind. I'll send a runner to fetch him, straightway. Will he be at your place?'

Some way beyond the end of Tower Street.

Lowering clouds made the warren of rat-infested passageways and narrow alleys dark and dismal. The torches we had brought to light the way, if we had to enter a tunnel – which I prayed we would not – were nigh worth kindling outside in this gloomy corner of the city. The outer walls of the Tower of London loomed large with the weight of years. Hovels and tumbledown shacks cowered like frightened children beneath its stone skirts, all of them crooked and left to rot. It was a wonder and a sorry one that folk lived here at all but it seemed they did.

Furtive faces peeked from broken doorways and lurking shadows made hasty retreat into yet darker, secret holes.

The stench was eye-watering. Flies swarmed. It seemed the scawagers ne'er ventured here to clean the streets. A dead dog, worm-ridden, had lain some days and none had removed it. Heaps of ordure blocked our way, making progress through this obnoxious labyrinth slow indeed with many a side-step and detour. And all the while, the storm clouds gathered above, closing out the light.

We four – Adam, Thaddeus, Gawain and I – found a court with a narrow alley leading off it, towards the Tower. It fit Mistress Alder's description well enough. At the end was a hovel: little more than a few timber palings nailed together. But it proved to be the concealed entrance, as I had been told.

'I cannot go in there.' I eyed the narrow cleft that led off into absolute darkness. 'I have been lost in these tunnels 'neath the Tower a year since. It was terrifying, blacker than hell itself. I will not do so again.'

'Come on, Seb. I never had you marked out for a coward,' Adam said. 'Besides, this time there are three of us and we each have a torch to light our way. And this can't be the same tunnel since the Tower is over yonder.'

'And how else will we unravel this mystery?' Thaddeus added. 'You want answers, do you not? As we all do.'

'Aye, but not down a tunnel... See Gawain? He has better sense. He wants no part of this, wise dog that he be.' It was true for Gawain's tail and ears were drooping and he had come but half a pace within the hovel. He whimpered at the prospect.

'Gawain can wait here for our return. Have courage, cousin: we'll come to no harm.'

'How can you know? Who can tell what dangers may lurk within? We be in search of an evil-doer. If he lies in wait for us...'

'How can anyone be lying in wait? Nobody knows we're coming.' Adam was peeved at my reticence.

'I do not like the feel of this place.'

'Stop it, Seb. I'm going in and Thaddeus is coming with me to sort this matter out, once and for all. Is that not so, Thaddeus?' My cousin seemed to have taken charge, eager for adventure.

The bailiff nodded agreement as Adam took flint and tinder and lit our torches.

'You can come with us, or wait here or go home; whatever you please,' he said, waiting as the flames caught and settled. 'Come along, Thaddeus. We've wasted too much time as it is.'

I watched as my cousin and my friend squeezed their way through the narrow entrance, pushing aside the nailed boards that had concealed it, disappearing from my sight. Only then did it occur to me: it was likely a black maze beyond; how would they find their way back out of the labyrinth?

'Wait! I have chalk to mark the walls.' I rummaged for the piece of soft white rock within my scrip. Afore I realised, I was hastening after them; chalk in one hand and a lighted torch in the other. A yard or two into the tunnel, I paused to mark a bold chalk cross upon the wall to the left hand, then followed on, hearing the footsteps and voices ahead of me. Every twenty paces or thereabouts, I marked another cross – Our Lord's symbol to guide us back to the light when this devil's enterprise was done.

It was as well that I had thought to use the chalk forewhy my torch illumined many a side passage, leading off on either hand, into oblivion. We might so easily take a wrong turning upon our return, for the tunnels seemed a nest of entangled serpents, all entwined. We were together now, Adam and Thaddeus having waited for me to catch up. Assiduously, I continued to mark the wall. In places, this proved difficult, where I had to scratch away the slime; in others, the stones were dry but crumbling to dust. I feared a roof fall might happen at any moment but kept silent regarding my anxieties. As it was, my cousin had named me for a cowardly fellow. It concerned me greatly that we had not the least idea of our destination nor what we would find there. How might we know if we were but seeking spectres and phantasms? Was there anything to be found down here? Mayhap, we were cursed to wander in this foul place, forever lost in darkness.

I checked my wild thoughts, meandering like these tunnels. All will be well, I told myself. I wiped sweat from my brow.

'Look to our torch flames,' I said. No longer bright yellow, they burned a dull, amber hue. 'If we hope to find some alchemical process being conducted, then that requires fire. Fire makes smoke and, since no one could see and breathe in thick smoke, there must be a vent or chimney through which it makes its escape. I sense we be too far underground by now for either case. If such work goes on here, it must be in one of the side passages closer to the entrance. Nobody would bring a still, furnace, charcoal and equipment so far as this.'

'They could put it in a barrow. The passages are wide enough,' Adam said, 'I think we should go a way farther. After all, these tunnels must have been built to serve a purpose once.'

'I don't know... 'Tis airless in here,' Thaddeus said, sagging against the wall, knocking loose a shower of dust which set us coughing. 'I'm getting breathless just walking.'

He was correct and Adam agreed.

'Call me coward, if you will,' I said. 'But I think we must go back. There be evil here; I sense it surrounding us. Besides, I do not feel so good.' Only as I spoke the words did I realise it was the case. My head ached and was rapidly filling with cobwebs, making clear thought more difficult by the moment.

'Let's get out of here,' Thaddeus insisted. 'Seb's right. I'm feeling strange too. Come on.'

The bailiff turned his back and began to retrace his steps. He held his torch, ever dimmer now, so it shone upon the wall, searching out the chalk crosses.

Much in need now of fresh air and – in my case – daylight, we went eagerly, although a strange lethargy began to drag at my heels. The others were slowing also and I found myself ahead of them both upon our retreat. Then came disaster.

Of a sudden, I could not see any chalk crosses. I searched the walls, frantic to rediscover our holy guidance. My first panicked conclusion dawned:

'Someone has followed us,' I cried, 'Erasing the marks I made. I know not which way… and what of the one who pursues us? Where is the devil? God save us! What can be done now? We be lost!' My head spun; a flood of despair and dizziness nigh knocked me to the ground as if a flesh and blood assailant attacked me. I wish it had been so. I might defend myself against a fist or a club but against these invisible foes, what could I do?

'On your feet, cousin,' Adam demanded, dragging at my arm. 'Come! We're not done for yet.' He and Thaddeus pulled me upright, though neither man looked much better than I felt. Sweat ran from Adam's face and his skin looked an odd hue in the ever-diminishing torchlight.

'We need to get out before the torches give up.' Thaddeus took a wheezing breath and was next to stumble. It needed all our strength to get him to stand. We were unsteady, staggering against one another like vintners who had garbled their own wares to excess.

'We must have taken a wrong turn,' I gasped. 'So no crosses…

if we keep going… upon an upward slope… we must reach the streets… once more.' I prayed my befuddled mind was making sense enough to get us out of this accursed place. Else we would die, cursed, down here.

Quite how we succeeded in reaching a barrier of splintered planks and managed to break out, into God's own precious daylight, I know not. We threw our fading torches aside, although I saw mine now flared up anew.

Thaddeus fell to his knees, casting up the contents of his belly. Adam lay sprawled flat upon the dirt, gasping like a landed trout, whilst for me the skies revolved and I could not decide which way was up or down. What a trio we were. Fortunately, none were there observing us in our privy hell. Feeling weak and poorly as we did, I expected we must appear parchment-pale, yet the contrary proved true: Adam was rosy-cheeked as a rouged strumpet and the bailiff's face was the hue of a ripe, Kentish cherry. I supposed that I likely looked the same – odd though it was.

Gradually, the world righted itself. Adam and Thaddeus recovered themselves, regained their usual complexions and my wits cleared.

'This cannot be the entrance where we went in,' I said. 'No hovel… no Gawain… and see the Tower? 'Tis much closer here. Do you know where we be, Thaddeus? I do not recognise this place.'

Thaddeus wiped his soiled lips upon his sleeve and looked around.

'This could be St Katherine's Lane, off East Smithfield.' He pointed to a church tower to our right hand. 'That looks to be the tower of St Mary Grace's Abbey, so, behind us…' He turned around, shielding his eyes from the sun, 'That would be St Katherine's Hospital… aye, and you can just glimpse the sparkle of the river beyond, through that stand of elm trees. See?'

'I believe you be correct, my friend. May our Lord Christ be thanked for His great mercy.'

Adam and Thaddeus both crossed themselves and added their 'Amens' to my prayer of thanksgiving.

'Well, that was a wretched and utter waste of our time, wasn't it? I propose we find the nearest decent tavern and find consolation in a gallon jug of best ale.' Adam brightened at the prospect.

'Not until I find poor Gawain. He must be fretting for us by now.'

'I doubt that. Likely he's already found a good dinner somewhere or other, filched a pig's trotter from a cookshop or a juicy bone from a butcher's place. Whatever his case, he's no doubt feeling better than we are. I'm never going into such a hell-hole again, Seb. You were right about that. If ever I'm foolish enough to suggest it, cousin, remind me how we fared this time.'

'Aye,' Thaddeus agreed. 'If any murderers, counterfeiters, rascals and misfits are lying low in there, they're welcome to it. I don't care if they escape justice; I'm not the one to fetch them out. I'll resign as bailiff if the mayor expects me to venture in after them ever again. And God curse the old hag who told us of those tunnels in the first place. I shouldn't be surprised to learn she's a witch, in league with Lucifer's hordes. You said it was the case, Seb, that she had a face covered with warts. Are they not the devil's marks?' He made the sign of the Cross – again.

'Mistress Alder be a washerwoman, not a witch. You saw her at Mallard's Court yourself, Thaddeus, and she admitted to knowing naught of what was in those tunnels. Do not blame her.'

'Perhaps I should arrest her,' Thaddeus suggested.

''Tis not her fault that we nigh came to grief, my friend.'

'No? Mayhap, I'll leave her be, unhindered, for now. If she is a witch…'

'Let sleeping dogs lie,' Adam said. 'A wise decision. Now, what about that ale? I'm parched.'

'Speaking of dogs: I shall search out Gawain first; then join you after,' I said. 'If I may find him…'

'We'll be in the Green Dragon Inn in the Minories,' Thaddeus said, familiar with London's streets through his duties as city bailiff. ''Tis the nearest I know that serves a goodly brew. Food's not bad either and I'm hungry. It must be nigh suppertime.'

'Aye, I know the place,' I said. 'I painted the signboard for it not so long since.'

As I left them to go in search of Gawain, a thunderbolt split the air and the first heavy raindrops landed like stones.

Chapter 18

Friday eve
The Green Dragon Inn, The Minories

THE RAIN pelted down, lightning lit up the sky and thunder growled. I had to drag poor Gawain along all unwilling and whimpering with fear of the storm. The Green Dragon Inn was crowded as every person with the least sense sought shelter. Little wonder that the place was thronged but Adam and Thaddeus had reserved a place for me at their board.

Gawain and I arrived, drenched and dripping like Monday's washing straight out the tub.

'You found him then,' Adam said, giving Gawain a piece of his cheese to cheer the creature after his soaking and divert his thoughts from the claps of thunder.

'Aye. I found him with little trouble, awaiting where we left him, at the other entrance, which was not so far from where we came out. I wonder how many other ways there may be into those tunnels for, clearly, neither be the entrance Mistress Alder described.' Having shaken off as much rain from my cap, hair and jerkin, I sat on the bench beside Adam, accepting gratefully the ale and platter he passed me.

'I'm not convinced the warty old witch told you true anyhow,' Thaddeus said. 'I saw her at Mallard's Court and didn't like the look of her. She's not to be trusted. I doubt this Hamo ever had a forge anywhere near where she sent us. Reckon she put a curse on us too.'

'Of course she did not, my friend. Mistress Alder be a most respectable woman.'

'Her legion warts say otherwise.'

'She cannot help those.' I took a bite of cold mutton, wrapped in bread with a slice of onion, relishing the savoury taste.

'And if she didn't put a curse on us, why did we fall ill of a sudden, all three of us? Answer me that, Seb.'

'Hey, move away,' Adam said, giving me a shove. 'You're making a puddle where you sit, cousin, and now it's soaking into my breeches. I'll look as though I've pissed myself when I stand.'

'Apologies,' I mumbled through a mouthful of food. I used my napkin to mop up the worst of the water off the bench. He should be thankful to have only a wet backside when I was soaked to the skin from head to foot, my soggy clothes clinging to me unpleasantly.

'So what about this wretch, Hamo? Are we going to look elsewhere for him, Bailiff?' Adam asked.

'I shall ask Mistress Alder to take us to the place,' I offered. 'And...'

'Oh, no, Seb. I want naught more to do with her,' Thaddeus said, thumping his fist upon the board to confirm it. 'I'm going nowhere that witch directs. Next you know, she'll turn us into rats and toads to dwell in those damned tunnels 'til the end of our days. No! I forbid you asking her anything.'

'I swear that she be naught of the kind...'

'And you haven't answered my question either. If she's harmless, why did we all get sick but recover once we escaped from her evil labyrinth? I've never felt so like to die any moment. I couldn't catch my breath and neither could you, so don't deny it.'

'I admit, I felt the same, Thaddeus, and cannot explain it. Mayhap, the air was tainted but why should that be Mistress Alder's doing? Foul airs occur without human cause: when the tide goes out, the river oozes its own vile miasmas and we do not blame elderly women for that, do we? Who can tell what horrors lay deeper within those tunnels, giving off some horrid distemper.'

'But I couldn't smell anything but damp and mould. This wasn't foul airs. An enchantment was sapping my strength, moment by moment.'

'I agree with Thaddeus,' Adam said. 'Something unseen was trying to kill us and if that's not witchery, I know not what else it can be.'

'Adam? Are you meaning that you also believe Ralf's woman to be a witch?'

'Well... I don't know, do I? Ralf hasn't come to any harm with her... unless... what of his bent back? Did she lay a curse upon him too?'

'Oh, what a mazy pair you be!' I threw my napkin upon the table, drained my cup and left the bench. 'I ne'er heard such silly childish ramblings and superstitious nonsense from two grown men I accounted rational and sensible. You speak as witless fools. Will you be blaming the untimely storm upon imps and hobgoblins and Adam's wet breeches on a warlock's wiles?'

'Nay, I blame you for that, Seb.' Adam was grinning but I had heard enough.

'Come, Gawain, let us depart this house of madmen. I have better things to do than hear a good woman slandered and accused of malicious deeds and infamy.'

I left the inn to walk home, through the rain, but I was wet already and it fell softly now the worst of the storm was passed. My return from the Green Dragon by the Minories meant that Crooked Lane was not upon my way. Nonetheless, I went there, to Mistress Alder's house, afore my courage failed me; whilst anger yet overrode Adam's and Thaddeus' pervasive superstitions in my head.

The washerwoman greeted me at her door. Her welcoming smile became a look of concern at sight of my half-drowned appearance.

'Come you in, Master Foxley, come you in straight. Let me

fetch you towels. Whatever brings you here in such weather? St Mary be praised, I fetched my dry linen in before the heavens shed their heavy burden. Here. Dry yourself, master.' She gave me two lengths of pristine linen and I set about stemming the small flood of water from my person.

Unfortunately, Gawain did what a wet dog be wont to do: he shook himself from nose to tail with utmost vigour, showering all about – notwithstanding a neatly folded pile of spotless laundry.

'My heartfelt apologies, Mistress Alder,' I said, dragging Gawain further from any other clean items he might despoil. 'I fear my dog has undone your hard work. How may I make amends?'

''Tis but rainwater. It'll dry and little harm done. Now, what you need, master, is a cup of my mead. Take off your cap and jerkin and I'll put them to dry. Then you can tell me why you've come.'

The clothes I could remove were hung to dry but, for decency's sake, I could not sit naked, so my hose and shirt had to dry whilst I wore them. But the mead was warming and my situation not so bad. Over the rim of my cup, I observed the woman as she worked, cutting bread and smearing it with honey. Her warts were undeniable but beneath them, her face was amiable, her mouth a kindly curve, her eyes bright. There was no hint of malice there. Adam and Thaddeus were sorely mistaken. Besides, had she not thanked St Mary for saving her linen from the rain, if not from Gawain's unfortunate ministrations. For a certainty, a witch would not let a saint's name slip from her tongue but choke upon it.

She set the bread and honey before me and bade me eat. I had eaten sufficient at the inn but it would be discourteous to refuse her hospitality.

'So, how may I help you, good master?'

'Much as you did afore, mistress.' I chewed and swallowed, sipping mead to wash down the bread. 'Bailiff Turner, my cousin, Adam, and I attempted to find Hamo's forge, following your instructions. We did not find it.'

'You went in those terrible tunnels? Just three of you? Did I not tell you to take an army?'

'Indeed, you did but since we failed to find him, we were not endangered, not by man, leastwise. However, we all three fell most unwell. We could hardly draw breath enough to escape the darkness. Our torches were dying also.'

'Are you certain you were in the right place? I know there's evil in there but Hamo's never suffered so.'

'Nay, mistress, I be quite uncertain of it. That be my reason for coming to you again. Would you be able to show me the place, forwhy I fear we went astray somehow in following your directions.'

'Never! What if that glary bear is there? I dare not take the risk, master, even for your sake, though I owe you for your goodness to Ralf.'

'You owe me naught, mistress. Ralf works well and more than repays me for having given him employment. But, mayhap, if you cannot show me the right entrance, in person – a reluctance I fully comprehend – you might describe it more precisely for me? You told me it was off Cutpurse Yard, in a passage called Furnace Alley.'

'Aye, so it is. Did you find the hovel that hides the way in?'

'We did. Or rather we found timber palings…'

'Nay. It was once a house, now fallen down, but more than a few planks. Are you sure you was in Cutpurse Yard and followed down Furnace Alley?'

'Well, there was none to ask the name of the place.'

'Did you go by way of Edwin's Alehouse next to the wheelwright's yard and see the ol' granary? It isn't used now 'cos thieves kept helping theirselves and the sacks o' grain got damp but you can still see the hoist for lifting the heavy loads. It sticks out like a broken arm above the door at the head of the steps, though they was wood and mostly rotted away. The granary's in Cutpurse Yard and the alleyway leads off in the opposite corner, half hid by an elder bush. You can't miss it.'

'I fear that we did. I recall neither alehouse, wheelwright, nor granary.'

'Then you was in the wrong place. No wonder you never found him or his forge. Will you try again?'

'In truth, mistress, I know not. None of us be eager to return to those malignant tunnels.'

'Aye, 'tis probably for the best if you don't. I wouldn't want Ralf to lose a second master, 'specially one as good and kindly as you, Master Foxley.'

''Tis generous of you to say, mistress. Now, if I may have my jerkin and cap, I will thank you right heartily for the refreshment and the directions and be upon my way.'

'They won't be dry as yet.'

'No matter. I shall be missed at home as it grows late.'

Saturday, the twenty-sixth day of June
The Foxley House

I had lain abed last night, Gawain snoring at my feet, weighing in the balance the pros and cons of venturing into the tunnels once more. Would either Adam or Thaddeus accompany me, if I dared? Should I even consider going alone? What would I do if Hamo was there? I had no right to arrest any man. What was I thinking? Me versus that huge mountain of strength? Was I quite mad?

By first light, I was dressed and ready to return to that sordid part of London. I had determined my task to find the forge - no more than that. I would confront no man but simply discover and confirm the place, according to Mistress Alder's more exact description, and then inform Thaddeus. He could decide what to do after.

I wrote a note and left it upon the kitchen board, informing the household that I had business to conduct and would be returned for dinner. I went out, armed with an unlit torch, flint, steel and charcloth but naught else. Gawain accompanied me but whether he would have courage sufficient to enter the tunnel, who could say?

Towards certain tunnels beneath the Tower of London

The morn was fresh and clear after yesterday's rain. The sun was yet unrisen but the eastern sky was enrobed golden with promise. The swallows were already swooping above St Paul's and a few early folk set to their daily chores. The proprietor of the Sun in Splendour tavern was washing down his step and hailed me as I passed.

My walk towards my destination was unimpeded by housewives a-marketing, or tradesmen vying for my custom. Thus I made swift progress – mayhap, swifter than I should have liked. It surprised me how easily I found an alehouse and a wheelwright's yard next door. How had we not seen them previously? The alehouse door was yet shut but the wheelwright was preparing for the day. I called out to him and he raised a calloused hand in acknowledgement but spoke not.

A few paces farther and a gap betwixt buildings opened into a court of sorts and there I espied the broken beam of a hoist protruding high above. I had come to the abandoned granary. Mistress Alder had told me true. Across the yard, an elder bush sprouted, lush amid the barren timbers of ramshackle tenements and tumbledown shacks. It seemed to grow from naught but was laden with creamy platters of flowers, struggling valiantly towards the light. Beside it, I turned along a narrow passageway. It looked well-trodden of late, wheel-ruts in the mud indicating a hand cart or barrow had come this way more than once.

At the end of the passage known as Furnace Alley – as I now had no doubt it was – stood the hovel, as described. Its door was but a memory, the remains of its rotted leather hinges hanging as ragged scraps from the jamb. All was dark inside... and silent. But the smell of burnt charcoal and smoke was obvious enough. I had found Hamo's forge. And there was a definite coppery tang also. Unsurprising, I suppose, in a place where metals are worked.

As my eyes grew accustomed to the gloom, I could make out a doorway opposite. I kindled my torch in readiness to enter the Stygian darkness, screwing up my courage.

'Coming?' I whispered to Gawain, wondering whether he would venture or no. I had, of necessity, to hold the torch in both hands as I trembled momentarily. I breathed deep and both hands and flame steadied. 'Come, Gawain. 'Tis not so bad as you fear.'

As I feared.

Except that it was. And worse.

A few yards in, the tunnel turned to the right and I could feel a source of great heat close at hand. The forge was in use, or recently so. I must have a care. Yet I could neither see nor even sense any movement. Perhaps I should leave now. If Hamo was absent but about to return...

At first, I thought the sound was my own heart pounding in my ears. Or Gawain. But then it came again: a moan, a gasping breath.

I eased forward, raising the torch.

'Is s...' I cleared my throat. 'Is someone there?'

No answer came. Then a groan.

'Who be there?' I took another step, squinting into the gloom. Then I saw it: a glint of something bright in the corner. Another rasping breath accompanied the clink of metal, followed by a glittering cascade in the light of my torch, a tumbling rush of metal and an agonised groan.

I had found Hamo the Smith in his own fiery lair 'neath a heap of coin.

Thinking there had been some awful mishap, I moved closer to see. I gasped. This was no mishap. No accident. The poor brute was slumped upon the floor, covered in blood, unable to move. The reason why? His right hand was raised above his head, fixed to a wooden workbench by a large nail, hammered through it. I turned away, sickened by the appalling sight.

'Help... me.'

I swallowed down the bile that rose in my throat and went to him.

'Get... it out,' he pleaded.

I looked about. Tools, unfamiliar to me, lay strewn around, haphazard. I chose something that looked to be for gripping and put my torch in a sconce on the wall. Then, applying all my strength, I attempted to pull out the nail. He screamed. I was too inept with the tools of another man's trade. Nausea threatened again as I felt and heard iron scraping upon flesh and bone.

'I be that sorry but...'

'Pull it out... damn ye.'

I tried again. This time, the nail came free and I stumbled back as he cried aloud.

He lay sprawled, nursing his wounded hand. I knelt beside him.

'I shall fetch aid for you. The wheelwright be nigh at hand. He will help.'

'T' late...'

I would get up to leave but he grabbed my arm with his good hand, pulling me down.

'Don't... go.'

'Who did this to you?'

At first, I feared he would not answer. His breathing rattled; his eyelids fluttered. He was correct: it was too late. Hamo was dying.

'Who did this to you?' I repeated. 'You shall have justice, if you tell me.'

'Bastards… baldsers…'

'Who? Say again.'

'Venisens…'

'Venison? Butchers? Do you mean butchers did this to you? Why would they?'

'Venison,' he repeated. Then he released his hold on my arm and fell limp. Whoever had done this to him, he could not tell of it now.

I stumbled outside, into sweet cool air, shuddering and retching. The sensation of iron pulling through flesh, scraping bone… I heaved again. Gawain whimpered; licked my hand.

''Fear not, lad. I be fine.'

It was not true. Bracing myself against a wall, I got to my feet, unsteady and weak at the knees. Much like yesterday, in some other of the tunnels. Nay. Not so. Rather, the feel of iron in flesh, grating on bone… I could not free myself of that. Looking down, I saw to my dismay the state of my attire. In the gloom, I had not realised but I must have knelt in a pool of blood. Flies were summoned to my hose as apprentices to a dinner bell, swarming, black upon crimson that had once been pale grey kersey. I surely stank like a slaughterhouse. How could I now dare to walk the city streets, clad like a butcher – or a murderer?

I leaned back against the wall and closed my eyes, willing my senses to cease reeling and the earth 'neath my feet to stand firm.

Gawain was barking.

'He's here! I've found him.' Strong arms held me as I lay in the mud. 'Seb! Seb. Wake up, damn it. Speak to me. Where are you hurt? You witless fool, why did you come here alone? Are you knifed?'

'Nay. Not my blood.' I pointed with a wavering finger. 'In there, Adam. Hamo… I found him dying.'

'Someone fetch water or ale to revive him,' my cousin called out.

Faces gathered around, looking down upon me. I could not think how they came to be here: all familiar yet unexpected.

'How did you find me?' I asked.

'Consulted the old witch. How else?'

'She be no such…'

'I know. I know. At least she told us true this time. As soon as I read your note, I guessed what you intended. I gathered a band of doughty fellows, all capable in a fight. Then we asked the old woman. And here we are. That's the story, in short. How long have you lain here?'

'I know not. It was barely dawn when I found this place but then… I cannot think on it, Adam…'

'Take time. Gather your wits. Ah! Ale. Just what you need.'

Of all the folk, the one who brought me ale was most surprising: John Rykener. Of course, he could brawl as well as any man, as my cousin knew to his cost. That he should concern himself to come to my aid… He held the cup to my lips and I drank gratefully.

'Good thing the alehouse is now open,' he said. 'We'll all need a cup when this is done. What say you, Adam?'

'Aye, and Seb can pay the reckoning.'

Rykener laughed that strangely high womanly laugh of his. Over his shoulder, I caught sight of others, milling about, waiting. Stephen Appleyard – strong and trusty. Jonathan Caldicott – my less than trustworthy neighbour but keen enough in a brawl. Bennett Hepton – how did he come to be here? And – could I be mistaken? My brother Jude leaned nonchalantly against the yard wall, inspecting his fingers and admiring his boots. I could well imagine he would have much to say later, concerning the trouble I had caused him; any inconvenience to others accounting for naught.

'The bailiff? Is Thaddeus with you?' I asked Adam when I had drunk some of the ale.

'Jack's gone to fetch him and the constables. Guildhall was out of our way. I didn't dare waste a moment. In truth, I thought we'd find you dead by Hamo's hand.'

Hamo's hand. My belly churned.

'Seb? You've turned waxen pale again. Don't you swoon away a second time. I'm not carrying you home. Finish your ale; it'll steady you.'

'I cannot get it out of my head... what I saw.' Aye, and the rest of that grisly experience. 'Have you ventured within?'

Adam nodded.

'I've seen.'

''Tis as with the others, is it not? Hartnell and Guy Linton... the same.'

'Don't concern yourself now. No doubt Thaddeus will require your story in full when you've recovered.'

I saw in my cousin's eyes, the way he could not face me right squarely but looked askance, he knew something but would not speak of it. What was it that he knew? Was this death different in some way? The accursed nail was the same... I covered my mouth with my hands and squeezed my eyes closed. I must not give in to it...

The Foxley House

My escort home was oddly assorted. Adam remained at Cutpurse Yard, awaiting Jack's return with the bailiff. Bennett Hepton went off to his fishmongering business and Stephen to his carpentry shop. Jonathan Caldicott disappeared into some tavern or other along the way, so I was assisted to Paternoster Row, blood-stained and disgusting, by two of the most finely clad fellows in London: my brother and John Rykener, one on either arm. They feared I would fall, most like, for I was not entirely steady on my feet. Rykener chattered like a monkey all the while, chuckling at his own jests and hailing every other passer-by by name. It seemed he knew more folk in person than

I had e'er met. Many folk stared at the state of me whilst others preferred to avert their gaze hastily and no blame to them.

Jude said naught to anyone but muttered under his breath. His brow was drawn down in a savage scowl; his mouth set straight as a bar. It did not bode well for me. Undoubtedly, I should suffer the full force of his anger soon, may Jesu aid me.

Rose flew to embrace me as I stepped into the kitchen. Her eyes were moist.

'I feared for you so, Seb. When Adam said what he thought your note truly meant, I was frightened of what might happen to you. Ralf told us what a monster this Hamo fellow is.'

'Was. Hamo is no more. There, lass, trouble yourself no longer.' I stroked her back as she held me.

'Oh, but what am I about?' She stood away from me and saw the stains, now drying rust-coloured. 'Are you hurt, my poor dear one? You look pale, indeed. Sit. Sit and let me pour ale for you. All of you,' she added, seemingly noticing Jude and John Rykener for the first time.

'I have taken no hurt, Rose, but I apologise for my pitiful state, my clothes...'

'No matter, so long as you are whole.'

'Thank you,' I said. I did not continue to voice the thought, the relief, the difference betwixt Rose's greeting and the way Emily would have berated and scolded me for my ruined hose. My wife used to have the greatest care for my attire and little to spare for the man who wore them.

Ralf and Kate joined us at the kitchen board, wanting to see for themselves that I was uninjured.

'I don't want to lose another master,' was Ralf's comment when I assured him I was well.

John Rykener made himself at home, admiring the well-organised kitchen, the freshness of new rushes strewn upon the floor and the absence of dust and cobwebs on the beams – such womanly remarks. A strange creature he that could fight as a man but consider aspects of housewifery as a woman.

Jude had yet to speak at all. I thought this an ominous sign. Like a weir holding back floodwater, he would burst forth at some point and, doubtless, I should be the soul engulfed in the tide of his anger, whether deservedly or no.

Thaddeus arrived after dinner – his timing gone awry this once – but it meant I was washed clean and presentable to greet him.

'There was a deal to do,' he explained, 'What with the coroner and the surgeon and the body. You might have spared me the note-taking, Seb, you heartless fellow.'

'You still do not have a clerk to serve you?'

'I've asked but the mayor's secretary says there is no allowance to pay for such a post. What's an over-worked bailiff to do but rely upon his friends? As you did this morn, so I heard, with half of Farringdon and Cheapside wards hastening to aid you. Adam told me what he knows of it whilst we were at the scene but I need your side of the tale too, Seb. I'm sorry but it has to be.'

'Then let us talk in the garden. There be ears I should spare the hearing of the details.'

The air in the garden plot was scented with mint, thyme and lavender. Bees hummed and the hens scratched with little enthusiasm, too hot to labour in their feathered coats. Gawain flung himself down, panting in the shade 'neath the apple tree, having chosen the coolest spot afore we could. I sat upon the grass beside him and Thaddeus joined me, having removed his heavy tabard of office. Rose brought us a jug of elderflower cordial, fresh made and cold from standing in the water trough. In so pleasing a place, it seemed wrong to speak of such matters as I must.

'What came to pass, Seb?' Thaddeus asked when the moment could be delayed no longer. 'Adam said you went back to consult that old woman yesterday?'

'I did. She gave me more ways whereby I might be sure of

finding the correct tunnel, which I did this morn right early, as soon as there was light to see. I wanted it over and done.'

'But you went alone. That was foolish, was it not?'

'I intended only to find the right place and be certain of it. Then I would fetch you, once I knew. I never meant to confront him.'

'So you found the yard, the passageway, the hovel. Why did you go into the tunnel?'

'I yet had no firm evidence that the forge was there within until I saw it. I smelled smoke but that could have come from a cooking fire. Once I had seen the truth of it – the furnace still hot and glowing – I turned to leave. But then I heard it.'

'Go on.'

'A man groaning in pain. I held the torch high. It was hard to make out anything in that gloomy, smoky lair.' I breathed deep, sipped the refreshing cordial and described to Thaddeus what I had found – every ghastly detail.

At some point, Jude came, bringing a cup and a stool from the kitchen to avoid grass stains upon his hose. He helped himself to cordial but did not interrupt.

'Could the fellow speak?' Thaddeus asked. 'Did he say anything to you before he died?'

'A few words. Naught that made sense.'

'Anything may help us find these damnable killers, Seb. Tell me what he said.'

'He said "bastards." That word seemed clear enough but does not help. Then he repeated it, or near enough, saying "baldsters" or "butchers" or some such, for butchery was what they did, most certainly. But he was fading. Likely he was slurring his words and meant "bastards", as afore. Then he repeated the word "venison" twice over, making a plural of it the second time: "venisons". I asked him what he meant but he was gone. I fear I cannot see that this assists us in any way, Thaddeus.'

'I believe it does,' Jude said, finding words to say at last. 'Not "venisons"; he meant Venetians. And not "baldsters", or whatever you think you heard, little brother. Baldesis is what he said.'

'Why would you think that?' Thaddeus asked him. 'You weren't there. How would you know?'

'Because it makes bloody sense; that's why.'

Chapter 19

Saturday eve
The Foxley House

THADDEUS STAYED to supper forwhy our discussion concerning Hamo's last words continued at length.

Jude told us of things he had learned in Firenze and Venezia in Italy – terrible things. Italy, he said, was run by the great banking families: the de' Medicis and the Frescobaldis in Firenze, the de' Medicis and their cousins, the Baldesis, in Venezia. Those who defaulted on their debts owed to these families went in fear of being 'nailed by the hand' and, if payment was not forthcoming after that, they could expect to be gutted like a Martinmas pig and left to die.

'So that's what they did to this damned fellow that you found, little brother,' Jude went on. 'And trust you to kneel in his spilled guts and ruin a perfectly good pair of hose. You've been in more scrapes than a parchment skin and, as usual, *I* have to rescue you. Don't know how you bloody survived in my absence.'

'I knelt in… Oh, merciful Jesu, spare me.' I felt the blood drain from my face but I would not swoon again. 'It was dark in there… I did not see…' So that was how this most recent murder differed from the others. I was glad I had not seen this detail.

Thaddeus spared me the worst of the moment by enquiring of Jude:

'Why don't the authorities stop them? I thought Venice had

271

a duke or someone to govern there.'

'The Doge, aye. They elected Giovanni Mocenigo to office last year, for life, and if he wants it to be a long one… Who do you think chooses and governs the Doge? The Baldesis. Money is power there, as anywhere, and the money lies in their hands. The Doge is in debt to them, like all the rest. He does as he's bloody told; else he'll suffer the same.'

'And you believe the Baldesis have committed these murders, here, in our own fair city?' My friend sounded both incredulous and affronted. 'How dare those devilish foreigners?'

'The nail in the hand is their mark of trade, as we have the Fox's Head. But you said, didn't you, little brother, the others were tortured?'

I nodded.

'Well, they likely got the information they wanted and traced a path back to the smith.'

'Mm, so they may have but they didn't get the man behind this counterfeit coin business. We did. Clement Mallard is in custody, telling all in the vain hope of saving his scrawny neck.'

'Thaddeus? You ne'er told me,' I said.

'Didn't have the chance, did I? Yestereve, he confessed his guilt concerning the false coin, all the while declaring he had naught to do with the murders. I believe he speaks truly. He admits that he lent sums of money to Hartnell, Linton and others he refused to name but, in each case, about one-third of the coin lent was counterfeit. Then he would demand payment of the sum wholly in true sterling, making a great profit. My investigations reveal that both victims had also borrowed money from others, often as not, simply to pay off debts elsewhere.'

'If they had borrowed from the Baldesis also,' I said, my wits sharper now, 'They may well have been repaying those debts, in part at least, with Mallard's false coin. The bankers would be losing money, finding their coffers refilling with counterfeit. They would likely know who had repaid them falsely and want to punish the offenders, torturing them to learn the source.'

'Almost doing my task for me but in the most brutal and criminal fashion.' Thaddeus tugged at his earlobe. 'We cannot let them continue in this way yet on what grounds can I arrest them? I have no evidence that the Baldesis are committing murders within my jurisdiction.'

'I doubt they are,' Jude said. 'They wouldn't do their own dirty work. They'd employ lesser folk to get their hands bloody. I wouldn't waste my time trying to prove them guilty, if I were you.'

'But Hartnell and Linton deserve justice. As does that wretch, Hamo, in truth,' Thaddeus protested.

I agreed with him. Such outrages should not go unpunished. Jude did but shrug.

'That's how it goes in Venezia,' he said. 'Naught you can do about it. It's the way it is with the likes of these banking families. I should know; being bloody married to them.'

'Then, mayhap, you could find out more… get proof of their involvement in these crimes.'

'Do I look like a bloody fool? Or a man eager to embrace an assassin's blade? Unlike you, little brother, I have more sense. You have to learn to let matters lie. Not every wasp nest needs poking. Not every midden has to be disturbed so you can test its foulness. You're a bloody idiot, Seb. Always were; always will be. That you've lived this long is a miracle.'

'By Jesu's mercy, I have. But you say, Jude, that the de' Medicis in – where was it? – Firenze? They do like the Baldesis?'

'So I've heard. Not that I've seen for myself. Why do you ask?'

''Tis just that the king's book, our great commission, be intended as a royal gift to a certain Lorenzo de' Medici in Florence. Is it the case that we be making so fine a piece for a murderer?'

Jude laughed and clapped me heartily upon the back.

'Does your delicate conscience prick you, if you are? What do you care who has your work, so long as you get paid for it?'

'If, indeed, we do… get paid, I mean.'

'The king will pay his bloody reckoning, surely? Duke Richard always does, as we well know. If the king doesn't settle his accounts, then why should anyone else ever feel obliged to?'

'Ah, now, Jude, 'tis you who be the innocent. Ask of any London merchant who supplies the Crown. They all complain in like wise: delayed payment, reduced payment, or sometimes naught at all. King Edward seems to think that royal favour be good enough; the honour of doing him service be sufficient recompense, though how that might put food upon a man's board or a shirt upon his back, the Exchequer does not explain. I hope for payment but my expectations be small.'

'If he doesn't pay you, then you must refuse ever to work for him again: no more royal commissions.'

'Refuse the king? You think I would dare?'

'I bloody would. Work for nothing? Why should I? Why should any right-minded man? You must turn down any future royal commissions, at least until the full cost of the present work is settled, else you'll be the one in debt to bloody usurers and bankers. I don't want to find you nailed to your desk in the workshop, your guts strewn on the floor.'

I cringed in horror at the prospect and felt my blood run chill. Mayhap, Jude was correct, this once.

'Well!' Thaddeus brought our morbid deliberations to an abrupt end and got up off the grass, brushing down his breeches. 'I don't think I need detain you further, Seb. If you could oblige me by putting all this in writing, I shall be grateful.'

'How much do you pay my brother for his services as clerk?' Jude asked, unexpectedly.

'I, er...'

'Even bloody tight-arsed Coroner Fyssher used to pay us sixpence a day for our note-taking and report writing.'

'I do it as a favour for Thaddeus as my good friend, *gratis,* when he be hard-pressed. I do not expect coin for it,' I said, hastening in defence of the bailiff.

'Then no wonder your damned purse is ever empty, little

brother. You're the biggest bloody fool in Christendom.' Jude also rose. 'However, I've got more important matters for a Saturday eve: wine jugs to drink dry and a wife to fuck. So, if you need me, you can likely find me at the Sun in Splendour, but only if it's a matter of life and death. Any lesser reason and you'll suffer my great displeasure and a soundly kicked arse. You have been duly warned.'

'The Sun in Splendour? Have you lodged there this while?' I asked. 'I was searching all over for you… all your haunts of old. And there you rest in the newest place.'

'That's where Adam found me and Rykener breaking our fast this morn and dragged us off to save your bloody skin – again. Me and Chesca will be there for another week or so yet, I dare say.'

I struggled to my feet to bid farewell to Jude and Thaddeus. Gawain did likewise.

'Give my kind regards to Mistress Foxley,' I heard Thaddeus say to my brother as they both left by way of our side gate.

It sounded strange: a reference to Mistress Foxley who was not Emily.

'I intend to give the wench a deal more than that,' Jude replied and laughed.

I gathered up the discarded cups and the empty jug and returned them to the kitchen.

'Nessie, there yet be a stool 'neath the apple tree. If you would please to fetch it in when you go shut up the henhouse for the night.'

She grumbled at my request. No precise words but a muttering and a sullen look, as though I had demanded some great unreasonable labour of her.

I said naught concerning her discourtesy but set down the cups and jug upon the board and returned to the garden to accomplish the task myself. Emily would not have done so but rather taken her broom to Nessie's behind. As I set the stool in its place by the board, Rose came down the stair, smiling.

'Little Dickon is sleeping like an angel, if you wish to go kiss him and bless him, Seb,' she said.

Seeing her sweet, gentle face, of a sudden, I felt a longing to kiss, not my son's cheek but her lips. Fool! Fool! I berated myself. You cannot. 'Tis not seemly for a widower of hardly two months standing.

It was as well that Nessie was there in the kitchen, a presence to temper my sinful desire.

Instead, I mounted the stair and went into the back bedchamber, Rose and Kate's room, where my son slumbered in his cradle in the corner. I sat upon the end of the bed and watched him sleep. So innocent. So dear. Rose cared for him lovingly, as if he were her own child. She cared for me, also, as I now realised. And I for her. Might we e'er be more than simply members of the same household, living 'neath the same roof? Could we be a true family some day? Were my growing feelings for her true? Or did I just want someone to fill the hole in my life left by Emily's passing and to be a mother to my children? Was it too soon to know for certain? So many questions whirled in my head.

'I would have your opinion, little one, if only you might speak.' I stroked his dark hair from his brow, ran my finger down his perfect cheek. 'What would you have Papa do, eh? You have a fond affection for her, as I do, I see that. But could it be more? Could you love her as your mother? Could I...'

I sighed and shook my head, then leant over the cradle and kissed his forehead. 'Think on it, my dear son. I would know your wishes. Sleep sound, little one.' I made the sign of the Cross over him. 'May the Lord Jesu bless you and keep you in safety through this night and always.' I blew out the candle and left him to his dreams.

I had another matter to attend, one I had nigh forgotten: choir practice. And I was late. The precentor would be wrathful. He be a hard man to please. We had two events of importance: the morrow, being the closest Lord's Day to the feast of the martyred saints, Peter and Paul, the latter being the cathedral's own patron, a special High Mass would be celebrated in the presence of Bishop Kempe. And then upon Tuesday next, the feast day itself, another High Mass and, so rumour ran, King Edward himself was to attend.

The precentor had instructed me a few weeks ago as to the pieces he required of me, insisting my attendance at practices was in no way to be shirked. Yet I had missed one or two, *mea culpa*. He would ne'er forgive me if I missed this day's final rehearsal. Thus, I made haste across the street to Paul's, at once cheered at the prospect of singing but wary of the precentor's ire.

Sunday, the twenty-seventh day of June
St Michael le Querne Church

Jude brought Chesca to St Michael's for Low Mass. I was pleased to see that he made the effort, if only to avoid the fines and penance that might be due, if he did not.

Dame Ellen and her fellow matrons made much of Chesca, welcoming her to the parish as the goodwife of Jude Foxley. I believe they hoped my errant brother was tamed at last. Father Thomas said the like to me as I craved his blessing at the porch upon leaving after the office was done.

'She's very young, this Francesca-Antonia,' Dame Ellen said, coming to join me as I paid my Lord's Day's respects at Emily's graveside. She nodded approval as I lay a posy of rosemary and lavender at the foot of the wooden marker. 'You think she'll do him any good, Sebastian? Where did he find her? She's not English born, is she? Where does she hale from? Not France, I trust? I wouldn't want their sort as my neighbour.'

'Fear not, good dame. She comes from Venezia – Venice, as we say. But, aye, I agree she seems over young but a determined lass nonetheless. She knows her own mind, I assure you.'

'She'll need to, to keep your brother in good order. Do you think she'll succeed? Of course, if he'd had any sense of honour and decency, he would have wed Rose a twelvemonth since. Now she would make any man a worthy wife. But this mere chick… what's she to do with a wayward arrow like him? Does she have a craft of her own? Can she cook, sew and keep accounts?'

'I be certain she can do the last, being a banker's daughter, if e'er there be any money to keep account of.'

'Ah! So that's the way of it, then.' Dame Ellen sounded as one who had received a great revelation. 'I bid you good day, Sebastian.' With that, the elderly woman bustled off to find her friends and advise them of this new intelligence.

No matter, I had made known neither privy secrets nor confidences.

'Go with God's grace, Dame Ellen,' I called after her afore resuming my contemplation and soul-searching at my wife's grave. But I received no better answer from my departed spouse than I had from my little son last night.

Mayhap, I should enquire of Jude. After all, it would be courteous to ask of him who had once been Rose's intended, though he had relinquished all rights to her by his marriage to Chesca. In truth, Adam might better advise me but Jude was still my brother, more fully my flesh and blood. Was I thus obliged to consult with him? I supposed that was the case.

I looked about the churchyard for him. Was this as good a time as any to discuss such a delicate matter with him? Everything was questions, questions, questions. But I saw him stepping into the street with Chesca on one arm and his new friend, John Rykener, upon the other. I determined that this was not the time, not with such company close by. I should have to maintain my patience a while and seek out my brother later. Upon the morrow, mayhap? I could not be easy, fretting so. I had to talk to someone.

St Paul's Cathedral

At home, I donned my chorister's gown and kerchief and scurried to St Paul's. The precentor was already shouting at the youngsters, bewailing their poor efforts at the scales to warm their voices on this special day.

'The Bishop wants to hear music, not this dreadful caterwauling.'

I looked at the lads' scrubbed faces: some angelic – like Will Thatcher that we had rescued not so long ago - others full of mischief. In either case, none were much put out by the precentor's complaints, they being accustomed to the tradition. I joined them, receiving a scowl for my tardy arrival but no comment.

We went in procession leading the ageing Bishop of London, his gold-trimmed vestments sparkling in the sunlight as we made our way across the precinct, through the crowds in their Sunday best but as dull as sparrows in comparison to his bejewelled mitre and flowing cope. The nave was thronged with congregants for this celebration of London's own saint, hot and wreathed in the blue smoke of incense. Their chattering stilled as we processed up the central aisle, led by the great gold Cross and acolytes. First, the young choristers, then the canons; I followed behind them, the precentor after me with the dean and chapter at his back. And lastly came Thomas Kempe in all his glory. Arthritic and creaking as he was, nonetheless, he knew right well how to put on a magnificent show.

In due course, my moment came when I stood in the chancel beyond the rood screen and sang my *Jubilate* with all my heart and soul. None in the congregation in the nave could see who sang but they would hear me and, I hoped, rejoice in the wondrous anthem as I did. After my opening solo, the rest of the choir joined in, like the angelic Host of Heaven, praising God. But the high point, literally, was my opening of the *Gloria,* a difficult piece with its rising crescendo to a top note that I doubted myself every time I could reach. But I did, confounding the precentor's expectations and fear of my failure. It was well done, though only I say so. The precentor would ne'er admit as much.

As we recessed, I caught sight of Adam above the heads of others, grinning at me. And Jude also. The rest were likely there but hidden from view, being not of so tall a stature. I hoped Rose had heard me. Rose. I confess, my singing had been for her as much as for the Almighty. I should beseech forgiveness for my sin.

Smithfield

When dinner was done – I complimented Rose upon a fine repast but, in truth, I do not recall what I consumed nor how it tasted – I took little Dickon to the Horse Pool at Smithfield. I sat him upon my shoulders. To hear him chuckling there on high was a joy, despite the handfuls of hair I might lose to his tight grasp.

Adam came with me, his longbow in hand. He had archery practice to attend at the eastern end of Smithfield by Aldersgate but, for some cause, he chose to accompany me by way of Newgate instead, although it made for a longer walk.

'What's amiss with you, Seb?' he asked, pulling at my sleeve.

'Amiss? Naught at all. Why?'

'Forwhy I've been speaking to you all this time, complimenting you on your fine voice earlier, and you ignore me like a deaf man. Clearly, your mind is elsewhere, upon other things. So, what's amiss, I ask again.'

'I have much to think on is all.'

'Not still worrying at those murders like a wormed tooth, are you? We've done our best with that business. Leave it to the bailiff now.'

'I was not thinking of that at all.'

'What then? It fills your head to the banishment of all else, whatever it is.'

'I cannot speak of it, for the present, at least. When I have determined my own heart, then I may tell you. But not yet.'

'Your own heart, eh? Well, the rest of us know full well where that lies.'

'You do not. I hardly know myself.' I made to stride away in protest but he caught me.

'Seb, dear cousin.' Adam turned me to face him and refused to allow me by. 'When that blind and witless heart of yours finally realises it belongs to Rose and hers to you, then we can have a sensible conversation concerning it.'

'You know? But I ne'er said a word about…'

'You don't have to. It's writ plain enough in your every glance and gesture towards her. For pity's sake, kiss her, embrace her and spare us all the suspense. You know you want to.'

'But does she? Besides, Emily be so lately departed. 'Tis too soon to be seemly.'

'Rose would wed you tomorrow, you know that.'

'Do I?'

'She loves you, Seb. I've known that since I came to dwell with you. At first, I hoped that she might think I would make a fine husband but swiftly realised my mistake. She would rather remain unwed than leave you.'

'But she was supposed to marry Jude.'

'And you think she was distressed when that didn't come to pass? Not at all. She was much relieved, cousin. And now you are no longer tied to Em, well… I can guess at her thoughts, if you can't.'

'Is it that you believe Rose loves me?'

'Always has, by my reckoning. She's likely waiting for you to realise the same.

'But…'

'No buts, Seb. I've got archery to attend and you've got the little fellow to entertain now we've straightened out the great matter that bewildered you so. Go to, cousin, enjoy your afternoon.'

And I did so with a light heart and a smile so broad it caused my jaw to ache. But I cared not.

The Sun in Splendour Tavern

They insisted that I went, Adam and Ralf, though I protested our purses could hardly bear the cost of an evening of drinking and wassail. And upon the Lord's Day 'twas improper, if few concerned themselves for such proprieties these days.

I discovered we had been invited by my brother – yet replete with coin by some means it was better not to investigate too nearly – and he was buying both the wine and ale for his guests. This generosity was so unlike Jude, I suspected some other reason beyond apparent conviviality. I was not mistaken.

I had consumed but half a cup of ale when that reason was made clear.

'Give us a song, little brother. I had almost forgotten your solitary saving grace, that you're the finest songster in London. Come now. Chesca wouldn't believe that it was you, doing the *Gloria* and the rest behind the screen. I promised her you'd sing to us in person and prove it. What will you give us? Something lively, eh?'

'I should have known you had some sly motive.'

'Now, Seb, you know you love to show off your talent. Look at the audience you have.' He swung his arm, gesturing to the tavern's legion customers. 'I told everyone you would entertain us this eve. You don't want to bloody disappoint them, do you?' He nudged me and whispered: 'I'll pass your cap around, earn us some silver and we can share the profits.'

'Not working on the Lord's Day! Jude, you cannot.'

'I'll keep it all then, if you're so fearful of offending. What will you sing? Stand on that bench so everyone can see you.'

'Jude, do not use me as your dancing bear, your performing monkey...'

'Oh, just get on with it and sing, damn it.' He turned to face those gathered. 'Harken all!' he cried. 'My little brother, whose fine voice sang the anthems in Paul's this morn, is eager to give you an evening of song. What say you? Shall he sing for you?'

'Yea! Yea!' The word rang out.

I was sore reluctant and about to refuse but then I saw Rose come into the tavern and find her place with Adam and Chesca. Oh well, mayhap, if I did not approve of earning money on a Sunday, I yet could sing solely to please the dearest of women with an easy conscience and if others heard, then so be it.

'Sing *The Nut-brown Maiden*, that always goes down well,' Jude said in my ear as he assisted me up onto a firm bench.

'Nay, not that. 'Twas my song to Emily. I shall not sing that again.' I steadied myself and breathed deep.

'*The Chaste Wife*, then. Everyone loves that.'

'Too lewd for the Lord's Day.'

'What of it. For Christ's sake, sing something. I promised them.'

So I sang of *The Wandering Minstrel* whose harp was his only love. A plaintive air and naught bawdy about it. The applause was sincere but muted.

'Sing us the one about the ploughman ploughing his fine furrow,' someone shouted.

I thought on it a moment. It was a seemly ballad. So I sang of the fellow who impressed his sweetheart with the straightest furrow, ploughed so deep, and his good seed sown abroad, fertile and sprouting. Why did they laugh and cheer so? I could not see why a hard-working husbandman toiling in his fields was a cause for such mirth. But the company loved it, clapping and stamping their feet in approval. Who was I to argue?

Jude handed me a cup to refresh myself.

'Thought you disapproved of such songs on a Sunday.'

'Such songs? *The Ploughman's Lay* be decorous enough.'

My brother burst out laughing and turned back to the audience.

'What shall you hear next?' he asked, still chuckling. My brother's humours oft eluded my understanding.

As I was singing a merry song about a foolish cobbler who dreamt he was a king, standing on the bench, I could see over the crowd towards the tavern door. It stood open to the warm twilight airs and beyond, outside in the street, I thought I saw shadows moving. Three dark shapes outlined against the paler stone of the building across the way. They did not behave like respectable citizens going home. I could but say they lurked. But I forgot them right swiftly in the loud cheers and cries of 'More!' and 'Sing another!' ringing out as I ended and reached for the ale cup.

The evening ended and I was much wearied with all that singing and would go home to my bed. But Jude had other concerns in mind.

'Come up to our chamber, Seb. Chesca will be sleeping soon enough. We can talk. I have things that need to be said. We haven't had the time 'til now. We can share wine, if the taverner will oblige at this hour.'

'I be that tired, Jude. Can it not wait until the morrow? As it stands, I shall be walking home in the dark and without a torch, risking the Watch questioning me, taking me for a hedge-breaker up to no good.'

'Then stay the night. We'll find you a pillow. After all, what've you got to go home to but a bloody empty bed, now the Moody Mare's not there, waiting to scold you at every turn? I'll wager, you're secretly pleased at your release from the serfdom of husbandhood.'

'How can you suggest it… and do not call her so.' Jude could rouse my anger as none else ever did and, perhaps, the more so forwhy there was an element of truth to his words, though I hardly dared admit it, even to myself. 'I shall leave now.'

But Jude took my arm in a strong grip.

'Come, little brother. I need your aid.'

'If 'tis money you want, do not ask. My coffers, my purse and the aumbry be all empty, as you know full well. I have naught left to live by, thanks to you. Let go my arm.'

But he kept hold, such that to pull away might tear my sleeve.

'Please, Seb. Please stay.'

It was a rare word indeed upon my brother's lips but 'twas rather the look in his eye that persuaded me. Desperation.

Chapter 20

Sunday eve, late
The Sun in Splendour Tavern

SO I stayed as Jude had asked. The chamber above the taproom at the Sun in Splendour was newly appointed with crimson hangings. It had two window casements and both stood open to the star-studded night. We sat over a wine jug by one window, without troubling to light a taper, the stars giving light enough for conversation. Whilst Chesca slept in the canopied bed, we talked of this and that, as brothers do. It had been a long time – years, mayhap – since we last spoke together in this manner. He told me more of his travels to distant lands. I told him of doings in London and our business prospects since his departure at the end of summer last. Yet none of these were the weight upon his mind.

'What did you wish to speak of to me, truly?' I asked, for the drink and weariness pressed upon my eyelids and I feared to fall asleep afore he said his piece.

'Oh, not much.' He shrugged as if he could hardly recall so small a matter now that he had the opportunity to tell of it.

'In which case, I have a subject to raise with you, Jude. It concerns Rose… she who was once your intended.'

'I bloody know who she is. And if you're going to tell me you fancy bedding her yourself, I say go to, little brother. It's about time you fucked a good woman. You don't need my permission.' Jude grinned hugely and poured yet more wine.

Outside, in the yard below, a dog barked and was swiftly silenced.

''Tis not like that. Why do your thoughts ever take the most sordid path?'

'Human nature. A man's natural urges.'

'When my twelvemonth of mourning be done, I would ask Rose to be my wife. I thought to tell you out of courtesy.'

'Can you wait so bloody long? I know you're more a monk than a man but...'

''Tis expected.'

'Must you do as everyone expects? You can swive the lass before you wed her, surely? But, is it that you're not certain she's of a like mind? Does she fancy a skinny pea-stick like you for a husband? Or has she a line of other handsome fellows queuing at the door? Is that it, little brother? You fear your bloody rivals will get in her bed before you? You want me to fend them off, chase them away for you?'

'Nay, Jude. My life be not as yours – '

There came a crash, a splintering of wood, then another. A man leapt through the open window, flinging me aside, overturning wine cups, stools and everything. The other window was likewise ill-used.

The two men seized Jude, wrestling with him just as a third barged through the door. Jude yelled and kicked out.

Chesca woke up, screaming.

I picked up a stool and swung it at the man who was twisting Jude's arm and dragging him against the shattered casement. The stool caught him on the shoulder and he let go of my brother and came at me, snarling, wielding a hammer. I brandished the stool and lashed out again, missing. He advanced, the hammer held high. As it came down, aimed at my head, I thrust out the stool, which took such a blow, the seat cracked and my arm shuddered with the force of it. I stumbled and fell. He advanced. The hammer rose again, his face flooded with murderous intent. I saw my death reflected in his eye.

I know not how but I gathered my legs 'neath me and threw myself forward. He struck out at me. But I caught him a lucky blow with the stool and he fell back, bleeding from a gash across his forehead. The hammer fell with a clang and I swooped to pick it up. It was a heavy weight in my right hand, a good weapon, and the stool to serve as my shield.

The other man loomed over Jude, wrenching him in an agonising grip from behind.

My brother dared not struggle for a long blade gleamed in the starlight, held at his throat. I watched, horrified, as his blood trickled darkly against the pale skin of his exposed neck.

'Put hammer off, or he die.'

From the corner of my eye, I saw the first man recovering, getting to his feet.

Chesca was still screaming.

But it was my brother's terror-stricken face that spurred me on.

No marksman I, this had to be accurate. I threw the hammer at the face of Jude's assailant. It hit him full square. He released hold of my brother and crumpled like an empty grain sack. The knife dropped from his grasp and skittered across the floor, disappearing 'neath the bed, out of reach.

Jude was upon him in an instant, removing the fellow's belt and using it to bind him to the foot of the bed afore leaping to Chesca's aid. Not that she was in need of it. The lass fought like a demon in a flurry of bedcovers, her assailant writhing and smothered beneath them.

I trussed up the half-stunned man, the one I had caught with the stool, as if he were a Christmas goose, taking Jude's example and using the wretch's own belt. He groaned and cursed. At least I had not slain him. Concerning the other, I was less certain, for his face was a mask of blood, black in the gloom, pooling on the woven rug. He lay still. I knew not if he breathed.

By the time the taverner, his wife, the tapster and the potboy, roused from slumber by the din, came hastening and squawking into the chamber like fox-fearing hens, it was all over.

I righted the stool – my sturdy defender, now split – and collapsed upon it. Then I saw a small object lying on the floor. It was an iron nail and I had seen its like three times previously.

It was a long night.

The man I had swiped at with my trusty stool would survive with a few bruises and stitches to the gash on his brow. The one who had held a knife to Jude's throat was less fortunate. The hammer had broken the socket of his eye. There was a deal of blood and the eye was likely blinded. But I felt neither remorse for my deeds nor the least compassion for the outcome. Let them suffer who had dared threaten my brother.

The third assailant, the one who had come through the door and attacked Chesca, suffered worst. It seemed our feisty Venetian lass went to bed armed with a stiletto – a lethal narrow-bladed dagger hid 'neath her pillows. She had used it to defend herself with considerable efficiency and the bedsheets were now gory and slashed, bearing witness to a ferocious fight. The wretch might not recover from his wounds, so Surgeon Dagvyle warned. If he succumbed, Coroner Fyssher would have to be involved, unfortunately.

Jude and I had no liking for Fyssher, having worked as his clerk, each in turn, and learned of his slapdash, heartless and idle ways in dealing with such cases. Chesca's defence would fall to us, if the fellow died.

I was deep in sleep upon my stool, leaning back against the wall, when someone shook me awake.

'Seb, wake up! How can you sleep with this turmoil all around you?'

I forced my eyes open reluctantly. The chamber was ablaze with daylight, too bright for my aching head. I never was a wine-drinker.

'Thaddeus? God be thanked that you're here; not Fyssher.'

'Aye, well, he might have to be summoned yet. But Dagvyle

wants to tend to your hurts now.'

'My hurts? I have none.'

Thaddeus raised my right arm and showed me a long, bloodied rip in my sleeve. I had been unaware of it. Then he touched my cheek and his thumb came away crimson. I realised my face was sore.

'My brother and Chesca?'

'Both safe. Like you, they have cuts and bruises. Jude complains loudest about his ruined doublet but his neck will heal without a scar, Dagvyle says.'

I sat quietly whilst the surgeon cleansed my injury with wine, stitched the cut, smeared it with honey and bound it in clean linen. He bathed my face and picked out splinters from my cheek, likely from the shattered casement when the men broke in. He gave me some ointment to apply myself, as needed.

The taverner announced that we could break our fast downstairs. But first, I bade the potboy go to my home, to inform Rose and Adam of my whereabouts and that I was quite safe. I feared the gossipmongers might already have spread abroad tales of murder and mayhem at the Sun in Splendour and would not have them worrying without cause. Emily ever used to berate me for not telling her where I was or what I was doing. Belatedly, I had learned my lesson.

'Go to the bookshop at the sign of the Fox's Head across the way, if you will,' I instructed the lad. 'Assure them all be well with Seb Foxley, his brother, Jude, and his sister-by-marriage.' I gave him my last halfpenny and told him to hasten. 'I hope you can afford to pay for breakfast,' I said to Jude. 'That be my last coin.'

'Don't know why you bloody wasted it. You could've shouted your message from here and they would've heard.'

'Aye, likely you be correct.'

Jude made to go down to the taproom, though I was unsure whether I wanted food. Rather, I enquired of the surgeon if he had a remedy for an aching head. He was then much concerned that I might have taken a blow to my skull. I told him, I thought not. I did not want to confess my wine-sodden brain for fear my testimony might be doubted when I answered the bailiff's questions later.

'I hardly credit what I did,' I admitted to Jude as he munched oatcakes beside the empty hearth in the taproom.

'What did you do? Last I saw, you were hiding behind a bloody stool.'

'But I… no matter. At least you came through it whole.'

'Whole? Have you seen the state of my best doublet? Ruined! And I have more bruises than time to count them. And the taverner expects me to pay for the wrecking of his bloody chamber. How am I to pay for that?'

'With the money you received from my singing last eve?'

'You jest, little brother. What do you suppose bought the jug of wine you were guzzling, eh? There might be a few pence left to pay for these oatcakes – and for the saints' sake, bloody eat some of them.' He pushed the platter towards me. 'Otherwise, I'm penniless as you are.'

'Who were they, Jude?'

'Who?'

'Those men, of course. They came for you, did they not?'

'They attacked you, too.'

'Only because I was there.' I bit into an oatcake and realised I was hungry. 'Likely, they believed you and Chesca would be sleeping, since we lit no candle. They intended to murder you in your bed, if not Chesca also. Who were they? And do not say you know not. This once, do not lie to me, Jude.'

'When do I ever?'

'Constantly. Now tell me the truth.'

'You slander me, little brother.'

''Tis no slander, unless it be false. Cease avoiding my question.'

Jude looked away, anywhere but at me. Then he spoke but so softly I had to lean close across the board to hear him.

'They were Baldesi henchmen.'

'I knew it.'

'Shh. Keep your voice down. I've been avoiding them for a week past.'

'They came armed with a hammer and nail. Did you know that?'

'I saw the hammer. Seemed an odd choice of weapon.'

I took the iron nail from my purse, where I had put it for safekeeping. I held it out to him in the palm of my hand. He did not touch it but looked at me with an appalled expression.

'They were going to nail your hand, just as they did with the others. Why? Did you also owe them money and repay them with false coin?'

'I wouldn't borrow from the bloody Baldesis if they were the last money-lenders on earth. I'm not bloody stupid.'

'So, if not money, there be only one other reason: Chesca. Tidings of what came to pass when you eloped with her from Venezia must have reached her relatives in London by now. Tell me, Jude. Forwhy, if that be the case, your life may yet be hazard.'

'Don't say that. What am I to do? That's what I wanted to talk to you about last night but I couldn't find the words… then it was too bloody late. They must have found out; discovered who I am. They've been following me. I don't know what to do for the best any longer. You've got to help me, Seb. I reckon I'm safe for a while with those bastards all in a sorry state but the Baldesis can afford to pay others.'

I almost told Jude he should have thought of that afore he stole Chesca away from her family, under cover of night. But it was too late to point that out now. It could not be undone.

'I cannot promise you any miracles but I shall make enquiries. I think you must be prepared to leave London though, for a while, at least. Would you be willing to work?' I chewed thoughtfully, attempting to recall the details of something I had overheard during a recent meeting of the guild at Stationers'

Hall in Amen Lane.

'Work?' He voiced the word as if it were a foreign tongue to him. 'What sort of work? The bloody guild banned me, if you recall?'

'Aye, which be why I can but enquire. At the last guild meeting, Master Collop said...'

'He that bloody banned me!'

I ignored his exclamation.

'Master Collop said he had received a request from Westminster. From the king's French-Italian Secretary, no less. The office deals with correspondence in those tongues particularly and a senior clerk there has died recently. They be asking for a likely replacement but, thus far, though a few know French, none with any knowledge of Italian has come forward. If I could persuade Master Collop that you would not bring the guild into disrepute, as you did afore, he might see fit to reinstate you and recommend you at Westminster. If your language skills be good enough? You may find safety at the king's court, you and Chesca. The Baldesis would not dare to attack you there, in a palace full of guards, with courtiers thronging every passageway and chamber. What say you? Shall I make enquiry?'

'I'd owe you a favour, Seb, if you did.'

'You owe me a tally's-worth of favours already. What matters one more betwixt us? I shall do what I may. Meanwhile, you best find somewhere to hide. Mayhap, Dame Ellen would give you sanctuary in our old lodgings. I believe they stand empty at present.'

'Take Chesca to that poky little hole?'

'I think safety be more important than comfort this once. Chesca will understand.'

'You don't know her.'

'True. But if lives – yours and hers – depend upon it...'

The Foxley House

Having eaten and taken the headache remedy, I went home. Thaddeus would know where to find me when he wished to question me but I hoped he might allow me pause to recover fully. Despite having slept upon the stool, I yet felt worn to the bone. Fighting for my life was not a common occurrence, Jesu be thanked, and I ached from head to foot. New bruises appeared by the minute, blackening tokens of last night's debâcle.

Besides, I had yet the king's commission to fulfil and, in addition now, a visit to Master Collop was required upon Jude's behalf. That conversation must employ diplomacy and careful wording on my part, if I were to persuade the Warden Master of the Guild to have my brother's name relisted upon the guild roll. What I could make of Jude's virtues to argue the case, I knew not. Knowing somewhat of the speech of Venezia and Firenze was little enough, yet I must create of that adequate reason. I would not lie to enhance his recommendation. To do so would reflect badly upon me, if he proved less than I made of him. I valued my position as a rising guildsman too much to take the risk, even for my brother's sake. Mayhap, that was selfish of me but I had the responsibilities of a household and business and a hard-won reputation to maintain, if I were to succeed in these things.

Having given but a brief tale of last night's happenings to everyone, enough to content them with the promise of a full accounting when Thaddeus arrived – as he surely would – I sat at my desk and arranged my brushes, determined I should paint a half-page miniature or two and think matters through more thoroughly afore he came. I did not. Rather, I fell asleep there, at my desk, my head upon my folded arms.

Adam roused me to say Thaddeus was come and dinner was about to be set upon the board. The bailiff's timing was perfect on this occasion – a rare day when it was otherwise but he was ever welcome with an invitation of long-standing.

'You should not have let me sleep so long, Adam. 'Tis a morn entirely wasted in slumber.'

My cousin shrugged.

'You looked exhausted. I hadn't the heart to drag you from your dreams.'

'Dreams? Nightmares more like.' I winced as I stood, wrenched joints and bruised flesh complaining. I vowed most fervently that ne'er again should I fight with any man. God be praised, I was not born into the knightly class with combat as my craft and trade. A sharpened pen was weapon enough for me. 'Does Thaddeus intend to eat afore questioning me? The subject hardly sits well with enjoying our repast.'

'So long as we get to hear all about it.' Adam looked far too gleeful at the prospect of a gory tale. 'You promised us and I can't wait to learn how you fought off a trio of murderous felons. You, of all people, the hero? Who would have thought it, eh?'

'Who says so? 'Tis unwise to pay heed to gossip. How often it befalls a fabric of fiction, errors and plain lies.'

I went through to the kitchen. The bailiff sat at the board but rose to greet me, bowing in fact!

'All hail, Sebastian Foxley, mighty Vanquisher of Foes.' He laughed. 'And how are the wounds of battle?'

'Do not make mock. I hurt too much. And I know not how you come by this ludicrous notion that I…'

'Your brother is telling the whole of Cheapside and Farringdon, all who care to listen, that you fought off three brutes and saved his life and Mistress Foxley's.'

'Why would Jude do that? Belittling me, come what may, be more his way. Besides, Chesca saved her own life without aid from any man, least of all me. I used a stool as a shield and threw the ruffians' hammer back at them. That was all. Oh, but I found this, Thaddeus.' I gave him the iron nail. 'That and the hammer may be evidence sufficient to solve our three murders.'

''Tis just like the others.'

'Aye, but unbloodied, God be thanked. I fear they intended the same gruesome end for my brother.'

'Is he likewise a debtor to the Baldesis?'

'He says not, but stealing away their daughter would likely do their name as much dishonour as counterfeit coins.'

'His new wife is a Baldesi? I didn't know that. Your brother lives dangerously, Seb.'

The conversation lapsed as Rose served us a fine dinner of beef spiced with anise and cinnamon, served with a green pea pudding and alexanders in batter – a favourite of mine, as she well knew. I suspected this meal was a thanksgiving for my survival. I ate my fill, content that Thaddeus kept his necessary enquiries 'til after, else it would be a pity to spoil such fine meats with talk of dour happenings.

After dinner, since it had begun to rain, Thaddeus and I retired to the parlour. It would not do for his notes to get wet, if we talked in the garden. However, I left the parlour door ajar and arranged the settle for the bailiff such that he had his back to the open portal. I was unsurprised to see that Adam and Kate remained in the passageway betwixt the parlour and the workshop since I had promised they should hear my story in full. No doubt but they would convey the details to the rest as soon as may be.

I told Thaddeus all that I knew and could recall. In truth, it was not well told forwhy the events had occurred so swiftly. It was no easy matter to untangle them and arrange them in sensible order. It seemed to have happened all at once and, likely, in time enough to recite but a handful of Paternosters. My telling took longer, even though I embellished naught.

'So you threw the hammer and it caught your brother's assailant in the face, or in the eye, to be precise?'

''Twas but luck where it struck him.'

'Jude tells it otherwise.'

'Oh? I do not think I misremember it.'

'He says you flew at the wretch, clouting him repeatedly until you could wrest him – Jude – from his would-be killer's hold.'

'I recall no such acts. Did the miscreant suffer so many blows?'

'Not according to the surgeon.'

'Then it must be the case that Jude yet suffers from the shock of it and tells it awry. I see no cause for him to make me out his most strenuous defender, exaggerating my deed. 'Tis quite unlike him.'

'Perhaps he would make you out a hero in recompense.'

'A hero?' Or – the uncharitable thought came to me of a sudden – a scapegoat, should the ill-doer die of his injury? Or the pot of honey to attract any other Baldesi wasps that might come seeking revenge? Nay. I must not do my brother such injustice. I set those unwelcome possibilities aside.

'Indeed. You're London's hero of the hour. Make the most of it, Seb. There could be a few free cups of ale in it for you at The Panyer or elsewhere.'

And, thus, my tale was told.

Epilogue

I N THE weeks following, we completed King Edward's gift
for Lorenzo de' Medici, Lord of Florence, in time for the
king's examination afore the merchant-ambassador's departure.
Vegetius's *De Re Militari,* though I say it myself, was the most
beautiful work to come out of the Foxley workshop thus far.
Mallard's emerald was an exquisite centrepiece upon the gilded
leather binding, set about with the rainbow colours of the
Ravenna mosaic tesserae. The miniatures and decorated initials
were sumptuous in the gold and vivid pigments and Adam's
script was faultless. We were justly proud of it.

Aye, and shocked, indeed, when four days after he had
collected the finished book, the royal messenger returned
with a letter of commendation, signed by the king in person,
and... a purse of coin! Such a wonder was that, I declare I stood
speechless upon its receipt and quite forgot my manners, failing
to thank the messenger until Adam spoke for me. I stared at the
purse in my hand in wonderment.

As to the felons Thaddeus had in his charge, in August,
Clement Mallard was tried upon a charge of treason, the coin
dies, stolen from the Tower, having been found in his possession.
Counterfeiting the coin of the realm carried the full penalty.
The vintner was drawn upon a hurdle to Tower Hill, hanged
upon the gallows tree but cut down alive to suffer the rest of
his punishment. None of us went to watch the spectacle, nor
to view his ugly head upon a spike on London Bridge. All his
goods and properties, including that little casket of gemstones,
were forfeit to the Crown.

The day following, two of Jude's Italian attackers were tried upon three counts of murder and three of assault upon us. Not that the assaults could add anything to the outcome – a man can die but once. They pleaded their lack of English as an excuse not to stand trial in court whilst the case was conducted in a tongue they did not comprehend. It gained them naught: the law does not care for a plea of ignorance. They were hanged until dead at Tyburn as common murderers but not afore they named the Baldesis as their paymasters.

The third of them, sorely wounded by Chesca's blade, lives yet. We pray he may survive for the required year and a day, as the law dictates, thus sparing Chesca any blame for his demise. He was tried, in his absence, whilst lying at St Bartholomew's Infirmary. He was found as guilty as his fellows but too sick to go to his execution. Whatever befalls, he be a dead man, one way or the other.

Naught could be done to prosecute the Baldesi bankers, the word of a pair of condemned felons proving inadequate evidence. But they have received written warnings from King Edward and Lord Mayor Gardyner that any future misdemeanour could result in expulsion from the city. I hope that be sufficient deterrent to save Jude's skin and, mayhap, mine also.

I have spoken to Master Collop concerning the chances of Jude's reinstatement as a guild member and the possibility of his clerkship at Westminster. But those outcomes lie in the future. As do our individual hopes for happiness: Adam united with Mercy Hutchinson and Kate's possible betrothal to Hugh Gardyner, a matter I raised with her father, Alderman Edmund Verney, a week past. He be thinking upon it but I believe he will approve and make approach to Lord Mayor Gardyner, as young Hugh's uncle and guardian – much to Kate's delight, if he does. Even Ralf be free at last to spend time with Mistress Alder, now she stands widowed by Hamo's death.

At present, Jude and Chesca have found lodgings in Fish Street. Bennett Hepton's house, next to his fishmonger's business, stands empty since Bennett wed Peronelle Wenham, as was, and now lives with his new wife close by Cheap Cross. Jude complains that he knows well why Bennett prefers to live elsewhere and the reason the lodgings have been empty this while, despite the low rent asked. Apparently, the stink of fish pervades all. But Jude can afford no better until he may work for his living – a situation he requires but dreads. He desires the earnings, yet taking direction and instruction from anyone but himself be not his way these days. He will have to learn that art anew.

And what of dearest Rose and me? Only time will tell.

Author's Note

Those of you who have previously read 'The Colour of Shadows' will have met John 'Eleanor' Rykener before. He really existed in medieval London but a century before this adventure is set. I have taken the liberty of moving him forward about ninety years since he is such a brilliant character. The authorities caught him posing as Eleanor, *in flagranti,* wearing skirts and lying with a man in a stall in a stable. They didn't know quite what to make of him – homosexual acts weren't illegal until Tudor times. The Church authorities might have burned him as a witch for wearing clothes unsuited to his gender – as they did to Joan of Arc – but the City of London, ever with an eye to commerce, merely fined him for 'misrepresentation', i.e. promising a service as a woman which he couldn't properly provide.

Did you enjoy Mistress Joan Alder's medieval turns of phrase to describe her one-time husband, Hamo: 'wallidrag', 'skabbit skarth', etc? They're all genuine Middle-English words and mean… well, exactly what you think they ought to mean. Great fun!

If you have read Seb's earlier adventure, 'The Colour of Murder', you will know about the maze of tunnels beneath the Tower of London. I can't find any mention of them in the history books and they don't appear on plans of the Tower. I only know they exist because an elderly lady who worked as a secretary for the Vintners' Company of London during World War II told me about them. The vintners kept their casks of wine in the tunnels that run under the Tower for safety from bombs during the Blitz and staff sheltered down there during air raids. One day, for a dare, the secretaries decided to explore the tunnels further and discovered an ancient network with blind alleys and hidey-holes. They didn't go too far for fear of getting lost but what they found was a novelist's gift. The Tower of London was once a royal castle and it's known that Windsor Castle and Nottingham Castle – and probably others – had escape tunnels constructed so the king could make his escape, if necessary, and that may explain this secret of medieval London.

In this current adventure, while in the tunnels, Seb, Adam and Thaddeus probably suffer the symptoms of carbon monoxide [CO] poisoning. CO is produced when fire burns in insufficient oxygen, so their own torches could have caused this. The bright red skin tones are produced by inhaling CO and the amber colour of the torch flames is also indicative. Reduced oxygen levels would have affected our heroes too. To medieval folk, who knew nothing of the chemistry, witchcraft would seem to be a likely explanation for the invisible assailant and possible killer.

Important Characters featuring in 'The Colour of Evil'

There follows below a list of characters that readers may find helpful.

The Foxley Household

Sebastian [Seb] Foxley – an artist, illuminator and part-time sleuth

Adam Armitage – Seb's cousin [actually his nephew] from Foxley, Norfolk, a scribe

Rose Glover – Seb's house-keeper, a glover [rescued by Seb in a previous adventure]

Dickon & Julia – Seb's children by his late wife, Emily Appleyard

Kate Verney – Seb's apprentice

Nessie – Seb's maid-servant

Jack Tabor – once Seb's apprentice, now Appleyard's

Gawain – Seb's 'colley' dog [medieval spelling of 'collie']

The City Authorities

Thaddeus Turner – city bailiff and Seb's friend

Angus the Scot – a constable

Thomas Hardacre – a constable

Seb's Fellow Stationers

Richard Collop – Warden Master of the Stationers' Guild and Seb's one-time master [real]

Hugh Gardyner – one of Collop's current apprentices, the
    lord mayor's nephew
Guy Linton – a stationer, once Collop's apprentice with Seb
Ralf Reepham – Linton's journeyman scribe, from Norfolk

Unexpected Arrivals

Jude Foxley – Seb's errant elder brother
Francesca-Antonia Baldesi-Foxley [Chesca] – Jude's
    Venetian child-bride

Friends and Neighbours

Stephen Appleyard – Seb's father-in-law [Emily's father], a
    carpenter,
Mercy Hutchinson – a widow from Distaff Lane, Julia's wet
    nurse & Adam's intended
Simon Hutchinson – Mercy's eldest son, a school friend of
    Will Thatcher
Nicholas & Edmund [Mundy] – Mercy's younger children
Dame Ellen Langton – once Seb's landlady and Emily's
    mistress as an apprentice silkwoman
Edmund Verney – an alderman, Kate's father
John/Eleanor Rykener – a cross-dresser [real]
Jonathan Caldicott – Seb's neighbour in Paternoster Row
Mary Caldicott – Jonathan's wife
Joan [Joanie] Alder – a washerwoman and friend of Ralf
    Reepham
Peronelle [Pen] Wenham-Hepton – a silkwoman, used to be
    Emily's co-worker
Bennett Hepton – Pen's new husband, a well-to-do
    fishmonger
Beatrice [Beattie] Thatcher – a silkwoman, used to be
    Emily's co-worker
Harry Thatcher – a thatcher, Beattie's husband

Will Thatcher – Beattie and Harry's son, rescued by Seb and Adam in a previous adventure

Other Londoners

Philip Hartnell – a cutler and thief
Clement Mallard – a wealthy vintner
Edward Phelps – Mallard's manservant
Giles Honeywell – a purveyor of stationery in St Paul's Cathedral
Thomas Kempe – the Bishop of London [real]
Geoffrey Wanstead – the bishop's man of letters
John Dagvyle – a surgeon [real]
Hamo – a smith, once Joan Alder's husband

Meet the author

Toni Mount earned her Master's Degree by completing original research into a unique 15th-century medical manuscript. She is the author of several successful non-fiction books including the number one bestseller, *Everyday Life in Medieval England*, which reflects her detailed knowledge in the lives of ordinary people in the Middle Ages.

Toni's enthusiastic understanding of the period allows her to create accurate, atmospheric settings and realistic characters for her Sebastian Foxley medieval murder mysteries.

Toni's first career was as a scientist and this brings an extra dimension to her novels. It also led to her new biography of Sir Isaac Newton. She writes regularly for both *The Richard III Society* and *The Tudor Society* and is a major contributor to MedievalCourses.com.

As well as writing, Toni teaches history to adults, co-ordinates a creative writing group and is a popular speaker to groups and societies. Toni is also a member of the Crime Writers' Association.

This novel is Toni's the ninth in her popular "*Sebastian Foxley Murder Mystery*" series.

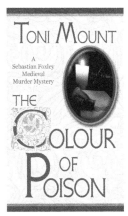

TONI MOUNT

A
Sebastian Foxley
Medieval
Murder Mystery

THE
COLOUR
OF
POISON

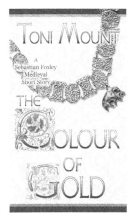

TONI MOUNT

A
Sebastian Foxley
Medieval
Short Story

THE
COLOUR
OF
GOLD

TONI MOUNT

The Third
Sebastian Foxley
Medieval
Murder Mystery

THE
COLOUR
OF
COLD BLOOD

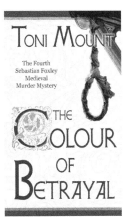

TONI MOUNT

The Fourth
Sebastian Foxley
Medieval
Murder Mystery

THE
COLOUR
OF
BETRAYAL

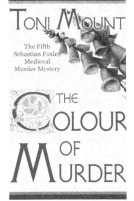

TONI MOUNT

The Fifth
Sebastian Foxley
Medieval
Murder Mystery

THE
COLOUR
OF
MURDER

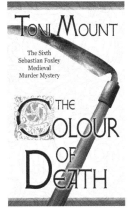

TONI MOUNT

The Sixth
Sebastian Foxley
Medieval
Murder Mystery

THE
COLOUR
OF
DEATH

TONI MOUNT

The Seventh
Sebastian Foxley
Medieval
Murder Mystery

THE
COLOUR
OF LIES

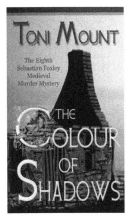

TONI MOUNT

The Eighth
Sebastian Foxley
Medieval
Murder Mystery

THE
COLOUR
OF
SHADOWS

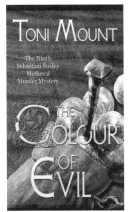

TONI MOUNT

The Ninth
Sebastian Foxley
Medieval
Murder Mystery

THE
COLOUR
OF
EVIL

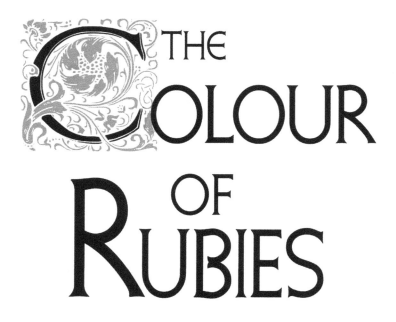

THE
COLOUR
OF
RUBIES

Prologue

The Palace of Westminster

B Y LISTENING at doors, lurking in dark corners and hiding behind faded tapestries, the espier had learned much to his master's advantage. He was now alone in the clerks' dormitory, foregoing a decent dinner to compose the letter. His hands were cramped with cold, no fire being lit in the hearth until the day's work was done. He kept stirring the ink to prevent it freezing. In the guise of a complaint about the English weather and the foolishness of the people with whom he had to live and work, whilst longing to see home, the intelligencer encoded his secret information for his master, Ludovico Sforza, Regent of Milan.

It was complicated to explain. Not that the use of Italian was a problem, being his native tongue, nor even the use of a cypher. The difficulty was the convoluted politics of kings, princes and dukes – how to explain the situation. Milan had had its eye on the Principality of Piedmont for years, lying as it did in a strategic position between France and the Italian City State. But Louis of France had similar intentions for Piedmont. The King of France was ever a thorn in Milan's side, thwarting any possibility of expansion.

But now King Edward had in mind a plan that would play well into Milan's aspirations – not that the stupid, bellicose English monarch would realise it. The espier had overheard a Privy Council meeting yesterday and learned this juicy morsel of intelligence. In his message, he revealed that King Edward was grown tired of his troublesome neighbour, the King of Scots and, since the treaty signed with them at York ten years before had now expired, he was determined to make war upon Scotland during this coming summer of 1480. By the terms of some Old Alliance, apparently, such action would require Louis of France to come to the aid of his Scots allies, distracting his attention to the northern end of his kingdom, far away from Piedmont. The espier did not dare to presume to tell his master that this would be the perfect opportunity to march the Milanese forces into Piedmont but Ludovico Sforza was an intelligent man: he would understand.

Having made a fair copy of his draft, the intelligencer signed it: *per mano dello Scudiero del Rubino*; 'by the hand of the Esquire of the Ruby', folded and sealed it. He would now deliver it to the courier in Lombard Street, in the City of London. As for the original draft copy, he tossed the paper into the hearth as kindling for the fire when it was lit, later.

The servant came to prepare the clerks' dormitory for the evening. His first task was to get the fire going, to warm the large chamber. But what was this? It looked to be a letter lying in the hearth. One of the clerks had been careless indeed. The servant could not read, so the words meant nought to him but he was a conscientious soul. He would give it to the Chief Clerk, whom he knew by sight. That should solve the problem. He would know what to do with the letter.

NEXT IN THE SERIES: THE COLOUR OF RUBIES

Chapter 1

Friday, the twenty-seventh day of January in the Year of Our Lord 1480 Westminster

WHAT A bloody miserable way to celebrate his nine-and-twentieth birthday.

He should never have come to work as a royal clerk. Secretary Oliver, who now ruled his days, was an utter bastard, sitting there, snug, amid cushions with the chamber's solitary brazier warming his feet whilst his eight clerks shivered at their desks before him.

The pen wavered unsteadily in Jude Foxley's chilled fingers. Pellets of snow beat against the glazed window such that candles were needed to work by even at mid-morn. Jude was unsure whether the ink was drying or freezing on the page as he wrote. It was hours since he last felt his toes, the cold leeching into his shoes from the bare flagstones of the King's Scriptorium.

Jude cursed Oliver and thought longingly of the Foxley workshop in Paternoster Row, back in London, where his brother Seb would also be cosy beside a glowing brazier, sipping mulled ale when he liked, taking time to leave his desk, stretch his back and walk about to thaw his feet. He should never have left.

He reached for a fresh sheet of parchment – the eighth or tenth, was it? He'd lost count of how many summonses to Parliament he had copied out, leaving a blank space for the name of the lord to whom each would be sent. Couldn't King Edward simply send out heralds to announce it? Damn it all. He'd never had such a tedious task, his mind as numb with boredom as his fingers with cold, aye, and his arse with perching on this misshapen wooden the stool with the split seat that pinched his buttocks. The draught blowing in the door gnawed at his ankles like a starveling rat every time it opened. That was the penalty he paid for being the newcomer to the scriptorium: the worst stool by the door. Mind, to sit by the window with icy airs rolling down the wall from the glass panes above wasn't much of an improvement, though there was more light to see what you were doing. Flickering candlelight glimmered off the wet – or frozen – ink of his last few words.

At the desk beside him, Piers Creed's teeth were chattering loud enough to be annoying. But then everything about Piers was irritating. Worst was his constant foul farting. God knew what he ate to cause such noisome stinks that so frequently disturbed his fellow clerks. The ominous purring rumble of another assault on the senses had Jude covering his nose with his sleeve in good time.

'For Christ's sake, can't you cease that?' Jude muttered from behind his sleeve which proved inadequate. 'Stop eating bloody horse-beans or whatever...'

'Silence!' Secretary Oliver bellowed from his exalted cushioned chair at the far end of the scriptorium. 'I've warned you before, Foxley. You speak again and your payment will be reduced by two pence since this is your second offence. Now get on with your work.'

Piers Creed is the bloody offence, Jude thought, stabbing his pen into the inkwell over hard and ruining the nib. But he knew better than to answer back to Oliver, the pompous bastard who served as the King's French and Italian Secretary. In truth, there wasn't much work for this particular royal office through the winter months, when ships weren't voyaging to foreign lands to collect or deliver correspondence. Hence, their current employment in helping out the clerks of the Lord Chancellor's office who were supposed to write out the innumerable summonses to attend Parliament before Easter.

Jude's much-exaggerated knowledge of Italian tongues had gained him this position – with his brother's aid – and now he wished most heartily that he hadn't bothered to lie about his skills. Still, the clerkship earned him coin in his purse. Besides, a month since, King Edward had celebrated Christmas in fine style, including everyone who worked at Westminster Palace in the feasting and entertainment. Jude had appreciated that, as did his young bride, Chesca – Francesca-Antonia Baldesi. She had made quite an impression at court, wearing her one remaining Venetian gown of silk and bits of finery, making quite a show. Men had been so envious of him with her on his arm, dancing with him, laughing at his wit. He grinned at the memory, reshaping his quill with his penknife. But Christmas seemed long ago now as he sat, freezing his bollocks off, scribbling endlessly even as the ink turned to ice in the well.

Christ be thanked for the mercy of the bell, calling them to dinner in the Great Hall.

'Coming, Piers?' Jude asked, setting down his pen and pushing back his stool which grated on the flagstones fit to set teeth on edge. Despite his vile personal problem, Creed was the closest thing to a friend Jude had made among the clerks since coming to Westminster.

'I've nigh finished this summons. I'll join you shortly. Save me a place at the board.' Creed went on scribbling without looking up.

Jude shrugged, gazing down on his industrious companion. The fellow's lank hair was sparse, his nose bulbous and his build so skinny he made Jude's lean-limbed brother Seb seem plump in comparison. In truth, Creed's only asset was that he made a splendid foil for Jude: a fine figure, broad of shoulder, taller than most, good-looking with a full head of fair hair.

At least, that was how Jude saw himself, refusing to

acknowledge that incipient and unwelcome roll of flesh that began to do daily battle with his belt buckle or, of late, the receding hairline Chesca took malicious delight in pointing out. ''Tis but a high forehead,' he'd told her, 'The sign of a large brain and great intelligence.' The young hussy had laughed, devil take her, and earned a slap for her mischief.

Mistress Baxter's Lodging House, Thieving Lane, Westminster

Chilled and miserable, Jude trudged home in the dark, through the deepening snow. But a surprise awaited when he returned to the upper chamber where he and Chesca dwelt at present, unable to afford anything better. He came bearing a cold supper of white bread and cheese, napkin-wrapped, filched at dinner. Living on a pittance, most of his fellow clerks did likewise, those who did not live at court. The unwed clerks had bed and board within the ramshackle parts of the palace but wives weren't allowed. Thus, Jude lodged in this single chamber with hardly space to spread his arms and a roof too low for him to stand to his full height of just six feet. Mind, at this rate, what with being bent over his desk all day at Secretary Oliver's behest and stooping here at Mistress Baxter's place, he'd be a bloody crouchback before he was five-and-thirty – not that he intended his life to go on in this dismal way for that long. He had plans.

Jude gawped at the sight that greeted him at the head of the rickety stair, Chesca decked in all her finery, her hair loose, gleaming, black as midnight, being the least of it. A good fire burned in the hearth, the room had been swept and the draping cobwebs removed. A table-board he'd never seen before was spread with a pristine cloth and all manner of food set out in pewter dishes: a whole salmon, jellies, cheeses and sweetmeats. And wine!

'Sweet Christ alive, Chesca. What have you bloody done?' Jude waved his arms to encompass the chamber. Even the bed was neatly made.

'Are you pleased, Jood? This for your birthday. I pouring wine for you... good wine, no dog's pees now.' She served him the red wine in a chased silver cup fit for royalty. God alone knew how she'd come by such luxuries. It was a fine Gascon wine, as had been served at King Edward's Twelfth Night feast.

Jude sipped it cautiously, wondering how much each swallow cost him. Money he didn't possess.

'Everything looks... so clean. Did you do it yourself?'

'You no spoiling it.' Chesca pouted like the child she was at just sixteen summers of age.

'You didn't, did you?'

'Servants clean. Baldesis no clean.'

'You're not a Baldesi now; you're a Foxley. We can't afford bloody servants... nor all this food and drink.'

'Your brother having servant; why no us?'

'You mean, Nessie? That foolish chit costs him more to feed than she does in labour. She doesn't count and answer my damn question, woman.'

'Mistress Basster. I paying her to making clean.'

'Mistress Baxter? You paid our bloody landlady to do the work? How much did that cost?'

'Leettle, leettle money, I swearing. Pleease now we eating good food.'

'Did you steal it or borrow the money?'

'An' I no meaning Nessie. Rosa – she serving or no?' Chesca changed the subject.

'Rose? She's a special case.'

Chesca cut flakes of salmon with her knife and arranged them on a piece of fresh white bread.

'I knowing. Nessie telling me how you an' Rosa were marrying an' you never coming to the church. Why you no coming to her? She fine woman.'

''Tis none of your bloody business! Besides, you should be grateful I never wed her, else I couldn't have saved you from that filthy old lecher your family wanted you to marry.'

Chesca sat in his lap and fed him the fine fish.

'You liking?' She raised her eyebrows in question, wriggled provocatively and began to unlace the doublet he wore beneath his clerk's gown. 'You liking other things more?'

'We're bloody eating, Chesca. I'm tired...'

'Never too tired. Eating later... after.'

'Don't take my clothes off, you little harlot. It's still chilly in here.'

'Warming in bed, Jood. Come now, husband.'

Thoroughly satisfied regarding all bodily requirements, Jude lay awake in bed, thinking – a bad habit of his brother's but, for the most part, one he rarely bothered to indulge. He reached out for his wine cup upon the floor, careful not to knock it over. Such good wine; how in Christ's name had Chesca paid for it? The possibilities stewed in his head, all of them bad. Had she taken up thievery? It seemed unlikely, seeing how much food and drink had appeared, as if by magick. Stealing on that scale could hardly have gone unnoticed. Maybe she'd run up a great account and he would suffer such a shock when the reckoning arrived with demand for immediate payment. God knows where the coin would come from in order to settle it.

But it was a third possibility that wormed its way insidiously into his head, like a small but venomous serpent: that somebody else had paid for everything. And why would that be? No one did favours out of kindness these days; they expected the favour returned – in full. He had nothing to give... but Chesca. What had the hussy done? Or rather *who* had she done? That little minnekin! If she'd lain in another man's bed, he'd kill the bastard, whoever he was.

Of a sudden, he was convinced he had struck upon the

truth and the rich food – paid for by some snot-nosed knave – roiled in his belly until he felt quite sick. He looked at his wife curled close beside him: young, beautiful, aye, and desirable, devil take her. In the fading firelight, she looked so innocent, sleeping like a well-fed kitten. No wonder the adulterous bitch hadn't answered his questions; avoiding the issue. Well, she'd bloody regret it; that was certain but he couldn't be bothered now. He turned his back on her and spent much of the long night plotting his revenge on the shit-monger scawager who'd cuckolded him, whoever it was. The worse the punishment he could devise for the pillaging prick the better.

Saturday, the twenty-eighth day of January

Beyond the frosted horn-paned window, as best he could make out, Jude saw a world shrouded white. Damn the snow. Damn the cold. His breath fogged the air even indoors. Last eve's welcoming blaze was now grey ash in the hearth with not a splinter of wood to revive it to life. His anger had likewise cooled overnight but he knew it wouldn't take much to rekindle it. One word amiss from Chesca and he'd skin her like a bloody cat so it was as well then that she slept on, huddled in the warm bed – no early riser she in any case but 'neath the blankets was the best place to stay on such a day. He'd wring the truth out of her later.

Jude donned his clerk's gown over almost every item of clothing he possessed: three shirts; doublet; jerkin; two pairs of hose and breeches. In so many clothes, he could hardly move and pulling on his boots proved a struggle. The debris of his birthday feast still littered the cloth. No point in wasting good food, whoever had paid for it. Jude cut a fat wedge of cheese which he put in his scrip for later, along with a handful of marchpane-stuffed figs. He piled flakes of salmon on a slice of white loaf and folded it to eat on his walk to work. It wasn't a mannerly way to break his fast but he didn't care. He swung his cloak around his shoulders and pulled his coif and plain clerk's cap as low over his ears as possible, cursed at finding his cheap gloves were splitting. Thank God it was Saturday, a half-day only of scribbling and shivering in that devil-damned place with Piers Creed farting and stinking beside him. It was no life for a red-blooded Englishman and definitely not for Jude Foxley.

Hard pellets of snow gusted in his face, stinging like icy sand. It was difficult to tell if this was fresh snow falling from the dour, leaden clouds, or simply blowing off the roofs. Underfoot was treacherous ice, hid by a soft layer of innocent-looking virgin white. He and others forced, complaining, from their firesides, slipped and slithered, ungainly. As Jude turned off King Street and entered Westminster Palace's outer courtyard through Great Gate, a fellow in front of him lost his footing and collided with a baker's lad carry a tray of still-warm bread, fresh from the ovens. Small loaves scattered in the snow but not for long. Folk swooped upon the scene of the mishap like scavenging kites and the bread disappeared, four *pains de main* finding their way into Jude's scrip to join the cheese and sweetmeats. Waste not; want not, as the old saying goes.

He trudged on towards the Exchequer Offices and the scriptorium adjoining the Great Hall. At the threshold of Secretary Oliver's cold little kingdom, he knocked the snow off his boots, shook it out of his cap, removed his useless gloves to chafe his numb fingers into life and prepared to work. The door whined like a lost soul – as it always did – when he pushed it open on its time-worn iron hinges.

As ever, first to arrive and last to leave, the industrious Creed was already at his desk, aye, and had begun his daily production of farts, to judge by the stink.

'Don't you have anything better to bloody do, Piers?' Jude greeted him.

'I'm not an idle layabout like the rest of you. Besides, since

Secretary Oliver entrusted me as key-holder, I have to be first here and leave last.'

'You have that wrong: he only gave you the key because you're so bloody eager to start work every morn. You give the rest of us a bad name, you foolish bugger. Here, have a sweetmeat.' Jude put a stuffed fig on Piers desk.

'What's this for? You want me to copy out your quota of summonses?'

'You suspicious old curmudgeon. 'Twas my birthday yesterday and a few morsels were left after.'

'Secretary Oliver'll be in a rage if he finds out we're eating at our desks, getting crumbs and grease marks on the parchment.'

'I won't tell him if you don't.'

'Oh, I don't know, Jude.'

'Well, damn it then, I'll bloody have it.' Jude took back the sweetmeat and ate it in two bites. 'Dilemma solved! Now, what's the old goat got for us this morn, eh?' he spoke through a mouthful of fruit and marchpane, wiping sticking fingers on his gown. 'More bloody summonses, no doubt.' He rubbed his hands together vigorously to warm them so he could hold a pen and sat on the stool with the split seat that pinched his arse if he didn't take care.

'Aye. He left us instructions to do another thirty: fifteen each.'

'What? Us alone? What are the other buggers doing, then?' Creed shrugged.

'Something just as boring, I suppose, when they get here. They'll be blaming the snow for their tardiness. They always do. Snow makes a fine excuse for being late to work.'

'Even those who live here? I had to walk from Thieving Lane.'

'That's not so far.'

'Farther than you had to come from your bloody dormitory above stairs. Oh, shit. My damned ink's frozen solid.' Jude threw down his pen in disgust. 'Well, I can't work 'til that thaws out.' He took the inkpot and set it beside the solitary brazier the clerks were permitted in their icy den. He stood close as he dare to the glimmer of warmth bestowed by the feeble glow of charcoal without scorching his threadbare gown. It had been his predecessor's cast-off and, therefore, was too short to keep his knees warm when he sat to write – yet another reason for complaint about his current employment.

'While you're waiting for your ink, last night, after you'd gone, Chief Clerk Sowerberry put a sheaf of papers on the shelf up there.' Creed nodded towards an untidy-looking pile of mismatched sheets in danger of sliding to the floor. 'He said we're to sort them out, see what's relevant and send them to the appropriate offices.'

Jude took the papers to his desk and began to straighten dog-ears and smooth out creases. Some were torn.

'Reckon this could all go for bloody fire-lighting.' He leafed through them, muttering under his breath: 'Laundry list... order for parchment... memo to self: "don't forget M's birthday"... another laundry list... an anonymous tailor's demand for payment... Whose stuff is this? Each one in a different hand...'

'Don't ask me. Mayhap, some servant was finally setting about cleaning behind a coffer. Could be years old, some of it.' Creed fidgeted and let out a long rumbling fart.

'Can't you go outside to do that, you disgusting wretch? I have to breathe in your bloody stink.'

'It's a penance we both have to bear.' Creed sighed and repeated the offence for good measure before dipping his pen to complete the document he was writing.

Jude made no answer, frowning over a paper. Smoothing out the wrinkles where it had been screwed up, he followed a line of wording with his finger, puzzling to make sense of it. It seemed to be in some Italian form but not of Venice, which he would recognise for certain, nor of Florence, with which he had some acquaintance. The hand was tiny, cramped and execrable with many crossings-out and insertion marks, dots and under-scoring.

'Something of interest?' Creed asked, finishing another

summons and reaching for a fresh parchment to commence with 'Right Trusty and Well-Beloved, We Greet You Well...' – the customary royal greeting.

'Doubt it. Someone's first draft for a letter home, by the look of it. Just rubbish.' Despite his words, Jude set the paper aside for perusal later, if he could be bothered. If it contained a bit of juicy court gossip, it might be worth the trouble to interpret. A few extra coins for 'information' could always be of use to a poor clerk with a spendthrift wife.

Their fellow scribes arrived in twos and threes, all blaming the weather for their late arrival, as Creed had predicted, moaning about the pitiful brazier that did nought to warm them. They, too, found their inkwells frozen – another reason to delay working, so they trooped off, in search of mulled ale whilst the ink thawed, the door screeching closed behind them.

'Hal, Lawrence, bring some drink for us!' Creed called out with little hope that they would, he and Jude being the lowest of the low in the clerks' unspoken hierarchy.

Unsurprisingly, the clerks returned without any ale for Jude or Creed.

'What have you two been doing?' Hal Sowerberry, the Chief Clerk, demanded. He was heavyset but of short stature, dark-browed. Jude hadn't liked him on sight, the pompous, puffed-up toad. Chief Groveller and Arse-Licker Extraordinary were better titles for him in Jude's opinion. And he possessed a nasty temper.

'More summonses. What else?' Creed told him.

'Foxley. What of you, you lazy cur? I don't see any summonses on your desk.' Sowerberry leaned back in Secretary Oliver's vacant chair, arms folded, making the most of their master's absence to sit close to the brazier.

'My ink was frozen as yours. Meantime, I've been going through a pile of waste papers from somewhere or other. You said to make certain there's nought important among them before putting it all on the fire. Wouldn't do to accidentally burn your love letters, Hal, from your latest mistress, would it now?'

'Shut your mouth, Foxley.' Sowerberry leapt towards him, fist raised.

Jude stood up, straightening to full height. Up on his toes, he added an extra couple of inches, towering over the angry clerk.

'Touch me, Sowerberry, and you'll bloody regret it,' he said, sounding utterly calm and composed. No note of ire in his voice.

'I'm your superior!'

'I don't care if you're Pope Sixtus himself,' Jude continued in the same easy tone. 'No man lays a finger on me.'

Sowerberry thought better of it and backed down but his scowl promised retribution to follow.

'You'll be the one in trouble when I inform Secretary Oliver of your behaviour.'

'*My* behaviour? You're the one threatening to strike me, you ridiculous little prick.'

Sowerberry had been goaded beyond bearing and went so far as to climb upon Jude's desk to get at him. His eyes blazed and his penknife was in his hand.

Jude stepped back, avoiding a clumsy thrust, laughing.

'Get off my desk before you fall and hurt yourself. We don't want blood splashing the parchment, do we? That would upset Secretary Oliver, wouldn't it? God knows, he might even chastise us, then we'd all be in tears.'

'Stop it, Jude, don't mock him,' Creed said softly. 'You're making matters worse with every word. You don't want him for an enemy. He's a sly one.'

The situation was ended by the entrance of Secretary Oliver himself, fur-swathed and red-nosed, sniffing. He croaked a greeting of sorts – or it might have been a reprimand, it was hard to tell – and slumped in his comfortable chair. Lord of all he surveyed here in the clerks' office, if he was afflicted by an excess of rheumy phlegm and a chill, then everyone else should be made to suffer the same. Leastwise, that seemed to be his purpose as he sneezed and coughed and spat his contagion right freely upon all.

Jude now had reason to be glad of his draughty place, farthest from the brazier, well away from Oliver. The fellow looked pitiful and, for once, uninterested in what his underlings were doing, whether working or wasting time. Creed, of course, was writing out yet more summonses. Such diligence should be commended, though it rarely was. More likely, poor Creed was derided by his fellows and given far more than his fair share of work.

'Take a breath, Piers,' Jude whispered, nudging him. 'They'll only give you more work to do if you finish those damned summonses. Look around: Sowerberry and the rest are doing nothing at all, fiddling with their cod-pieces, picking their noses, scratching their arses. We're the only ones working.'

'I'd rather be doing something to pass the time 'til dinner.'

'Here, take a look at this.' Jude handed Creed the creased paper that caught his attention earlier. 'What do you make of it, eh? Interesting?'

'Not much, in truth,' Creed admitted after a deal of squinting and thumb-chewing. 'Italian tongues aren't my strong point. What do you think it says?'

'I best not tell you too much. 'Tis a love letter to King Edward's latest mistress. We don't want that to become common knowledge, do we now? The king might throw us in the Tower of London and feed the key – or us – to the bloody lions in the Menagerie.' Despite his words of doom, Jude was laughing, watching Creed's horror-stricken face. 'I'm jesting, Piers. Don't take everything so damned seriously. Of course, it's not a bloody letter from the king. Why would it be when the king doesn't know any Italian? If he did, he wouldn't need me and I wouldn't be freezing my bollocks off in the pest hole. See sense, you daft fool.'

'What does the letter say?'

Jude shrugged.

'Ah, now, 'tis a difficult hand to make out, is it not? I'll take it home; work on it there. I can hardly concentrate here, what with you farting and him sneezing all the time.' Jude cocked his chin at Secretary Oliver who appeared to have nodded off.

''Tis most conscientious of you, to work at home when you'll not be paid for it.' Creed sounded surprised – as well he might – if not impressed.

'That's me, Piers: a most hard-working fellow indeed,' Jude said as he surreptitiously folded the letter out of sight, beneath his desk, and slipped it into the sleeve of his gown. In truth, he had no idea what it said; his Italian was not that good. But to keep up the pretence of fluency, he had his secret assistant. Chesca.

OUT LATE 2021

Get your FREE BOOK!
https://www.madeglobal.com/authors/toni-mount/download/

Historical Fiction

The Sebastian Foxley Series - Toni Mount
The Death Collector - **Toni Mount**
Struck With the Dart of Love - **Sandra Vasoli**
Truth Endures - **Sandra Vasoli**
Cor Rotto - **Adrienne Dillard**
The Raven's Widow - **Adrienne Dillard**

Historical Colouring Books

The Mary, Queen of Scots Colouring Book - **Roland Hui**
The Life of Anne Boleyn Colouring Book - **Claire Ridgway**
The Wars of the Roses Colouring Book - **Debra Bayani**
The Tudor Colouring Book - **Ainhoa Modenes**

Non Fiction History

The Turbulent Crown - **Roland Hui**
Anne Boleyn's Letter from the Tower - **Sandra Vasoli**
Jasper Tudor - **Debra Bayani**
Tudor Places of Great Britain - **Claire Ridgway**
Illustrated Kings and Queens of England - **Claire Ridgway**
A History of the English Monarchy - **Gareth Russell**
The Fall of Anne Boleyn - **Claire Ridgway**
George Boleyn: Tudor Poet, Courtier & Diplomat - **Ridgway & Cherry**
The Anne Boleyn Collection I, II & III - **Claire Ridgway**
Two Gentleman Poets at the Court of Henry VIII - **Edmond Bapst**

PLEASE LEAVE A REVIEW
If you enjoyed this book, *please*
leave a review at the book seller
where you purchased it. There is
no better way to thank the author
and it really does make a huge
difference!
Thank you in advance.

Lightning Source UK Ltd.
Milton Keynes UK
UKHW041328310321
381312UK00001B/34